"I have nowhere to go. No money. Nothing."

Jack Fletcher studied her, then casually stuck his hands in the pockets of his jeans. "You're welcome to spend the weekend on my couch, although I don't guarantee the springs."

Caroline's nails dug into her palms. "Thank you. I appreciate your kindness."

"No, you don't. You'd like to take my offer and ram it down my throat."

She stared at him. "If you know that, then why invite me into your home?"

"It's in the job description. The more of a pain in the ass you are, the harder I have to try to help."

She blinked. Had he really called her a pain in the ass? That hardly fit her image of how priests were supposed to talk. Caroline gazed at him. Then she lowered her eyes.

There was at least one blessing in this ridiculous, humiliating situation: Her father-in-law would have no chance of tracking her, buried in this priest's apartment. Which meant that she had something like twenty-four hours to get her act together and plan some way to get down to Grand Cayman.

And liberate five million stolen dollars.

"Exciting…colorful characters…a moving and emotionally enriching work." —*Affaire de Coeur*

JASMINE CRESSWELL

NO SIN TOO GREAT

To Lorraine!
With very best wishes
Enjoy!
Jasmine Cresswell

MIRA BOOKS

ISBN 1-55166-147-0

NO SIN TOO GREAT

Copyright © 1996 by Jasmine Cresswell.

MIRA and the star colophon are trademarks of MIRA Books.

Printed in U.S.A.

To the three new men in my life:
Steve, Skip and Dom.
This one's for you!

One

Even before she touched him, Caroline knew that Dayton Ames was dead. His handsome face was contorted in a rictus of pain, and spittle had congealed in a crust at the corner of his mouth. One eye had rolled back in the socket to stare blindly at the ceiling. The other eye had slipped sideways, creating the horrible illusion that he leered at her from beneath a half-closed eyelid. Dear God! How in the world had he managed to die so painfully without making enough commotion to wake her?

She was normally a light sleeper—her current life-style demanded it—but she hadn't heard or felt a single movement. What if Dayton had tried to ask her for help, and she had slept on, unaware?

Paralyzed with shock, it took Caroline several seconds before she gathered her wits sufficiently to lean across the bed and gently close Dayton's eyes. She smoothed his hair from his forehead, an unexpected lump in her throat. Poor Dayton! He'd had a minor problem with his heart, but he'd prided himself on his physical fitness and he was only forty-eight, much too young to die. His business ethics had been lousy, his morals nonexistent, but in some of the little ways, he'd been a kind man. Caroline wiped at a stubborn tear. In other ways, of course, he'd been your basic dick, one of the successful male chauvinist types she knew all too well. His concept of marital fidelity extended—just—to the point that he had never taken another woman to bed at the same time as his wife.

Caroline edged away from him, shivering in the chill of the air-conditioning. For someone who prided herself on her competence, she was feeling unacceptably dithery and disorganized. To put it mildly, this was a situation that was going to require careful handling.

Captain Of Industry Dies In Bed With His Mistress. She could see the headlines now. Oddly enough, given that her entire relationship with Dayton had been so carefully calculated, she couldn't decide if she wanted to read those headlines or not.

Her temples pounded with a grade-A headache. Her mouth was bone dry and her thoughts kept fading into fuzziness. Worst of all, her heart felt as if it was racing forward, then coming to an abrupt, grinding halt. Still, she couldn't let events overtake her. Supine surrender to fate was part of the old Caroline. For the past year, she'd been able to roll with the punches and stand up, swinging purposefully.

Fighting grogginess, she got out of bed and reached for her robe. No luck. All she could see were her satin teddy and one of her shoes, discarded last night en route from the dining room to bed. Dayton's shirt was on the floor next to her teddy. She had a sudden vivid memory of Dayton kissing her passionately while she unfastened the buttons of his shirt and pulled it from his shoulders. She'd been laughing, teasing him, almost comfortable in his company. At first, Dayton had been tense and somber, as he often was, his competitive instincts all focused on dominating her with the flashy expertise of his sexual techniques. Then he'd lightened up and started to laugh, joining in her teasing. They'd laughed a lot, in the end. Irrationally, and despite her disapproval of all that he stood for, Caroline was glad that Dayton's last few hours had been filled with laughter. If she believed in hell, she'd have been worried that Dayton didn't have many more hours of laughter ahead of him.

Overwhelmed by an emotion she couldn't bring herself to identify, she picked up his shirt and put in on, wrapping it tightly around her body. Astonished, she realized that she'd started to cry in earnest, dry, heaving sobs that hurt her throat and made her nose run.

A wave of nausea caught her by surprise, and she slumped on the bed. What in the world was wrong with her? She couldn't be hungover. She made it a rule never to drink more than a single glass of wine when she was working, and she certainly hadn't broken that rule last night—so what was going on?

Caroline didn't realize someone had come into the apartment until she heard the tap-tap of high heels on the marble tiles outside the master bedroom suite. And she had no time to move before Felicity Van Haas, otherwise known as Mrs. Dayton Ames, came into the bedroom.

Intimidatingly elegant in a beige linen suit, cut just low enough around the neck to avoid being dowdy and accessorized with a Gucci purse and pearl earrings, Felicity stopped in the doorway. Her gaze flickered disdainfully over Caroline then blurred and focused somewhere in the middle distance. A faint flush darkened the well-preserved beauty of Felicity's fair complexion, the only visible sign of embarrassment or anger at encountering her husband's mistress. In *her* bed.

"I think you'd better leave," Felicity said, her voice low and perfectly modulated. "Dayton, I'll wait for you in the library."

Caroline realized that Felicity couldn't see her husband's face from where she was standing; she had no idea he was dead. It would be easy to just stand up and walk away, leaving Felicity to discover on her own that her husband wasn't going to be joining her in the library, or anywhere else. In the split second she had to make a decision, Caroline told herself she had no reason to protect Felicity. In fact, she had several excellent reasons for wanting to hurt her. But somehow, she couldn't quite bring herself to be that brutal. Not now. Not when Dayton was dead.

Caroline stood up, clutching the sheet and the bedpost so Felicity wouldn't be able to see how shaky her knees were.

Never let your opponent see your weakness. Phillip had taught her that. One of her ex-husband's few useful legacies.

"Mrs. Ames, I'm sorry—"

"Just get out. Don't insult me with apologies."

Caroline drew in a deep breath. "You don't understand, Mrs. Ames. I'm sorry, but Dayton...your husband...is dead."

Felicity didn't move for a full minute. Finally she turned her head a fraction of an inch and allowed her eyes to meet Caroline's. She didn't step into the bedroom. "Dead?" she repeated, her voice dull with shock. "What do you mean, he's dead? He can't be dead! We just had lunch together on Thursday."

Caroline cleared her throat, resisting an insane impulse to put her arm around Felicity Ames's shoulders. "I'm sorry," she said quietly, moving to one side so that Dayton's face could be seen from the doorway. "I think he must have had a heart attack. Or maybe a stroke."

Felicity cast a single quick glance toward the bed. For a second, she paled, then her mouth hardened, and Caroline knew exactly what she was thinking. She was wondering if her middle-aged husband had died from overexertion, trying to impress his twenty-nine-year-old mistress with his sexual prowess. Caroline pushed away an uncomfortable twinge of guilt. Dammit, she had no reason to feel guilty! Their sexual encounter last night had been typically energetic, but Dayton had fallen asleep peacefully enough.

There was no way to reassure Felicity, no way to counter the look of loathing that had flared momentarily in her eyes. Any explanations would simply make matters worse, so Caroline shrugged and said nothing. These days, she spent a lot of time saying nothing.

Felicity remained equally silent. Her movements jerky, her face impassive, she walked to her husband's side of the bed and stared at him, making no move to touch him. Caroline would have thought she was feeling nothing at all if she hadn't seen a pulse throb in Felicity's neck and her fingers tighten convulsively around the gold chain of her purse.

"Have you called anyone to report this?" Felicity asked, her gaze once again settling on a spot somewhere to the left of Caroline's ear. "The paramedics? A doctor?"

"No, I only just found him—" Caroline broke off and tried again, not wanting to sound callous. "I only just woke up," she said stiffly. "Dayton must have died during the night. I'm very sorry, but I didn't wake up when . . . it happened . . . so I can't tell you anything more."

"On-balance, I'd prefer not to hear the details of my husband's dying moments from a whore," Felicity said.

Caroline didn't even blink. She'd been trained in a hard school, and on the insult scale, that one scarcely registered a blip. "I'll get dressed," she said, bending to pick up her teddy and her solitary shoe.

"Use one of the guest bathrooms," Felicity instructed.

Caroline hesitated, then gestured toward the master bath. "My makeup and toothbrush are in there."

"Collect them and get out."

Making a wide circle around Felicity, Caroline walked into the master bathroom. She avoided looking in any of the floor-to-ceiling mirrors. With a reckless disregard for spills and damage, she swept her makeup and personal belongings into the Louis Vuitton overnight bag Dayton had given her.

Felicity was still standing by the bed when she came out, but neither of them acknowledged the other's presence by so much as a flicker of an eyelash.

Caroline's skin was washed with a wave of heat. She wasn't sure whether she was furious with Felicity or ashamed of herself. Maybe both, she thought wryly. In retrospect, she was beginning to think she had plenty to be ashamed about. And it didn't help that she still felt so woozy. Her head was pounding, and she had a weird fleeting impression that she had to walk very carefully past Felicity and hold her head high, or she would explode.

Desperate as she was to escape from Dayton's apartment, and even more so from his widow, Caroline showered before she dressed and took the time to apply a quick, expert layer of makeup. Thank goodness, she felt marginally less woozy after cleaning up. Felicity Ames intimidated her, and Caroline needed the protection of looking reasonably put together, even though she still felt as if she was flying apart. Of course, however hard she labored, she could never hope to emulate Felicity's understated elegance and classically perfect good looks.

Blood will out, as her adoptive father loved to say. And Caroline's mongrel bloodlines left much to be desired. Still, if she was going to be condemned as a whore, she might as well try to look like an expensive whore.

She always planned ahead, so she had something to put on that was more suitable than the strapless black dinner dress she'd been wearing the night before. She'd anticipated a typically hot Chicago summer day, and she'd packed a full-skirted dress of semi-sheer muslin that tied at the cinched waist with a woven belt of bright Mexican cotton. She hadn't brought a slip, and she knew that as soon as she moved into the light, the outline of her legs would be quite clear. That tantalizing transparency was the whole point of the outfit, of course. She had great legs, and she'd learned to capitalize on her assets. Except that this morning, the dress didn't appear sexy; she was afraid it appeared vulgar.

Caroline shrugged. What can't be cured must be endured. That had been a favorite saying of one of her nannies, and she'd incorporated it into her philosophy of life while still a teenager. Odd how these little snippets of memory survived long after the nanny herself—one of at least a dozen—had been forgotten. Between her parents, her ex-husband and her nannies, she was a walking dictionary of dubious proverbs.

She left her overnight bag on the living room table, then folded Dayton's shirt into a neat rectangle and carried it to the master bedroom. The door was closed. She knocked quietly.

For twenty seconds or so, there was no response. Then Felicity spoke. "Who is it?"

Felicity knew damn well who it was, and the curt question rubbed Caroline raw in places she hadn't even known were wounded. She reacted with self-protective cruelty. "It's Dayton's mistress," she said, her voice satisfyingly firm and cool. "Presumably I'll have the honor of being the last in that long and expensive line."

The door was flung open so hard that it crashed against the wall. Felicity's calm was obviously a thin, precariously maintained veneer. "Get out," she said through clenched teeth. "Leave now."

Caroline held out Dayton's shirt. "I thought you might want this."

"Keep it. Burn it." Felicity closed her eyes and turned her head away.

The infuriating prick of sympathy came again. Caroline shoved it aside. "Whatever you say, Mrs. Ames." She forced herself to speak calmly. "I probably shouldn't leave right away. Would you prefer me to wait in the kitchen? The paramedics might want to ask me some questions. They may have to fill out a police report and they'll need my input."

"I want you to get out of here," Felicity said. "Right now."

"But what will you tell the police? The paramedics?"

"You can leave that to me," she said. "And you can be sure I won't mention your presence, so you won't be involved. Goodbye, Caroline."

Surprised, Caroline glanced up. "You know my name?"

For the first time, Felicity's control over her expression broke completely. Her cheeks burned and her eyes darkened with fury. "Yes, I know your name," she said. She stepped back from the bedroom door and slammed it in Caroline's face. The bang reverberated through the silent apartment.

For an instant, Caroline was afraid she was going to be sick right there in the hallway, in the middle of Dayton's expensive Persian rug. Then the nausea passed. Hell, what was one more slammed door in a lifetime of slammed doors? Lifting her shoulders in an indifferent shrug, she collected her overnight bag and walked out of Dayton Ames's apartment.

Two

By the time she arrived at her own apartment, Caroline was running on overload, her nerves jumping with a potent mixture of excitement and dread. Dayton's unexpected death had pushed forward her schedule by more than two weeks, and she wouldn't be able to use the getaway scheme she'd planned with such painstaking care.

That realization gave her definite pause. Improvisation was dangerous where Joe was concerned, but Dayton's death had left her with no choice. Despite her continuing wooziness, she knew one thing with crystal clarity—she needed to be out of the country by the following morning, before Dayton's personal bank accounts were examined and before the newspapers started to carry reports of his recent financial transactions. The Dayton Fund was big enough that the *Wall Street Journal* and the *New York Times* were sure to give broad coverage to any problems that were uncovered. And once the story was reported in New York, Caroline knew she would no longer be safe. Joe lived in New Jersey, and he skimmed the *Times* every day.

She shook off a tiny shiver of terror and told herself how fortunate it was that Dayton had died late on a Friday night. She had the whole weekend ahead of her to get a jump on disappearing. Presumably none of Dayton's partners would go through his office papers for at least twenty-four hours, not even Christopher Van Haas, Felicity's father, who was Dayton's official business partner and the executor of Dayton's will.

Still, she couldn't count on having much of a grace period once the auditors moved in and examined Dayton's files. Joe almost certainly knew she'd been Dayton's mistress—it was inconceivable he would not—and with Dayton dead, Joe would make it his business to find out where she'd gone, even if, by some miracle, he didn't connect her with the missing money. As a matter of principle, Joe always liked to know where his victims were.

Fear marched down her spine in icy steps. Caroline fought the urge to throw a change of clothing into a suitcase and simply take the first flight out of Chicago. Planning, she warned herself. None of this is going to work without planning.

As soon as she'd taken another shower, scrubbed off all her makeup and changed into jeans, she started calling the airlines. Marriage to Phillip had taught her a lot, and ever since the day when she'd finally worked up the courage to leave him, she made her travel arrangements directly with the airlines, using a credit card issued in a false name.

While she was trying to hide from her father-in-law right after the divorce, Caroline had discovered that obtaining multiple credit cards was easy. The national enthusiasm for enticing consumers to buy goods they couldn't afford made their acquisition a breeze. And, provided you paid them off on time, once issued, they were never recalled. Currently she was using a card that was billed to Ms. Jeanne Matalin, secretary—a character she'd invented out of thin air about four months ago. Since there was no reason for Joe to know about Jeanne Matalin, Caroline was optimistic that her airline booking in Jeanne's name would go unnoticed.

She could have flown straight to the Cayman Islands from O'Hare, except that the airlines insisted on seeing a passport and matching ticket before allowing passengers to board an international flight. Since she had no documents for Ms. Matalin other than the credit card, international travel under that name was out.

All was not lost, however. A fake passport was just one of the many elaborate preparations she and Lionel had made. So she booked a flight to Miami as Jeanne Matalin, then called a different airline and made a reservation in the name of Sally Decker, nurse, for the short flight south from Miami to Grand Cayman. She didn't make a hotel reservation—one less booking fed into a central computer system, one less booking that could be tracked to her or to either of her aliases.

Caroline hung up the phone feeling reasonably content with her travel arrangements as far as getting *to* Grand Cayman. The weak link in the chain was the return segment of her journey. Ideally, she'd hoped to have a customs official in Grand Cayman paid off to guarantee that there would be no examination of her hand baggage. But Lionel hadn't completed those arrangements yet, and she sure as hell wasn't going to take the risk of contacting him again until she had the money.

She wished she could talk to Lionel, explain to him why she'd brought forward her plans, but she couldn't, and there was no point in wishing for the moon, as dear old nanny number six or seven would have reminded her. Dayton's unexpected death meant that she had to leave town before all the details of her plan were in place. She decided she'd get to Grand Cayman first and then worry about smuggling the stolen bearer bonds back into the States. Lord knew, Lionel's network of corrupt drug-dealing friends stretched throughout the hemisphere, and paying a petty customs official in Grand Cayman to look the other way should be all in a morning's work for him. The situation wasn't ideal, Caroline realized, but it was the best she could manage under the circumstances. Dayton was dead, and she had to get out of Chicago before Joe started to show an interest in her movements.

Caroline knew her evasive tactics were rudimentary and wouldn't stop an experienced investigator from finding her, but they might slow Joe's people down, perhaps for as much as a week. And a week was all she would need. Please God, let that be enough. Once she had retrieved Dayton's stolen money, she would bury herself so deep that even Joe wouldn't be able to trace her. Until it was too late.

Caroline had spent the past three months perfecting her plans, and she should have felt elated that the payoff now waited right around the corner. With Dayton out of the picture, in some ways her task was a lot easier. At least he wouldn't be on her trail, as well as Joe. Part of her thrummed with an excitement and yearning she could barely keep in check. Another part couldn't believe she would succeed in getting to the money before Joe.

Don't think about the money, she warned herself. Concentrate on getting out of Chicago. She poured some ice water and rubbed the sweating glass over her forehead.

The planning process would be a mile easier if her stomach hadn't been churning, her heart racing and her head aching. Oddly enough, she even felt an undercurrent of worry about Felicity. The fact that Dayton's wife would be publicly humiliated when the truth came out about his business dealings ought to have been a matter of complete indifference to Caroline. But she couldn't quite shake the feeling that Dayton's wife didn't deserve to pay so dearly for the sin of marrying the wrong man and being born to the wrong father.

She and Felicity were sisters under the skin, she reflected with bitter irony. Neither of them had had the smarts to realize they were choosing husbands who were certified assholes.

But there was no time to dwell on Dayton's death or Felicity's problems. Caroline had enough problems of her own. And she had a lot to do. She set about methodically destroying every scrap of paper that recorded her life and activities over the previous six months. When she was finished, she had a black plastic garbage bag full of shredded paper to take to the dump, and a wallet containing her fake passport, nine thousand dollars in traveler's checks, a thousand dollars in cash and a driver's license from when she'd lived in New York City. Fortunately, her New York license was still valid, so she cut up her Illinois one and tossed it into the garbage bag along with the rest of her trash.

Her recent past safely consigned to oblivion, she packed two suitcases, trying her best to choose clothing that was inconspicuous—not an easy task given that most of her wardrobe had been bought for the express purpose of seducing Dayton Ames.

She'd visited the Cayman Islands five years before, with Phillip, and she knew it wasn't exactly the vacation paradise of the Caribbean. At the time of their trip, naive and still infatuated, she'd wondered why Phillip had chosen to vacation on an island where only seven miles of beach were free of iron and lava rock and the nightlife consisted mainly of expatriate Brits playing bridge. Later, after they were married, she'd realized that Phillip hadn't gone to the Cayman Islands because of the turtle farms or the cramped beaches. Like most other visitors, Phillip had gone there to take advantage of the banking facilities.

The islands were a British protectorate, and the colonial authorities had a surprisingly practical attitude to the funds sliding in and out of their jurisdiction. They pocketed the profits and asked as few questions as possible—a system that dismayed the IRS and US Customs but made many American citizens very happy. Including Dayton Ames, as Caroline had discovered early in their acquaintance.

Her packing done, she completed the remaining preparations to leave her apartment with the ease of hard-won experience. She had designed her living arrangements so she would be free to disappear at a moment's notice. She had no pets, no living plants and no food supplies to speak of. She'd had a goldfish once, a self-important creature with a long tail she'd called Humperdink. She'd given Humperdink away when she realized that he was the first thing she went to check on when she came home, and that she'd fallen into the habit of talking to him. The fact that she'd actually missed the silly creature merely confirmed that she'd made the right decision in giving him away. Caroline didn't trust emotional attachments, even to goldfish.

By five-thirty, the household chores were finished and the apartment was pristine. She'd vacuumed every surface and thrown away the dust bag along with her shredded papers. Whoever came looking for her—Joe or the police—would be hard put to find any proof she'd ever lived there.

Despite being tired, she didn't sleep well that night, and she got up early on Sunday morning so she'd have time to read the newspaper before leaving for the airport. She called and arranged for a cab to pick her up at nine-thirty, then walked to the corner of Fullerton and Clark to pick up a copy of the *Chicago Tribune*.

Dayton's obituary was the lead story on the front page of the business section. She read it while she drank the last of her orange juice from a disposable cup. The headline was printed in large, bold type: Dayton Ames, Founder And CEO Of The Dayton Fund, Dead At Age 48.

The subsequent story gave no hint of any scandal surrounding Dayton's death. Felicity hadn't exaggerated when she'd informed Caroline that she would take care of everything. As far as the *Tribune* was concerned, Dayton Ames, pillar of society and captain of finance, had died peacefully in his sleep. Alone.

The report explained that Mrs. Ames had been spending the night with Lucy, her teenage daughter, and a few young friends at the Ames's suburban home in Winnetka. She had returned to the city early on Saturday morning, as planned, and discovered her husband dead in their bed.

The *Tribune* informed its readers that Dayton Ames was active on the board of the local United Way and that his death was a grievous loss to the Chicago philanthropic community. The newspaper pointed out that his company, the Dayton Fund, controlled investment assets in excess of three hundred million dollars, and that the burial service would be private.

Arrangements for a memorial service would be announced at a later date.

The bare-bones account of Dayton's death was exactly what Caroline had hoped to read. Thanks to Felicity's desire to conceal the truth about her husband's infidelity, nothing had slipped through that was likely to attract the interest of an investigative reporter from the national media, at least for the next few days. Of course, when the irregularities in the fund came to light, it would be a different story. But by then, Caroline would be long gone.

She crushed her paper cup and tossed it into the garbage disposal, finally allowing herself to hope. It looked like she was going to get the forty-eight-hour window of opportunity she so badly needed.

Her house phone buzzed, indicating that someone was at the door. She picked up the receiver, trying to quell a quick leap of her pulse. She had to stop assuming that every ring of the bell presaged bad news.

"Hello."

"The Yellow Cab you ordered is here, ma'am."

"I'll be right down. I just have to collect my luggage."

"Yes, ma'am. I'll be waiting for you."

Caroline glanced at her watch. The driver had arrived three minutes early, he spoke perfect English and he'd called her ma'am. Twice. Any one of those things would have been surprising; a triple combo was truly amazing. Life was looking up. She smiled, her first smile in twenty-four hours. Maybe, if she got *really* lucky, the cab's air-conditioning would work. Miracles had been known to happen, even in a Chicago cab.

Engine running, the Yellow Cab was waiting at the curb right outside her front door. The driver's window was down—which didn't bode well for the state of his air-conditioning system—but at least he was on the job, standing next to the open trunk, waiting to take her luggage and smiling politely.

"Thanks," Caroline said, handing over her suitcase. "I'll keep this carryon bag with me."

"Sure thing, ma'am." The cabby slammed the trunk and put his hand firmly beneath her elbow. "This way, ma'am."

Caroline's stomach clenched, and she jerked her elbow, not attempting to be subtle about her wish to be released from the cabby's hold. Far from relaxing, his grip tightened.

"Let go of me," she said, instantly afraid. She hated to be touched.

"Sorry, ma'am, no can do." His polite smiles vanished, and he opened the rear door of the cab, propelling her forward, off the curb.

In the blink of an eye, her mild fear became full-fledged terror. Joe! Dear God, how had he found her so fast? The answer came in a trice. Her phone. He'd bugged her stupid phone. This cab was a setup, which was why it had arrived early.

She struggled with the strength of desperation, but the driver was tall and strong and obviously an expert in the techniques of urban abduction. What else would she expect from one of Joe's employees?

There were a couple of pedestrians down the street, and Caroline tried to scream, but her abductor clapped his hand over her mouth, muffling the sound almost before she could draw breath.

She bit his palm, hard and deep. He didn't even wince, much less pull away. She managed to direct a backward kick toward his groin, but he sidestepped and she didn't connect.

"Stop it, bitch," he said, and shoved his knee with brutal force into the small of her back, leaving her no choice but to step into the cab. She had no doubt he would knock her unconscious—or break her back—if that's what it took to bring her in. Joe's orders had a way of being obeyed.

Another man she didn't recognize was already seated in the rear of the car. He grabbed her hands and pulled her inside. She toppled across his lap, face-down in his crotch, and the driver slammed the door behind her, springing behind the wheel and accelerating from zero to forty in about ten seconds flat.

As soon as the cab started moving, Caroline scrambled into an upright position and edged to the corner of the seat. The man sitting next to her leered suggestively. She tugged down the hem of her skirt, struggling to regain control of herself. How could she possibly have thought it would be so easy to get away? What an absolute fool she'd been to believe that Joe was no longer keeping her under surveillance. With a sinking feeling, she accepted the likelihood that she'd probably never been out of his sight since the day of Phillip's funeral.

The man next to her patted her thigh. "You should leave your skirt up, babe," he said, grinning. "You got great legs."

She responded with silence and a blank stare. The man chuckled. "Reckon Dayton Ames had hisself a good time with them legs. What do you reckon, Steve? You reckon Mr. Ames had fun with them legs?"

"I reckon you should keep your mouth shut," the driver replied. "Act more respectful to a member of your employer's family."

So they knew who she was, Caroline thought, and that she'd been Dayton Ames's mistress. No real surprises there. If Joe had been keeping her closely watched, he certainly knew where she'd been spending many of her nights.

"Where are you taking me?" she asked. That was all she could manage before her voice cracked with fear.

"We're taking you for a nice ride," the driver said. "Ain't that right, Gerry?"

"Right," her seatmate agreed. "A real nice ride. To the best part of town an' all."

Caroline looked out the window, more to hide her panic than to confirm where they were going. She wasn't reassured to see that the kidnappers were telling the truth: they were heading toward the Gold Coast, not into some hideous South Side slum. But then, she'd never really considered the possibility that these were two drug-crazed addicts looking to indulge in a little rape and robbery. She'd known right away that they were sent by Joe.

"Why are you taking me for a ride?" she asked when she could breathe freely enough to catch her voice. "Are you going to tell me what this is all about?"

"You know that better'n we do," Gerry said. "The boss, he don't take us into his confidence."

Unfortunately, Gerry was right. She probably *did* know more about what was going on than they did. Caroline bit back a bubble of hysterical laughter. She was so damn scared, she was incapable of showing even a trace of emotion in case she started shrieking and couldn't stop.

"How long has Joe been in town?" she asked, trying to make the question sound casual.

Neither of the men answered. Caroline spread her hands flat on the cracked leather seat. She could feel the sweat congeal beneath her palms. She swallowed and concentrated on regulating her breathing.

Steve glanced at her in his driving mirror, and his mouth twisted into a sneer. "Almost there, sugar. Ready to put on your best party smile?"

For reply, Caroline laced her fingers tightly together and stared out the window.

"Snooty, aren't we?" Steve said. "Guess that's what comes of marrying well."

Gerry snickered. "Yeah, but she didn't do so good out of the divorce, did she?"

No, Caroline thought bleakly. I didn't do good at all.

The cab turned into an alley alongside Bloomingdale's on North Michigan Avenue. Steve used an electronic access card to gain entry to the underground garage, then parked the cab in the handicapped space right next to the elevators. Joe had apparently found himself a home in one of Chicago's most elegant buildings. That knowledge worried Caroline. She couldn't think of any reason he'd be spending much time here, other than because of her. His business interests were all in New Jersey.

With a casualness that she found more chilling than any angry threat could possibly have been, Steve pulled back his jacket to show her the nine-millimeter semiautomatic tucked into his belt.

"Me and Gerry, we each got ourselves one of these fancy new pieces," he said. "Now, you come upstairs without making no fuss, and we won't have to use either of them, right? Then you'll stay alive, and we won't have Joe yelling at us, right? And everyone will be real happy." He smiled. "You want us all to be happy, sugar, don't you?"

"Sure," Caroline said. "I just love making everyone happy."

"Let's move it, then, sugar. The boss is waiting. And he sure don't like to be kept waitin'. But you know that, don't you? You and Joe must be real old friends by now."

Caroline didn't answer, she couldn't have found her voice even if she'd wanted to answer. Steve used a special key, and the elevator carried them directly to the penthouse floor. The doors opened onto a private lobby, decorated in the style usually favored by lawyers who wanted to be sure prospective clients knew their fees were stratospherically expensive. Joe's taste had never been subtle or understated.

The sliding mahogany doors leading into the penthouse stood open, and Steve propelled her straight inside, across a carpet that had probably once graced the floor of an imperial residence in China.

She only realized how much she'd dreaded this meeting when they emerged from the vestibule and came into the living room. A familiar, silver-haired man stood looking out the living room window, apparently admiring the panoramic view of Lake Michigan. He didn't turn around at the sound of their approaching footsteps, waiting instead in silence until Caroline and her escort had walked all the way across the room. Then he turned. And smiled.

With an effort that broke sweat on her forehead, Caroline kept her face expressionless and her gaze locked with his. She hoped he didn't see her tremble, but speaking was more than she could manage.

Unfortunately, despite her efforts, she knew he saw precisely the effect he was having on her, and that made him smile even more broadly. He stretched out his hands in a parody of affectionate welcome. "Caroline, my dear child. How good to see you again after all this time."

Avoiding his hands, she forced out a reply. "A year, Joe. It's only been a year."

"At my son's funeral." Joe's voice cracked with grief that still sounded as fresh and new as it had when Phillip's lifeless body had been found gunned down on a Brooklyn street. "And not a word from you since."

"We met in court," she said tautly.

He ignored her comment. "I guess I should be grateful you had the courtesy to come and see your own husband buried."

"Ex-husband," she said. "Phillip and I were already divorced when he died."

Joe's swarthy complexion darkened to an alarming shade of purple. "I don't acknowledge your divorce," he roared. "We're Catholics in my family, and so are you. You converted when you married Phillip."

"I know I did." She'd agreed to a lot of things when she married Phillip that she later regretted. Caroline drew in a deep breath. "Look, I'm sorry, Joe—"

"You had no right to divorce my son." He scowled at her, anger still unabated two years after the divorce. "What more did you want from my boy? There was nothing he wasn't willing to do for you."

"Except give me respect and trust—"

"What the hell are you talkin' about? My boy, he was crazy mad in love with you!"

Caroline pressed her hands flat against her sides. "Joe, we've been over all this before, so many times—"

Joe brought his arm down in an angry chopping motion. "My boy was educated, with a degree from the same fancy school as you, and better grades, too. He was a good provider, gave you a nice home, kept you in pretty clothes. He didn't even chase after other women, although they all wanted him and you weren't willing to give him the time of day. He swore to me on my mother's grave that he never had another woman once he was married to you."

Caroline knew there were some arguments that couldn't be won, so she didn't reply. She might have been dumb enough to believe she'd shaken Joe Rossi from her life these past six months, but she wasn't dumb enough to tell him that his only son—his murdered son—had been a chronic liar.

Joe scowled, infuriated by her silence, then flapped his hand at Steve and Gerry. "Wait outside," he said. "Go on. I'll call you when I need you."

The men left. Once he was alone with her, Joe seemed to relax, at least a little. He usually managed to behave with cheery benevolence when things were going his way, and the ease with which he'd commanded Caroline's presence had apparently pleased him. He gave her another smile, this one genuinely admiring.

"Let's talk about nicer things, eh, *cara?* You're looking good, Caroline, very good. Blond hair suits you. Goes with those cool gray eyes of yours. Real high-class. I like a woman who takes care of herself."

"I *need* to take care of myself," she said coldly, refusing to feel demeaned by his scrutiny of her body and the lingering glance he gave to her legs. "My face and figure are my only remaining assets."

Something about her tone apparently didn't ring quite true. The look Joe shot her was sharp and probing. But then, he hadn't gotten to his current position by being a fool, as Caroline knew all too well. She held her breath but, for whatever reason, he decided not to challenge her.

"You want a drink?" he asked, gesturing toward a well-stocked bar. "I can call the girl and get you ice tea or a Pepsi if you don't want the hard stuff."

"Nothing, thanks. I really need to be leaving if I'm going to catch my plane." She glanced pointedly at her watch, as if they didn't both know there wasn't the faintest chance in the world of her flying to Miami. Or on to Grand Cayman. "I'm in a bit of a hurry, Joe. Was there some special reason you wanted to see me?"

"Not special, exactly. Like I told you, *cara,* you're family. We need to chat every now and then. That's what families do. Spend time together." He beamed at her, a perfect picture of the benevolent, kindly father-in-law, anxious to make her feel welcome.

She hated him in that moment, hated him more than she'd believed she could hate another human being. But she wouldn't give in and ask him the question she knew he wanted to hear from her.

"Thank you for your interest, Joe." Her voice shook from the effort of not broaching the one subject she most longed to broach. She'd be damned if she'd let him see her grief. Or any profound emotion at all. She stretched her mouth into a smile. "As you can see for yourself, Joe, I'm well. And keeping busy."

His smile tightened. "Warming that bastard Dayton Ames's bed."

There was genuine anger in Joe's voice. Caroline wasn't sure if it was directed at Dayton or at her. Knowing Joe, probably both. As his son's widow, she was expected to remain chaste and grieving for the next forty years. She realized, with a tiny shock at the childishness of her own motives, that part of the reason she'd become Dayton's mistress had been a need to defy Joe in the way most likely to annoy him.

"Dayton paid well," she said, her voice carefully neutral, as if Dayton's generosity explained everything. She cocked her head and spoke politely. "I didn't realize you knew him, Joe."

"Then you're nowhere near as smart as I always thought you were," he snapped, annoyed by her self-control. "What the hell did you need Dayton's money for? What clever little scheme are you concocting in that too-smart brain of yours, Caroline?"

Her stomach clenched with terror. There could be a dozen different reasons for Joe's question. None of them boded well for her plans, but she managed a credible pretense of a shrug. Nowadays, it was very hard for anyone to discern what she was feeling, even an expert like Joe. She'd repressed her emotions for so long that if she ever tried to respond normally—to feel naturally—she would probably discover she'd forgotten how.

"What do you think I needed his money for?" She looked Joe straight in the eye, injecting the note of resentment he probably would expect from her. "You may remember that my divorce settlement left me a little low on cash. I believe I received a thousand dollars and my car. That sort of money doesn't take a woman too far these days."

He grunted. "You have a college degree." Joe wasn't being sarcastic, she knew, not entirely. Like many first-generation Americans, he had a naive faith in the power of a college education. Phillip's law degree had been a source of supreme pride to his father. "Why didn't you get a regular job?" he demanded. "The way I remember it, you were always Miss High and Mighty, preaching to Phillip about the value of hard work and honest labor."

She forced her mouth into a tiny, mocking smile. "Well, Joe, it seems that Phillip converted me to his values rather than the other way around. Like I said, a girl has to live, after all, and trainee accountants, with no experience to speak of, just don't pull in the kind of money that a well-paid mistress can earn for herself. You can't blame me if I decided to go after the big bucks."

"As a whore? You think I like hearing that my son's widow is earning her living on her back?"

"I didn't know you cared, Joe."

He ignored the mockery in her voice. "Of course I cared. My son's widow . . . I expected more respect for his memory."

"Well, you were the person who first claimed that I had no morals," she said. "You shouldn't have given me ideas." She shrugged. "The fact is, Joe, I had expenses to meet, and my parents weren't about to help me out, that's for sure."

To her astonishment, she saw that he was inclined to believe her. The mention of her parents had been a convincing touch. He certainly knew that Mr. and

Mrs. George V. Hogarth IV weren't likely to be forking out spending money to their errant, disowned daughter.

"You could have come to me," he said, sounding tired. "Whatever our differences, if you'd played your cards right, you could have had anything you wanted from me after my son died."

"Could I?" she asked, shocked into rashness. "Seems to me, Joe, you'd have given me everything except the one thing I wanted." Her voice broke but she recovered quickly, furious at the momentary lapse. "Let's cut to the chase, shall we? You didn't bring me here to chat about old times. So what do you want from me?"

Joe walked over to the window, indicating that she should come and stand beside him to admire the view. She obeyed, trying not to show her revulsion at their proximity. Or her fear. The sun had turned the waters of Lake Michigan into a dazzling silver mirror. The beauty made her feel sad. It had been a while since she'd stood still long enough to watch the reflection of sun dancing across water.

Joe broke the silence. "Why did you book a flight to the Cayman Islands?" he demanded, as if he didn't already know the answer. "What you want to do down in that place?"

So she'd been right, Caroline thought bleakly. Joe had been bugging her phone. There was no other way for him to know this fast that she'd booked a ticket to Grand Cayman. She'd checked her apartment regularly, and she could have sworn it was clean, which just went to show that amateurs didn't have much of a chance when they went up against the pros. Obviously, she'd missed one of Joe's high-tech micro minibugs. So much for Jeanne Matalin and the anonymous credit card.

There wasn't a hope in hell Joe would believe she was hightailing it down to Grand Cayman for a spot of recreational sun and surf.

"I keep my own personal accounts there," she said. "Dayton paid well, but he worked me damned hard for the past six months. I saw no reason to cut the IRS in on my profits."

Joe gave no sign whether he believed her or not. "You're not the only person Dayton's been screwing," he said abruptly.

Her mouth went dry. "What does that mean?"

"He been screwing me, too. The bastard's been ripping me off on a regular basis."

Joe never revealed information without a purpose, so why was he telling her this? What did he hope to discover? "How come?" she asked, deliberately making herself sound confused. "How could he cheat you?"

"He's been milking that fund of his. I put good money into that damn fund, expecting it to come out clean, and that bastard was creaming off half the profits."

How the hell had Joe found that out? Dayton had been so proud of the fact that he'd used only the most sophisticated skimming techniques to rob his boss. "I wouldn't know anything about Dayton's business dealings," Caroline said, amazed that her voice managed to squeak its way past her shaky vocal chords. "I was Dayton's mistress, not his financial partner."

Joe scrutinized her with unnerving intensity, but Caroline hoped his prejudices would work in her favor. In his heart of hearts, Joe didn't really believe that women were capable of understanding the workings of a multimillion-dollar mutual fund, and it was outside his vision of the world to accept that Dayton Ames would be stupid enough to confide details of his financial transactions to a woman he was paying to bed. Still, he had a peasant's instinct for knowing when he was being cheated, even if he couldn't quite see how, and Caroline suspected he sensed she was lying about something. He just wasn't quite sure about what.

"Lionel's dead," he said, with one of his sudden changes of topic designed to throw her off guard. "He died two weeks ago. We had a real nice memorial service in Brooklyn last Saturday."

His ploy worked, just as he'd known it would. For a split second, Caroline's heart stopped beating. *Lionel's dead.* The words echoed deep inside her soul. Her despair was so overwhelming that she wanted to howl with the anguish of her lost hopes. A scream was already rising in her throat when she fought it back, grabbing frantically for her self-control. The scream died, emerging as no more than a tiny whimper of distress.

She unclenched her teeth so she could speak. "I'm sorry to hear that. How...how did he die?"

"An accident."

She licked her lips. Sure. And Elvis was working at a supermarket in Las Vegas. "What sort of an accident?" she asked.

"It was very sad, a tragedy, really." Joe looked mournful, and the irony was that he probably felt genuine regret. "He fell out of the window of his mother's apartment. The poor guy busted his neck, and his spine was shattered in three place—"

"No, I don't want to hear any more!" Caroline clamped her fist over her mouth, swallowing bile.

"Sorry, I didn't mean to upset you." Joe held out a glass of club soda, all kind solicitude. "Here, *cara*, drink this. I knew you and Lionel were close and all, but if I'd realized you still cared so much, I'd have broken the news more gently."

She took a sip of the club soda, her teeth chattering against the rim of the glass. "It doesn't matter," she said wearily, and at that precise moment, it really didn't. If one of Joe's employees fell out a window, it was a safe bet he'd been pushed. She knew Joe hadn't discovered how profoundly Lionel had betrayed him last year, or Caroline herself would be dead. Which meant that Joe had arranged for Lionel's murder because he'd learned what she and Lionel had been planning to do with Dayton's stolen money.

So why had Joe told her Lionel was dead? Was he warning her that her plans had no chance of coming to fruition, or threatening her with a similar fate? Caroline didn't really care. In every way that mattered, she already felt as good as dead. With her careful plans in ruins, she wasn't sure what she had left to live for.

The club soda fizzed and popped its way into her stomach, and she had the oddest sensation that her insides had vanished, leaving her hollow. Her skin no longer felt like the outer layer of a real person. Instead, it was a shell of pain, wrapped around the void that had once been Caroline.

"Come home, Caroline." Joe's voice was surprisingly kind. "Stop fightin' me, because you can't win. We both know you can't win."

She knew he was right, but his confidence that he'd defeated her stiffened her spine. She wasn't quite ready to surrender. Not yet. Dammit, despite everything, she wasn't dead yet, and some tiny, stubborn voice whispered that there was more than five million dollars in Dayton's account in Grand Cayman, and she was the only person alive who knew how to access it. With that kind of money, all things were possible. Joe himself had shown her the bitter truth that, in the last resort, everything is for sale, even justice.

She drew herself up to her full height and squinted down her nose at Joe in her best prep-school manner. There were some advantages to being raised in a wealthy, blue-blooded family, she thought wryly, even if you were adopted.

"Go fuck yourself, Joe," she said with exquisite politeness. She swiveled on her heel and walked to the door without waiting to see his reaction. If he really lost his temper, he was quite capable of shooting her in the back. Right now, she wouldn't have cared if he had.

Gerry and Steve were waiting outside the door, expressions avid. They'd most likely been listening at the keyhole. She thought there was something vaguely comic about the whole situation, but she was too tired to work out exactly what.

"Show's over, folks," she said. "Excuse me, please. It's time for me to go home."

Steve stared at her, then glanced toward Joe. "Boss? You want us to take her someplace?"

She didn't want to ride with Gerry and Steve. She wanted—quite desperately—to be alone. "I can find my own way—"

"Take her back to her apartment," Joe yelled. "Leave her in the middle of Michigan Avenue. I don't care what the hell you do with her. But keep on her ass. I don't want her out of your sight." He slammed the door behind her so hard that the Lalique crystal vase across the hallway shook on its stand.

Caroline wondered why Joe was so angry. He had no cause to feel annoyed with the outcome of their meeting. In all the ways that mattered, he'd won.

The door jerked open again. "Caroline!"

Something about the way Joe spoke her name made her turn around. "Yes?"

His beautiful dark eyes—so like Phillip's—gleamed with cruelty. "Andrew sends his love," he said.

She stared at him, speechless with pain, and he closed the door once more, this time with infinite softness. He gave no sign at all that he heard the frantic pounding of her fists on the mahogany panels. No sign that he heard her pathetic sobs.

Joe liked solitude to savor his victories.

Three

If Gerry and Steve spoke to her on the ride to Lincoln Park West, Caroline didn't hear them. She huddled in the back seat of the car and heard only the drumbeat of Andrew's name echo in her heart.

When they arrived at her apartment, Steve stayed at the wheel of the car and Gerry got out to escort her to the door of her building.

"You got the key to get in?" he asked.

Caroline saw his mouth move and realized he'd asked a question, so she nodded, although she had no idea what he'd said. To her relief, it seemed she'd given the right response. Gerry grunted and walked to the car without saying another word.

She watched Steve turn the car into a narrow service alley across the street from her apartment building. He parked at the curb, angling the car for a clear view of her doorway. The knowledge provoked no reaction in her, no sense of alarm, no desire to evade their scrutiny. Logical thought and emotion were temporarily beyond her.

After five minutes of staring aimlessly in the direction of their car, Caroline realized that the sun was making her sweat, so she finally turned and took a step toward the covered porch of her building in search of shade. The move was purely reflexive. As she turned, her foot knocked against something solid, and she tripped, almost falling. She glanced down and saw her suitcases. Gerry must have tossed them right by her feet.

She stared at the two cases blankly, as if they were alien objects from outer space. She vaguely recognized that she ought to do something with them but couldn't decide what. She walked around them, then dragged them into the lobby of her apartment building. They were pink and gray tweed and very heavy. Too heavy to carry anywhere, Caroline reflected hazily. Besides, why would she need suitcases? She wasn't going to make her trip to the Cayman Islands anytime soon. Not with Joe watching her every move. Joe and Gerry and Steve and lord knew how many other goons, all watching her, twenty-four hours a day. She was trapped, unable to access Dayton's money without alerting Joe, unable to make her move until she had the money.

Emotion returned and self-pity overwhelmed her. Six months of hard work as Dayton's mistress all gone to waste. She couldn't get to the money, and worst of all, Lionel was dead. Not only did his death lie heavy on her conscience, but she had no idea how she was going to replace him. Now that she no longer had daily contact with Joe's organization, how would she ever find somebody willing to work for her on the inside? More to the point, how could she justify tempting another man to almost certain death?

Blindly, she stared through the building's glass doors into the sun. *Andrew sends his love.*

She closed her eyes, fighting tears. Her rules for herself were strict, and they didn't allow tears for Andrew, just as they didn't permit her to think about the past. She'd vowed last Christmas that she simply wouldn't put herself through the torment of remembering ever again.

Caroline stared at her suitcases. Since she couldn't think why she would need them, she left them standing in the middle of the lobby, tweed memorials to her vanished hopes.

There didn't seem to be any point in staying in the lobby of her building, so she walked outside and wandered aimlessly toward the nearest crossroads. Steve and Gerry drove out of the alley, following her. She waited through three changes of traffic lights, unable to decide which way to turn. She wasn't trying to think up some clever scheme to avoid the tail. On the contrary, she was paralyzed, the effort of making a decision almost beyond her powers.

Left, right or straight ahead? The choice seemed too difficult. So many options, all without purpose. In the end, she crossed Fullerton and turned north, still without any sense of her destination, except that she had no intention of spending the night in her apartment. The idea of returning there, to the place she'd thought was so safe, revolted her. However long she searched for electronic bugs, however many she removed, she would never be sure she'd found them all, and she would feel Joe's presence in every pore of her body. Her flesh crawled at the thought.

She walked briskly now that she'd chosen a direction, her eyes darting from side to side, busily absorbing information about her surroundings, although her brain refused to process it. The street remained a meaningless blur of people, cars and storefronts, which she couldn't manage to shape into a coherent picture. At the periphery of her vision, she was constantly aware of Steve and Gerry, but she couldn't quite remember why this was a problem.

The blankness of her mind shifted and reformed into a semblance of coherence, recoiling from the loathsome knowledge that for weeks—perhaps months—Joe had kept her under close surveillance, and she'd never once spotted a tail. Good grief, it was humiliating to think of how she'd deluded herself into imagining she was in control when actually Joe had been pulling all the strings, sitting at the heart of his lair, laughing at her pathetic moves.

Caroline trudged on, indifferent to the blazing midday sun, until her legs felt wobbly and the sweat pooled at the base of her neck and dripped between her breasts in a steady trickle. Even so, when she did finally stop, it was only because a couple of teenagers on inline skates careened into her, and only the quick action of a bystander prevented her being knocked into the road, right into the path of oncoming traffic. And Gerry and Steve.

Dazed, but feeling no sense of alarm at the accident narrowly averted, Caroline thanked the bystander and the small crowd of onlookers who'd gathered to see if she was all right. Vaguely, she was aware of Steve turning the car at the traffic light and looping around to tail her again. A bus rolled up to the sidewalk and she started to get on it, then got off at the last moment, dizzy with indecision. The two boys on skates swooped past again, showing off to three giggling girls who'd just stepped off the bus.

Caroline was forced to move, somehow becoming tangled in the group of giggling girls and swooping skaters. When the girls turned into a vest-pocket park and the skaters moved on, she noticed she was walking down a side street that was dank and strewn with garbage. But at least she'd lost Steve and Gerry, giving her a narrow window of opportunity to hide herself while she reformed her plans.

Undeterred by her surroundings, she trudged on, stopping only when an old woman stepped right in front of her and Caroline realized she didn't have the energy to circumvent the unexpected obstacle.

"You look wore out, hon," the old woman said. "You okay?"

Was she okay? Caroline blinked, thinking hard. Hell, she was still standing, wasn't she? That must prove she was okay.

"I'm fine," she croaked. "Thanks." She would have walked on, but she found her legs, having stopped, couldn't seem to start again. She lurched forward and clutched the woman's arm for support.

"You look like you need a rest, hon. There's a bench over there by the park gate. You wanna sit down?"

Caroline frowned. She didn't want to sit. She wanted to have a drink. "Thirsty," she said to the old woman. "I need a drink." That didn't sound very polite. "Please," she added.

"What you need, hon, is to go home and sleep it off before you gets yourself into real trouble."

How could you sleep off a thirst? Caroline felt herself sway, and realized she was about to faint.

"Drink," she repeated. "Please, I need a drink."

The old woman shrugged. "It's your funeral, hon, but I bin down the road you're takin' and it don't work out so good."

"Coke," Caroline said. "I just want a Coke."

The woman turned away, her face wrinkled with disapproval. "I guess alcohol's better'n Coke. The bar's thataway."

Caroline forced her legs to move. She staggered to the side of the road in the direction of the woman's pointing finger. Then she propped herself against the wall of the building and peered owlishly at the window. A blinking neon light displayed the outline of a pitcher of beer.

Thirsty as she was, Caroline knew she didn't want to drink beer. Beer made her sick to her stomach. With exaggerated care, she formed another thought. If this was a bar, it would serve soda as well as beer. And if she went inside, she could order a Coke. The effort of thinking with sustained logic left her exhausted. She

staggered to the bar door and leaned on it with her full
weight. It opened and she stumbled through.

The smell of stale cigarette smoke and spilled beer
made her gag, but she was too thirsty to care. She
clung to a wet tabletop to stop herself falling and sa-
vored the cooled air blowing over her, drying the sweat
on her forehead and chest. God, it felt wonderful!
Quickly, she hauled herself upright and crossed to the
bar, flopping onto a stool. Then she leaned forward
and laid her head on her arms. Boy, was she ever tired!

After a few moments in the air-conditioning, her
brain started to work rationally again, and she realized that she'd come dangerously close to collapsing
from dehydration and heat exhaustion. She wondered how far she'd walked and where she was.

She lifted her head and the bartender, a thin man
wearing a red shirt, eyed her warily. "Yeah? What can
I get you?"

"Diet Coke," she rasped. "Large. Extra ice."

He served her in silence, pushing the glass toward
her and shoving a plastic straw in amongst the ice
cubes. She sipped with ravenous thirst, and gradually
the pounding in her ears faded and her eyes began to
function normally again.

She looked around, crunching ice cubes. Her impression of the bar didn't improve on closer inspection. She'd chosen a heck of a place to overcome her
heatstroke, Caroline thought ruefully. The smoke
clogging the air wasn't all from tobacco, that was for
sure, and the general squalor of the place suggested
that the last thorough cleaning had been some time

around 1970. The only other women in the bar both sported tattoos on their muscled forearms and wore skintight athletic shirts that molded their nipples and revealed scoops of pasty white skin. The dozen or so men clustered around a pool table wore mean expressions, dirty jeans and leather knuckle-dusters. All of them had hair longer than hers. Bikers, she thought gloomily, and definitely not the sort who collected toys for tots over the holiday season.

There was an old-fashioned black pay phone by the door, and she debated calling a cab, then decided against it. She didn't want to wait here—wherever *here* might be—a minute longer than necessary. It would be ironic if, having survived her latest encounter with Joe, she succumbed to the random violence of a gang of bikers.

Draining the last of her soda, she tried to mentally retrace her route so that she could locate where she was. She remembered turning north when she left Lincoln Park, so that meant this bar was most likely somewhere uptown. Uptown was the sort of neighborhood that changed its personality block by block, covering a range of possibilities from dangerous through mildly sleazy to respectable streets of expensive yuppie town houses. She apparently had landed deep in a sleazy part.

The el train ran through here somewhere or other, but she didn't feel up to coping with public transport at this point. If she made her way over to Ashland, she should be able to find a café where it would be perfectly safe to wait for a cab. Although where the blazes she would direct the cabby to take her was an interesting question. Some out of the way motel seemed like the best bet.

Long-term decisions could be left for later, she decided. Whatever new plans she made, they couldn't be fulfilled sitting in a grungy bar, sucking on ice cubes. Caroline pushed herself into a standing position, dismayed to find that her legs still felt wobbly and that she'd developed outsize blisters on both heels. Walking to Ashland was not going to be a comfortable stroll. Which was probably appropriate retribution for having behaved like such an idiot. She shouldn't have gone to pieces over a simple meeting with Joe. His reentry into her life had caused a setback, but she'd find a way to cope, just as she always had.

Seeing that she was ready to leave, the bartender gave the counter a swipe with a stained towel and leaned across to take her glass. "That'll be two bucks," he said.

She'd forgotten about paying for her soda. Good grief, did she have any money? Caroline patted her side. Her purse was still slung over her shoulder, safely zippered shut. Thank heaven for small mercies. In those few minutes after Steve and Gerry left her on the sidewalk outside her apartment, she'd been quite capable of dropping her purse next to her suitcases and walking away without a cent to her name. It was bad enough that by now the suitcases would be gone, which meant that she'd kissed goodbye most of her favorite clothes. It would have been disastrous if she'd also lost her cash, her charge cards and her fake passport.

The bartender was waiting to be paid. She unzipped her purse and pulled out her wallet, remembering a split second too late that she was carrying nothing smaller than a fifty-dollar bill.

This was definitely not the ideal place to be flashing a wad of fifties, but she had no choice. She pulled out a note, trying her best to hide the stack of similar bills in her wallet.

"Can you change this?" she asked as casually as she could.

To her relief, the bartender made no comment. He took the bill, rang up No Sale on the till and handed her two twenties and a five. "That's all the change I got," he said.

"That's okay." Caroline didn't believe him about the lack of change, but she knew she'd gotten off lightly. Very lightly, in fact. Five bucks wasn't such a bad price to pay for a soda, if that was what it took to get her out of this bar safely. She stuck the change in her purse, zippered it shut and walked quickly to the door, relieved that nothing worse had happened. In retrospect, she realized she'd behaved with almost criminal stupidity. True, she'd had a rough twenty-four hours, but that didn't excuse her behavior. She'd spent the past several months training herself to cope with precisely this sort of situation.

Andrew sends his love.

Was it true, Caroline wondered as she left the bar. Had Andrew really talked about her? Said that he loved her? Or had Joe invented the supposed message just to torment her? If so, he was succeeding. Mightily succeeding.

Stop thinking about it, she ordered herself. Don't hand Joe that much of a victory. You're breaking the rules.

She blanked out the intrusive images of Andrew and Joe and walked toward the intersection, doing her best to ignore the pain of her blisters and keeping to the scant shade provided by shop awnings and decorative overhangs. Since she wasn't allowed to think about Andrew, she filled her mind with possible plans for getting her hands on Dayton's money, all of which she discarded as fatally flawed. She might be able to escape Joe's scrutiny long enough to get out of Chicago. But she didn't have a chance in hell of landing in the Cayman Islands without him knowing about it. One of his people would be on her tail before she had a chance to pick up her luggage and exit the immigration hall.

The blister on her left foot had grown into a pulsating blob of pain, and she bent to move the strap on her shoe to a more comfortable position. In a moment of sudden quiet, she heard the thud of footsteps coming up fast behind her. She spun around, recognized two men from the bar and knew she was in big trouble. She didn't attempt any heroics. She yelled at the top of her lungs for help and started to run, but she hadn't taken more than a couple of steps before one of them grabbed her, clapping his hand over her mouth and dragging her into a deserted side street.

I already did this once today, she thought wildly. I don't want to do it again.

She kicked and bit and struggled, but to no avail. The man hooked his arm around her windpipe and squeezed. Her breath vanished with terrifying abruptness, and she felt her body go limp.

On the verge of passing out, she realized that the second man had snatched her purse from her shoulder and had found her wallet.

She heard him whistle. "Hot shit!"

"What's she got?"

"Jeezus! Must be a thousand bucks in here. Where the hell did she get it?"

"Who cares?" The man holding her swung her around and landed a vicious uppercut to her jaw. "Stupid bitch. Stupid rich bitch. Who the hell cares how she got it?"

Caroline choked, coughing and retching as he flung her away from him. She crashed into the wall. She didn't exactly feel her head bang against the bricks, rather she heard the crack reverberate inside her skull.

Red dots swam across her vision. She shook her head. The red dots danced and the world tilted. From a spot just above her head, she watched herself slide down the wall and crumple into a boneless pile on the hot pavement. She wanted to scream, but no sounds emerged.

Voices spoke from high above her. "Someone's coming. Move your ass outta here."

"Ha! I ain't stupid, you know. Gimme my share of the money first."

Blackness swept over her in sickening waves, then parted for an instant. She saw a booted foot swing toward her. She lay helpless, knowing exactly what was going to happen. The boot connected with her gut and her ribs exploded in a sunburst of excruciating new pain.

She closed her eyes. Another blow was aimed for her breasts, but it was hastily delivered and she barely felt it. Far, far away she heard more shouts and the sound of running feet.

The thud of footsteps disappeared into blackness, leaving only blissful silence and release from pain. She sank gratefully into the void.

The fingers on her forehead were cool. The masculine voice in her ear was warm, almost gentle. "I've sent for the paramedics. They'll be here very soon." She felt the cool fingers pick up a strand of her hair and smooth it away from her face. "You're going to be fine, trust me. We'll soon have you fixed up as good as new."

Trust him? She didn't even trust herself, let alone a perfect stranger. Caroline would have laughed except that it hurt to laugh, so she kept silent, not attempting to open her eyes. The less she said, the less she could inadvertently reveal.

And revelations were always dangerous.

"Can you tell me where it hurts?" The cool fingers moved again with feather lightness across her face, their touch inexplicably soothing. Against her better judgment, she responded by turning her cheek toward the man's hand. A thumb brushed over her mouth, barely touching it, and the warm voice spoke again.

"I bet you're thirsty. I've sent Marcus for some ice water, and he should be back any minute. A sip or two will help to make you feel better. I hope."

Water sounded like a great idea, but Caroline still didn't speak. Instead, she completed her silent inventory of pain: a headache that was damn near splitting her skull, ribs that felt as if they'd been used for football practice and feet that would need Band-Aids the size of watermelons before she could stand on them. Otherwise, she felt amazingly okay. The thieves, it seemed, had been scared off before they could do any really serious damage. She had reason to be grateful to this warm, husky voice. Later, if she was sure it was safe, she might say thank you.

"I think you can hear me," the voice said. "Could you manage to open an eye or wiggle a finger or say hi, maybe?"

She was curious enough about the owner of the voice to force open an eyelid. Light blazed painfully inside her skull. She quickly closed her eye again. Good lord, the sunlight hurt!

"Hey, that was great." The voice spoke with what Caroline considered excessive cheer. Hadn't the stupid man noticed that she closed the damned eye almost the instant she opened it? His fingers rested lightly against her cheek, letting her know he was still close by. "Are you ready yet to tell me where it hurts the most?"

She opened her eye once more, this time cautiously, squinting against the sun. "Everywhere," she said.

He actually had the audacity to chuckle. "Well, that's comprehensive," he said.

"Also accurate." Her voice rasped over her desert-dry throat. Feeling a little stronger, she opened her other eye and blinked several times until her vision cleared.

A man, maybe in his late thirties, maybe as much as forty, was seated on the pavement alongside her, his expression solicitous. Despite her woozy state, she saw at once that he was quite astonishingly handsome. His eyes were an intriguing color somewhere between hazel and green. His hair was dark brown, shiny with health and long enough to show a hint of wave. His nose was straight and of classical proportions, narrow at the bridge and flared at the nostrils. His ruggedly squared chin provided just the right touch of masculine aggression, and he topped off his roster of perfections with a smile that packed enough boyish charm to give Brad Pitt a hard run for his money.

All in all, Caroline decided, he was the second most handsome man she'd ever seen in her life.

Which, given that Phillip was the most handsome man she'd ever seen, didn't exactly recommend the man to her.

He gave her a cute, lopsided smile. "The good news is, you've only been unconscious for a couple of minutes," he said. "The bad news is those men who attacked you managed to get away."

In the overall mess that constituted her life, the men from the bar seemed a relatively minor problem. "My head...aches," she said.

"Nothing seems broken, but don't move, not if it hurts." He touched her hand, grasping it gently in lieu of a handshake. "I'm Jack Fletcher, by the way. It's good to have you back with us."

She didn't tell him her name. She never gave out personal information until she was sure she wouldn't regret it. And men who looked like her ex-husband weren't exactly at the top of her list of people she wanted to confide in. "My ribs..." she muttered, deciding her best bet was to pretend she was still nearly incoherent with pain. "They...hurt...like hell."

"One of the guys who attacked you landed a couple of pretty good kicks before I could reach you." Jack Fletcher ran his hands over her rib cage with impersonal efficiency. "Hmm...I can't tell if anything's broken. I made it halfway through med school, but I guess that isn't far enough to be useful."

She mumbled something incoherent, although she was pretty sure her ribs were just bruised. Phillip had broken her ribs in three places on one memorable occasion. She could recall exactly what that felt like, and how difficult it had been to breathe. This was nowhere near as bad.

"We have painkillers in the office," Jack Fletcher said. "But you probably shouldn't take them until we're sure there's no risk of concussion."

A couple of aspirin sounded like a terrific idea. Caroline decided it was safe to start recovering. "I'm sure I don't have a concussion," she said, levering herself up on one elbow. "In case you haven't noticed, I'm perfectly coherent."

"Hmm. How many fingers am I holding up?"

"Four. And your T-shirt says you ran in the 1994 New York Marathon."

"It lies," he said. "And I'd still wait for the paramedics if I were you—"

"There's no need. I can move." She spoke curtly, irritated by her state of vulnerability. She hated to be caught at a disadvantage, and she couldn't think of a much bigger disadvantage than lying on the sidewalk, bruised and beaten, while a handsome man condescendingly offered help.

She tried to stand, and he caught her just in time to prevent her falling and giving her head another crack on the concrete pavement. She collapsed into his arms with such force that she sent both of them reeling against the wall. She ended up with her head resting on his shoulder and her body thrust against his. Which was considerably more comfortable than lying on the pavement, but otherwise a decided change for the worse. Caroline loathed physical contact unless she controlled it.

To her surprise, the man didn't take advantage of her near fall to stroke her back or indulge in a little foreplay under the guise of soothing her hurts. Instead, he shifted his position slightly so that she was still cradled in his arms, but her weight was supported more by the wall than his body. Odd, Caroline thought. In her experience, men as handsome as Jack

Fletcher never passed up the chance to make a move on a woman. Unless he was gay, of course.

"I think maybe we'd better wait for the paramedics before you try your next maneuver," he said, his voice still warm and friendly, but impersonal. "Next time I might not be able to catch you."

Definitely gay, Caroline decided, which some women might consider a waste of spectacular good looks and a great body, but which she considered a point in his favor.

"I can walk if you help me," she said, her tone fractionally more relaxed. "You must be as tired of standing out here in the sun as I am."

"Let's wait for Marcus, shall we? Since I sent him in search of ice water, you may as well take advantage of his services. I'd prefer not to have to listen while the paramedics yell at me for moving a patient with a concussion."

"We already decided I don't have a concussion."

"*You* decided. I'm taking a strictly neutral position on the subject."

Her forehead wrinkled into a scowl, but he ignored her glare, staring behind her to the end of the street "Ah, great! Here comes Marcus now."

A black youth, about fifteen or so, jogged into view and came to a halt at her side. He handed her rescuer an oversize plastic cup and a bundle of white rags.

"Here, Father. I tore up an old shirt."

"Thanks, Marcus. Actually, nothing seems to be bleeding, so we don't need the rags. Any sign of the paramedics?"

Father? But the boy was black and the man was white. Caroline stared from one to the other. "Is he your son?" she blurted.

Marcus and Jack Fletcher both grinned. Jack answered, "In a manner of speaking. I'm a priest, and Marcus is living with me for a few months." Seemingly unaware of the bombshell he'd just dropped, he handed Caroline the water. "Here, drink a couple sips of this. I think you'll feel better."

"You're a priest?"

"Yes," he said. "I'm a priest."

Caroline stared at him with as much loathing as if he'd sprouted fangs, horns and cloven hoofs. She pulled away from his grasp and supported herself by leaning against the brick wall while she took a gulp of water.

Good grief, a priest! This was definitely turning out to be one of the more spectacularly awful weekends in her life. After her experiences trying to free herself from Joe and Phillip, Caroline's esteem for the clergy had sunk to a spot slightly below drug dealers and snake-oil salesmen.

"Why aren't you wearing your uniform?" she demanded, not bothering to hide her hostility.

"Sometimes we're given time off for good behavior," Jack Fletcher said mildly, as if he hadn't noticed her rudeness. "And I just came back from playing basketball."

"I appreciate the help you've given me," she said stiffly. "Unfortunately, since all my money was just stolen, I'm afraid your reward for this good deed will have to come strictly from heaven.''

Her dislike permeated her voice, and she saw the merest flicker of reaction in his eyes before he responded with undiminished courtesy. "Professionally speaking, I'd say heavenly rewards are the best kind, wouldn't you?"

"No, not at all." He was looking at her with an infuriating hint of sympathy, as if he knew she was hurting inside. She swung around to avoid his gaze. Now that she knew he was a priest, Jack Fletcher made her skin hot and prickly with discomfort. "Personally, I'm all in favor of cash settlements," she said.

He showed no inclination to argue. "Cash can certainly be useful on occasion."

"I didn't know priests were allowed to think about the attractions of money."

His eyes gleamed with rueful laughter. "I have days when I wonder if we think about anything else. Have you any idea how much it costs to run a ninety-year-old stone building with a heating system that dates from 1920?"

Marcus spoke up. "You through with the water, Father? I need to get back. Some of the kids are wild today."

"Yes, thanks, Marcus."

From the corner of her eye, Caroline saw Jack Fletcher turn and give Marcus a high five. *Priest earns heavenly Brownie points by taming the neighborhood gangs,* she thought sarcastically.

"Thanks for the quick service," he said to the boy. "Let the others know that I'll be available to help out with homework in about ten minutes or so, will you?"

"Uh-huh. Sure, Father." Marcus turned politely to Caroline. "I'm glad you're okay, miss. We thought you were dead meat for sure when we saw those guys beatin' up on you. Father Jack tried to catch them, but they had too much of a head start."

Marcus sounded so earnest, so anxious to please, that Caroline felt a faint flicker of some emotion she could barely recognize. She thought it might be gratitude. She shifted from one blistered foot to the other and eventually managed a smile that was almost sincere. "Thanks for your help, Marcus. I sure do appreciate it. I'd have been in big trouble without you."

"You're welcome, but I didn't do nothin' much. Father Jack, he scared those thieves off. Catch you later, miss." Marcus loped toward the end of the street. Where, Caroline noticed for the first time, a very large church stood guarding the west corner of the intersection.

Father Jack—ridiculous name—glanced at his watch and sighed in resignation. "The paramedics are taking too long to get here. I guess that means they've gone to St. Luke's Catholic Church again."

Puzzled, Caroline looked toward the church at the intersection. "That isn't St. Luke's?"

"It's St. Luke's, all right, but it's an Episcopal church. We're about ten blocks from the Catholic St. Luke's, and we're a permanent source of confusion to the authorities."

"You could change your name. Or the Catholics could change theirs."

"We've all considered it, but a lot of the parishioners at both churches are attached to their old name, and they hate the idea of giving it up." He gave her a friendly smile that Caroline didn't trust for a single second. Why would he feel goodwill toward her when she'd gone out of her way to be rude to him?

"Are you an Episcopal priest, then?" she asked. "Not Catholic, I mean."

"Yes." He shot her a quizzical glance. "Does that make it better or worse as far as you're concerned?"

She didn't pretend to misunderstand his question. "I don't know. I'm not sure if I understand the difference between Episcopalians and Catholics."

"Well, there are several, but I guess you could sum it up best by saying about four hundred million, give or take a million or so."

She stared at him. "Four hundred million what? Dollars?"

"Not dollars. People. The Roman Catholic Church has almost half a billion members worldwide. The Episcopal Church has about seventy million." He grinned. "If you count some of them twice."

She almost returned his smile. Then she realized she was asking him questions because she liked to listen to the sound of his voice. She stopped immediately.

When she didn't say anything further, he subjected her to another searching look, but at least he made no more personal comments. Instead, he gestured toward a building at the side of the church. "If you're sure you can walk, we probably ought to go to the parish house and give the paramedics a call.''

"I can walk and I certainly don't need the paramedics. All I need is a hot shower and some clean clothes, and I'll be fine.''

"In that case, I'll call Emergency and cancel. No point in bringing the medics over here if you don't need their services.''

"I'll be fine,'' she repeated. "You should definitely cancel.''

"Do you need an arm or would you prefer to walk alone?''

"Alone, thank you.''

He watched, pacing his stride to hers, as she hobbled the hundred yards or so to the church buildings. Caroline told herself that she didn't regret refusing his help, although her blisters were damn near killing her. He stepped in front of her as they reached the parish house and held open the door. On closer inspection, Caroline revised her opinion that he was the second most handsome man she'd ever met. He was, she decided, even better looking than Phillip. He managed the mingled look of sincerity and wry humor far better than her ex-husband, and there were a couple of interesting crinkles around his eyes that added character. Shuddering, Caroline turned away.

Father Jack was all bland politeness when he spoke. "You're welcome to use the facilities if you'd like to wash up. And we have a phone in my office if you'd like to call for a cab to take you home. You probably shouldn't use public transport until you've had a chance to rest for a few hours."

Although his manner remained courteous, his voice had lost the warmth Caroline had found so comforting. Her gaze locked for a brief moment with his before turning to fix blankly on the gray stone facade of the church. The stark reality of her situation struck her like a blow, and she suddenly grasped the appalling dimensions of her problems. Summed up in a few words, she was penniless, jobless and soon to be homeless.

She'd left her suitcases in the lobby of her apartment, an open invitation to theft, and her carryon bag was presumably still at Joe's. She certainly couldn't remember seeing it after Gerry and Steve bundled her into the cab. Her purse had just been stolen, along with her traveler's checks and her cash. Yesterday evening she'd personally destroyed most of the documentation that proved she was Caroline Hogarth. In effect, she had no money, no credit cards, no checkbook, and her passport and driver's license had most likely been flung to the four winds by the men who grabbed her purse. Even if she borrowed money from Father Jack and returned to her apartment, she had no key to get in, and nothing to eat or drink once she arrived there. The monthly lease on the place expired in six days, and with no checkbook and no credit cards, she couldn't even access the pathetic few hundred dollars she'd left in her checking account.

Jack Fletcher didn't say anything, but Caroline could feel him watching her. He must be used to dealing with bums, beggars and harlots down on their luck, she thought acidly. He could probably spot somebody about to plead for charity with one of his sparkling green eyes closed.

The longer she stood there, the more she hated the thought of having to beg for handouts, but her situation was truly desperate.

He finally broke the silence. "You look worried," he said. "Are you sure there isn't some way I could help?"

For a long time now, all Caroline had had to sustain her self-image was her pride, and that was about to be pulverized. She swallowed a huge lump in her throat. "I need money," she said through gritted teeth.

"For the cab?" he asked. "Of course, I should have thought. Come on inside and I'll get you something from petty cash. Would twenty bucks see you through until Monday?"

She stepped into the linoleum-floored hallway and was met by the typical institutional smell of disinfectant overlaid by stale coffee and polish. In the distance, she heard a phone ring and the hum of young voices, arguing amically about a dictionary. Caroline drew in a gulp of air. "I don't need money for a cab," she said.

"Then what do you need it for?"

"Everything." Her cheeks grew hot and her stomach churned with shame, but she wouldn't allow herself to look away. "I have nowhere to go," she said. "No money. Nothing."

Jack Fletcher didn't respond as she'd expected. "What's your name?" he asked. "You never told me."

She had no idea why she answered him truthfully. "Caroline," she said. "My name's Caroline Hogarth."

He held out his hand and she shook it reluctantly. "Hi, Caroline, nice to meet you. Are you new in town?"

"Not exactly."

"But you don't have anywhere to live?"

"The lease on my apartment runs out in six days. But I can't go back there." She swallowed another huge bite of pride. "I'm afraid to go back there."

Jack Fletcher leaned against the wall, his hands stuck casually in the pockets of his jeans. "My apartment's just around the corner, and the couch in my living room converts into a bed. You're welcome to spend the weekend with Marcus and me, although I don't guarantee the bedsprings on the couch."

She would more willingly have spent the weekend with Godzilla, but at the moment, Godzilla wasn't issuing invitations and Jack Fletcher was. Her nails left little half-moons where they dug into her palms. "Thank you," she said. "I appreciate your kindness."

The laughter returned to his voice. "No, you don't," he said. "You'd like to take my offer and ram it down my throat."

She stared at him. "If you know that, then why are you willing to invite me into your home?"

"It's in the job description," he said. "The more of a pain in the ass you are, the harder I have to try to help."

She blinked. Had he really called her a pain in the ass? That hardly fit her image of how priests were supposed to talk.

The hum of voices from the back room was interrupted by an outraged yell and the sounds of an escalating scuffle. "Gotta run," Jack said. "The washroom's down the hall, second door on the right. When you're cleaned up, maybe you could come and help drill some of the kids in their spelling. They need all the individual attention they can get." He exited through a pair of swinging doors and the sounds of fighting stopped like magic.

Caroline stared in disbelief at his disappearing back. He expected her to spend the afternoon helping a pack of badly behaved kids with their spelling? He couldn't be serious. Besides, she needed to rest. She still had a pounding headache.

She walked slowly toward the washroom. There was at least one blessing in this ridiculous, humiliating situation: Joe would have no chance at all of tracking her, buried as she was in the stronghold of a do-gooder Episcopal priest. Which meant that she had about twenty-four hours to get her act together and plan some way to get herself down to Grand Cayman.

And liberate five million stolen dollars.

Four

Teenagers doing homework were definitely one of humanity's less appealing subspecies, Caroline decided, pushing a limp strand of hair off her forehead and rubbing her tired eyes. This particular group seemed to have only a passing acquaintance with the fundamentals of arithmetic and no acquaintance at all with the basics of grammar and spelling. Still, there was something endearing about the way they accepted her presence and assumed that she would know how to help them solve their problems.

Caroline Hogarth, problem solver. Now there was a concept funny enough to make anyone laugh, even a homeless woman with a splitting headache.

Caroline walked around the clusters of tables, helping any kid who looked frazzled—anyone except a thin, nervous girl who was accompanied by her son, a toddler with melting brown eyes and a six-tooth smile that damn near broke Caroline's heart. She gave the teenage mother a wide berth, moving away every time the little guy looked as if he might toddle toward her, and tried not to register the fact that his name was Ramon.

Jack Fletcher was paying her no attention at all, which was what she wanted, of course. At any given moment, he seemed to be helping a minimum of three kids, and he always looked as if he was enjoying himself. He had a deep, quiet laugh that the younger teens responded to with huge grins and the older ones with quick, teasing banter. When Caroline realized she was staring at him, waiting to see his smile, she got up and turned away so fast she knocked a pile of textbooks onto the floor.

Jack was at her side before she had the first book back on the table. "Are you okay?" he asked, in a low voice that sounded full of sympathy. "Maybe I shouldn't have put you to work, but I thought it was the best way to make sure you stayed awake."

He was great at creating the impression he cared, Caroline thought cynically. If the ruling powers of the Episcopal Church had any smarts, Father Jack would be promoted to bishop in charge of fund-raising in no time at all. Donations would increase exponentially.

"My head still aches," she said. "And my rib cage is trying to decide whether the left side hurts more than the right or vice versa." She had no idea why she admitted so much. Confessions of weakness were always dangerous, especially when you hadn't figured out your opponent's angle.

"You need to rest," Jack said. "I'll get Marcus to walk you home. Sorry I can't come myself, but Kathleen Williams, our church secretary, is on vacation, and I'm learning all over again how much she does to keep things running smoothly."

"I can wait until you're free—"

"I've promised this crew pizza once they've finished their homework, so it'll be a couple of hours or more before I can get out of here. And you need some peace and quiet. If you'd like to lie down, the living room couch is all yours." He pulled a bottle of generic painkillers from the pocket of his jeans. "Here, you could probably use a couple more of these."

"Thank you." Caroline swallowed the pills with a sip of water. She knew she sounded cold and ungrateful, but she didn't trust him for a second. His voice might be kind and his offer generous, but she'd developed a sixth sense for knowing when people were scrutinizing her—and Father Jack was subjecting her to an inspection intense enough to make her stomach contract with nerves. She wondered if he had observed her while she'd been working with the kids. How unsettling to think that he might have been keeping her under surveillance and she hadn't noticed. How did a priest acquire a skill like that? More to the point, why would he need to?

Before she married Phillip Rossi, she'd been a fool who trusted everyone. Nowadays she trusted nobody except people like her father-in-law, who could be relied on to behave like sewer rats on any and every occasion. Last year, when her parents believed the evidence Joe presented in court, Caroline had finally accepted the simple truth that people always let you down sooner or later. The fact that Jack Fletcher was a minister of religion didn't change his ultimate unreliability as far as she was concerned. Priests, in her experience, were definitely not on the side of the angels.

She set down the cup of water, still not looking at him. "I'm ready to leave," she said.

She expected Jack to play kindly Father Confessor and try to placate her with a syrup of meaningless words, but he didn't. "I'll find Marcus," he said and strode down the corridor, leaving Caroline to wait uneasily by the door to the parish house, staring at his retreating back. Damn, but she hated not being able to predict what he would do! It was years since a man had managed to surprise her.

Still, Father Jack wasn't likely to figure in her life for longer than a weekend, so she didn't really need to agonize about his motives. But it bothered her that she couldn't fathom what sort of payoff he was expecting in return for his offer of hospitality. Since he knew she had no money, sex was the obvious answer, but he gave no sign that he was planning to demand sexual payment. In fact, he scarcely seemed aware of her as a woman. If he didn't want sex or money, what the blazes did he want?

She scowled ferociously in the direction Jack had taken, then heard a little voice start to cry. Caroline looked down and reacted without thinking. She bent and scooped a crying Ramon into her arms, murmuring nonsense words of reassurance and tickling his tummy until his tears stopped and he started to smile. He hadn't yet lost his baby plumpness, and he felt warm and solid in her arms. Unable to resist, she nuzzled her cheek against his. Ramon pulled back, rubbing his eyes with knuckles padded by endearing little dimples of fat. Knowing she ought to put him down, she unfolded his fingers and blew a noisy raspberry into his chubby palm. His laugh was so rumbling and infectious that she laughed in return, ignoring the cramping pain in her stomach. She started to play a game of patty cake with him when she heard the swing doors open somewhere behind her.

Jack Fletcher was coming back.

She quickly sat Ramon on the floor and stared into the middle distance as if she'd never even noticed the toddler. When Jack walked past, Marcus in tow, she was studying a chip in her nail polish with fierce concentration.

She needn't have been so defensive, so worried that Jack would be intrigued by her interest in Ramon. The priest settled at the table without saying a word or even glancing at her. Within seconds, Ramon had clambered onto Jack's knees, and one of the ninth graders was hanging over his shoulder to ask about a math problem. Jack plunged into an explanation, and Caroline acknowledged wryly that he'd managed once again to confound all her expectations. She was so accustomed to being the center of attention—even though the attention came from people who wished her ill—that she'd forgotten what it felt like to be just one of the crowd. In his own way, Jack Fletcher was surprisingly good at delivering reminders of the virtue of humility.

Marcus must have been anxious to deliver her to the apartment and get back to the parish room before the pizza arrived, as he set a fast pace the three blocks home, not attempting to make conversation until they arrived.

"This is where we live," he said, pointing to a two-story apartment building, which stood out from its neighbors because it was freshly painted in gray with white trim. "Nice place, huh?" His voice throbbed with quiet pride.

"Very nice," she lied, hiding her dismay. The building was a featureless 1950s cube, with all the visual appeal of a county jail spruced up for a government inspection. She hated to think where Marcus must have lived before, if he viewed this place with such favor. Somebody was obviously making an effort to keep the courtyard swept clean, but an empty cigarette pack had already blown in through the iron fence, along with a couple of torn candy wrappers. A tub of geraniums was trying hard to survive the exhaust fumes from passing traffic, and a spindly sapling made a valiant attempt to cast some shade on the concrete paving slabs.

Caroline found the attempts to prettify the yard vaguely pathetic. They made her think of an old woman whose makeup is so thick it simply emphasizes the wrinkles it's supposed to cover.

Marcus seemed aware of no such shortcomings. He marched up the short path to the door of the building, humming beneath his breath. He picked up the empty cigarette package and candy wrappers and carefully pinched off a wilting leaf from the scraggy geranium. Glancing possessively around the yard, he flashed Caroline a proud grin.

"Next year we're gonna plant a lot more flowers," he said. "Ain't nobody round here—there isn't nobody around hear that steals my flowers. It's a real cool neighborhood."

"Where did you live before?" she asked.

"South side," he said, his face shuttering. He swung around and pointed to the sapling, his smile returning. "Me and Father Jack, we bought that tree from the Walmart garden center." He pronounced the Walmart name with reverence, as if it was a famous horticultural center noted for its exotica. He patted the thin trunk of the sapling. "It's gonna be a maple tree one day, with red leaves and syrup and everything. I never had no place—" He broke off, once again correcting himself. "I never had any place to make a garden before."

Caroline looked from his hopeful, smiling face to the scraggy geraniums and cracked paving stones and overcame an absurd desire to cry. "Well, this sure looks like a great place to start one," she said, following him into the cramped lobby of the apartment house. "There's lots of space in the front yard for you to fill with plants next spring."

"Yeah, growin' things is okay. With flowers and trees, you can make a place look real fancy." Marcus unlocked two heavy-duty safety locks on a dark green steel door, the number 104 stenciled in white. "We live in this apartment right here on the ground floor. You can come on in."

She followed him into the apartment, which was low-ceilinged and utilitarian in design but more spacious than she'd expected. The walls were painted a restful shade of rich ivory, and new vertical blinds hung in the windows.

"This is the living room," he said, ushering her into the center of the large room. It was decorated with comfortable furniture in various shades of beige, the monochrome dullness enlivened by an assortment of bright throw pillows and houseplants set on the windowsill and on the modular shelving units that covered an entire wall.

Marcus rearranged a trail of philodendron leaves so it got more light and frowned in concentration. "I guess if you wannna sleep, we'd better find you a pillow and some sheets."

The concept of sleeping on sheets seemed to be a recent one for Marcus, and he grinned, pleased with himself for having remembered.

"Sheets would be great," Caroline said. "Thanks, Marcus, you're being very helpful."

"No problem." He disappeared down a narrow hallway, emerging with an armful of bed linen. "We got two bathrooms," he said, gesturing with his chin. "The sink, the shower, everything works in both of them." He clearly considered functioning plumbing cause for comment. He indicated a closed door. "This bathroom is Father Jack's, and we mostly use it for visitors. It's kinda more picked up than mine, if you know what I mean."

Caroline felt herself smile. "Yes, I know what you mean," she said, taking the sheets from him. "Thanks again, Marcus."

"You're welcome. I guess there's a clean towel in the cupboard under the sink in Father Jack's bathroom. We just done laundry. We do laundry twice a week." Marcus sounded astonished at this frequency. He set the pillow on the arm of the couch and heaved a sigh of relief at having completed his duties as host.

"That's it, then, miss. I'll see you later, 'cos I sure don't want to miss out on that pizza. Father Jack, he's the worst cook in the whole world."

"How comforting to know he isn't totally perfect," Caroline muttered.

Marcus shrugged. "Nobody's perfect, right? But Father Jack, he's a cool dude." He picked up a Walkman and a pair of earphones from the kitchen counter. "I'll lock the door, but don't put up the chain or nothin', or we won't be able to get in if you're sleeping. You don't have to worry none. This neighborhood's real safe. Hasn't been nobody shot here or nothin'. Not this entire year. The dealers, they all stay over on Wilton. Ain't no—there isn't no gangs 'round here." He adjusted the earphones over his baseball cap and shuffled out of the apartment, body swaying and fingers snapping in time to some inaudible beat.

Caroline waited to hear Marcus's key turn in the locks, then she picked up a pencil and notepad lying next to the phone and made her way to the kitchen. She had no time for sleeping, however tired she might feel and however much her head was aching.

As she hoped, there was a sturdy Formica table pushed against the wall at one end of the small kitchen, the ideal place to sit and make a list of what she needed to do. Her first task was to get her hands on sufficient cash to pay for a plane ticket to the Cayman Islands. Which wasn't going to be easy, since she needed to be out of the country as soon as possible. Joe Rossi might have lost track of her for now, but he'd pick up her trail before long, even here, hidden away with Father Goody Two Shoes.

So how was she going to earn a couple of thousand dollars in the next three or four days? Caroline could think of only one way, and she didn't much like it. Prostitution was an ugly word for an even uglier transaction. Despite her six-month affair with Dayton Ames, the idea of selling her body to fulfill some rich man's sexual fantasy left her sick and shaking, but she ordered herself to stop emoting and face reality. Just because she'd known Dayton Ames for several weeks before she went to bed with him didn't change the fact that—in unvarnished terms—she'd been his whore. And a whore was a whore, no matter where and with whom she plied her trade. So what difference did it make if she had to prostitute herself for a second time, with a different man?

Caroline drew in a deep breath, fighting nausea. Life often presented unpleasant choices, and you just had to get on with it. She needed money—lots of it, and fast. Her body, she'd discovered, attracted rich men who were willing to pay for their pleasures. In her current situation, squeamishness was not an option.

Teeth clenched, she went to make a notation on the pad and realized she'd snapped the pencil in two. She unclenched her teeth, placed the broken pieces neatly in the trash, found a ballpoint pen on the kitchen counter and pulled the notepaper toward her for the second time.

Money, she wrote and underlined it. She moved over to the right-hand column. By Wednesday at the latest.

She continued jotting down everything she needed to do, ordering her thoughts in the process. These notes were strictly for her own benefit. She must make sure they were destroyed before saintly Father Jack came home.

Jack let himself into the apartment, walking quietly in case Caroline was asleep. He saw at once that his concern was unnecessary: the sofa was empty and a set of sheets lay unopened against the cushions. Caroline Hogarth, it seemed, had decamped. Disappointed but not very surprised, he cast a swift glance around the living room, wondering what she'd stolen on her way out. Women as beautiful and obviously well-educated as Caroline didn't end up in this part of town unless they had oversize personal problems, usually connected with drugs or alcohol.

From the moment he'd first seen her being beaten up, he'd guessed her problems were rooted in some sort of substance abuse. Given that, he'd been downright foolish to send her home with Marcus. Addicts stole to support their habits, and he should have known better—he *did* know better—than to let her loose in his apartment without supervision.

Maybe he'd let his guard slip because, although Caroline was homeless and penniless, usually sure signs of an addiction that was out of control, nothing else about her behavior had validated his early suspicions. She didn't smell of alcohol or cheap perfume covering up the alcohol, and she had no needle marks anywhere on her arms. Her hair looked freshly washed, and her nails were carefully manicured. Addicts usually had nails bitten right down to the quick. He'd watched her closely while she worked with the kids and he'd realized she was tense as hell. She hadn't exhibited any of the physical symptoms, though, of someone craving a hit or a drink, and she hadn't tried to scrounge a cigarette, which was usually the first essential crutch for someone needing something more satisfying.

Still, Jack thought, addicts learned to be master deceivers, and Caroline Hogarth—if that was her real name—was a smart woman, clever enough to hide the symptoms of her addiction, at least on early acquaintance. Too bad she'd skipped before he had a chance to recommend one of the twelve-step programs run by St. Luke's. Although, if she wasn't ready to take charge of her life, she couldn't be bullied into trying, however much he wanted her to make a fresh start. After two years at the seminary and eight years as a priest, Jack had finally stopped believing he could save the entire world if he only worked hard enough. Nowadays, he realized it would be a terrific achievement if he managed to help a few people to save themselves. And, sadly, it looked as if Caroline Hogarth wasn't going to be one of those few people.

Jack told himself to forget about her and count his blessings. At least the TV was still in its usual place, surrounded by his collection of books and Marcus's plants. He made a quick check of his bedroom, pleased to find his CDs and stereo equipment in place.

Given that Marcus would think civilized life had ended if he could no longer watch such cultural treasures as *Baywatch* and *Beverly Hills 90210*, Jack should have been delighted that Caroline had left without stealing anything. Perversely, though, he felt restless rather than happy, aware of having failed a woman who badly needed his help. Somewhere beneath Caroline's veneer of sophisticated callousness, he'd sensed a core of rock-solid integrity.

Jack shook his head ruefully. Yeah, right. More likely what he'd sensed wasn't Caroline Hogarth's integrity but a surge of his own lust, brought on by the fact that she had the longest, sexiest pair of legs he'd seen since one of the prison guards stole his copy of the 1985 *Sports Illustrated* swimsuit calendar. Jack cast a wry glance at his current desk calendar, a gift from a dear old lady parishioner, with a different Bible quote for every day of the year. Somehow, he knew it would never supplant the swimsuit calendar in his affections.

The air-conditioning in the apartment was working with its usual lack of efficiency. Jack stripped off his T-shirt and doused his head under the cold tap in his bathroom, trying to cool off before he tackled the difficult task of preparing dinner. He should have eaten pizza, but the kids had all been hungry and he'd given them his share.

Slinging a towel around his neck, he decided to drown his frustrations in a can of Dr. Pepper. Being a priest in a parish like St. Luke's didn't leave much time for soul-searching. Most of his parishioners were struggling so hard to keep themselves employed and their neighborhood viable, that he sometimes felt like he put in twenty-five-hour days helping them keep the streets free of drug dealers and the apartment buildings safe to call home. Instead of wasting time analyzing his feelings about Caroline Hogarth, he needed to start on the schedule for next month's block patrol and for the teen pregnancy prevention program he was trying to develop with a counselor from Planned Parenthood. He preached commitment and responsibility; she preached condoms. Jack just hoped to God the kids listened to the counselor's message if they weren't willing to listen to his.

He pushed open the flimsy louver doors that separated the kitchen from the living room and stopped in his tracks. Caroline Hogarth hadn't run away, after all. She'd fallen asleep at the kitchen table, her head resting on her arms, a notepad and pen half hidden beneath her hair. Even sleeping, she radiated an aura of tension that was palpable.

Jack crossed to her side. The notepad she'd been writing on had skewed around as she slept and was pointing directly toward him. He saw a list, divided into two columns, the left-hand column clearly legible. He couldn't avoid seeing a series of subheads, although the accompanying notations in the right-hand column were hidden beneath her hair. Which was, he noted absently, quite exceptionally beautiful—thick, blond and wavy.

He glanced at the scratch pad. *Clothes,* he read. *Passport, Bank Account, Plane Ticket.* This was followed by *Parents?* which was crossed out by a black line drawn with such force that it cut right through the paper. Further down the page, three words had been enclosed in a doodled circle of scrolls and curlicues: *Sex for Sale.*

Those telling words hadn't been crossed out. Caroline's parents, it seemed, evoked a much stronger negative reaction from her than the idea of selling sex. Jack wished he could find that shocking, or at least surprising, but of course he couldn't. Anything about parental neglect and cruelty he hadn't learned in jail he'd learned since becoming a priest. The vast majority of the kids selling themselves on street corners—boys and girls alike—came from abusive homes.

He was wondering whether to leave Caroline sleeping or try to move her somewhere more comfortable when she made a snuffling sound deep in her throat, and he realized she was waking up. For a second or two after she opened her eyes, her gaze was soft and blurred with sleep. She stared at him drowsily, and he thought she smiled, but her expression sharpened almost at once. Although she remained slumped in the narrow kitchen chair, he could see her muscles tense as she asserted control over her body. When she finally lifted her head, her expression was blank. Her defenses, Jack guessed, were being dragged firmly back in place.

She followed the direction of his gaze to the scratch pad half-hidden under her arm. When she realized he must have read at least some of the notes she'd written, her cheeks paled. Her fear filled the space between them, so intense it was little short of terror. What *else* did she have written on that note pad? Jack wondered.

Her self-control was amazing, however, and she gave no outward sign of her inner turmoil. She simply sat up straighter in the chair, watching him from narrowed, calculating eyes. She looked, Jack reflected, as if it had been half a lifetime since she trusted anyone.

"Hi," he said, trying to sound friendly and cheerful, hoping to lessen whatever threat she thought he represented. "How are you feeling?"

"Fine." She snatched the notepad, crumpling the top few sheets of paper. She clutched the wad in her fist, obviously determined that he should get no more glimpses of what she'd written.

He kept his smile and his distance. "At least tonight the sofa should feel good in comparison to this hard table."

Her mouth twisted into a mocking parody of his smile. "A silver lining to every cloud, is that right, Father?"

"Not always," he said. "Nowadays, a lot of clouds are filled with acid rain."

He knew his answer annoyed her, but instead of scowling—her earlier tactic for expressing disapproval—she leaned back and linked her arms behind the chair back so that her breasts thrust against the thin, crumpled cotton of her blouse, threatening to pop the buttons. She should have appeared ridiculous, or at the very least crude. What she actually looked like was sheer sexual invitation bundled in a delectable package waiting to be unwrapped.

Jack ordered himself to think mature, uplifting, priestly thoughts. He failed miserably. *Lord, you can quit with this test already. Trust me, I've gotten the message.*

She knew exactly the effect she was having on him— and despised him for it. "What can I do for you, Father?" she asked, her voice sultry, but her blue eyes sparking with contempt. "You sure do look—hungry."

"It's been a long time since my last meal," he said neutrally.

She wouldn't let him maintain the fiction that they'd been talking about food. Her gaze drifted downward and fixed mockingly on his naked chest. His stomach muscles clenched, and he could almost feel sweat break out wherever she looked.

She moistened her lips with the tip of her tongue. "I like your outfit, Father Jack. I'll bet it's a real hit with the potluck supper crowd."

If he hadn't witnessed her earlier flash of fear, Jack would never have guessed how hard she was working to project the illusion of a callous, street-smart woman. As it was, he sensed that her control was barely skin deep and that the sexual invitation was entirely phony.

"Thanks," he said blandly, recovering some of his poise. "I'm glad you approve. The towel is from Sear's Bath Shoppe if you'd like to try for the same look."

"It isn't your towel that's so special, Father, it's all that bronzed muscle and naked chest." She reached up and squeezed his forearm, her gaze deliberately sultry as she walked her fingertips up his forearm. "Mmm, mmm, what pretty biceps you have. Where do you go to work out, Father Jack?"

Every time she called him Father, it was a blatant insult. He couldn't decide if her scorn was directed at him as an individual or at the priesthood in general. Most likely both.

Jack gently disengaged his arm from her clasp. "I swim at the local Y," he said with a calmness he didn't feel. Her come-on might be faked, but it was damned effective. "I also play basketball with the local high school kids whenever they take pity on me and let me sub on one of their teams. How about you? Where do you work out, Caroline?"

She yawned, stretching with calculated provocation. "I get all the exercise I need in bed," she said. She leaned forward across the table, her voice throaty with pseudo intimacy. "I've been told by my partners that I have a really spectacular routine."

"Is that so?" Jack's efforts to sound casual were failing more and more rapidly. After twenty months in the state pen, he'd heard, seen and defended himself against almost every form of sexual come-on known to humankind—from hookers brought in by corrupt guards all the way to homosexual gang rapes threatened by prisoners with too much time on their hands and too little outlet for their sexual energy. He wasn't easily shocked, and he was even less easily turned on. But for some reason, Caroline had managed to get right under his skin, where she seemed to be triggering the release of gallons of male hormones.

He reached into the fridge and pulled out two cans of soda, offering her a drink with a display of indifference that was ninety percent sheer illusion. "You should try the Y some time," he said, sitting in the chair opposite her. "You might find that it provides better all-around muscle tone than exercising in bed."

She frowned, taking the can with an angry mutter of thanks. "Aren't you supposed to deliver me a sermon on the sin of fornication and the torments of hell?" she demanded.

Jack shrugged. "Would it do any good if I did? If so, let me know, and I'll get right on it."

For an instant, he thought he saw a flash of reluctant amusement in her eyes, then she looked down, hiding her expression. "You don't talk like a priest," she said accusingly.

"I try," he said. "I've been told I do weddings and funerals real well. If you're in the market for either of those, my rates are very reasonable."

She took a sip of soda and stared at him, eyes puzzled. She'd forgotten about her provocative pose, and she suddenly looked tired and scared. Jack realized to his chagrin that he found her vulnerability even more erotic than her aggression.

Lord, if You could please move on to a different test, I'd sure appreciate Your cooperation. The next time one of the kids tells me sexual abstinence is too hard, I promise to listen with less condescension and a great deal more sympathy.

He took a quick gulp of ice-cold soda and tried to think like a priest instead of a man who had just realized that ten years was much too long to be celibate. Caroline crossed her legs and leaned toward him invitingly. Jack wiped a trickle of sweat with his towel and decided it was time to change the direction of their conversation.

"Do you have somebody you would like to call?" he asked. "Friends or family who might be worried about you?"

Her face shuttered instantly. "No, thanks," she said. "There's nobody I need to call."

He recognized her closed expression. He'd used one just like it for most of the first year he spent in prison. He guessed that it masked equal amounts of fear, anger, regret and bitter hurt.

"What about your parents?" he pressed, curious to see her reaction. "Don't they need to know where you are?"

Caroline's gaze flickered for an instant to the crumpled wad of notes she still held in her hand. Jack was sure they were both thinking of the heading *Parents* which she'd crossed out with such vicious force.

When she looked at him again, her deadpan expression had been replaced by a taunting smile. "My father lives in Seattle and my mother's dead."

"I'm sorry."

"Don't be. My mother's been dead since I was thirteen. She and her boyfriend were found shot in their trailer over the Thanksgiving holiday weekend. There was so much alcohol in their systems that the police never could decide whether they committed suicide, had a fight and murdered each other, or whether the guns went off by accident when they were stumbling around in a drunken stupor. Personally, I favor the drunken-stupor theory. It fit so well with everything else I ever heard about my dear old mom."

Heard? Did that mean she'd never met her mother? Jack was too smart to ask and invite the inevitable rebuff. Caroline needed to realize she wasn't going to be able to shock him by telling lurid stories about her past.

"I spent nearly two years in the state pen doing time for killing a man," he said, and had the dubious satisfaction of seeing her flinch.

"You murdered someone?" she asked. "Wh-who did you kill?"

"A junkie who was too desperate for a fix to defend himself. I beat him to the ground, and then when he tried to crawl away, I dragged him back and pummeled my fists into his body until he died."

"It was an accident, then." She sounded oddly hopeful, as if—despite her earlier scorn—she didn't want to believe him guilty of cold-blooded murder.

The DA had called it manslaughter, but Jack forced himself to admit the truth that had kept him awake through so many dark nights of the soul. "No, it wasn't an accident. I lost my temper, and at the time I was beating him up, I wanted to kill him."

She stared at her hands. "How did you get such a light sentence, then?"

"I had a good lawyer, I guess." In fact, his family and friends had tried to appeal the sentence, claiming it was outrageous that he should do time for trying to prevent his wife's murderer from taking aim and killing again. Jack, in despair over Beth's death, had refused to cooperate in their efforts.

He leaned back in his chair and spoke quietly. "Okay, are we through trying to shock each other with horror stories from our résumés? If so, maybe we can have a friendly conversation, like regular folks who're interested in getting to know one another a bit better."

For a long time she stared in silence at her Dr. Pepper. She didn't look up when she finally answered him. "I don't know if I remember how to do friendly conversation."

He thought that might be the first wholly truthful thing she'd said to him since they met. "I think it goes something like this," he said, stepping carefully through a conversational field that he suspected was strewn with land mines. "Since we've already exchanged introductions, we cut straight to the chase. It's dinnertime, and I'm starving. So I ask if you can cook, and I wait in a state of high anxiety until you reply."

She hesitated for a moment. "I can cook," she said. *Thank you, Lord.* "Wonderful, terrific. You're doing great." His smile was entirely genuine. In this household, anyone who could cook was a treasure. "Next question. Would you be willing to make dinner tonight? Before you reply, I should warn you that, in your own self-interest, there is only one correct answer to that question."

She almost responded to his smile. Then she turned away, and he could see nothing but her back—*and* about forty-five inches of leg silhouetted through the thin cotton of her skirt. Jack winced. Since meeting Caroline, his mind had been running on an alarmingly single track.

"What do you want me to cook?" Caroline asked the kitchen sink. "I think my gourmet skills are too rusty for anything elaborate."

"If you can heat soup without burning the pan, you're way ahead of me." Jack pulled open the fridge door, gesturing with a flourish. "Anything you see is yours to command."

She edged past him and peered into the fridge. Her eyes widened. "Wow, with these supplies, I can see loads of exciting possibilities." She pulled out a loaf of bread that had mold visible through the plastic wrapper and a lettuce that was hovering in a state somewhere between limp and putrid. "How would you like your sandwich, Reverend? With a stomach pump or with antibiotics?"

"There's more food in the pantry," he said, taking the offending items from her and tossing them into the garbage. "Also, you could check the freezer. I know we bought chicken pieces the other day." He shrugged, embarrassed and apologetic. "I seem to have a blind spot where cooking is concerned. The logistics of getting a nourishing, good-tasting meal onto the table have always defeated me."

"Given your profession, you could always pray for divine assistance," she said dryly.

"Believe me, I've tried. So far, the answer seems to be something along the lines of 'Buy a cookbook. Read and learn.'"

He was absurdly pleased when she responded with a chuckle. But she sobered abruptly, as if laughter broke some self-imposed rule of conduct. "Will Marcus be here for dinner?" she asked.

"No, he's going with a friend to the movies, and then he's sleeping over at his grandmother's apartment."

"Okay." She opened the freezer and pulled out a package of chicken pieces. She brushed off a layer of frost and examined it dubiously. "At least you have a microwave to defrost it," she said. "And I saw a couple of onions in the fridge that might not cause instant botulism."

Chicken and onions wouldn't precisely have been Jack's choice of dinner menu, but he doubted if there was anything she could cook that would be worse than what he would have prepared for himself. Besides, he wanted to give her something constructive to do. He had a gut feeling she would be more at ease once she'd cooked a meal for the two of them, and at the moment, he wanted her to relax even more than he wanted to eat something good for dinner.

"I have a couple of schedules that need to be worked on," he said, pushing open the door to the living room. "I'll be in here. Holler if you need me."

"Yes, I will." She called him back as he stepped over to his favorite armchair. "Reverend..."

Her Reverends sounded marginally less hostile than her Fathers. "Yes?"

"Thank you," she said, her voice stiff and clumsy, as if it had been a long time since she felt the need to say those words. "Thank you for taking me in and letting me spend the night here. I would... I would have been in a difficult situation without your help."

"You're welcome. I'm glad I happened to be in the right place at the right time."

She hesitated, and he was sure she was poised on the brink of revealing something important. Then the moment passed. "I'll call you when dinner's ready," she said, bending to pull a saucepan from the cupboard next to the sink.

A button on her blouse finally popped open as she straightened, and she fastened it absentmindedly. Taking a rubber band from one of the drawers, she tugged her hair away from her face into a casual ponytail. Her eyes took on a sudden sparkle as she reached for the chicken pieces, and her cheeks were tinged with pink, as if she was excited to be doing something as ordinary as cooking dinner. A strand of hair hadn't quite made it into the rubber band and kept flopping over her forehead. Jack fought the almost irresistible urge to tuck it behind her ear. Caroline, he decided, was one of those rare women who looked more sexy the less she tried.

He escaped to the safety of the living room and started work on his speech for Planned Parenthood. Avoiding Temptation, he wrote, and underlined it. *Don't put yourself in situations that you know you're not going to be able to handle responsibly.*

All things considered, that sounded like terrific advice.

Five

Caroline knew she was smiling, an unusual state of affairs for her these days, but Jack's expression was so blissful it was comic. "Everything okay with dinner?" she asked.

Jack sighed with exaggerated ecstasy. "Not okay," he said, putting down his fork. "Wonderful. This is a real treat, Caroline. I'd forgotten how great home-cooked food can taste."

His compliments pleased her more than they should have. If Jack had forgotten the pleasures of eating home-cooked food, she'd forgotten until tonight how much she enjoyed preparing dinner for a friend.

"Your pantry turned out to be a treasure trove of goodies," she said. "There was even a jar of sun-dried tomatoes lurking at the back of the top shelf."

"That must have come from Meg, my sister. She sends me care packages every six months or so, along with a cookbook. She's an eternal optimist. She keeps telling me that if you can read, you can cook."

"She's right, you know. Just do what the recipe says, in the order it tells you. And voilà, as Miss Piggy would say."

Jack shook his head. "Never trust a philosopher whose snout is longer than the space between her ears. I'm living proof that the skill to burn water develops in the womb and is merely refined over the years to new levels of incompetence."

She laughed. "Maybe you should start with something really basic—"

"Marcus is working on it. He's teaching me how to use the microwave, and I'm doing okay, provided I don't have to rotate the platter too often. He swears I'll be able to make butter-flavored popcorn with no scorched kernels by the end of the summer."

"Wow, what a goal!"

"Yeah, real high-concept stuff. Trouble is, Marcus is humoring me. Secretly, he knows I'm doomed to failure."

She laughed again, taking a final bite of chicken and feeling more relaxed than she had in months. With Dayton Ames, she'd eaten some of the finest gourmet food the most elegant restaurants of Chicago could provide, but she couldn't remember a meal in the past year that she'd enjoyed more than this one.

"You haven't heard the best news," she said, getting up and taking their plates to the kitchen. "I made a dessert. Peach cobbler to go with the vanilla ice cream you had in the freezer."

If she'd told him he'd been given a free pass through the Pearly Gates, he could hardly have looked more delighted. He watched with barely concealed longing as she took the bubbling, golden-crusted dessert from the oven. "That's a work of art, not a cobbler," he said. "Where did you learn to cook such great food?"

"In college," she said, her smile fading. The past was forbidden territory, and she never allowed strangers to enter it.

He leaned against the doorjamb, arms crossed, stance casual. He was too sensitive not to have felt her resistance, but he chose to ignore it. "What was your major?" he asked. "Catering? Hotel management? Food service?"

"None of the above." She didn't tell him she'd graduated from Princeton with a degree in finance. Summa cum laude, although it had taken her six years to get her act together and stop changing her major just to annoy her parents. She'd really been a serious pain in the ass when she was younger, she reflected ruefully. She was struck by the uncomfortable thought that her adoptive parents might have had some grounds, however slight, for believing the myriad lies Joe Rossi had told about her. Growing up, she'd taken care to paint herself to them as a rebel. Had it been totally unreasonable of them to believe her rebellion had eventually evolved into outright dereliction of duty and neglect of her family obligations?

Jack watched her set the dessert on the table and handed her a serving spoon. "All I learned in college was how to find a fast-food restaurant that was open after midnight," he said. "How come you learned to be a gourmet chef?"

He seemed to have a hard time knowing when he'd been snubbed, Caroline thought, not at all sure why she answered him truthfully. "I lived off-campus with two roommates for my senior year. Anna Marie was Italian, from New Jersey, and Melissa was Chinese, from Hong Kong. They were both fabulous cooks and they argued constantly about the merits of Chinese food versus Italian. They spent the weekends cooking, trying to prove their respective points. I kindly offered my services as judge and jury, and gained ten pounds in two months eating the evidence."

He laughed. "Who did you declare the winner?"

She raised an eyebrow. "You don't think I was dumb enough to resolve an argument that was producing the best meals this side of New Orleans? I just made appreciative noises to both cooks and tucked in."

"And then asked them to give you their recipes? Or watched them at work in the kitchen?"

"Something like that." Volunteering information about her past was such an unusual experience she felt like a diver plucking up courage to jump from the highest board after a year in retirement. She took the plunge. "After sampling a few of their meals, I noticed that noodles are an integral part of both Italian and Chinese cuisine—"

"Because of Marco Polo," Jack said, scooping a second helping of ice cream onto his crumble. "He went to Asia in the thirteenth century and brought the technique for making noodles from China to Venice."

Caroline chuckled. "Well, that's one version of what happened."

"There's another?"

"Sure there is. According to my friend Anna Marie, you have the story twisted around. In her version, Marco Polo showed the Chinese how to cook Italian noodles—and they weren't very good students."

Jack grinned. "And what did Melissa have to say about the Italian version of history?"

"You definitely don't want to know. It would shock your priestly ears."

"I doubt it, but I'm beginning to see that you were smart to hang low, pass no judgments and eat the evidence."

"You betcha. Anyway, at a certain point—probably right around the time I realized I could no longer close the zipper on my jeans—I got curious as to how you could take the same basic ingredients and end up making them taste entirely different. So I persuaded my roommates to teach me their secrets."

"You were obviously a great student," Jack said, savoring his last mouthful of peach crumble. "Not to mention a diplomat of the highest order. Now that you're free to speak the truth, which food do you prefer, Chinese or Italian?"

She wrinkled her nose. "Why choose between perfections? As far as I'm concerned, the ideal dinner is assorted dim sum followed by tiramisu, heavy on the whipped cream." She sighed and patted her stomach. "Followed these days by multiple hours sweatin' to a Kathy Smith workout video."

If Jack remembered that she claimed to get all the exercise she needed in bed, he was too tactful to remind her. For a priest, he didn't seem to be big on re-criminations and moral lectures.

"Right now, it's hard to believe anything could taste better than the meal we've just eaten," he said. "But feel free to try to change my mind. I'm up for dim sum any time. Or whatever goodies you feel moved to cook. I could work up a prime appetite for an old-fashioned American hamburger, with onion rings on the side and lots of catsup."

"Now?" Her mouth hung open. "You could eat a hamburger now?"

"Well, maybe not right this minute, but I'd give favorable consideration to the offer of a midnight snack."

"I can't believe what I'm hearing!"

"You have to understand I'm making up for years of culinary deprivation. You're definitely the answer to a hungry man's prayers."

He grinned, hazel eyes sparkling with an intriguing hint of green, cute dimple softening the angular strength of his face. Caroline realized she'd fallen into the trap of returning his smile each time he looked at her. She should have known better. Jack's smile appeared so warm and open and honest that it tricked you into thinking he must be warm and honest inside, too.

A dangerous illusion, believing that a person's looks were a reliable guide to his character. Her ex-husband had not only been as handsome as the Reverend Jack Fletcher, his smile had been heartbreakingly winsome and appealing, his dimple even cuter than Jack's.

She'd learned, within months of their marriage, that Phillip reserved his sweetest, most tender smiles for the occasions when he planned to beat her. Phillip, unlike many spousal abusers, never lashed out in blind rage. His attacks were reserved for cold, calculated punishment of Caroline's imagined sins. If he decided that she'd been too friendly with some man—a conclusion he reached almost every time they went out together—he would delight in sending her subtle signals of an impending attack, signals that other people interpreted as affection. His smile had been a cruel secret weapon, recognized only by the two of them. He'd used it to instill fear and to keep her subjugated.

The memories crowded in, threatening to overwhelm her. She took a quick swallow of water, trying to calm herself. A broken nose, a fractured wrist, multiple cracked ribs and uncounted bruises could give a person a whole different perspective on smiles and dimples, she thought grimly.

"Are your ribs hurting you again?" Jack asked, "I can get you a couple more painkillers if you like. You haven't taken anywhere near the safe limit for the day."

Caroline realized she'd wrapped her arms around her body in an unconscious gesture of self-protection, which explained why Jack seemed to be reading her thoughts. Still, it bothered her that he was so perceptive, so quick to spot the shifts in her mood. She prided herself on understanding what made a man tick. She didn't like to think a man might understand her. Without a barricade thick enough to protect her thoughts and feelings, she felt naked.

"I'm fine," she said, letting her hands fall loosely into her lap and shaping her mouth into a convincing imitation of a smile. Nowadays, she could lie with her body language almost as effectively as she lied with her words. "Thanks for the offer, but I don't need any pills."

Jack's gaze remained steady. For a moment, she had a horrible feeling he wasn't deceived, that he knew she was hurting, inside and out. She was relieved when he turned away and reached for her empty dessert bowl.

"It's good to know you're feeling okay," he said. "I'm still a bit concerned that you weren't checked out by the paramedics."

"Don't be. I'm barely bruised."

"Sometimes the physical bruises are the least things to worry about," he said. "It's the unexpected violence that haunts us because it makes us feel so helpless."

"I'm not helpless," she said curtly, pushing her chair away from the table and getting to her feet. "Shall I make coffee?"

"I'll take care of it," Jack said. "Even *I* can brew coffee. You rest for a while, Caroline. You're probably more tired than you realize. Getting beaten up takes it out of you."

His sympathy made her skin prick with nervous tension. She clenched her teeth. "I'm quite capable of helping you clear up—"

"Yes, of course you are, but there's no reason you should. You made dinner, now it's my turn to do some work." Jack glanced at his watch. "It's almost ten o'clock. Why don't you watch the local news and see if the weather forecasters have anything exciting to say? We badly need some rain to cool things off around here."

"Try praying," she said flippantly.

"I did. Now I'm waiting to find out if the answer is yes, no or maybe." He looked at her quizzically. "Prayer is a dialogue, you know, not a one-way system for ordering gifts and benefits."

It was the first time he'd delivered anything that sounded like a sermon, and it made Caroline squirm. She wanted to look away, but somehow Jack managed to hold her gaze. His eyes weren't in the least like Phillip's, she acknowledged, and the difference was much more than a question of color. Her husband's dark brown eyes had been sexy and full of laughter. But the laughter had been cruel, and the sex had been rapacious. Jack's hazel eyes were also sexy and full of laughter. But they seemed to promise laughter that would be shared and sex that would warm the heart instead of chilling the soul.

Caroline spun away with an angry shrug, not because she felt annoyed, but because she found herself aching to ask for Jack's help. After all that had happened over the past year, she was appalled by her susceptibility to a pair of flashing eyes and a sexy male body. Good grief, how many times did she need to have a lesson repeated before she finally grasped the message?

Behind her, she heard Jack say her name. When she didn't respond, he put down the dishes he'd been carrying into the kitchen and followed her across the living room. She forced herself to turn and confront him, ordering herself to see him as the man he was, not as the man she yearned for him to be. Everyone had an angle. What was Jack's? The fact that he was an ordained priest was no guarantee of integrity. To her certain knowledge, her father-in-law had two priests and a bishop in his pay. Churches were human organizations, and their ministers could be corrupted just like the employees of any other worldly institution.

He didn't look corrupt, she'd grant him that much. Jack was damn good at playing the role of would-be friend and counselor. The longing to trust him swept over her again, and she spoke quickly, an aggressive edge to her voice. "What do you want?"

He perched on the arm of the sofa and glanced at her reassuringly, almost as if he understood why she needed to sound so belligerent.

"You don't know me, Caroline," he said, his velvety voice wrapping her in a cocoon of false warmth and security. "There's no reason for you to trust me and no way I can convince you that I deserve your trust. But if you should happen to feel pushed to the wall over the next couple days, and you decide you don't have anyone else to turn to, remember I'm here, and that I'd like to help. No strings attached. No pay-backs required."

As an ex-con, he must know what it felt like to buck the system, Caroline reflected. He must know what it felt like to beat your head against the system's over-lapping layers of bureaucracy, inefficiency and out-right corruption. He, of all people, might understand what it was like to see justice trampled underfoot by courts and judges who rewarded the corrupt and pe-nalized the honest. The urge to share her burdens, to confide in him and plead for help, was so overwhelm-ing that for a single dangerous instant she could feel Andrew's name quivering on the tip of her tongue. What would happen if she told him about the stolen money Dayton Ames had hidden in his offshore bank account? Would he understand why she had to get to Grand Cayman and take that money? Would he ac-cept that she had no other choice?

When she realized what she was thinking, she pressed her hand against her mouth, shoving back the words, panicked at how close she'd come to confid-ing in him.

Jack touched her briefly on the arm. "It's okay," he said, getting to his feet. "Don't look so threatened, Caroline. Nobody's going to force you to talk until you're ready, least of all me." His mouth quirked into a smile. "The folks in my profession did away with the rack and the thumbscrew three hundred years ago."

Caroline recovered her poise. "The only reason I'm not talking to you is that there's nothing useful for me to say."

"Right." Jack didn't pretend to believe her. "You know, Caroline, when you can't risk trusting anyone else, I've found that God makes a great listener."

Caroline thought of all the times she'd begged and pleaded with God, willing to promise almost anything if she could just be reunited with Andrew. As far as she could tell, God's answer had been one cruelly slammed door after another, one hope after another hammered into the dust.

"I'm glad you've been so lucky," she said with undisguised bitterness. "Personally, I've come to the conclusion that God is in acute need of a hearing aid."

Astonishingly, Jack laughed. "I've had moments when I would agree with you," he said. "Trouble is, I suspect we're the ones with the hearing problem. The answer is coming through loud and clear. We're just not willing to listen."

She would never accept that she had to spend the rest of her life separated from Andrew. To think of him living in Joe and Angela Rossi's household made her sick to her stomach. There was nothing she could say about that to Jack, of course, so to end the discussion, she picked up the remote control and fumbled with the buttons.

"I'd better switch on the TV if you want to hear the weather forecast," she said. "The news must have started by now."

Jack accepted the change of subject without comment. "I'll be in the kitchen," he said. "If they announce that World War Three is imminent, give me a shout. Otherwise, I'll stick with the dishes."

Images of Andrew crowded in, just as they always did when she allowed herself to think about him even for a moment. Caroline steeled herself to push the images away. She sat on the couch and stared at the television without seeing more than a blur of lines and colors. When the shapes finally formed into recognizable pictures, she saw that the commercial break was over and the news was starting. She tried to pay attention.

Inevitably, the lead story was a fire, complete with standard pictures of flames roaring into the night sky. The news anchor informed Chicago viewers that a strip shopping mall had burned down in a suburb west of O'Hare airport and that arson was suspected.

The cameras switched to another news reader, an attractive African-American woman. She announced that a south-side housing project had reported its two hundredth shooting incident of the year. Fortunately, the three victims were all expected to recover from their wounds.

The program cut to a commercial. A young woman informed viewers that her father sold more Ford cars than any other dealer in Illinois. An airline invited viewers to soar to new heights at rock-bottom prices. Caroline yawned and decided to mute the sound until the weather forecast came on. She was searching for the appropriate button on the remote when the string of advertisements ended and a picture of Dayton Ames flashed onto the screen. Her finger froze over the control.

"Questions continue to be raised about the unexpected death on Friday night of Dayton Ames, founder and manager of the multimillion-dollar investment fund bearing his name."

Dayton's photo disappeared and was replaced by a shot of the entrance to his apartment building on Lake Shore Drive. "Preliminary reports from the medical examiner suggest that his death in the luxury penthouse atop this building might not have been from natural causes."

The picture shifted again, this time to a shot of a perky young reporter outside a police station. Fumbling with her notes, Ms. Perky gave a toothy smile to the camera. "Police this afternoon refused to elaborate on the precise cause of Mr. Ames's death. However, they do have some leads they are actively pursuing. They hope the public will help them to locate a young woman who was seen leaving Dayton Ames's apartment early on the morning of his death. She was described as being in her late twenties or early thirties, slightly above average height. She's slender, blond, and has blue eyes. The police witness described her as, quote, real good-looking, end quote."

Caroline realized that the sounds of dishes being stacked in the dishwasher had stopped and that Jack had left the kitchen. She let out her breath with infinite care and tried to adjust her stiff body into a pretense of relaxation.

Jack didn't say a word. If she hadn't been tested a dozen times in the past, Caroline would never have been able to sit quietly, gazing at the screen with an expression she hoped was somewhere between bored and sleepy. She knew Jack had moved across the living room and was standing directly behind her because she could sense his presence with every cell in her body. She had no idea how he was reacting to the news report, and she didn't dare look around to check.

Transfixed, she stared at the television as a police sketch flashed onto the screen, showing a somewhat generic-looking woman with teased blond hair hanging loose around her face, wearing a transparent outfit that bore only a fleeting resemblance to the cotton dress Caroline had been wearing when she left Dayton Ames's apartment. The witness—whoever that might be—clearly was no fashion expert.

Caroline repressed a shiver. If Dayton hadn't died from natural causes, then what and who had caused his death? And anyway, how could he have been murdered when she had been with him all night? She'd slept deeply, but surely not so deeply that someone could have crept into the bedroom and killed Dayton without her sensing the intruder's presence? Damn, what a mess! Her only consolation was that the police picture was so vague it would be difficult to identify her as the woman they were looking for.

Then she remembered Felicity Ames, and her heart sank. Felicity was a proud woman, concerned about her status in the ranks of Chicago high society, which was presumably why she'd wanted Caroline out of

Dayton's apartment before the police arrived. She would shrink from public exposure of the cracks in her marriage and resist acknowledging that Dayton Ames had died in bed with his mistress. But whatever the cost to her pride, Felicity would surely respond to a direct police plea for information. Now that the authorities were questioning the precise cause of Dayton's death, how could Felicity conceal the fact that she had found Caroline in bed with her husband's dead body? She would leave herself open to charges of obstruction of justice if she failed to report Caroline's presence in Dayton's apartment.

Until this moment, Caroline had assumed her chief problem was keeping out of Joe's clutches long enough to beg, borrow or steal the money for a plane ticket to Grand Cayman. Now she realized that keeping herself hidden from the police might be almost as big a challenge as keeping herself hidden from Joe Rossi.

"The police are very anxious to talk with this woman," Ms. Perky continued, speaking from a split screen alongside the sketch. "They seem confident that she will be able to shed light on the mysterious circumstances surrounding Dayton Ames's death."

The newscaster from the studio broke in with a question. "Do the police have any idea at all who this woman might be?" he asked. "Is she considered a suspect in the death of Mr. Ames?"

Ms. Perky adjusted her earpiece and gave a beaming smile. "Not officially, Larry. The police aren't saying anything more than that the preliminary coroner's report suggests Dayton Ames's death might not have been from natural causes, and they want to speak with this mystery woman in order to further their investigation."

"I expect we'll be hearing more of this story in the days ahead."

"Yes, I'm sure we will, Larry. The police intend to make a statement when the initial results of the autopsy become available, most likely in the middle of next week."

"Thank you, Kristine."

"Thanks, Larry. Now it's back to you in the studio."

The news once again gave way to advertisements. Acutely aware of Jack's presence behind her, Caroline tried to make some casual comment, or at least to move, but her body seemed frozen into its current pose, her legs curled under her in mock comfort.

While she was still trying to unlock her paralyzed muscles, Jack strode across to the television and switched it off without even consulting her. In the ensuing silence, her breathing sounded heart-stoppingly loud.

With an effort that broke sweat along her spine, she managed to bring her head up so her gaze met Jack's. "Why did you switch off the TV?" she asked, her lips moving stiffly as she tried to imitate normal speech. "I thought you wanted to watch the weather forecast?"

"Later." Jack sat on the couch. He was vibrating with tension, she noticed, a symptom that in Phillip's case had always been the precursor to a violent outburst of rage. Caroline felt a quiver of fear as intense as it was visceral. The realization that Jack was probably looking for an excuse to lose his temper was all the spur she needed to jolt her paralyzed muscles into action. She jumped up from the sofa and edged away, trying to move smoothly so as not to inflame him.

Jack fulfilled her worst forebodings. He grabbed her hand and dragged her back, his movements rough with barely controlled anger. Shoving her onto the sofa, he leaned across her, pinning her against the cushions with the weight of his body. Then he put his finger under her chin and tilted her head so she was forced to look at him.

He spoke grimly. "Hardball time, Caroline. I want the truth, no more evasions. Did you know Dayton Ames? Are you the woman the police are looking for?"

She replied through gritted teeth, wondering what she'd do if he hit her, desperate enough to risk finding out. "Get off me, Reverend Fletcher. Get off me right now."

There was an infinitesimal pause before he reacted. "I'm sorry," he said. He backed off, sliding across the couch so their bodies were no longer touching, although he remained close enough to grab her if she tried to run.

She huddled as far from him as she could, cowering into the cushions, hating the fact that she felt so intimidated, and aware at some deep level that part of her fear wasn't caused by Jack, but rather by her response to him. When he'd held her pinned to the sofa, excitement had raced beneath her fear, a dangerous undercurrent in a raging river of emotions. She was appalled that she could feel even a hint of sexual desire in this situation, and for this man. She shoved the sensation aside, adding sexual desire to the huge pile of emotions that were permanently off-limits.

Jack ran his hand through his hair, breathing hard. "I'm sorry," he said again. "I was out of line to crowd you like that, way out of line. You have every right to be angry. But I need some answers, Caroline. The truth, please. Are you the woman who was seen leaving Dayton Ames's apartment building?"

She didn't hesitate in her lie. Eyes wide, she stared straight at him in a careful simulation of honesty. "What? No, of course not. Don't be ridiculous, Jack—"

"I'm not being ridiculous. The woman in the police sketch looks exactly like you."

"Like me?" She gave an impatient laugh that sounded almost like the real thing. "Oh, come on, Reverend, this conversation's so silly it's getting boring."

He was unimpressed by her acting, implacable in his questions. "The woman in the police drawing looks *exactly* like you, Caroline. Shall we go to the nearest police station and ask them what they think about that coincidence?"

"That seems a major waste of time to me, but we can go if you like." She managed a shrug, although she was ice cold with terror. "If you say the woman in the sketch looks like me, I'll agree that maybe she does. She also looks like ten thousand other women in the Chicago area who happen to be blond, blue-eyed and thirty-something.''

''Even if that was true, which it isn't, you're forgetting something important. Those other ten thousand women aren't afraid to go home. You are. You told me so yourself.''

Confidences were always a mistake, Caroline reflected, especially when they were truthful. In the wake of her kidnapping and the beating from the bikers, her defenses had been down and she'd given Jack far too much personal information. But he wasn't going to get anything more out of her. She linked her hands in her lap and stared at them in silence. Belatedly, she was remembering all her own rules about keeping quiet and not providing ammunition that could be fired at her.

Jack leaned forward, careful this time not to come into actual physical contact with her. Oddly enough, the artificial distance between them made her even more aware of him.

''I need some answers, Caroline. You're educated, intelligent, beautiful—and homeless. Why?''

''My money was stolen, remember?''

''Yeah, I remember. But why can't you call someone and ask them to spot you a hundred bucks until you can get to the bank on Monday and establish your credit? If you're not running from the police, why do you need to camp out with me?''

From the day three years ago when she first decided to divorce her husband, she'd been forced to live a lie. From the day last year when her father-in-law defeated her in court, she'd almost never told the truth. These days, tall tales tripped from her tongue with the skill of a professional story-teller. All she needed to do was invent some plausible tale and tell it to Jack. But tonight the lies wouldn't come with their usual fluency, and the longer she took to reply, the more impossible it seemed to come up with anything even remotely convincing.

"Caroline?" He spoke softly, his voice taking on the warmth and sympathy that made her so edgy and uncomfortable. He crooked his finger under her chin, forcing her once again to look at him. But this time his touch was gentle, a caress instead of a threat.

"Caroline, let me help you," he said. "I know from experience that just putting your problems into words can often make the burden seem a little bit less."

She closed her eyes; he looked so damned strong and trustworthy that she was afraid of what might happen if she continued to look at him. Even with her eyes shut, her mental picture of him remained disturbingly clear. She wondered what would happen if she leaned forward, rested her head on his broad shoulders and told him everything. The idea made her feel giddy with a potent combination of alarm and anticipation.

She felt the brush of his fingers against her closed eyelids. "You're crying," he said. "Caroline, please tell me what's wrong. I can't bear to see you hurting like this."

He was right: she was crying, and that was forbidden. She sure was overindulging in prohibited activities tonight. She blinked fiercely, and when she opened her eyes she managed to look at him with a reasonable facsimile of her old self-protective mockery. If the barrier felt a bit thin, well, it was better than no protection at all.

From some intuitive level, she grabbed at the knowledge that aggression was her best defense against Jack Fletcher—and against her dangerous longing to trust him.

She leaned forward and spoke with exaggerated huskiness. "I can't go home because my husband threw me out, Father Jack. He says I'm a whore." Which was true enough, in its own twisted way. Phillip had made that accusation a hundred times.

Jack's expression betrayed no reaction. "Are you a whore?" he asked coolly.

She swallowed hard, just once. "Why, yes, Father, I guess I am."

The acknowledgment hung starkly in the air between them. Jack stared straight into her eyes. "I don't believe you," he said. "You don't have the eyes for it. They're still alive."

She shrugged, not trusting herself to speak. He picked up her left hand and ran his thumb over the base of her ring finger. "If you're married, where's your wedding ring?"

"I pawned it," she said with complete honesty. "I needed the money." Sometimes, with Dayton Ames, it had amused her to tell the truth and make it sound like a lie. The same trick didn't work with Jack. She didn't find her truthful lies in the least amusing.

He turned her hand over. "No indentations, no tan line. No sign that you wore a wedding ring any time in the recent past. I don't think you have a husband, Caroline, much less a husband who threw you out of the house early this morning. And if you pawned your wedding ring, you did it months ago."

She couldn't afford to have Jack continue with his questions. Come on, she chided herself. Why the hell can't you come up with a convincing story?

She drew in a quick, sharp breath. "You're right. I'm not married, not legally anyway. But I was living with this man. He promised to marry me, but we fought, and he threw me out. My family disapproved of our relationship, and now I have nowhere to go."

"Gee, I'm real sorry to hear that," Jack said. "What was your lover's name? Dayton Ames?"

"No! No, it wasn't Dayton Ames."

Jack framed her face with his hands. "You know something, Caroline? You're a lousy liar."

"I'm not!" she protested, hot with frustration, infuriated that Jack wasn't more gullible. Damn it, she was an excellent liar, one of the best. "You just aren't willing to believe the truth when you hear it. For a priest, you have a shocking lack of faith in your fellow human beings."

Jack smiled grimly. "I have tremendous faith in my fellow humans—most of the time, you can count on them to behave badly. Were you with Dayton Ames the night he was killed, Caroline?"

"Of course I wasn't! I don't even know the stupid man!"

"Is that so? Among the many useful things prison taught me is this. The louder the jailbird squawks, the less likely he is to be innocent. Same rule works on the outside, too. You're squawking way too loud, Caroline."

"I'm not squawking, I'm telling you what happened. My lover threw me out of our apartment this morning, and now I have nowhere to go."

Jack stood up and walked toward the phone. "I guess that's it, then. You don't intend to answer my questions truthfully, so I have no choice but to call the police and let them sort out what's really going on here."

"No, please don't! You're wrong about me, Jack, dead wrong!" She ran after him, snatching the phone out of his hand and slamming it into the cradle.

He whipped around, pushing her against the wall. "Then prove it, damn you! Tell me the truth about why you can't go home, about why you don't have a soul in the world you can ask for help when you get beaten up by a pair of thugs."

She stared at him, desperately considering and discarding various lies.

They realized in the same moment that their bodies were touching from chest to thigh, and that Jack was unmistakably aroused. They sprang apart, their movements as jerky as if they'd been stung by bees. Over the drum of her heartbeat, Caroline suddenly understood that there was only one way she was going to stop Jack asking questions she couldn't answer, only one way to silence him.

Throwing her head back, she closed the gap between them and ground her hips against him in explicit invitation. He shuddered, his eyes closing as she rocked against him. She drew in a quick, triumphant breath, relieved that she hadn't been mistaken, hadn't misread the signals. Jack Fletcher wanted her. Wanted her badly enough that she would be able to make him forget what it was they'd been talking about.

She didn't allow herself to think or to consider the implications of her actions. Afraid of breaking the mood by speaking, she reached for the zipper of his jeans and started to glide it slowly downward. For a moment, Jack froze, but just as she got the zipper all the way down and started to stroke him, he opened his eyes, capturing her fingers with a hand that wasn't quite steady.

"Caroline...I think we should stop this right now." His voice was firm, but he was having a difficult time zipping his jeans. Whatever Jack might say, his body was sending her a vastly different message, and she knew exactly how to put him over the edge. Marriage to Phillip had taught her a lot more than how to duck a swinging fist.

"Why should we stop?" She didn't need to make her voice low and husky; it was that way already. "We're consenting adults, and this is what we both want, isn't it?"

"No," he said. "It's not what you want at all."

Odd that he should consider her feelings. Odd, but irrelevant. Sex was a tool she used to tame the men she encountered, not an experience she expected to enjoy. "You're wrong," she said, linking her hands behind his head and exerting the slight downward pressure necessary to bring his mouth into contact with hers. "You're a very...stimulating man, Jack."

She slanted her mouth expertly beneath his. As she'd expected, his resistance vanished the instant she kissed him. What she hadn't expected was the flare of excitement in the pit of her stomach, the sudden intoxicating sensation of spinning dizzily in space.

Thrown off-balance by her reaction, she melted deeper into Jack's arms. His body was muscled and firm, the strong center of a universe that had turned molten at the edges. She felt hot little sparks of pleasure everywhere he touched. When he started to unbutton her blouse, her nipples tingled with anticipation, and she heard her breath squeeze out of her lungs in a soft moan of longing.

In the same instant she realized she'd lost control of their encounter. Jack was in charge of this kiss, not her. Horrified at the way he'd somehow tricked her into surrendering power, she fought the waves of pleasure, clamping her lips tightly together and pummeling his chest.

"Stop it," she said, panicked by the sensations he was producing. "Please, you must stop. You were right. This is a mistake."

He drew away from her, turning sharply so she could see only his back. Then he shoved his hands through his hair, his movements jerky and uncoordinated.

"I'm sorry," he said, when he finally faced her again. "You deserved something a whole lot better from me than that."

She was struck by the discomfiting thought that perhaps Jack had deserved something better from her than to be subjected to an emotionless exploitation of his sexual needs. She quickly dismissed the thought. A person in her position couldn't afford too much moral sensitivity.

She treated him to a hard-edged smile. "We kissed, Reverend, that's all. No sinful fornicating or anything else to get your bishop hot under his clerical collar. What happened wasn't that big a deal."

"I disagree," Jack said. "I let you down and I'm sorry. You should have been able to count on me as a friend, and I blew it."

"Great confession, Father. You do that really well." She spoke quickly to cover the little ache throbbing deep inside her.

"Yeah, I've had lots of practice. Plenty to confess." He threw her a look that made her stomach lurch. "You know what you do really well, Caroline?"

"No, but I'm sure you're going to tell me." She waited for him to say lie, or cheat, or hide the truth.

"Kiss," he said, and walked into his bedroom, slamming the door behind him.

Six

Jack emerged from his bedroom just as she finished tucking the corner of the sheet under the sofa cushions. "You'll need these," he said, handing her a plastic grocery sack. "The women's guild at the church keeps a few toiletries on hand for emergencies, and I brought some home for you. And I found a T-shirt of mine for you to sleep in."

"Thank you." She managed to take the sack without looking at him, relieved to see a package of underwear resting on top of the other supplies. When you possessed nothing except the clothes on your back, it was surprising how exciting a toothbrush and a twin-pack of stretch nylon panties could be.

"You're welcome. Good night, Caroline."

"Good night." She heard him turn into his room and thought it would be safe to look in his direction. He happened to glance up at just the wrong moment. Their eyes locked, and she felt heat sweep through her.

She knew she needed to say something flip and casual, but her mind seemed fresh out of witty remarks. No doubt because it was too busy sending floods of unwanted hormones swirling through her system. She latched onto the first thought that floated up from the swell.

"I need to wash my clothes," she said. "Where should I hang them to dry?"

"The bathroom's fine. They should dry overnight, and there's even an iron in the linen closet. Top shelf, left-hand side. Another present from my sister."

"Taking care of you sounds as if it's a full-time job for her."

He grinned. "You don't know Meg. She's mayor of Goose Run, Montana, and controls all four thousand citizens with a rod of iron. She's also the mother of three teenagers and the unflappable wife of an absentminded genius who invents gadgets in their basement. Trying to whip me into shape is a minor sideline for Meg, something she takes care of between orange juice and coffee at breakfast."

"She sounds exhausting," Caroline said. Having grown up with a mother who organized most of the volunteer activity for the city of Chicago and presided over all the major events in the social calendar, she knew what it was like to exist in the wake of somebody who didn't understand the concept of leisure or the value of the occasional idle moment.

"Meg's fun to be with," Jack said. "I don't find her exhausting, but I only have to cope with her in small doses. I've often wondered how her kids handle that pace on a daily basis." He glanced at his watch and stepped into his bedroom. "I guess I'd better get some sleep. We always start the week off at St. Luke's with an eight o'clock Mass on Monday mornings, so I'll be leaving here around seven-thirty tomorrow. I'll try not to disturb you."

"Don't worry, I'm an early riser and a sound sleeper." The knot that had developed in her stomach was bothersome. Even more bothersome was the way her throat ached every time he looked at her.

"Great." He hesitated a moment. "Caroline, much as I enjoy your company, you obviously can't spend the rest of your life sleeping in my living room. Tomorrow we need to talk about your plans for the future."

"Yes, I guess we do." The ache in her throat was expanding, making it difficult to breathe.

"Maybe we could have a chat some time around mid-morning, after Mass and before Marcus gets back from his grandmother's?"

She swallowed hard. "Yes, of course, that'll be fine with me if it's convenient for you. I know I need to get my life back on track."

She thought she'd managed that reply rather well, but something in her voice must have betrayed her insincerity. Unlike her ex-husband, Jack wasn't self-centered enough to be lulled by the appearance of total submission.

He was at her side in a moment, forcing her to turn around. "You're going to run, aren't you?"

She kept her eyes averted. "No, of course not. I haven't anywhere to go...."

"That's true," he said quietly. "I hope you understand *how* true. The streets are dangerous, Caroline, and only fools try to hide out there."

She could have told him that the dangers of the street were obvious and the dangers to be found inside a home more subtle but no less deadly. She didn't, of course. This evening had already provided her with a crash course in the risk of honest communication.

"Jack..." It was the first time she had called him by his name rather than by his title, and she let her voice catch as she said it. Though she couldn't be sure that pathetic little break was entirely acting. "Jack, it's been a terrible day. I'm really tired, and I still need to do my laundry. Could we hold off on any more discussion until tomorrow?"

She knew she sounded convincing, in part because she genuinely wanted to rest. Annoyingly, Jack showed no sign of being deceived.

"Sure," he said. "But just a friendly reminder, Caroline, in case you feel the urge to take a midnight stroll. I spent one year, nine months, three weeks and four days in jail. Trust me, I sleep real light, and I move *real* fast."

Her chin snapped up. "And I've spent six years in hell, Reverend Fletcher. Trust me, if I really wanted to take a midnight stroll, you wouldn't have a clue that I was leaving."

Jack's eyes gleamed. "Gee, aren't we both just too tough and street-smart for words?" He shook his head, clearly irritated by his burst of sarcasm. "Scratch that. Let me start over. Of course, you have every right to leave here if you choose to do so. But you're a smart, beautiful woman, Caroline, and I'd hate to see you get hurt because of a few temporary problems in your life. Would you please stay here in my apartment until we can work out somewhere safe for you to go? Some place where you can make a genuine fresh start?''

Caroline refused to let herself react to his conciliatory tone. In the space of a few hours, Jack had provoked more emotional response from her than Dayton Ames had unleashed in the entire six months of their relationship. Which meant that, for all his friendly smiles and soothing words, Jack was a dangerous man.

She was too tired to keep the necessary watch over her tongue, so she opted for escape. She grabbed the sack of toiletries and headed toward the bathroom. ''I need to get started on my laundry,'' she said. ''You can safely assume that with all the clothes I possess in the world drip-drying over your bath, I won't be going anywhere, at least for now.''

''Do I take that as a promise not to leave before I get back from church?''

''I guess so,'' she said tiredly. Even she could hear the doubt in her voice, so she added the necessary lie. ''Yes, it's a promise, Reverend. I won't leave before you get back from church.''

''See you tomorrow, then. Take your time in the bathroom. I'll use Marcus's.''

Her hands were shaking, she discovered as she squeezed paste onto her new toothbrush. Jack's fault, of course. It was those dratted laugh lines at the corners of his eyes. They made it damn near impossible to refuse him anything, even when she knew he was inviting her to wade straight into the middle of a quicksand. If she carried on this way, by tomorrow she'd be ready to tell him her life story in exchange for one of his irresistible smiles. Or one of his kisses.

She yanked so hard at the button fastening her skirt that it almost popped off. Her skirt and blouse were crumpled and dirty, but neither was actually torn, except for the rip she'd just made at the waistband of her skirt. Since these two items constituted the only outfit she possessed in the world—God only knew what had happened to the jacket she'd been wearing when she left for the airport—she might as well make an honest woman of herself and wash them.

She turned the linen skirt inside out, automatically patting the pocket in the side seam for tissues or other junk. Her fingers encountered a small, stiff object. Good lord, how had she missed this earlier on? Heart pounding, she reached in and pulled out a shiny rectangle of red plastic.

My bank card, she thought, staring at it in awe. She had no memory of slipping the card into her pocket, but presumably she'd done it at some point during that blank period of time after Joe's henchmen dumped her on the sidewalk outside her apartment.

She ran her thumb over the bumpy letters of her name. Her real name, unfortunately. Because of her relationship with Dayton Ames, she hadn't used this account much in recent months, except to pay the rent on her apartment. As best she could recollect, it still had well over a thousand dollars in it.

Caroline stared into the mirror over the sink and realized she was white with excitement. I can withdraw two hundred dollars with this card, she thought. In each and every twenty-four-hour period, I can go to a bank machine and withdraw two hundred dollars.

Or, more accurately, she could withdraw two hundred dollars a day until the police tracked her down, which they would likely do very shortly, maybe as early as tomorrow. She couldn't count on having many more days of freedom, since Felicity Ames would undoubtedly inform the police that the woman they wanted to question was Caroline Hogarth, who'd been with Dayton Ames the night he died. As soon as Felicity Ames spoke to the authorities, Caroline's chances of getting her money would be zero.

Her choice seemed quite clear. If she waited, this bank card would be useless. On the other hand, if she used the account tonight, she'd be two hundred dollars richer by tomorrow morning.

Two hundred dollars would be a tidy sum to have on hand, but it wasn't enough to buy her ticket to the Cayman Islands. Her feverish brain tossed up another thought. If she arrived at a bank machine a few minutes before midnight, she could withdraw two hundred dollars right away. Then, at a minute or so after midnight, a new day would start and she'd be able to withdraw another two hundred dollars, making a grand total of four hundred dollars.

Four hundred dollars! In her present situation, it sounded like a small fortune. Caroline glanced at her watch. Ten-forty-five, which meant that in just over an hour, she might have enough money to buy a plane ticket to the Cayman Islands. A whoop of glee burst from her throat, and she quickly turned on the tap to drown the betraying sound in a gush of water.

It was premature to start celebrating. She had no idea where to find a bank machine, and this was not the best part of town to wander around in, searching aimlessly. More importantly, even when she *had* a plane ticket, she would still need a passport to board any plane destined for the Cayman Islands. How in hell was she supposed to get a passport with the authorities hot on her tail? Calling her congressman and claiming a family emergency wasn't likely to cut it. That was for respectable people, not fugitives wanted by the law.

Take each problem as it comes, Caroline told herself, returning her new toiletries to the plastic bag. Money first, passport second. She stripped off her remaining clothes and stepped under the shower, needing to cool off. Hope after a period of total despair was dangerous because it made a person reckless, and she couldn't afford to behave recklessly. Mistakes always had to be paid for. Look at the price she was paying for making the stupid, elementary mistake of assuming the phone in her apartment was safe from Joe's wiretaps.

The water sluiced refreshingly over her tense muscles and sticky skin, soothing the throb of her blisters. Whatever else might or might not happen over the next couple of days, she needed to use her bank card tonight, Caroline decided. And that meant she was racing against time if she was going to get to an automatic teller machine before midnight. She didn't doubt Jack was a light sleeper, and to escape from the apartment without alerting him, she'd have to lull him into letting down his guard.

She hurriedly swished her blouse, bra and panties through the shower water, squeezed out what she could, then hung them over the towel rail. Jack had said he would use Marcus's bathroom, but if he came in here over the next half hour or so, she didn't want him wondering why she hadn't washed her clothes. With luck he wouldn't notice that her skirt was missing from the items drying on the rail.

She toweled off at high speed, slipping into a new pair of panties and Jack's T-shirt, which was oversize and skimmed her thighs. Carrying her skirt over her arm, she walked into the living room. The door to Jack's bedroom was closed, and there was no sign of light. Darkness didn't guarantee that he was sleeping, however, and she didn't want him coming from his room to check if she was in bed. She deliberately bumped into the coffee table and muttered a mild curse under her breath, just loud enough that he would be aware of it if he happened to be listening.

The couch springs gave an obliging squeak as she stretched out on the cushions, and she smiled faintly. If Jack *was* waiting to hear her turn in, these few sounds should convince him that she was well on the way to slumber. Yawning, she switched off the lamp on the end table next to the couch and made the rustling noises of somebody trying to get comfortable on a narrow bed.

When she stopped moving, quiet blanketed the apartment, disturbed only by the distant wail of police sirens and the muted hum of traffic. Jack was apparently not a man who snored or even snuffled. The silence emanating from his bedroom was so complete it began to make Caroline uneasy. How had he learned to sleep so noiselessly? In jail? Or was it a priestly attribute he'd picked up at the seminary? She hoped like hell that he *was* asleep, and not lying in wait for her to make a move toward the front door.

She yawned again, fighting drowsiness. What did priests wear to bed, anyway? Jack looked like the sort of man whose natural inclination would be to sleep nude. But presumably priests were supposed to keep their bodies modestly covered at all times. Or maybe that was nuns. Either way, whether Jack slept in an ankle-length flannel nightshirt or buck naked, there was absolutely no reason for her to be wondering about it. Male bodies, particularly the priestly variety, were none of her business. All she wanted from Jack was for him to stay asleep.

Caroline wriggled around on the couch until the springs creaked again. Then she lay very still, all thoughts of Jack rigorously banished, and stared at the illuminated dial of her watch, waiting for it to say eleven-twenty. She had no idea where she'd find an automatic teller machine, but she planned to make her way over to Ashland and work down from there. Ashland at least had the advantage of being a high-traffic area, and a street with a cash dispenser was likely to be well-lighted. She wasn't a fool, and she knew the risk she was running of being mugged or raped, or worse.

However, there was no point in dwelling on risks that couldn't be altered. She calculated it would take ten minutes to reach Ashland and another ten minutes to locate an automatic teller machine. That gave her a twenty-minute cushion before midnight. The timing seemed just about right to maximize opportunity and minimize risk.

At precisely eleven-twenty, Caroline sat up and swung her feet to the floor. She listened intently. Not a sound came from Jack's bedroom. Carefully, she pulled on her skirt, tugging it up under the T-shirt and silently closing the zipper. Before she took her first step away from the couch, she shut her eyes and counted to twenty. When she opened them, there was a significant improvement in her night vision. So far, so good.

She listened again for sounds of Jack stirring. Nothing. Sandals in hand, she crept toward the kitchen. While she'd been cooking dinner, she'd noticed two keys hanging on a hook by the fridge. One of them was almost certainly a front door key. Once she'd gotten her money from the automatic teller, she needed to get into the apartment without Jack knowing she'd ever been gone. Whatever the disadvantages of bunking down in his living room, she didn't want to waste any of her precious four hundred bucks on a motel room.

Months of learning how to avoid Phillip had made her adept in the art of moving silently. She slipped into the kitchen, closing her hand over the keys to prevent them from jingling as she lifted them from the hook. She slid them into her skirt pocket, where they nestled next to her bank card. For good measure, she helped herself to the can of WD-40 that she'd noticed in the cupboard under the sink.

Can in hand, she emerged from the kitchen. Everything remained quiet. No sign of a light, and Jack's bedroom door was still safely shut. Like a shadow, and making no more sound, she glided the final few feet to the front door. Very carefully, she sprayed WD-40 on the bolt that reinforced the heavy-duty lock, waiting for the roar of a passing truck to cover the faint hiss of pressurized spray squirting from the can. Freshly lubricated, the bolt slid open without a hint of sound. Holding her breath, she turned the lock. Not a squeak betrayed her action.

With a silent sigh of triumph, she stepped into the lobby, her entire attention concentrated on the difficult final task of closing the apartment door without making a sound.

"A damn fine escape job." Jack's voice came pleasantly—terrifyingly—from behind her. "I had no idea you were on the move until the front door opened. I suppose there isn't a hope in hell you'll tell me where you're going?"

She whirled around, so shocked at being discovered that she felt dizzy. "Wh-what are you doing out here?"

"Waiting for you." He closed a slender book and slipped it into the hip pocket of his jeans. "You're about fifteen minutes earlier than I expected. I figured you'd give me at least one full hour to say my prayers and fall safely asleep before you made a run for it."

She was still off-balance with shock. "Why are you waiting for me?" she asked. "You have no right—"

"I have the right of any friend to try to stop you from harming yourself."

"You're not a friend! I don't have . . . I don't want friends." Anxiety made her voice change pitch. "Stop trying to control my behavior, Reverend. I'm an adult, capable of making my own decisions."

"True, but I can offer advice, and this is it. Don't go out tonight, Caroline. You'll get hurt, you know, one way or another."

"Thanks for caring, Reverend," she said with heavy sarcasm, aware that the minutes to midnight were ticking away and she didn't have time to stand here arguing with him. "But this is a free country, and I have a right to go anywhere I please, even after midnight and even if I'm likely to get hurt. It's my choice, and I'm choosing to go out. Let me pass."

"Sure, if you feel that strongly about it." He stood aside, gesturing politely for her to pass him. "The lobby door is stiff. You'll have to push hard on the handle before it will open."

Why was he capitulating and letting her go? Caroline walked uncertainly toward the main entrance, her worst fears realized when she saw that Jack was following close behind.

"What are you doing?" she demanded, as if it wasn't quite obvious. "Where do you think you're going?"

"You know where I'm going. I'm coming with you."

"Damn you! I don't want you to come with me!"

He smiled, his courtesy unruffled. "I can understand why. I don't imagine you'll do a very hot trade with me standing right next to you."

Her head jerked up. "What are you talking about?"

He touched the white band around his neck. "In case you haven't noticed, I'm in uniform. Thought I might get in a little street-side preaching. You've no idea what a depressing effect a dog collar has on most johns. Except the ones who're gay and assume I'm out there in costume, waiting to be propositioned."

He thought she was sneaking out to turn tricks! Caroline almost laughed. She felt sure there must be an ironic moral to all this, although right now she was in no mood to search for it. "Stop trying to save me, Reverend. Go preach somewhere else. You have no right to impose your moral values on me—"

"It's a free country," he said softly, tossing her own childish words at her. "I have the right to go anywhere I please."

"Not if you're harassing me, you don't."

"How about if I'm keeping you from performing a criminal act? In case you've forgotten, prostitution is illegal. Shall we go check out our respective rights at the local police station, Caroline? And while we're there, I'll suggest they have their witness in the Dayton Ames case take a look at you. I have this strong feeling he'd say you look *real* familiar." He smiled with as much amiability as if he was offering her a choice between chocolate cake and fudge brownies. "Shall we go to the police? Or shall I come with you? How does that sound?"

"It sounds like coercion," she said tightly.

"Yeah, doesn't it, though?" Jack continued to walk next to her, whistling "Onward Christian Soldiers" beneath his breath. She could cheerfully have murdered him.

There was no way she could force him to leave her alone. Even if she ran, he'd soon catch up with her. Father Jack looked as if he spent far more time working out in the gym than preaching from the pulpit. Which meant that she could either tell him what she planned to do or she could kiss goodbye all hope of getting her hands on four hundred perfectly legal dollars.

With her choice presented in those terms, it was no choice at all. If she was going to get to the Cayman Islands, she needed to use her own bank account tonight. Reluctantly, Caroline spoke up.

"I'm not planning to spend the night turning tricks," she said through clenched teeth. She took her bank card out of her pocket and waved it under Jack's nose. "I'm planning to withdraw money from my bank account. Quite legal and very tame. Disappointed, Reverend?"

"Not disappointed," he said. "Relieved and puzzled. Why wait until it's dark, when you're likely to get mugged? Why the need for secrecy?"

"I only found the bank card a little while ago when I went to wash my skirt, or I would have gone earlier." Irrationally, she wanted him to believe her. Given that she was despised, doubted and disowned by almost everyone who knew her, she was surprised by her sudden desire to convince Jack she hadn't taken advantage of his generosity.

"I wasn't lying when I told you I had no money," she said tightly. "Until an hour ago, I thought this card had been stolen along with everything else from my purse."

"I understand." He didn't point out that she hadn't really answered his question, that she hadn't explained why she needed to rush out in the middle of the night to withdraw money that, presumably, would still be in the exact same place the next morning. She found his failure to probe troublesome. She'd noticed earlier, over dinner, that the fewer questions he asked, the more she wanted to explain. She clamped her lips firmly together and strode forward.

"You're walking mighty fast," he said. "Do you know where we're going?"

She decided to ignore his use of the word *we*. "I figured there must be a money machine somewhere in Ashland."

"Yes, there's a bank about three blocks south of here, with a machine in the lobby. It'll take us less than ten minutes to get there."

She couldn't help a quick, anxious peek at her watch. Eleven-forty. Thank goodness. It seemed there was still time to get to the machine before midnight. She sneaked a sideways glance at Jack, worried about everything he wasn't saying. His reticence was beginning to make her nervous.

"You don't have to come with me," she said. "I'm used to taking care of myself."

"Humor me," he said. "I'd only lie in bed imagining you raped or murdered. Besides, it's a beautiful night for walking and I enjoy your company."

"Be careful, Reverend. That sounded almost like a request instead of an order."

He smiled. "Every so often, I'm smart enough to remember that honey attracts more flies than vinegar."

"The problem with that cute piece of folk wisdom is that either way the flies end up dead."

His voice was quiet. "Is that what you're afraid of, Caroline? That you're going to end up dead?"

She looked at him for a second, then turned her head sharply, staring at the litter-strewn street. How did he do it? she wondered. How did he manage to cut through her defenses the instant she let down her guard even a fraction? With two quick questions, he'd managed to bring her face to face with her own darkest fear, the possibility that Joe would arrange for her to be murdered before she could rescue Andrew. It was the dark monster that prowled her dreams.

"We all die sooner or later," she said. Her effort to sound unconcerned didn't quite succeed.

"True, but most of us hope it will be later, not sooner." He didn't allow himself to be diverted into an abstract conversation about the human condition. He honed right in on what they'd been talking about. "Why are you scared, Caroline? Who are you running from?"

The only thing in the world that scared her more than her father-in-law was the urge she'd developed to confide in Jack Fletcher. She was so close to telling him the truth about Andrew she shook with the effort to remain silent. She was frantically searching for a lie big enough and bold enough to put Jack off track when she realized she was staring at a familiar object in the scraggy bushes that marked the division between one apartment building and the next.

"My purse!" she exclaimed, making a dive for it. "Jack, it's my purse!"

Logically, she knew the purse was going to be empty, that the bikers would have thrown it away only when they'd taken everything that might be of value to them, but she couldn't help feeling a surge of hope as she lifted the flap. Her passport might be there. *Please, God, let it be there.* The bikers would have no use for a passport.

"It's empty," she said, her voice dull.

"I'm sorry." Jack gave her arm a consoling squeeze. "Let's look around, though. They might have tossed your credit cards somewhere nearby. Quite often, thieves only want cash."

They didn't find any credit cards, but Jack found the small satin bag that held her makeup a few moments later. He dusted off fragments of leaf and dirt before handing it to her. "Hey, this may not be credit cards, but it deserves at least a little smile," he said. "My wife always used to say that with lipstick and her favorite eyeshadow, a woman is ready to conquer the world."

My wife. He'd said the words with such warmth and tenderness that Caroline felt an absurd surge of envy. She hadn't realized he was married, but she was determined not to ask him any questions. She didn't allow herself to get involved in other people's lives. But by banishing all thoughts of Jack's wife and her own missing passport, she managed the requested smile.

"Thanks," she said, taking the makeup. "This is turning out to be a big night. We've not only found my favorite purse, but I'll soon have money to put inside it."

"You're becoming a woman of property," Jack said, smiling. "Look, there's the bank on the next corner."

They still had five minutes until midnight. As they walked the last few hundred yards to the bank, Caroline pretended to check if her makeup had been damaged. Feigning a murmur of delight as she held up a small vial of Chanel perfume, she used her other hand to find the key she'd been searching for. The key to a safety deposit box in a large, impersonal, downtown bank.

From her point of view, it was a very important safety deposit box, although it contained no money, no jewels, nothing that could be sold or traded on the open market.

The box contained nothing but papers. A letter from her ex-husband, written the week before he died. And a signed confession from the hit man who'd been hired to gun Phillip down.

Though delighted to have the key in her possession, Caroline knew it represented something that was so dangerous she doubted she'd be able to work out a way to exploit it safely. If she told Joe Rossi she knew who had murdered his beloved only son, he would move heaven and earth to ensure she shared that knowledge with no one except him. He might even let her see Andrew in exchange for such a valuable name.

Trouble was, once she gave Joe the information he craved, her life expectancy would be measured in hours, perhaps even in minutes.

Knowledge was a dangerous thing for people with secrets. Ignorance might not be bliss, but as Caroline understood all too well, knowledge killed.

Seven

Joe was not in a good mood. He hated Chicago—hated the broad sweep of streets, the smooth facade of the tall buildings, the endless expanse of Lake Michigan, rippling below his windows. It was unnatural having that much water thousands of miles away from an ocean. At least he *thought* Lake Michigan was thousands of miles from an ocean. It took long enough to get here on the goddamn plane. Joe knew the roads and byways of New Jersey better than he knew the wrinkles on his wife's tits. Other than that, his grasp of geography was hazy.

Sometimes he regretted that he'd had so little schooling. If his father had been something more than a no-account *soldato* trying to claw himself a place in the local Family, maybe he'd have lived long enough to ensure that Joe got himself an education.

But then again, maybe he would have done no such thing. Joe Senior hadn't been good for much beyond banging the heads of petty crooks to make sure they paid their dues on time. That and banging his wife, leaving her with a permanently stuffed belly. When his father got killed in the line of duty, Joe was twelve. He already had six younger brothers and sisters. If his father hadn't come to a blood-spattered end on a Newark sidewalk, Joe would probably have been the eldest of a dozen ill-fed, ill-housed Rossi kids.

Joe had shouldered the burden of providing for his siblings without a murmur of complaint. They were his blood; he owed them a living. His two brothers, born within ten months of each other, had barely enough brains to make one smart person, but he'd found them both jobs in his organization, and they were good family men who knew their duty. In some ways, as things turned out, it was lucky they were too stupid to be anything but loyal. The struggle to get himself promoted from Atlantic City *capo,* to *consigliere* for the whole of New Jersey had extracted a price too terrible to think about. The profits to be made from the drug trade had played merry hell with relationships within the organization, and Joe needed to have a few loyal dumb asses he could count on. His brothers fit the bill perfectly.

His sisters he'd married off before they could cause him trouble, and he'd made sure every one of them was a virgin on her wedding night. Nowadays, there weren't many men who could boast that they'd kept all the women in their household pure. But Joe believed in the old ways, and he'd seen that his sisters were protected the way women should be. He'd chosen his brothers-in-law, handpicked each of them, and a damn fine job he'd done of choosing.

Only Phillip, flesh of his flesh, bone of his bone, had defied him.

Joe sighed, the pain of his son's death as fresh as if it had happened yesterday instead of over a year ago. If Phillip had married the nice Italian Catholic girl Joe had selected for him instead of that uppity WASP bitch Caroline Hogarth, life would've turned out real different for all of them.

And now Caroline was threatening him again. Threatening him by planning to run off with the money Dayton Ames had stolen. For the sake of his career, to protect his hold on power, Joe couldn't allow that to happen. The five million dollars was important, but far more important was what it represented. With Lionel dead, the only people within his organization who knew that Dayton Ames had been ripping him off were his accountant and one of his brothers-in-law. That was why he'd come to Chicago, to arrange for Ames to be taken care of, all nice and quiet, nobody from his organization involved, at least not directly.

For now, he had things under wraps, and there was no danger of somebody taking advantage of this minor screwup and organizing an attack on his leadership. But if Caroline Hogarth succeeded in getting away with the money Ames had stolen, Joe would be finished as *consigliere* for New Jersey.

A leader was only respected as long as he was successful. It was bad enough that everyone knew his daughter-in-law had made a horse's ass of him by going to bed with Dayton Ames when his son's body was scarcely cold in the ground. Far worse if word got out that he'd let her get away with five million dollars of organization money. Joe's reputation wouldn't be worth shit if that happened.

He turned from the window and held out his glass. The girl he'd had sent up poured more Scotch without having to be told. Seemed like she was a fast learner. Pity the men he'd been given to work with here in Chicago weren't half as quick on the uptake as she was. Bunch of dick heads, the lot of them. Still, he was operating in somebody else's territory, and he could understand why the local bosses didn't want him to bring in his own people, even though he'd told them his pursuit of Caroline had nothing to do with Family business.

Which was true, in a way. Dayton Ames was strictly business, but making sure Caroline didn't get out of control was something real personal. Joe didn't like to admit he'd made mistakes, but if he'd known his daughter-in-law was going to be this difficult to handle, if he'd known she wouldn't come home where she belonged and take up her domestic duties in his household, he'd have had her killed right after Phillip's funeral. And now, dammit, he couldn't get rid of her because it looked like she might be the only person in the world who knew how to access Ames's secret accounts in the Cayman Islands.

Just thinking about how his great plans for Dayton Ames had been screwed up made Joe's stomach burn. He scowled at Steve and Gerry, who were lounging around as if they'd done what they were told to do, instead of fucking up for each and every one of the past thirty-six hours. Monday afternoon, and they still hadn't found Caroline! He was furious that they'd come back empty-handed. Again.

"What do you mean, you can't find her?" he demanded. "What the hell you been doing for the past two days? Getting a suntan?"

"Chicago's a big city," Gerry said, like he was providing secret information. "Bigger than any town in New Jersey, Joe, that's what you gotta take into account. The girl's got two million places to run and hide without ever leaving the city."

Bigger than any town in New Jersey. The stupid runt. "You'd better *hope* she didn't leave the city," Joe spat out. "You got somebody good in charge of watchin' the airport? I'm telling you, that bitch is gonna head for the Cayman Islands first chance she gets."

"We got Vic and his people," Steve said. "But O'Hare's a big airport, biggest in the world, and we can't watch every gate twenty-four hours a day."

Joe counted to ten. Jesus, he had the patience of a saint! "It's because Chicago's a big city with a big airport that you two were supposed to be watchin' her," he said. "And we know she wants to get to the Cayman Islands because that's where she called and booked a ticket to, remember?" No point in letting these two jerkoffs know that he had other reasons, aside from the wiretap, for suspecting that Caroline would head for the Cayman Islands as fast as she could.

Steve finally seemed to realize he and Gerry were in real trouble. Quick on the uptake, he wasn't. Cut off the guy's balls and shove 'em down his throat, he might notice you were carrying a knife.

"You told us to take her home, Joe, and that's what we did. We kept an eye on her and followed her, just like you said. But we didn't have no backup and when she got on that bus, we never managed to find where she got off. How the hell was we supposed to know she'd disappear? She didn't look like she was trying to hide from us. She looked like she wasn't hardly with it, if you know what I mean."

Steve sounded sullen, not even smart enough to know that when you've screwed up, you need to start kissing ass like there's no tomorrow instead of wasting time trying to defend yourself.

Joe swallowed a gulp of Scotch, hanging on to his temper by a thread. It wasn't time to let loose on this pair of losers. Not yet. "I told you to keep on watchin' her ass, Steve. You've been doing it for six months now. Somehow, I figured even a two-year-old kid would be smart enough to know I told you to watch her because she was likely to make a run for it."

"She can't have gone far," Gerry said hopefully. "She left her suitcases in the lobby of her apartment building, and she hasn't been back there, we made sure of that. She hasn't set foot in her apartment since we picked her up for you on Sunday morning."

Joe could feel the blood pounding in his head. "That's because she's cleaned the place out! There's nothin' there she needs, you stupid assholes! Can't you understand that Caroline Hogarth is a smart woman?

She's fixed up a place to stay if she ever needed one, and that's where she's run to.''

"We sent Clive Burroughs to talk to her father at the bank," Steve said. "And we checked with the housekeeper out at his place in Winnetka. Real nice place they've got, but Caroline hasn't been in touch with them. Her mother's been in Europe, and she only got back like two days ago.''

Jesus Christ almighty, did they really think Caroline Hogarth was dumb enough to try to get help from her parents? After the way they'd publicly disowned her? Joe felt his temper crest hot and hard inside him. "I *told* you, she doesn't have nothin' to do with her family. They're disgusted with her.'' He threw his glass into the empty fireplace. "Damn it all, you find that bitch before she takes off for the Cayman Islands, or I'll slice your hearts out and feed them to the fuckin' fishes. Goddamn lake has to be good for something.''

He noted with satisfaction that Steve and Gerry exchanged frightened glances. Seemed like they'd finally gotten the message that they needed to take their fingers out of their noses and start doing some work.

"Look, Joe, we understand this is important," Steve said. "We've put a lot of men onto this. But you've gotta understand that the police are lookin' for her, too. Felicity Ames didn't say nothin', but you forgot about.... What I mean is, we didn't get to the doorman across the street in time, and he told the police he'd seen Caroline leaving Ames's place the morning after he died. She came out the back way, right past the entrance to this guy's building. Now every cop in Chicago is out lookin' for her. Stands to reason, she's layin' real low."

"I can read," Joe said with heavy sarcasm. "Even if I couldn't, I saw her picture on every TV channel in the city. I know the police are looking for Caroline. *You* better find her first." He felt aggrieved just thinking about how Steve and Gerry's inefficiency was causing him so many problems. "I didn't think I'd have to worry about witnesses," he said. "I expected to have Caroline right where I could find her, whenever I *wanted* to find her."

"But, Joe, we brought her to you once. If you wanted to know where she was, why didn't you keep her right here, with you?"

Because I don't know which bank Dayton Ames hid the money in, you stupid shit. Because other people screw up all the time. Because I have to keep watching her to try to find out where Ames stashed that five million dollars. The fact that he didn't know what Ames and Caroline had done with his money was acid in his soul. The fact that stupid punks like Gerry and Steve were beginning to wonder why he was so obsessed with Caroline Hogarth made the acid doubly strong.

He forced a smile. "I told you, boys, I need Caroline to lead me to somebody I'm lookin' for. Somebody on the Cayman Islands who done me wrong." That was the closest he was willing to come in explaining his actions. "So, if you're anxious to get that bonus we talked about yesterday, start searchin' a bit harder. Lure Caroline out of hiding, keep on her ass, and I'll make sure she's followed to Grand Cayman. Then you'll get your bonuses.''

If they'd had the brains of a baboon to share between them, Steve and Gerry would've started to see connections between Ames's death and Joe's obsession with Caroline's whereabouts. Fortunately, they didn't.

''She's got time on her side, Joe. She can just lay low till things cool off some.'' Gerry fiddled with his earring. Sometimes Joe wondered if the guy was a damned faggot, the way he dressed. ''She won't come out of hiding until the police call off the heat, you can bet on it.''

Joe thought for a minute and decided that, for once, Gerry might have a point. Even morons occasionally got it right.

''If the cops are turning the heat up too high, then you need to cool it,'' Joe said. ''Cool the heat and smoke her out into the open.''

''How we gonna do that?'' Gerry asked. ''We can't buy off the whole damn police force.''

''Why not?'' Joe asked sourly. ''We're spending enough money on them.'' He sat down, letting his gaze roll over the girl they'd sent up to him from one of the escort services run by the organization in Chicago. She was standing next to the portable bar trolley, Scotch and a bucket of ice cubes in reach, waiting patiently to serve him. He saw the solution to his problem at once, and wondered why he always grasped things so much quicker than other people.

"The police are lookin' for a tall, slender blond with long legs, blue eyes, right?"

"Right, Joe." Gerry nodded.

"So we'll give 'em just what they're looking for." He gestured to the girl, who was tall, blond, had long legs, blue eyes and looked like real class. It was only when she opened her mouth that you realized why she was earning her living as a hooker instead of on a soundstage in Hollywood.

He patted her on the knee. "Put the bottle down, sugar, I need you to do me a little favor."

She knelt in front of him and her hand reached automatically for the zipper of his fly. He brushed it away, impatient with her stupidity. God, he hoped her smarts included more than knowing when to serve Scotch without being told.

"Not that," he snapped. "Now sit down and listen up good. You've got a story to learn, and you better get it right. What's your name again, sugar?"

"Michelle." She licked her full, red lips, her eyes bright with fear. Joe found her fear a turn-on, but unfortunately, he didn't have time to play right now. He patted her bottom.

"Well, Michelle, honey, this is your lucky day. I'm gonna tell you how you're gonna earn yourself a thousand dollars a day for the next few days, and a bonus when you're all done."

She looked nervous. "Vic promised me this was just a regular appointment. He knows I don't let nobody beat me up."

Joe smiled. "Honey, nobody's gonna beat you up and spoil those pretty little tits of yours. Nobody wants you to do anything difficult. All you got to do is walk into a police station and tell them you're the lady they're lookin' for."

"What lady? What lady are they lookin' for? Are they goin' to put me in jail?"

"I doubt it. We'll send one of our lawyers with you. Trust me, Michelle, honey. It's gonna be the easiest money you've ever earned."

Caroline surfed through the entire selection of TV channels while Jack was at church, but despite her determined flipping between various news programs, she didn't hear a word about Dayton Ames, much less a repeat bulletin seeking information about the unknown woman who'd been seen leaving his penthouse.

She hadn't really expected the death of Dayton Ames to be featured on national news programs two days in a row, but she couldn't make up her mind whether this silence from the local stations indicated a rare stroke of good fortune or whether it presaged some future disaster of unknown dimensions. Based on experience, she ought to prepare herself for the worst. Over the last couple of years, the light at the end of the tunnel had invariably turned out to be the headlights of the oncoming train.

Somehow, though, she wasn't worrying as much as she should about the reasons for Felicity Ames's inexplicable failure to turn her in to the police. In fact, if it wasn't for the nagging anxiety of having told Jack her real name, she would be feeling absurdly optimistic for a woman who was on the lam from both the mob and the police and whose worldly possessions fit inside a plastic grocery sack and a medium-size purse. Perhaps some of her good cheer could be attributed to the early morning call to the airlines that had elicited the information that a "vacation special" round-trip ticket to the Cayman Islands could be purchased for a mere $369. Not wanting to risk accessing her bank account again, that meant she had a whole thirty-one dollars to blow.

The apartment conveyed a peaceful air of summer laziness. Clad only in underclothes and her borrowed T-shirt, Caroline rummaged through the pantry and found all the ingredients to make raisin muffins. She swiftly mixed the dough, thinking how pleasant it would be to share the morning newspaper with Jack while they munched on warm muffins and sipped freshly brewed coffee.

Reality, though, intruded on that agreeable daydream. Jack had already announced that they were going to spend the latter half of the morning discussing what she planned to do with the rest of her life. Even if he brought home a newspaper, they weren't going to be sitting at the table, bickering cheerfully about who got the comics and who got the movie reviews. She was going to get a stern lecture on the merits of finding honest work and learning to cope with life's problems by a more constructive method than running away.

She permitted herself an ironic smile that faded into wistfulness. She wondered how Jack would react if she told him there was no need for a discussion or a lecture, since her plans for the immediate future were already laid. She planned to fly to the Cayman Islands, steal five million dollars, pay off assorted lowlifes and hightail it to New Zealand before either the police or Joe's pals could organize themselves to stop her.

Not a schedule that left much room for honest hard work and moral self-renewal, she thought wryly.

She had just finished showering and changing into her newly ironed clothes when she heard the sound of a key turning in the front door lock. Jack. The prospect of his return caused an annoying flutter in the pit of her stomach, but it was Marcus who came into the living room, not Jack. He was accompanied by an attractive girl about his own age. Or at least, she would have been attractive if her expression had been less sullen.

"Hi," Marcus greeted Caroline with a casual wave. "This is my cousin Evonne. She's come to talk to Father Jack. Evonne, this is Caroline. She's stayin' here for a few days."

Evonne barely managed a nod of acknowledgment before turning her blank gaze toward the window. Marcus sniffed the air, oblivious to the tension Evonne had brought into the room.

"Hey, what smells so good?" he asked, making for the kitchen. "Have you been cooking? Man, something sure smells good."

"Yes, I've been cooking." Caroline smiled. "In this household, it's pretty easy to see what you have to do to be popular."

Marcus's eyes glowed. "Hey, man, this is so great. I can't believe you can cook! Evonne, guess what, Caroline made muffins." He stopped exclaiming and tried to look both starved and mournful. "Gran wasn't feelin' too good, that's why I came home early. We didn't have breakfast this morning."

"We had cereal," Evonne said.

"There was no milk," Marcus said, casting his cousin a frustrated glance.

Evonne didn't respond and Caroline took pity on him. "The muffins should be cooled by now. They're cinnamon raisin, if you want one."

"Oh, man, I can't believe this. This is like before Gran got sick. Real home cookin'." Marcus loped into the kitchen and emerged with a muffin in each hand. "Evonne, you wanna muffin?"

"What?"

"A muffin. Do you want a muffin?"

She shook her head. "No, thanks. I already ate breakfast, remember?"

"Nope." Marcus looked at the second muffin and grinned at Caroline with a total lack of repentance. "Oh, well, I guess it's too late to put this extra one back now." He spoke through a mouthful of raisins. "Mmm, mmm, good. Hope Father Jack persuades you to hang around for a while, Caroline, you sure are a great addition to the household." He flicked crumbs from his T-shirt and took another huge bite of muffin. "I'm off now," he said thickly. "Tell Father Jack I'll be back by bedtime, okay?"

"Wait!" Caroline stopped him as he sauntered to the front door, munching on a muffin, Walkman hanging from the back pocket of his baggy pants. "Where are you going, Marcus?" It was really no business of hers where he went, but the question was instinctive, a throwback to her own upbringing.

He took his time swallowing the last bite, demonstrating the typical teenage reluctance to convey any personal information that wasn't bludgeoned out of him. "I'm goin' over to Antoine's place for a while, okay? We're gonna ride the bus out to Schaumburg, maybe go to the mall. We're just gonna hang out. I don't have summer school until tomorrow."

He looked the picture of innocence, but his voice told a different story. "Would Father Jack approve of that plan?" she asked. "Does he like you and Antoine hanging out?"

Marcus shuffled his feet. "Antoine's okay," he said defensively. "Just because his older brother got busted, it don't mean Antoine's gonna start dealin' or nothin'. Antoine's cool."

Caroline had no trouble translating that answer. Antoine was trouble. "Why don't you call your friend and invite him over here?" she suggested, hoping for a compromise. "You can shoot some hoops at St. Luke's. Maybe there'll be enough guys to get up a game."

"Antoine don't have no phone," Marcus said. "Can't ask him nothin'."

She noticed that since they'd started talking about Antoine, Marcus's grammar had deteriorated, and his words had slurred. She suspected the mistakes were a deliberate provocation, so she ignored them. "Well, if your friend doesn't have a phone, you could walk over to his place and ask him if he'd like to have dinner with us. I bet he would."

Marcus sneered. "You'd lose your bet, lady. Antoine don't want to hang out at no priest's apartment."

"Then I guess you can't hang out with Antoine," Caroline said crisply. "Because you live in a priest's apartment."

Marcus's eyes flashed angrily. "I'm sixteen," he said. "I can go where I want, do what I want. Ain't nothin' you can say to stop me. You got no rights over me, lady."

Alarmed at the speed with which their exchange had escalated into a confrontation, Caroline felt her cheeks grow hot. Marcus's petulant answers sounded embarrassingly like some of the answers she'd given Jack the night before. She only needed Marcus to mutter that America was a free country, and he'd be her perfect echo. No wonder Jack had treated her outbursts yesterday with a sort of resigned tolerance. He probably viewed her as an overage escapee from one of his youth groups.

She might have sounded immature last night, but she was wise enough to know that there was no way to argue or threaten Marcus out of hanging out with his friend. She also knew that the wrong words at this moment could send him straight onto the street—and straight into trouble.

"I'm baking stuffed pork chops for dinner," she said, improvising rapidly. "And we're going to make ice-cream sundaes for dessert. All the toppings you can think of. Cherries, chocolate, fudge, chopped nuts, the works. Are you sure you and Antoine wouldn't like to join us?"

Marcus paused, obviously torn between defiance and teenage appetite. To her relief, ice cream won the debate. Or perhaps, like her, he was secretly glad for an excuse to end an argument he hadn't really meant to start. He shrugged, avoiding her gaze as he conceded. "Okay, I'll ask him. We'll be here around three, okay?"

Four hours from now. It was the best she could hope for, and she knew it. In fact, she considered it proof of Marcus's basic maturity that he was able to climb down so easily from his perch of offended dignity. "I'll expect you at three," she said. "We'll have dinner early. I'm looking forward to meeting your friend."

"Yeah, right." He hunched his back and nodded to his cousin, who was sitting on the sofa staring vacantly at the blank TV screen, apparently impervious to the argument going on around her. "Bye, Evonne. Catch you later."

She blinked. "What?"

"Bye," he repeated. "See you later."

"Yeah," she said. "Later, dude."

An uncomfortable silence descended after Marcus left. "Would you like a Coke?" Caroline asked his cousin, simply for something to say. "I don't suppose it will be long before Father Jack gets back. He said he'd be here right around this time."

Evonne continued to stare at the TV screen. "No, thanks," she said after a long pause. "I'm not hungry, I don't want a muffin."

Caroline refrained from pointing out that she'd offered a Coke, not a muffin. Evonne's gaze was so empty, she wondered if perhaps the girl was not very bright. She spoke gently. "Is something wrong, Evonne? You look as if something's bothering you."

Evonne jumped up. "Nothing's wrong. I need to be goin'," she said. "I shouldn't have come. There's no reason to take the Reverend's time—"

"I'm sure he'd like to see you," Caroline said, realizing in a rush that Evonne's blank expression resulted not from lack of intelligence, but from some problem that was so overwhelming she couldn't focus beyond it. "You came all this way, Evonne. Don't leave without talking to him."

"No, there's nothing he can do," Evonne said. "Don't tell him I asked to see him, or he'll come around to Gran's, and she's feelin' real poorly."

There was no reason in the world to get involved in Evonne's problems, Caroline told herself. On the contrary, there were about a thousand reasons why she should not—chief among them the fact that she'd managed to make such a total screwup of her own life that she had no business butting into anybody else's.

Whatever problem Evonne was wrestling with, Caroline was unlikely to have any insights worth sharing. Besides, she'd almost precipitated a disaster sticking her nose into Marcus's affairs. Where teenagers were concerned, she had no experience and no natural expertise.

Determined not to meddle, she smiled with polite indifference as she escorted Evonne to the front door. "Unless he asks, I won't mention anything to Father Jack about your coming here," she said.

Evonne stepped into the lobby. "He won't ask, and Marcus won't say nothin'."

The girl turned away, but something about the weary droop to her shoulders made Caroline's stomach knot with concern. Dammit, she couldn't let her just walk off without making any attempt to help her. She was just a kid, a mixed up teenager, and Lord knew, Caroline could empathize with that. She'd been thoroughly mixed up at Evonne's age. She ought to be able to lend a sympathetic ear at least until Jack arrived. How much harm could she do?

"Evonne!" she called out. "Don't go. I'd really like some company right now. Couldn't you stay a while?"

Evonne looked around, and Caroline saw the faintest of shudders rack her frame. "No, I can't stop—"

Evonne pressed her hand to her mouth, and Caroline was hit with sudden understanding. "Here," she said, grabbing Evonne's hand and rushing her toward the bathroom. "This way."

They made it just in time for Evonne to throw up. Caroline didn't say anything while the girl washed her face and rinsed her mouth with peppermint-flavored mouthwash. Her skin, a much lighter shade of brown than Marcus's, looked ashen, with a sickly yellow tinge across her cheekbones. She leaned against the bathroom wall, her eyes closed, arms drooping, as if she lacked the energy to move even to the nearest chair.

Caroline put her arm around Evonne's waist and guided her to the couch. "Rest here for a while," she said quietly. "I'll pour some cola into a glass. If you let the bubbles dissipate and then sip it slowly, you'll find it helps with the nausea."

Evonne sank onto the sofa, too drained to protest. Caroline came back with the soda and a slice of dry toast. "Sorry, we're fresh out of crackers," she said, putting the plate in front of her. "Toast was the best I could come up with."

"I can't eat," Evonne said. She shivered. "It makes me feel sick to eat." Her voice rose with a quiver of incipient hysteria.

"That's okay." Caroline didn't press her, just pushed forward the glass of cola. "Do you know why you're feeling so sick? Do you have stomach flu, maybe?"

"I don't have the flu." Evonne watched the bubbles fizzing and popping in her glass. "You know what's wrong," she said bleakly. "I'm pregnant."

Caroline had guessed, of course, but she still felt a jolt of shocked sympathy. She put her hand over

Evonne's in an automatic gesture of comfort. The teenager's fingers were icy, as if her circulation had stopped.

Caroline gently chafed her hands. "How old are you, Evonne?" she asked.

"Seventeen." She paused for a moment. "Almost seventeen. It's my birthday in three weeks."

If she was telling the truth, she was at least a year older than Caroline had thought, but still much too young to be facing the prospect of single motherhood. "What about the baby's father?" she asked. "Does he know you're pregnant?"

"Yes, he knows." The glass rattled as Evonne set it onto the table. "He wants to marry me. That's why I came to see Father Jack, to arrange for us to be married right away. Jamal says the sooner we get it over with, the better."

Get it over with. Not a promising way to describe an upcoming marriage ceremony. "Jamal? Is that your boyfriend's name?"

"Yes." Evonne broke off a piece of toast, but she didn't eat it.

"You don't sound too happy at the idea of being married," Caroline said.

"I don't want to get married, not even to Jamal, but I guess we have to, now I'm pregnant. That's what Jamal says. It's his baby as well as mine. We have to raise it right."

She sounded depressed rather than relieved that her boyfriend was willing to take his share of responsibility. News articles Caroline had read and television programs she'd watched suggested that many teenage girls got pregnant because they yearned for something small and helpless to love. Evonne, apparently, was an exception.

"Wouldn't Jamal be a good father?" Caroline asked. "Is that what's worrying you?"

"No, he'd be a fine father, I guess." She seemed startled by the question, as if she'd never considered the qualities a father might need. Perhaps she hadn't.

"Then I don't quite understand the problem."

Evonne took a sip of soda before replying. "Jamal and me, we don't want to get married and have children. We want careers," she said. "I want to be a nurse, and Jamal, he wants to be an optician."

"An optician? That's an interesting choice."

"Yeah, his little sister, she don't see so good, that's what got him interested in being an optician."

"It takes a lot of studying to be an optician," Caroline pointed out, feeling the need to inject a note of reality into the discussion.

"It's not like studying to be a doctor," Evonne said quickly. "It don't take forever. Jamal could earn good money by the time he's twenty-three. Once I graduate from nursing school, we could afford to rent a real nice apartment, move to the suburbs even. Jamal's sister, she's married to a teacher. She lives in the suburbs, in Evanston."

Caroline was touched by the mixture of practicality and idealism in their plans for the future. "Which high school do you attend?" she asked. "Is Jamal in the same class as you?"

"Next year I'll be a senior at George Washington High, but Jamal's already graduated. He was valedictorian." Evonne sighed. "All I have to do is make a B average and I can go straight into the nursing program at Illinois State." Her eyes shone with momentary pride. "That should be pretty easy. The last two years, I made straight As, even in chemistry, and that's my worst subject."

"You must be very proud of keeping up such good grades," Caroline said. "And your family must be thrilled by all your hard work."

Evonne smiled bitterly. "Proud of me? Stuck up bitch, that's what my mama called me. Just because I wouldn't give her any money for her pimp—" She broke off abruptly, playing with the toast on her plate. "I thought I was different, you know? I wasn't gonna get pregnant. Not me, I was the smart one, the girl with her head screwed on tight. I wasn't no dummy, sayin' yes to a boy just so's he could get my name tattooed on his arm and show it off to his friends, boasting he's a daddy now, and Evonne Banks is the girl he made it with. Not me, no ma'am. I was gonna make it out of the projects and get me a real life, a career, do somethin' to help other kids, left behind without nothin' to hope for." She gave another bitter smile. "So here I am, pregnant, not married and not even through high school. Just like my mama and my sister. Just like Marcus's mama, and just like all the other girls from the projects."

"Not quite like every other girl," Caroline said quietly. "You're smart, you've studied hard, and nobody can ever take your education away from you, because it's there inside your head. And Jamal's different, too. He hasn't tattooed your name on his arm and walked away. He's willing to take on his share of responsibility for what's happened. He must be pretty special, and he must think you're something special, too."

A spasm of pain crossed Evonne's face. "He *is* special," she said. "That's why I can't let him marry me. I realized that while I was sittin' here, waitin' on Father Jack. Jamal's got a full scholarship to Northwestern University starting in September. How's it gonna help anybody if he sacrifices his whole future just so he can support me and the baby by working at Pizza Hut for five lousy bucks an hour? There's no point in ruining both our lives. If I go on welfare, at least Jamal can still have his dream."

"Have you considered having an abortion?" Caroline asked. "Sometimes, for some people, that's the best choice."

"And for the baby?" Evonne asked with unexpected fierceness. "Would an abortion be best for the baby, too?" She twisted her hands, kneading them in silent despair. "I should have an abortion, I know I should. I know it's the practical answer, but I just can't do it. Not to my baby." Overwhelmed with misery, she covered her face with her hands, tears seeping through her fingers. "We used a condom," she whispered. "I didn't want to get pregnant, but I love Jamal so much. I didn't even like doin' it very much, but he wanted me so bad...."

Her tears changed to sobs. The harsh sounds tore into Caroline. Without stopping to question what she was doing, she pulled Evonne into her arms, rocking her, trying to soothe the agonized flood of tears. Life was so damn cruel, she thought. Why did a good person like Evonne have to face such a brutal choice? It was easy to say that if she and Jamal had waited to have sex until they were married, they wouldn't be facing such horrendous decisions. The reality, though, was that teenagers, seething with lust and hormones, were rarely capable of exercising restraint unless intense social pressure forced them to do so. Looking back on her own tumultuous adolescence, Caroline knew that it was luck, not good judgment, that had kept her from facing exactly the same sort of dilemma as Evonne.

Evonne's racking sobs finally subsided to sniffles and the occasional hiccup. Caroline handed her a wad of tissues. "Here," she said.

"Thanks." Evonne wiped her eyes and blew her nose. "I'm sorry about that. I guess there hasn't been anyone to talk to except Jamal, and he's so worried, he only makes things worse."

"What about your family?" Caroline asked. "Is there anyone who could help?"

Evonne took another tissue. "Gran's sick, so I can't talk to her. She has diabetes, and her kidneys are failing. That's why Marcus is living here with Father Jack. Gran used to come to St. Luke's when she was well, but she can't cope with any more trouble right now."

Evonne didn't mention her parents, but if her mother really had called her own daughter a stuck-up bitch she didn't exactly sound as if she'd be a rock of strength in the current situation. Still, Caroline felt obligated to ask. "It's a shame about your grandmother, but what about your parents? Is there any way they could help you?"

"No." Evonne shrugged. "My dad left home when I was three. Right now, if he isn't in jail, he's most likely high on something or hiding from his probation officer. And Mama . . ." She shrugged again.

Caroline wasn't deceived by those careless shrugs. For the first time in a couple of years, she spared a moment to consider the fact that her own problems might be severe, but plenty of other people had to face situations that were just as painful and just as dangerous. She badly wanted to help Evonne, but this wasn't exactly something that could be fixed by a hug, a kind word and a metaphorical Band-Aid.

Caroline decided that since she had zero experience in giving advice to troubled teens, the smart course was to refrain from suggesting solutions until Jack got home. After all, he was a priest, trained to counsel people in times of crisis. He would know how to handle this, if only to point Evonne in the direction of the professional help she needed.

Even as she delivered herself a lecture on the wisdom of keeping out of other people's business, Caroline knew she wasn't going to heed her own advice. Still, she was amazed at the suggestion she heard herself making only seconds after resolving to say nothing at all.

"You know, Evonne, there's one option you may not have considered. Have you thought about putting your baby up for adoption? Father Jack probably knows of a reliable agency that would help you find a couple who are longing to become parents. They might be able to give your baby a wonderful home."

Evonne hesitated for no more than a few seconds before shaking her head. "I couldn't," she said. "I'd rather have an abortion than give up my baby to strangers. I couldn't bear to spend the rest of my life knowing that I was separated from my own baby."

"Even if you knew that was the best thing for him? Or her?"

"It wouldn't be," Evonne said with absolute conviction. "No way my baby's gonna grow up with strangers, knowing his mama didn't love him enough to keep him."

"If your baby was adopted at birth, the parents wouldn't be strangers," Caroline pointed out. "To your baby, they would be the only mother and father he'd ever known." Her mouth felt dry and her stomach was turning somersaults, but she realized with a sense of profound shock that she really *did* think adoption might be the best solution for Evonne, for Jamal and for their baby. Which was the ultimate irony, considering she'd spent most of her adolescence blaming her adoption for every one of her manifold teenage miseries.

"I was adopted," she said, surprised that she was volunteering such an intimate piece of information to a girl she scarcely knew.

"You were?" Evonne looked at her with a spark of fresh interest. "I guess it turned out real fine for you," she said. "Your adoptive parents must have loved you a lot."

Caroline didn't say anything, and Evonne looked at her anxiously. "Did they love you?" she asked. "Are you glad you were adopted?"

It had taken Caroline years to face the truth. Even now it was hard to admit. "Yes," she said, her voice cracking. "I'm glad I was adopted. My birth mother wouldn't have been able to care for me, and my biological father wasn't willing to raise me, even though he had plenty of money. My adoptive parents gave me a stable home to grow up in, and they paid for a great education, wonderful clothes, terrific vacations—"

Evonne was much too smart not to hear what wasn't being said. "But did they *love* you?" she persisted. "That's the only thing that really matters, isn't it?"

Caroline was twenty-nine years old, and she still wasn't sure if she knew the answer to that question. "Yes," she said at last, giving her adoptive parents the benefit of the doubt. "My adoptive parents loved me." As best they were able, she added silently. Another unexpected qualification popped into her head. As much as I would let them.

"My baby's situation is different from yours," Evonne said, still unconvinced. "Jamal wants to marry me. He's willing to take care of me and the baby, not like your father. And I'm responsible, not like your mama."

"Yes, that's true." Caroline winced at the unwitting cruelty of Evonne's words. "But you and Jamal are very young. If you both sacrifice all your hopes and dreams to make a home for the baby, how long do you think it will be before you start getting mad at each other? Before your relationship stops being friendly and turns into something sour and hostile?"

Evonne didn't answer, but her face gave her away. She became preoccupied with scrunching up tissues, and Caroline didn't need to be a mind reader to guess that the stress of her pregnancy had already set Evonne and Jamal arguing.

"Consider this," Caroline said softly. "How happy can your baby be, Evonne, if you and Jamal secretly resent each other for everything you've both given up? And once the two of you start blaming each other for what's happened, how long do you think it will be before you start taking out your frustrations on the baby?"

Evonne gasped. "I would never hurt my own baby," she protested. "I would always love my baby. Always."

"Maybe," Caroline said quietly, not disputing her point, although she knew there were copious statistics to prove Evonne wrong. "Maybe you'll always love your baby, however tough times get. But how long will it take for you and Jamal to stop loving each other once you abandon your dreams?"

Evonne's eyes filled with fresh tears. "I don't know what's the best thing to do," she said. "There's no right answer, is there?"

"There's an answer that's right for you," Caroline said.

Evonne shredded another tissue. "Whatever I decide, I'll always wonder if I did the right thing. When I look back, there'll always be regrets."

"Maybe," Caroline said, taking Evonne's hand and holding it tightly. "But all you can do is make the best choice you can and then move on. You need to find a choice you can build on, not a choice that's going to wall you in."

"I have to talk to Jamal," Evonne said. "We never discussed adoption. I don't know how he feels. Maybe his family would help us out. They're really nice folks. His sister and her husband might take the baby for us—"

The ring of the phone interrupted them, and Caroline waited for the answering machine to pick up the call. A crusty voice spoke into the machine. "Jack, this is Frank Donohoe. Bad news, I'm afraid. They've ID'd a female fatality from an accident a couple of nights ago on the Kennedy Expressway. I'm sorry, Jack, but it's Kathleen Williams, the secretary at St. Luke's. Thirty-four, light brown hair, five feet seven. Her family's been notified, but as you probably know they're all out in California, and they want the body shipped west for the funeral. They're hoping you can take care of closing down her apartment. Give me a call, will ya? Sorry to have to give you this news."

The machine clicked off just as Jack let himself into the apartment.

Caroline's first highly irritated thought was that he got better-looking every time she saw him. Her second thought, more irritated still, was that his priestly robes looked astonishingly good on him. She'd half expected him to appear out of place wearing a cassock, as if he was playing dress up. Instead, he looked natural and even alluring. She reluctantly admitted that the long black robe imparted an aura of power she found both imposing and disturbingly erotic.

Evonne seemed afflicted with no such embarrassing and inappropriate emotions. She greeted Jack warmly but with deference, as if he was a cross between a kindly uncle and a favorite teacher. From the desperate, pleading glance she threw Caroline, it was obvious that she didn't want any mention made of her pregnancy.

Jack gave Evonne a quick, affectionate hug. "How's my favorite super student?" he asked. "And how's the summer job going at the library?"

Caroline saw the strain behind Evonne's smile. "Okay, thanks, Father. The library gave me thirty hours last week, and the money sure helps."

Jack noticed the strain, too, and his manner became more focused and more reassuring. "I'm glad you stopped by, Evonne. Did you come to see Marcus, or did you need to chat with me about something special?"

"No, nothing special. I know you're busy, Father—"

"Not that busy," he said. "Besides, if you need my help to take care of something, that'll give me an excuse to escape from a very boring meeting." He gave her a quick grin. "In fact, thinking about that meeting, maybe you could invent a problem, huh?"

Evonne managed a thin chuckle. "Sorry, Father, I can't help you out. I have to get home or my mother will—or I'll be late for work. But I'll come and see you next week, honest. Bye, Father. Bye, Caroline. Thanks." She almost ran from the apartment.

"Exit one unhappy teenager," Jack said, closing the door. He gave Caroline a wry glance. "Any chance you know what that was all about?"

"Some," Caroline said. "We talked for a while. She's a bright kid."

"Any chance you're going to tell me what she said?"

"None. But if she doesn't come back within the next couple of days, I think you should give her a call and encourage her to speak with you."

He grimaced. "Are we talking major problems here?"

Caroline hesitated. "Not immediately life-threatening," she said.

He sighed, showing the first sign of real weariness since she'd met him. "Evonne's a good kid, with a big heart and a sharp mind. And a mother who only stops inhaling crack long enough to give some lowlife a blow job to pay for her next hit. I've tapped every support system I know, but I figure it's still less than fifty-fifty that Evonne'll make it to graduation. You can only fight against so many obstacles.''

Right now, with a baby on the way, fifty-fifty were better odds than Caroline would have given. Jack looked depressed and she wished she could cheer him up. Instead, she had more bad news to pass on, about Kathleen Williams. She hoped Kathleen hadn't been a close friend.

''Someone called Frank Donohoe left a message on your answering machine,'' she said. ''He wants you to call him.''

''Frank? Sergeant Donohoe?'' he asked. ''What's up?''

She should have realized from the tone of Donohoe's message that he was a police officer. The fact that Jack Fletcher was on a first-name basis with a local cop didn't exactly flood her with confidence about his apartment being a refuge from the long arm of the law. But she supposed it was inevitable for a priest in a neighborhood like this to have ongoing contacts with the local police station.

Caroline gave a silent sigh of relief that she hadn't decided to pick up the phone and answer in person. Her distrust of the police was bone-deep, but she never made the mistake of underestimating their power. A corrupt cop could arrest her just as easily as an honest one.

''I'm sorry, Jack, Donohoe didn't have good news. It's about the church secretary, Kathleen Williams I believe her name was. You mentioned that she was on vacation when you first met me.''

Jack swung around, his face muscles taut. "Was?" he repeated, walking over to the answering machine. "What's happened?"

"I'm so sorry, Jack, but she's dead. She was killed in a traffic accident on the Kennedy Expressway."

He closed his eyes for a minute, and his movements stilled. One look at the shock and misery of Jack's expression was enough to tell Caroline that Kathleen had been important to him.

He pressed the replay button on his answering machine, then listened to Donohoe's message in grim silence, his gaze bleak.

The message tape rewound itself and clicked off. "Poor Kathleen," Jack said finally, his voice not quite steady. "She must have been on the way to the airport. She was going on vacation, and she was so excited. She spent the last two years saving up for a trip to France. Now she'll never get to see Paris." His voice broke slightly on the final word.

Jack was a priest, which meant that he dealt with death all the time. It was crazy for Caroline to feel the need to offer him comfort, but she tried anyway. "Maybe for Kathleen, heaven will turn out to be a trip to Paris, with Dom Perignon champagne waiting in her hotel room and a handsome Frenchman eager to take her on a stroll down the Champs-Elysées."

Some of the bleakness left Jack's eyes. "That would be Kathleen's definition of heaven, all right. Especially if the Frenchman is wearing a beret and humming a love song."

"What would your definition of heaven be?" she asked, hoping that she could keep that dreadful sadness out of his eyes.

He gave her a small smile. "I take it you're not interested in serious theology here?"

"Definitely not. My dream of heaven would be lying on the grassy bank of a wide river, with hot sun shining out of a blue sky and a tall tree for shade. And absolutely, positively no bugs. Maybe one puffy white cloud, scudding gently in the breeze. Just so you remember that sometimes it rains, even in paradise."

"I like the no-bugs part," he said. "But I'd prefer newly waxed skis, a mountain covered in fresh powder, no lines for the chair lift and an orchestra playing the last movement of Beethoven's *Ninth Symphony* when I reach the bottom."

She shook her head, smiling. "Oh, boy, that sounds way too energetic for me. I think I'll stick to my riverbank. And no music, just the sound of water rippling over stones."

"How about people?" he asked. "Would you be alone on your grassy bank?"

"No, Andrew would be there," she said, mentally adding the image of his small, sturdy body to her idyllic picture. He was picking her a bunch of daisies, his brown curls gleaming in the sunshine. As far as she was concerned, heaven without Andrew was a contradiction in terms.

"Who's Andrew?" Jack asked.

Her idyllic picture vanished in the blink of an eye. Her mouth opened and closed again without making a sound. She stared at Jack in appalled, horrified silence.

He'd done it again, she thought frantically. Without any apparent effort on his part, Jack had made her break one of the strictest rules in her entire code. She'd said Andrew's name out loud. The name nobody, not even Joe Rossi, had managed to force from her in almost a year. The name she wasn't even allowed to think.

The name of her son.

Eight

Jack discovered that he was jealous of Andrew. Not in a casual, fleeting way, but with primitive gut-eating force, the like of which he hadn't felt since he was in high school and his girlfriend was successfully propositioned by one of the linebackers on the football team.

It was crazy to be this jealous of a woman he'd only just met, especially one who had gone out of her way to indicate that she regarded sex as a commodity to be traded. But then, reason had very little to do with his response to Caroline. For a while in church this morning, he'd managed to get his feelings into perspective, but it seemed that the beneficial effects of his lengthy conversation with the Almighty were already wearing off, drowning in a flood of testosterone and lust.

"Who's Andrew?" he asked again, hoping she might trust him enough to tell him the truth.

Caroline swallowed. "Oh, he's...nobody important."

Her voice died away on the final word. The lie was so patent she couldn't possibly expect him to believe it. His temper—the demon that had killed a man—

flared high. He walked past her in silence, afraid of what he might say if he spoke to her directly and even more afraid of what he might do.

The temptation to grab her and kiss her until she forgot about Andrew was overwhelming, and he suspected she wouldn't protest all that much if he did just that. But her lack of protest wouldn't really signify consent or genuine desire, much less indicate that she liked him. He'd be exploiting her vulnerability, and she'd simply be using her sexual expertise to deflect his curiosity and shield her secrets. Jack's brain understood this quite well. He wished other parts of his anatomy would get the message.

He heard her go into the kitchen, but he continued to ignore her and dialed Frank Donohoe's number, surprised to find the detective at his desk.

They exchanged somber greetings. "I'm sorry about Kathleen Williams," Donohoe said. "We talked a couple of times and she seemed like a real nice lady."

"She was a terrific lady and a very good friend," Jack said, feeling a sharp spear of grief cut through him. "She'll be badly missed by everyone at St. Luke's, especially me. How did it happen?"

"To put it in a nutshell, she was in the wrong place at the wrong time. I'm real sorry, Jack. Sometimes life sucks, big time." Donohoe fell silent for a second or two. "It took us a while to make the ID because there were three women in the car, all about the same age, all smashed up pretty good."

"There were two other victims, as well?" Jack said. "Good grief! It sounds like a really bad crash."

"The other women weren't killed," Donohoe replied. "Still, it was a bad accident. Half a dozen cars involved. The expressway looked like LA after the earthquake. All caused by a drunk driver with four prior convictions and no license. His car jumped the median. Ploughed straight into the car Kathleen Williams was in, knocked it fifty feet down the expressway. It's a miracle there weren't more people killed."

There were miracles and then there were miracles, Jack thought grimly. *Lord, help me through this. I'm having a hard time accepting that Kathleen had to die.*

"What about the other women who were in the car?" he asked. "Are they going to make it?"

"The hospital says yes, although they've got a broken leg, a ruptured spleen and three broken arms between 'em. Some vacation, huh?"

"The nightmare variety," Jack said. "What about the drunk driver who caused the whole mess?"

"Died this morning," Donohoe said laconically. "Good riddance to him, I say, although I know you're not allowed to agree with me in your line of work. As far as I'm concerned, the world's a better place without him. Pity he had to take Kathleen Williams with him, is all."

"Yes, she'll leave a big gap at St. Luke's." And in his life, Jack added silently. The friendship between him and Kathleen had been one of those rare male-female relationships where warmth, respect and affection had been untinged by any hint of sexual attraction. His job meant that he had a huge circle of people who depended on him, but he had too few friends. He was going to miss Kathleen very badly. He cleared his throat. "You've notified her family already, Frank?"

"Yeah, sometimes this job really stinks, you know? The mother was incoherent with grief, but the father asked if you would pack up her apartment and send them the personal stuff. They can't face doing it themselves. They'll reimburse you for all the expenses and they want to make a memorial donation to St. Luke's in her memory. Sounds like they aren't short of a nickel."

"I can certainly take care of the packing. The problem is, I don't have a key to Kathleen's apartment—"

"That's easy to fix, because I have all her keys. We salvaged her purse from the wreck. Come around to the station when you have a moment and I'll release everything we took from the car to you. We pulled what was left of her suitcases from the trunk, too. You may as well take care of that along with the rest of her stuff. They said to give her clothes to Goodwill, by the way. They just want the books and the knickknacks. And any records and papers, of course."

Jack could think of few things he wanted to do less than sort through the intimate personal possessions of a woman he'd considered one of his closest friends. He massaged the knotted muscles in the back of his neck. Frank Donohoe was right, sometimes life sucked, big time. At moments like this, it required a major leap of faith to reassure yourself that God really did have the affairs of the universe under control. Despite all the theology courses he'd taken, Jack still didn't understand why kids had to grow up starving in Ethiopia and slaughtering each other in Cabrini-Green, any more than he understood why Kathleen had died. God's eternal purpose sometimes made for a damned awkward fit with human common sense.

Activity was the best cure he'd discovered for tempering the grief of losing someone you cared about. If Kathleen's parents wanted him to close up her apartment, he'd better get the keys so he could start the moment he had a couple of free hours. Confronting the reality of Kathleen's death would be the first step in learning to accept it. "Are you going to be at the station for a while?" he asked Frank.

Donohoe grunted. "Sure am. My shift lasts another four hours, unfortunately."

"Then I'll stop by in the next half hour or so and pick up Kathleen's keys," Jack said. "This is one of those jobs that will only get worse the more I think about it."

"Yeah." Donohoe grunted again, this time in sympathy. "Sometimes I think your job's almost as bad as mine."

"Worse. You only have to tell people the bad news. I have to tell them the bad news and then give them a reason to hope. I have to try to explain why terrible tragedies happen to good people. And sometimes, my friend, that can be damned hard."

After he hung up, Jack stood for a moment or two with his hand resting on the receiver, remembering Kathleen as he'd last seen her, flushed with excitement about her upcoming trip, exclaiming in rueful horror about her passport photo, which she claimed made her look like one of the ghouls from a Halloween horror movie. She hadn't been in the least comforted when he told her he thought it was quite a good picture. In fact, she'd told him he was a sadist to suggest such a thing. The memory of their banter made his chest tighten with regret.

When he finally turned around, Caroline was standing behind him, a plate of cinammon-scented muffins in one hand and a coffeepot in the other. The sunlight slanting through the blinds caught the gold in her hair and turned it to fire. She was so damn beautiful that he felt as if his breath had been snatched from his lungs. He stared at her, unable to speak and even less able to understand why she made him feel this way.

"I baked some raisin muffins for us," she said. Her voice was husky and uncertain, almost as sexy as her body. "And I made a fresh pot of coffee. I know you didn't have breakfast before you left."

"I was saying Mass," he replied. He sounded curt because he was still having trouble breathing. "It's normal for a priest to fast before taking Communion," he added by way of explanation.

He kept his gaze fixed on the muffins rather than on Caroline—that way there was some possibility that his brain would permit semicoherent conversation. The physical impact she had on him was disorienting in its intensity. What was even more bewildering was the sense of intimacy he experienced whenever she came near. Which was absurd, particularly given that he wasn't entirely sure she'd told him her real name, much less the truth about anything else. Perhaps he was discovering a new and intriguing form of intimacy, he thought wryly, one that required neither knowledge nor trust. Because the fact was that he didn't trust Caroline Hogarth, not as far as she could stretch her long, slender, entirely gorgeous legs. And yet in some extraordinary way he felt closer to her than he'd ever felt to Kathleen, despite the fact that he'd worked side by side with Kathleen for three years and genuinely liked her.

Caroline set the muffins and coffee on the table, which was already laid with place mats and paper napkins. For whatever reason, she seemed intent on proving her domestic credentials.

"I heard some of what you were discussing with Sergeant Donohoe," she said, pouring him coffee and giving him a warm smile that was in marked contrast to the icy brush-off she'd used to close the earlier conversation about her friend Andrew. "If you need some help to organize your friend's apartment, I'd be happy to volunteer." She smiled charmingly. "After all, I have nothing more useful to do over the next couple of days, and it's a sad task for you to do alone."

Jack might not know much about Caroline Hogarth, but he knew enough to mistrust this seemingly guileless offer. He ate some muffin, which was delicious, added cream to his coffee and returned her smile with one as friendly and insincere as her own.

"What a kind offer," he said, wondering just what motivated it. Perhaps Caroline was hoping to pick over Kathleen's belongings and replenish her empty wardrobe. He tested the idea. "She was about your size, I guess, so I'm sure you'll be able to find plenty of her clothes to fit you."

Caroline's cheeks suffused with angry color. "I'm not interested in Kathleen's wardrobe," she said hotly. As always on those rare occasions when she told the unvarnished truth, she immediately seemed to regret it. She looked away, and in a couple of seconds she had her smile back in place, although Jack sensed the smile cost her dearly in willpower. She flicked her hair away from her face, gave an embarrassed little laugh and generally managed to present a convincing picture of humble gratitude. It was a great performance, but Jack was so sure the humility and gratitude were faked that he felt tempted to applaud.

"I spoke too quickly," she murmured. "In my position, I can't afford to refuse Kathleen's clothes, can I? I have nothing to wear except this skirt and blouse, so I guess I need to swallow my pride and say thank you for what's offered."

"That might be a wise move," he said, her insincerity stinging him into unusual sarcasm. "I'm sure Kathleen's parents would consider you a deserving recipient—somebody who's destitute, dependent on charity, unable to take care of herself..."

She lowered her gaze, but not quite in time to hide the flash of fury. "It's...very generous of her par-

ents, and kind of you to suggest that I'm a worthy recipient—"

"Cut the crap, Caroline," he said softly. "I'm getting real tired of your lies." He leaned across the table and forced her to meet his gaze. "Entertain me.
Tell me what devious plot you're hatching. I confess,
I can't begin to imagine how Kathleen and her apartment come into it."

"Don't be crazy. There's no plot—"

"Then why are you so anxious to help me pack up
Kathleen's apartment? I'm willing to bet my next
month's paycheck that you don't have more than a
passing interest in replenishing your wardrobe."

"You'd lose your paycheck," she snapped. "I'm
wearing the only clothes I possess in the world. Of
course I'm interested in getting some more."

"Then why do I have this strong feeling that you've
been nearly jumping out of your skin with tension ever
since I spoke to Frank Donohoe? What did you hear
that's got you so excited?"

She took a fraction too long to answer. "You're
sensing my ambivalence, I expect. It's uncomfortable
to think that I'm going to get new clothes because a
young woman who was blameless and well-liked died
in a tragic accident."

He didn't doubt that her explanation was at least
partially true, but that was the trouble with Caroline.
She was much too smart to lie all the time, or even
most of the time. The trick was to sort out the kernels
of truth from the overall package. She wanted something that belonged to Kathleen. If it wasn't clothes,

what could it be? Was she hoping to steal some money? Credit cards? Had she figured out from what she'd heard of his conversation with Frank that Kathleen's purse had survived the wreck?

It would be easier to work out what Caroline wanted from Kathleen's belongings if he could decide precisely what she was trying to conceal, but so far he hadn't a clue. Which was surprising since his years in jail and as a priest had combined to give him a fairly good handle on human secrets in all their multitude and variety.

Jack didn't attempt to pressure her with questions. Experience had shown him that given enough rope, most liars soon hanged themselves. He decided to give Caroline all the equipment she needed to make herself a fully functioning noose.

"Come on," he said, pushing back his chair and holding out his hand. "Let's go to the police station and sign out Kathleen's personal effects. I'm sure you'd like to come with me."

He pretended not to notice the infinitesimal flick of a muscle in her jaw when he mentioned the police station, further evidence that Caroline was torn between wanting to go with him and wanting to avoid encountering any officers of the law.

"It's hot," she said. "I'm not sure I should come—"

"I insist," he said mildly. When her head jerked up, he smiled. "I'd enjoy your company."

She wasn't deceived either by his mildness or by his smiles; she knew he was testing her. But her desire to pick up Kathleen's personal effects outweighed her reluctance to visit the police station. "All right," she said with an attempt at nonchalance. "I'll come. I could use the exercise."

He glanced at his watch. "Marcus is due home around five or six. Right now, it's barely noon. We should have time to make a preliminary check of Kathleen's apartment once I have her keys. At least we can decide what needs to be shipped home to her family and what can be boxed up for Goodwill."

"Actually, we have less time than you think," Caroline said. "Marcus will be here at three, and I promised to cook dinner tonight for him and a friend."

"He called to say he'd be home early?" Jack asked. "That's a first."

She shook her head. "He didn't call. He came home with Evonne because their grandmother isn't feeling too well, and I had the impression he was bored at his grandmother's place—"

"He might have been. His grandmother's a wonderful woman, but her apartment's small, and if she's sick, there isn't much for Marcus to do. Where's he gone now?"

"He decided to go to the mall with his friend Antoine."

Jack's mouth tightened. Antoine was high on the list of friends he wished Marcus didn't have.

"Don't worry," Caroline said quickly. "I made Marcus promise he and Antoine would come home by three."

"Antoine's coming here?" Jack was genuinely impressed. "How did you manage that feat? I've been trying to get Marcus to bring him here for weeks."

"I offered a bribe," she said, smiling. "I promised to cook dinner for everyone, and Marcus's appetite was stronger than his desire to rebel."

"That's great news," Jack said, surprised at how efficiently Caroline had handled the situation. "Thanks for your tact—"

She set the muffins in the fridge. "How do you know I was tactful?"

"You must have been. Marcus is like most kids his age—say the wrong thing and you can send him into a major temper tantrum. Trouble is, these days when he gets mad, he doesn't lie on the floor and drum his heels. When he wants to stir things up a bit, he lets me know he's considering buying a couple of rocks from the friendly crack dealer at the corner of Antoine's apartment building."

Caroline winced in sympathy. "Raising a teenager in this neighborhood must be a terrifying responsibility," she said. "I sometimes wonder how I—" She cleared her throat. "I sometimes wonder how people cope with such a daunting task," she finished smoothly.

You almost had to admire her, Jack thought. When she set her mind to it, she covered up with an expertise that suggested years of practice. "Do you have any experience coping with teenagers?" he asked. "Are you a teacher, Caroline?"

"No," she said. "I was an accountant."

She looked momentarily furious with herself for having revealed that bit of information. *Was* an accountant? Jack wondered. Before she switched to the more lucrative trade of selling her delectable body? Or before some other major development in her life?

"An interesting profession," he said.

"Not very. There's not much you can do with columns of figures except add them up. I originally worked as a financial analyst—" She hurriedly switched to their previous topic. "Actually, Jack, we'll have to go shopping before I can start cooking. I bribed Marcus shamelessly with promises of ice-cream sundaes, and I have none of the supplies we need. Can we make a trip to the supermarket?"

"Sure," Jack said. "My bank balance is in one of its rare states of health. And thanks for being smart enough to come up with an effective bribe. Antoine and Marcus have been friends since they were in grade school together, but Antoine's at a dangerous place in his life right now, and it scares me when Marcus hangs out on his turf."

Caroline grabbed an elastic band from the drawer, twisted her hair into a loose braid and fastened it with the band. "I'm ready," she said.

For such a beautiful woman, her lack of concern about her appearance was startling. Or perhaps she already knew that she looked stunning whatever she did. "Give me a couple of minutes to change," Jack said. "It's too hot to go out in a cassock."

AN IMPORTANT MESSAGE FROM THE EDITORS

Dear Reader,

Because you've chosen to read one of our fine romance novels, we'd like to say "thank you"! And, as a **special** way to thank you, we've selected <u>three more</u> of the <u>books</u> you love so well, **and** a Free Picture Frame to send you absolutely <u>FREE!</u>

Please enjoy them with our compliments...

Editor,
The Best of the Best

P.S. And because we value our customers, we've attached something extra inside ...

PEEL OFF SEAL AND PLACE INSIDE

EDITOR'S
FREE GIFT
SEAL

HOW TO VALIDATE YOUR EDITOR'S FREE GIFT "THANK YOU"

1. Peel off gift seal from front cover. Place it in space provided at right. This automatically entitles you to receive three free books and a lovely Picture Frame decorated with celestial designs.

2. Send back this card and you'll get 3 of "The Best of the Best™" novels. These books have a cover price of $5.50 each, but they are yours to keep absolutely free.

3. There's no catch. You're under no obligation to buy anything. We charge nothing—ZERO—for your first shipment. And you don't have to make any minimum number of purchases—not even one!

4. We call this line "The Best of the Best" because each month you'll receive the best books by the world's hottest romance authors. These are authors whose names show up time and time again on all the major bestseller lists and whose books sell out as soon as they hit the stores. You'll love getting them conveniently delivered to your home...and you'll love our discount prices.

5. We hope that after receiving your free books you'll want to remain a subscriber. But the choice is yours—to continue or cancel, anytime at all! So why not take us up on our invitation, with no risk of any kind. You'll be glad you did!

6. Don't forget to detach your FREE BOOKMARK. And remember... just for validating your Editor's Free Gift Offer, we'll send you FOUR MORE gifts, *ABSOLUTELY FREE!*

YOURS FREE!

*This lovely Picture Frame is decorated with celestial designs—stars, moons and suns! It's perfect for displaying photographs of that "special someone" in your life and it's sure to please! And here's the best part: the frame is yours **absolutely free**, simply for accepting our no-risk offer!*

THE BEST OF THE BEST™: HERE'S HOW IT WORKS

Accepting free books places you under no obligation to buy anything. You may keep the books and gift and return the shipping statement marked "cancel". If you do not cancel, about a month later we will send you 3 additional novels, and bill you just $3.99 each plus 25¢ delivery and applicable sales tax, if any.* That's the complete price, and—compared to cover prices of $5.50 each—quite a bargain! You may cancel at any time, but if you choose to continue, every month we'll send you 3 more books, which you may either purchase at the discount price...or return at our expense and cancel your subscription.

*Terms and prices subject to change without notice. Sales tax applicable in N.Y.

"Don't take too long or we won't have time to pick up Kathleen's belongings before we go to the grocery store."

"We could always wait until tomorrow to get Kathleen's stuff," Jack said. "The supermarket's more urgent."

Caroline's face was fixed into an expression of mild interest, but he could almost hear the frantic pounding of her heart. "Don't we have time to do both?" she asked.

Jack took pity on her. For whatever reason, she was desperate to get her hands on Kathleen's belongings. "Yes, I guess we do," he said, disappearing into his bedroom. "I need to pick up Kathleen's keys as soon as possible."

"Did they retrieve her purse?" Caroline asked after him, "Or her suitcase from the wreck? We should get them, too."

For a split second, Jack went still. Then he zipped up his jeans and resumed his search for a T-shirt. So it *was* Kathleen's purse Caroline was after. The suitcases had been an afterthought, thrown into the conversation when she realized she'd sounded way too eager to get her hands on Kathleen's purse. Did she want the money or the credit cards? he wondered. Or something else? And how did she expect to steal anything without him noticing?

If he asked her, she would respond with lies, and Jack didn't want to listen to any more of Caroline's lies. He thrust his arms into the clean shirt and walked out of the bedroom. It would be easy enough to keep tabs on Kathleen's purse, so he'd soon be able to see for himself what Caroline wanted with it or from it. He was giving her the rope, and so far, she seemed to be looping it exactly as anticipated. Into a large noose.

"In fact, they did find them," he said. "We'll pick up everything the police have." He crossed to the apartment door, smiling at her as if he didn't have a suspicion in the world. "Keys, purse, suitcases, the works. Come on, my car is parked at the church. Let's go visit Frank Donohoe."

She'd given herself away, Caroline thought bleakly. Kathleen had been en route to France, which meant that she must have been carrying a passport. The unexpected chance to get what she so desperately needed was too great for Caroline to let pass. Unfortunately, she'd been a fraction too anxious when she mentioned Kathleen Williams's purse, and Jack had picked up on it right away. The fact that he hadn't attempted to quiz her made her twice as nervous. She'd have to be more careful if she was going to succeed in the incredible feat of getting herself to the Cayman Islands.

She wasn't used to the men in her life listening so closely to what she was saying. Her adoptive father had been too busy making money and maintaining his social position to spend much time with her. Phillip had had no interest in delving beneath the surface of her words. Joe could never accept that any woman had sufficient brainpower to deceive him. And Dayton Ames had viewed all their conversations as a form of sexual foreplay. She'd gotten careless, assuming that it was enough just to mouth the right words.

With Jack, using the right words wasn't enough. Intonation mattered. He listened to her carefully enough to hear every crack and nuance in her voice. In different circumstances, such sensitivity might have been very appealing. Right now, it was a damn nuisance. Deceiving him would be impossible if she allowed herself to get too excited. But it was difficult to remain cool when it seemed that she might be on the brink of solving her most intractable problem. Presumably Kathleen's passport was sitting in the police station, tucked into her handbag, waiting to be picked up by Jack. And stolen by Caroline.

She drew in a gulp of air and forced herself to walk sedately beside Jack. She wouldn't think about the darn passport for the next few minutes. That way, even if the wretched man was telepathic, he wouldn't be able to guess what she was thinking.

"This is my car," he said, unlocking the passenger door of a white Toyota Tercel. "I keep it here at the church because the parking lot's marginally safer than on the street."

She got in, wriggling on the hot seat, trying not to dwell on the fact that they were about to drive to a police station. Sergeant Donohoe had sounded like a kindly man, and he was a friend of Jack's. Cynically, Caroline wondered who was paying him off and how much it cost to have him turn a blind eye when asked to do so.

Quite apart from her general mistrust of police officers, what would she do if somebody recognized her as the woman wanted for questioning in the Dayton Ames case? She was running the most appalling risk by accompanying Jack into enemy territory, and yet she couldn't let him make the trip alone. Not only would she arouse his suspicions if she refused to go with him, she could imagine any number of scenarios in which, for one reason or another, the precious passport didn't make it home with him. She couldn't let that happen.

Despite her frequent appearances in court and her many hours spent in the company of off-duty cops on the take, Caroline's acquaintance with police stations was limited to movies and television. She walked into the Uptown precinct expecting chaos and drama. What she found were shabby offices, a pervasive smell of sweat masked by disinfectant, no sign of any criminals and two bored desk officers in the entrance hall who seemed to be drowning in paperwork.

She and Jack were directed inside the station. Jack was on first-name terms with at least half the cops on duty and was obviously an old friend of Sergeant Donohoe. They greeted each other warmly.

"For some reason, this accident's really sticking in my craw," Frank said. "Guess I've scooped one too many mangled bodies off the highway, and I think it's time to do something about it. If you want to start one of your infamous committees, Jack, I'll volunteer to collect the county-wide statistics on drunk drivers for you. Between the two of us, maybe we can get some legislation passed down in Springfield that'll make drunks think twice before they get behind the wheel of a car.''

Jack pretended to cock his head. ''Did I hear that right? You're actually volunteering to serve on one of my church committees?''

''There's no need to make a big deal out of it. It'll be easy to get those figures off the computer and stick 'em into a flow chart. Got my own PC at home now, you know.''

Jack gave him a mock punch. ''You're a good man, Frank Donohoe.''

''Yeah, well, put in a word for me with the man upstairs, okay?''

''My pleasure.'' Jack's eyes gleamed. ''Of course, direct communication usually works best, you know.''

''Yeah, so I heard.'' Donohoe scowled. ''You really are a pain in the ass, you know?''

''I should. You tell me that all the time.'' Jack gave the sergeant another affectionate thump. Then he put his hand beneath Caroline's elbow and urged her forward. ''This is a friend of mine, Caroline Hogarth. She's volunteered to help me sort through Kathleen's personal belongings.''

Oh, God, he'd given the police her real name! Now they'd know just where to come looking for her when Felicity Ames told them what had really happened the morning after her husband died.

Caroline shook the sergeant's hand and tried to smile as if she wasn't a wanted criminal.

Donohoe eyed her with unabashed interest. "I didn't know priests were allowed to have friends who look as good as you," he said, shaking her hand. "If he gives you any trouble, you turn him in to me, okay?"

"It's a deal." She did her best to return smile for smile and to reveal none of the tension she was feeling. The effort produced beads of sweat all the way down her spine. "It's nice to meet you, Sergeant, but I'm sorry it has to be for such a sad reason."

His expression abruptly sobered, and as she'd hoped, her remark sent him back to business. "I have the file right here," he said, reaching into his desk drawer. He picked up the phone and asked somebody called Danny to bring up Kathleen's suitcases and her pocketbook.

He hung up the phone, simultaneously opening the file. "I'll make this as quick as I can, Jack, but there's a fair few pieces of paper to sign. Damn bureaucrats come up with a new form to fill out every time you turn around and sneeze."

A policewoman strolled by and glanced toward Jack, doing a double take that rubbed Caroline's lacerated nerves raw. When they'd walked through the station, Jack had provided her with a certain amount of protective cover, since he was a familiar sight and people simply waved to him and went back to work. Now that the two of them were sitting down, Jack's presence had a less desirable effect. People seemed intrigued by the idea of him escorting an unknown woman into the station, and they wanted to get a good look at her.

She tried to blend into the surroundings. She could only hope that people were so busy speculating on the nature of her relationship with Jack that they wouldn't have time to wonder if she looked familiar. So far, her luck seemed to be holding.

Jack signed the last paper and Caroline suppressed a sigh of relief, grateful when a commotion in the doorway behind them made everybody turn to stare. She hoped that whoever had just been arrested would continue to protest loud and long, drawing attention to him rather than her.

Jack and the sergeant looked toward the source of the noise, and Jack's body tensed.

"Caroline!" he exclaimed in a low voice. "Look! Isn't that one of the bikers who attacked you? Take a look at him, quick!"

Her stomach plunged in rapid freefall to her toes. She swiveled and saw at once that Jack was correct. The handcuffed man lumbering into the room behind a young police officer was without doubt one of the men from the bar who'd stolen her purse and beaten her up.

The unexpectedness of seeing her attacker, on top of all the other tension, was too much for her. A tiny gasp escaped before she could bite it back.

Donohoe didn't even notice. Jack noticed at once. "It's him, isn't it?" he demanded. "One of the men who beat you up?"

She had enough presence of mind to cut off her instinctive denial. "I'm not sure," she said, relieved that she had a legitimate excuse for the quiver in her voice. "He looks familiar, but I can't be sure. Everything happened so fast...."

The biker glared at Caroline, looking as though he'd be quite willing to serve an extra few months in jail for the privilege of finishing the job he'd started a couple of days earlier.

"Wait a minute here," Donohoe said. "Have I got this right? Are you two saying that man attacked you, Ms. Hogarth? That he beat you up? Do you know him, then?"

The formal way the sergeant addressed her was warning enough that his questions were no longer casual. "What's the problem?" the biker yelled, saving Caroline from finding an immediate reply. "What you starin' at? You got a problem with somethin'?"

The police officer who was with him shoved him into a chair and told him to shut up. The biker subsided, still glowering in Caroline's direction. Everyone in the room looked at her with renewed interest. It was exactly the sort of attention she couldn't afford, and she forced herself to look away from the biker and meet Sergeant Donohoe's gaze.

"I was robbed a couple of days ago by a pair of bikers," she said. "Father Jack came to my rescue."

As she'd hoped, the sergeant's attention switched to Jack. "You get a good look at the perps?" he asked. "Is that gorilla one of them?"

Frustrated, Jack shook his head. "I don't know, Frank. I only saw the men who attacked Caroline from a distance."

"You want to press charges?" Donohoe asked her. "We'd love to have an excuse to lock the bastard up for a few days. And right now, I don't think we have enough to press charges. Mitch is getting ready to let him go."

Caroline's thoughts raced as she tried to imagine how an honest citizen with nothing to hide would behave in this situation. But the task was beyond her. It had been so long since she'd had nothing to hide that she couldn't remember what it felt like. All she knew was that she had to get out of this police station before somebody connected her to Dayton Ames.

She cleared her dry throat. "I'd love to press charges," she lied. "But the honest truth is that I'm not absolutely sure he's the man who attacked me." She pressed her hand to her throat, trying to look flustered, honest and innocent. Three lies in one facial expression. She smiled shakily. "Unfortunately, Sergeant, one biker looks a lot like another as far as I'm concerned. I've no idea if this is one of the men who attacked me."

Thank heavens there was some justification for her claim. The biker was bearded, long-haired, had tattoos all over his arm and wore jeans, boots and a sleeveless leather jacket decorated with chains. In fact, he could have served as a poster boy for bikers everywhere.

"I suppose it's no good asking why you didn't report the incident?" Donohoe asked tiredly.

"What was the point?" she replied. "I knew I'd never be able to identify the men who did it. And we all know that there was no chance of getting my money back."

"You'd be surprised. Jack, you should've said something, persuaded her to make a report." The sergeant delivered a brief lecture on a citizen's duty to report crimes. Then he sighed as if realizing he was trumpeting a lost cause. "We'll get him sooner or later," he said. "That sort haven't got the sense to keep out of trouble. I just hope he doesn't beat some woman to death in a drunken temper before we finally get to him. That's what he's in here for, you know. Beating up his woman."

"That's a crime, isn't it?" Caroline couldn't help asking. "Why can't you arrest him?"

"Sure, it's a crime, and we did arrest him. But the woman he beat up refuses to press charges. That leaves us nothin' to do."

The sergeant couldn't have known how much of an impact his words had on her. She felt a wave of fury and guilt wash over her at the injustice of the biker going free while she was forced to hide from the law. Her anger was all the more powerful because she had no way in the world to express it.

Jack put his arm around her shoulders, looking at her with eyes that for once held no reproach, only sympathy. "You okay?" he asked quietly.

She was cracking up, tearing apart, hurting from head to toe. She smiled. "Thanks for asking. I'm fine, Jack, really."

Donohoe looked intrigued, but was again distracted, this time by the arrival of the officer who'd been sent to retrieve Kathleen's belongings. He came in lugging a battered suitcase and a transparent plastic sack with an oversize shoulder purse tucked beneath his arm.

"Her things got messed up pretty good," the new arrival said. "One of the suitcases is trashed. I put everything from there into this bag, even the stuff that's torn. I didn't know what you might want to keep."

"Thanks," Jack said. "That was very helpful of you, Officer."

"Yeah, you're welcome. Maybe you'd like to carry the purse, miss? Then the reverend can carry the rest of the deceased's belongings?"

Caroline managed not to sound too eager. "Yes, I'll do that." She reached for the purse with hands that barely trembled. Unfortunately, it wasn't as easy to control the sweat that was breaking out in a thin line across her forehead.

Time to go. Let's move it, Jack. I want to be out of here.

The officer was very young, quite good-looking, and he obviously fancied himself a pro with women. He stared at Caroline with the practiced eye of a man who was accustomed to success with the opposite sex.

Suddenly his routine appraisal sharpened into recognition.

"You look real familiar," he said. "Haven't we met someplace before?"

Caroline fought her way out of a suffocating fog of fear. "I don't think so," she said. She produced a cheeky smile. "But I sure wish we had. I bet we'd have had a good time."

He laughed, appreciating her banter, but unfortunately he was smart as well as handsome. "I know I've seen you somewhere." He frowned, continuing to stare at her. "Are you a model? Maybe I've seen you in a magazine or on TV."

She laughed, her insides cracking with terror. "I wish," she said. "That would be an exciting career."

"Caroline's an accountant," Jack said, putting his arm around her in a gesture that spoke unmistakably of possession. "But I'm always telling her she could be a model if she wanted." He smiled at her, as if their relationship was intimate enough for them to have chatted frequently about her career—and her appearance.

The young officer's eyes widened, and he backed off. No wonder, since Jack had made his claim perfectly clear. He rammed home the message by extending his hand and pointedly ending the discussion. "Thanks, Officer, for saving all Kathleen's belongings. Her family will appreciate getting them, I'm sure."

"Yeah, right. You're welcome."

Jack leaned across the desk to shake the sergeant's hand. "Frank, we have to get going. Caroline's cooking dinner for a crowd tonight, and we still have to go grocery shopping."

Caroline had no idea why Jack was choosing to protect her from police scrutiny. But right now she didn't understand anything. Her thought processes had frozen. One thing could be said about life with her father-in-law: it had provided her with plenty of experience in functioning when her brain was paralyzed by fear. She had only the vaguest awareness of the three men chatting, of Jack picking up the suitcase and the bag of clothes, of the young officer taking the forms Jack had signed. Despite the fact that she was incapable of rational thought, her body continued to move. She felt her mouth shape words and realized she was saying goodbye to Frank Donohoe. The young policeman chuckled and she realized—incredibly— that she must have made a joke. Then, with a relief so overwhelming it made her tremble, they were parting company from Donohoe, walking down the corridor, leaving the police station.

And Kathleen's purse was still hanging from her shoulder.

They stepped out of the dank air-conditioning of the police station into the heat of the asphalt lot where they'd left Jack's car. He strode over to it in silence, unlocked the trunk and tossed Kathleen's belongings inside. Then he opened the car door and waited for her to get in.

Her hands stroked the comforting shape of Kathleen's purse, lying in her lap. She leaned back on the hot seat, waiting for the heat to unfreeze her brain.

Jack jump-started the process. He put his hands on her shoulders and pulled her around until she was facing him, so close that she could see the shadow of his beard just starting to grow.

"Okay," he said, and his voice was low, deadly with determination. "This is it, Caroline. Why were you so terrified in there? Tell me the truth about your relationship with Dayton Ames. Did you kill him?"

Nine

Caroline knew exactly how she needed to respond. She knew what to say to appear ignorant of Dayton Ames and all his dealings. Knew how to inject the faint note of exasperation into her voice that would best convey innocence. Knew how to confuse Jack by exploiting the sexual tension that underscored their confrontations. She knew exactly what she had to do, all right. But instead of doing it, she stared at Kathleen Williams's purse in her lap and thought about how tired she was of lying.

"Caroline, please trust me."

She squirmed as Jack's voice took on the dangerous note of kindness that always tempted her to believe he truly wanted to be her friend. "Let me help you," he said. "Talk to me, Caroline, explain what's going on in your life. Nothing ever seems quite as bad once you've shared it with someone who cares."

She didn't look at him, afraid she might cry. Ever since she'd met Jack, for some ridiculous reason tears seemed to lurk no more than a heartbeat away.

"I didn't kill Dayton Ames," she mumbled. If she hadn't been on the verge of crying, she would have laughed. She sounded about as credible as Ted Bundy claiming that the women he dated all died of natural causes.

"I didn't kill him," she repeated, more fiercely this time because she was tired of being accused of crimes she hadn't committed. Tired of pretending to be hard and cold and indifferent when she felt so fragile inside, hovering on the brink of shattering into a thousand jagged fragments.

Jack rolled down the windows of the car, and a welcome breeze rustled through the leaves of a nearby oak tree, cooling her hot cheeks. Instead of pressing her for more information, he leaned back in the driver's seat and started talking.

"My wife's name was Beth," he said with seeming irrelevance to the conversation. "She was a human dynamo, five feet tall, bright red hair and the stamina of fifteen people packaged into a tiny, hundred-pound body. When we met, she was already a fully trained nurse, with a graduate degree in emergency care, and I was a first-year med student struggling to remember the difference between a fibula and a tibia. She was amazingly patient with my ignorance."

"How did you meet? In the hospital?"

"Yes." Jack smiled. "We bumped into each other rushing down a corridor in Cook County Hospital, and it was love at first bump. We were married within six months, and the next three years were the happiest of my life. Beth was one of those special people who are so involved in life that you feel energized by being near them. I don't mean that she rushed around creating a constant whirl of activity, she just made every moment seem full . . . complete. Then, with no warning, it was all over."

He fell silent and Caroline broke another of her cardinal rules by asking him a personal question. "What happened? Did she . . . did she get sick?"

"No, she was murdered—killed by some junkie who came into the emergency room and shot a bullet into her heart at point-blank range. I can still see the blood pumping out of her, gushing in obscene squirts over the guy who'd killed her, soaking his clothes in bright red blood. Beth's blood."

"Oh, my God, Jack, no! How horrible for you! And for your wife, what a terrible way for her to die . . ."

His mouth twisted into a travesty of a smile. "The worst of it is, the guy who killed her was so far out of it, he probably never knew what he'd done. I'm not sure he even realized he was holding a gun, much less that he'd squeezed the trigger. Talk about a pointless killing."

"I'm so sorry, Jack." She instinctively reached out to touch him. She cradled his hand in hers, desperately wanting to offer comfort, realizing that comfort in such circumstances was almost impossible to give. She tried to think of something reassuring to say, but there were no words that didn't sound trite and overused. "I'm so sorry," she said again.

Jack's hand clenched within her clasp. "When I realized Beth was dead I went insane," he said. "I'd come to the hospital to drive her home, so I was waiting in the emergency room and I saw the guy run up and shoot her, but to this day, I don't remember what happened after the bullet hit Beth and all the blood gushed out. They told me later that I jumped him, fighting for the gun and screaming all the while for the doctors to come and save Beth.''

"But they couldn't save her."

"No, she was dead before even I could reach her, and I was standing scarcely ten feet away. So I took out my rage by throwing punches at the junkie who'd killed her. Not that it was much of a struggle, by all accounts. I was twenty-seven years old and a fitness freak. He was a heroin addict, close to starving, riddled with disease, and I guess he'd exhausted what strength he possessed getting to the hospital and killing Beth. When a couple of orderlies finally managed to restrain me, he was lying on the floor, dead of a heart attack, and the gun had skidded across the linoleum, six feet from either of us. God knows how soon he'd dropped it. The autopsy found evidence of nineteen different blows to his body that I must have inflicted, a couple of them without question after he was already dead."

"And that's why you went to jail?" Caroline asked. "Because you got into a fistfight trying to wrestle a loaded gun from your wife's murderer? Under the circumstances, it doesn't seem very fair. In fact, it sounds downright perverse—"

"If I hadn't hit him so many times, the DA wouldn't have pressed charges. But there were witnesses who came forward and said I kept on pummeling him long after he'd dropped the gun and collapsed on the floor.

I was out of control when I was beating him up, or I'd have realized he'd stopped resisting. But at that point I'd totally lost it. I had no idea what I was doing."

Jack stared out the window, but she knew he wasn't seeing the parking lot or the shabby facade of the police station. He was seeing some horrific scene indelibly printed onto his memory. She knew because she had a scene of her own that replayed with sickening regularity: two social workers, escorted by two police officers, coming to her door and demanding that she hand her son over to Joe Rossi, who stood behind them. Andrew had screamed in terror when Joe tried to take him away, his heels dragging on the carpet and his chubby fists flailing uselessly against Joe's chest. Her last glimpse of him had been of his contorted body, twisted around in Joe's arms, his little hands outstretched, begging her to save him.

"Mommy, Mommy. Mommy, Mommy." He was only two and a half, and he hadn't been able to find words to express his fear at being torn from all that was loved and familiar. So he'd just kept calling to her, over and over again, until the elevator doors closed and his sobs faded into the distance, leaving her alone with the endless echo of his cries, the pitiful theme song for a hundred subsequent nightmares.

She sat very still, waiting for the agony of the memory to pass.

"I've noticed that when tragedy strikes people, there's always one trivial detail that seems to stick in their mind," Jack said. "You know what was the worst thing for me about Beth's murder? It was the fact that they never could put a name to the junkie who killed her. It eats at me, knowing her death was so senseless, so random, that she was murdered by somebody who had no official identity. And then I took his life away, which was the only possession he had left."

"You didn't rob him of something he wanted to keep," Caroline said. "He obviously placed no value on his own life."

"Maybe not, but that doesn't mean he wasn't valued by God. And it certainly doesn't mean I had the right to kill him."

She twisted in the seat and looked him straight in the eyes, the pain of losing Andrew set aside in a burst of indignation. "Jack Fletcher, I know you're too sensible a man to be torturing yourself over what happened that night. Tell me I'm right, please. You aren't nursing a guilt complex over the fact that you attacked your wife's murderer? A drug addict who was armed with a loaded gun and too high to know if he was pulling the trigger? How many lives in that emergency room did you save by taking his gun away?"

He smiled wryly. "Maybe a half dozen. Maybe none. But thanks for making me sound so noble."

"You *were* noble."

"No, I was out of my head with rage, but I've come to terms with what I did that night, although I'll always regret what happened." His mouth quirked into a tiny smile. "Beth would have wanted me to take the guy home and show him that there are better ways to deal with life's problems than shoving a needle in your arm.''

"We can't all be saints," Caroline said, aware of an absurd twinge of jealousy for the multiple perfections of Jack's dead wife. "It seems to me the DA's office could have furthered justice and saved the taxpayers a lot of money by deciding not to prosecute you. If I were you, Jack, I'd quit with the guilt—it seems totally out of place."

He grinned. "Yes, ma'am. But don't worry, I stopped tormenting myself with guilt right around the time I was strip-searched for the first time and one of the prison guards made a pass at me. That was when I switched from feeling guilty to being mad as hell. I was furious with God for taking Beth from me and so damn sorry for myself that I was convinced nobody had ever suffered torments as dreadful as mine."

"What stopped you feeling sorry for yourself?" she asked, genuinely curious. "The anger?"

"At first. But listening to the life stories of the other inmates soon wised me up to what a prize pain in the butt I was being. I began to realize that prison was either going to make me or break me, and I'd be damned if I would let it break me. Half the guys in the pen had suffered more injustice by the time they were in kindergarten than I'd suffered in my entire life. Except that most of them never went to kindergarten. And they sure as heck didn't have two loving parents, one doting sister, an expensive education and a network of caring friends all waiting to support them the moment they got out. If they were real lucky, maybe in their entire lives they had one relative or a teacher who'd tried to help them. And that was the fortunate few. By the time I got out of jail, I realized that I wasn't interested in becoming a doctor any more. In the past couple of hundred years, we've learned to do a pretty good job of caring for people's bodies. As far as taking care of our souls, we don't seem to have progressed very much. I wanted to try to do something about that.''

Caroline definitely didn't want to start a discussion on the state of her soul. ''It's great that you have a supportive family,'' she said, ''but I think you're underestimating the amount of self-pity you're entitled to feel. Prison is a terrible place, no matter what.''

He shook his head. ''Grief is okay. We all have occasions when we need to grieve, and I sure needed to grieve for Beth. There's a part of me that will always miss her, will always wonder why she had to die. But self-pity doesn't get you anywhere, except locked into useless bitterness.''

His words struck a chord that Caroline reluctantly recognized. Was that what she'd been doing for the past six months? she wondered. Wallowing in self-pity and mistaking it for grief?

No. The denial was immediate, if not a hundred percent convincing. She wasn't indulging in self-pity. Her forced separation from Andrew was genuine cause for grief. To lose your son would be terrible in any circumstances. To lose him because your father-in-law had paid off witnesses and bought perjured testimony was justifiable cause for rage. Moreover, she wasn't sitting around, indulging in useless bitterness or empty recriminations. She was fighting with all the resources at her command to get Andrew back.

"I told you about Beth for a reason," Jack said, breaking into her painful thoughts. "I know from personal experience that it isn't easy to trust people when you've been let down. But however abandoned you feel, Caroline, I've felt that way, too, so I can empathize with whatever you're going through. The first six months I spent in jail, I would have killed myself if I'd been smart enough to figure out a way to do it. I felt utterly alone, with nobody in the world to help me."

"You had God," Caroline said.

"But I didn't want God," he replied, sounding amused by his earlier self. "I wasn't born with a religious vocation, you know, and I certainly wasn't blessed with what you might call spiritual maturity. Until Beth died, my concept of the Almighty was a gentleman with a rather testy disposition who got nasty if you didn't show him the proper deference. A sort of not-too-jolly Santa Claus with an erratic record in the gift-giving department."

Caroline knew her own concept wasn't much more profound, and she found herself smiling at Jack with rueful sympathy. "I guess that isn't the best sort of deity to get you through a dark night of the soul."

"Or anything else, for that matter." Jack met her gaze, his expression sobering. "God doesn't send help down to us on a white cloud, with angels to announce its arrival," he said. "He uses ordinary people and shows them how to help each other."

She thought of her adoptive parents, who'd accepted the lies Joe told about her because they'd always suspected that her socially inferior genes would cause trouble. She thought about her college buddies and her society friends, and how they'd all turned away from her after the fiasco of the custody hearing. "Right," she said, not attempting to hide her bitter sarcasm. "I've seen His magic touch at work many times."

"Sometimes it's hard to see what's right in front of our noses," Jack said. "Friends turn up in the most unexpected places." She wanted to look away, but he held her gaze. "Try to think of me as a friend, Caroline, not as an opponent you've got to outwit. When you've been to the bottom of the pit, you discover that you can't get out unless someone offers you a helping hand. Here's my hand, if you need it. I'm willing to wait as long as necessary for you to reach out and take it."

She stared at his outstretched hand in tense silence. She wanted so badly to trust him, to believe that she could tell him the truth and he would still be there for her. But when all was said and done, he was a priest. Even though he'd spent time in jail, even though he'd lost his temper and killed a man, he was a minister who'd promised to live by the rules of his church. How could he overlook the fact that she'd become Dayton Ames's mistress for the express purpose of robbing him? How could he condone her plan to use stolen money to rescue Andrew? How could he continue to hide her from the police if he knew she was the last person to see Dayton Ames alive?

The answer was that he couldn't, but it was a measure of how far her feelings toward him had changed that she spent several minutes contemplating the possibility of asking for his help. Even when she'd dismissed the idea completely, she still hated to destroy the intimacy growing between them, despite the fact that in her position, intimacy was a luxury she knew she couldn't afford.

"I didn't kill Dayton Ames," she said, miserable at the inadequacy of her response, even more miserable that it was so important to her that he accept her word. "Jack, I swear to you, I didn't kill him."

"I believe you," he said.

"Thank you—"

"Why shouldn't I believe you? So far, at least according to anything I've heard, there's no evidence the man was murdered."

She shifted restlessly on the hot car seat. "It's obvious the police think he was, whatever the official word might be."

"How do you know what the police think? And why are you so interested in the fate of a man you claim you've never met?"

Caroline shivered, despite the hot sun. Jack was right, of course. The official word on Dayton's death was simply that it was being investigated. She, of all people, ought to be confident that the autopsy report would come back stating he'd died from natural causes. Given that she'd shared Dayton's last night, slept in his bed, eaten what he'd eaten, drunk what he'd drunk, how could he have been murdered? And yet, at some point during the past twenty-four hours, she'd come to believe the impossible. Dayton Ames had been murdered—and she was being set up to take the fall.

"Do you trust me, Caroline?" Jack asked.

She didn't know what trust meant anymore. But as much as she trusted anyone, she supposed she trusted Jack. "Of course—"

"Then tell me why you were seen leaving Dayton Ames's apartment building that morning. Had you spent the night with him?"

Caroline felt weariness drape her like a leaden overcoat. "The police aren't looking for me," she said, the lie coming tired and limp from her lips. "You're mistaken in thinking I'm the woman the police want to interview. I have nothing to tell them. I know nothing about what caused Dayton Ames's death."

"I didn't ask if you had anything to tell the police," Jack said softly. "I asked if you'd spent the night before he died with Dayton Ames."

"And I've told you I didn't know him, so how could I spend the night with him?"

As if to prove she was lying, Danny, the police officer who'd half recognized her, emerged at that moment from the police station, car keys suspended from one hand, whistling tunelessly as he walked toward the parking lot and his car. He caught sight of Caroline and Jack, and his eyes lit up. He waved at them with enthusiasm.

"Hey, wait up!" he called, jogging toward their car. "I've just remembered where I saw you, Miss Hogarth!" He bent to peer in the open car window, grinning cheerfully.

Was the guy a sadist or a lunatic or what? Caroline licked her dry lips. "You have?" she asked.

"Sure have. It was on a wanted poster." He rolled his eyes, inviting her to share the joke. "You know, the one that was issued in connection with the Dayton Ames case. Blond woman, late twenties, five-seven, slender, long legs." He surveyed her legs in silent appreciation.

"We know the one," Jack said coolly. It was fortunate he said something, because Caroline was speechless.

Danny cocked his head. "You know, that sketch sure looks just like you, Ms. Hogarth. I knew I recognized you from somewhere. The similarity's really amazing."

This was totally insane, Caroline thought. "Are you going to arrest me?" she asked. "Or do I just get hauled in for questioning?"

Brazen it out, she decided, that's the best I can do. After all, what grounds do they have to hold me? Adultery isn't a crime in Illinois—is it?

"Guess we can't hold you today, Ms. Hogarth." Danny laughed. "The woman we were looking for turned herself in. Didn't you hear? I saw a news flash just as I was getting ready to leave the station. Michelle Roche is her name. Seems she was Dayton Ames's mistress." He leered cynically. "Now ain't that a real surprise?"

He touched his hand to his forehead in a mock salute. "Bye, Father Fletcher, Ms. Hogarth, I'm outta here. There's a cold beer with my name on it waiting in my fridge." He turned and headed toward his car.

Caroline graciously accepted Jack's apology for his groundless suspicion that she was the woman who'd been seen leaving Dayton Ames's apartment building. At least, she hoped she accepted it graciously and with a proper air of injured innocence. Since she was running on automatic pilot, it was hard to be sure.

The woman the police were looking for had turned herself in. Her name was Michelle Roche. What in the world was going on? Who was Michelle Roche? Was it possible that Dayton had kept another mistress, one she hadn't known about, who was also tall and blond? It seemed almost inconceivable, given his workaholic schedule, not to mention the hours he spent with her and the efforts he made to maintain the facade of his marriage.

And where was Felicity Ames? Why was she keeping silent through all this? Or perhaps she wasn't, Caroline thought frantically. Just because the police chose to make no public announcements didn't mean that Felicity Ames had told them nothing about Caroline's role in her husband's life—and death. What if Felicity had already given the police her name? What if police officers all over the city would soon get word to bring in one Caroline Hogarth? Danny and Frank

Donohoe would know exactly where to find her. In her desperate quest for a passport, she'd taken herself straight into the lion's den.

Jack said something, and Caroline mumbled a noncommittal reply. A few seconds later they were on their way to the supermarket. Fortunately, since they were short of time, they rushed through the shopping, picking up supplies for dinner and discussing nothing more significant than which variety of instant stuffing to buy and how much chocolate they needed for fudge sauce. To her vast relief, Jack left her at the door of the apartment with the sacks of groceries—and Kathleen Williams's purse—before driving to the church to park his car.

The second she was inside, Caroline set the groceries on the kitchen counter and tore open Kathleen's purse, ashamed of what she was doing but unable to afford the luxury of moral squeamishness. As she had so desperately hoped, there was a plastic folder in one of the zippered inner sections, flanked by a shiny new wallet.

Her fingers cold with guilty anticipation, Caroline took out the wallet and the red plastic folder. The wallet contained credit cards, an Illinois driver's license, a social security card and a hundred dollars—everything Caroline would need to temporarily assume Kathleen's identity, plus some welcome extra cash. The red plastic folder had two transparent interior pockets. An airline ticket occupied one pocket. A passport occupied the other.

A passport... she had the passport she needed! Steadying herself against the counter, Caroline studied the picture of the dead woman with fierce concentration. Kathleen wasn't pretty, but she wasn't plain, either. In fact, she had possessed no really distinguishing features. Her mouth was small, her teeth even, her eyes blue-gray and her light brown hair neither straight nor curly. In this picture, she happened to be wearing it back in a style somewhat similar to Caroline's.

Other than the hairstyle and eye color, she looked no more like Caroline than any other woman who was the same age, a similar weight, and had more or less the same coloring. Given the circumstances, however, she and Kathleen were more alike than Caroline had any right to expect. With sufficient makeup, skillfully applied, she might be able to produce a resemblance that was enough to get her through passport control at O'Hare airport and on board a plane to the Cayman Islands. In her experience of busy international flights, the inspection given to most people's travel documents was superficial unless the officials had reason for suspicion. And Caroline would move heaven and earth to make sure they had no reason to suspect her. She knew these documents represented her one and only shot at getting out of the country.

Even with Kathleen's passport, she didn't dare calculate the odds of making it as far as the Royal Bank of Cayman, where Dayton Ames had opened numbered accounts to stash his ill-gotten gains. As for getting back into the States, carrying five million dollars' worth of stolen bearer bonds, she preferred not to think just yet about the problems she would face.

United States customs officials would be the least of what she had to contend with. Joe would be her biggest worry. Her father-in-law knew she was trying to get to the Cayman Islands, and he must suspect why. He was undoubtedly furious that Steve and Gerry had lost track of her. Ironically, the bikers from the bar had done her a favor when they attacked her, delivering her into the anonymity of Jack's apartment. But her present safety was temporary, an illusion. Joe and his henchmen would be scrambling to track her down, and they would have drawn a tight ring of security around the airport. She hadn't yet managed to slip the leash.

Joe wouldn't try to stop her from flying to the Cayman Islands, of course. She would step onto the plane without knowing whether or not she'd been spotted. The passenger seated next to her might be a tourist or a businessman. He could just as easily be one of Joe's people with instructions to follow her until she led them to Dayton's stash of loot. Then they would kidnap her. And probably kill her, once they were sure they had recovered all Dayton's money.

Caroline had been imprisoned within the tendrils of her nightmare for so long she had forgotten what it felt like to live without fear. Even so, between the police and her father-in-law, the next twenty-four hours were going to be uniquely terrifying.

Six months of deceiving Dayton Ames had trained Caroline to keep one ear constantly open. On a couple of occasions, it was only her acute hearing that had prevented Dayton from finding her knee deep in his personal financial files. So despite concentrating on the contents of Kathleen's purse, she registered the muted sounds of someone walking across the court-yard and realized Jack was returning.

She quickly scooped all Kathleen's belongings into the purse. By the time she heard the door opening, she'd shoved the purse into a corner of the counter near the phone and had hurriedly upended a grocery bag, jamming a tub of ice cream into the freezer and milk into the fridge.

"Hi, Caroline, I'm home." Jack walked into the kitchen and gave her a companionable smile. "Man, it's hot out there."

"Hi, yourself," she said brightly, tearing the husks off ears of fresh corn with feverish energy. Since Jack knew nothing about cooking, she hoped she was giv-ing a fairly convincing portrayal of somebody who'd spent the past few minutes working hard to get a meal started. She fought the urge to chatter inanely and smile too brightly, sure signs of a guilty conscience.

She glanced at the clock on the microwave. "It's nearly three-thirty. Marcus is late." She pulled a face. "Lucky for me. Dinner's going to take a while."

Jack might know nothing about cooking, but he knew far too much about human nature. "How un-naturally cheerful you sound, Caroline. A man with a suspicious mind might think you were up to some-thing."

She managed a carefree laugh while mentally damning his perception. However, she hadn't survived her marriage and spent months double-crossing Dayton Ames without acquiring some skills. "I'm enjoying being domestic," she said. "Do you consider that getting up to something?"

"Probably not." He paused. "I've put Kathleen's suitcase and belongings in my room. Maybe once Marcus is in bed we can sort through her clothes and find some that fit you."

"Thanks, I'd appreciate that." She turned away, unable to meet his eyes. Deceiving Jack was nothing at all like tricking Dayton Ames. There was no sense of secret triumph, merely a sick feeling that she was behaving badly.

She was relieved when a scuffle of feet sounded noisily outside the apartment. "That's probably Marcus and his friend," Jack said.

She laughed again. "Marcus and his friend—and possibly an elephant or two by the sound of it." Quit with the hearty laughter, she warned herself. You're overacting.

"You're a lucky lady," Jack said quietly. "They arrived just in the nick of time, didn't they?"

"What do you mean?"

"That there's nothing like a couple of teenage males around for making adult conversation impossible. And I have the feeling you're very anxious to avoid adult conversation."

Fortunately, Marcus let himself into the apartment before she could fall into the trap of defending herself. Marcus muttered a surly greeting and announced that he and Antoine were bored and wanted to go swimming. Antoine didn't openly dispute this statement, although he looked as if his preferred entertainment would have been knifing people in a dark alley. The tattoo of a grinning skull on his chest was not friendly.

Jack smiled at Antoine suggesting mildly that Marcus might like to rephrase his announcement as a request. He then asked Caroline if she objected to being left alone to cook dinner. She assured him that she didn't, and barely managed to restrain herself from bursting into a rousing Hallelujah when Jack agreed to accompany the two boys to the Y.

"Be back by six," she said. "I'll see you later, guys. Work up a healthy appetite, mind. I'm cooking a huge meal."

She could have sworn she sounded as innocent as Mrs. Cleaver, but Jack—damn him—looked at her through narrowed, suspicious eyes before saying amiably that they would be home at five-thirty.

"I'd like to eat early, if that's okay with you, Caroline. I have a mass of paperwork waiting to be dealt with, not to mention sorting through Kathleen's belongings. Where did you put her purse, by the way?"

Caroline was proud of the vague, uninterested way she peered around the kitchen. "I guess it's on the counter," she said. "Yes, there it is, over there."

Despite her performance, Jack shot her another deeply suspicious glance before going into his bedroom to collect his swimsuit. Marcus emerged from his room, stuffing a towel and a suit into his gym bag. Antoine shuffled his feet and lit up a cigarette, offering one to Marcus.

Aware of Jack's eyes boring into him, Marcus shook his head. "No, thanks."

"All set, then," Jack said. "See you at five-thirty, Caroline."

"Enjoy yourselves," she replied, sighing with relief when the door closed behind them. She had almost an hour and a half to make good her escape.

Her sense of urgency mounted as she hurriedly combined the contents of Kathleen's purse with her own and stashed perishable groceries in the refrigerator. She stuffed the pork chops at the speed of light, removed the silk from the corn and peeled the potatoes she'd planned to serve mashed with gravy. It was crazy to waste time preparing dinner when she should be making an immediate dash for the airport, but she couldn't bear to think of Jack and the boys coming home hungry and being greeted by nothing but an empty apartment. Marcus had touched an exposed emotional nerve, and she was almost as reluctant to disappoint him as she was to betray Jack's generous hospitality. If only there was some way to stay... but of course there wasn't. Michelle Roche—whoever she might be—had provided Caroline with a narrow window of opportunity, and she'd be crazy not to grab it. Lord alone knew what Michelle's motivations had been in surrendering to the authorities, but Caroline had no intention of hanging around long enough for the police to find out they had the wrong woman in custody.

With the chops baking and the vegetables cooking, she steeled herself to invade the privacy of Jack's bedroom. She would attract just the sort of attention she was trying to avoid if she checked in for a flight to the Cayman Islands without any baggage. Repugnant as it was to betray Jack and steal from a dead woman, she had no choice except to take Kathleen's suitcase. Getting Andrew out of Joe's clutches took precedence over every moral imperative. Sometimes, in the long nights when sleep seemed impossible, she would torment herself with images of the man her son would become if his upbringing was left to Joe and Angela Rossi. The images were horrific enough to make petty theft seem unimportant.

To her relief, Kathleen's suitcase was standing at the end of Jack's bed, and she took it without looking left or right. She muttered an apology to the dead woman, hoping she would understand. *Kathleen, I'm sorry, you know I don't want to do this. But Andrew's just a little kid, and he's got nobody to look out for him except me.*

Stomach knotted with fear, Caroline spent twenty precious minutes in the bathroom, first scrubbing her face clean, then applying makeup in careful layers— toning down her pink cheeks, then plucking her eyebrows into a thin, straight line before powdering them so that her whole appearance became paler and more muted.

She worked for a solid eight minutes on her eyes, trying to find a way to make them appear smaller, more like Kathleen's. Eventually, she decided she'd achieved the closest approximation she was going to get. The lips were easier. All she needed to do was use a brown-tinted lip gloss she found among Kathleen's cosmetics, and the resemblance was more than passable.

Caroline was no makeup wizard, but on the whole she was surprised and pleased by the result of her labors. She doubted if she looked anything at all like the real-life Kathleen, but she *did* look quite a bit like Kathleen's passport photo. Perhaps the similarity would be enough to fool the people she needed to fool.

The apartment was beginning to fill with the appetizing smell of roasting meat. She basted the pork chops, checked the stuffing, drained the corn and mashed the potatoes. Then she turned the oven down low, covered everything with foil and set it all inside the oven to keep warm. The meal would dry out a bit, but from what Jack and Marcus had told her, it would still be better than anything they could have cooked for themselves.

She knew there was no explanation she could give for why she was leaving, no apology she could offer for the innumerable ways in which she'd taken advantage of Jack's generosity. She scribbled three or four different goodbye messages, then screwed them all up and tossed them into the garbage. When there are no adequate words, she realized, silence became the only acceptable choice.

Refusing to stop for one final look around, Caroline hooked Kathleen's purse over her shoulder, picked up the suitcase and quietly let herself out of the apartment.

She refused to ask herself why she was crying.

Ten

Joe would never have admitted it, but he found Felicity Ames intimidating. He knew instinctively that the black linen dress she was wearing had cost more than he allowed his wife, Angela, to spend on dresses in an entire season, even though it didn't have a stitch of embroidery, a single sequin or even a ruffle around the neck. He resented her power to make him feel coarse and uneducated. No wonder Dayton Ames had been double-crossing his partners, Joe thought acidly. It took a lot of money to keep a high-class ball breaker like Felicity clothed and happy.

Joe was of the opinion that American men had allowed their women to get totally out of control in recent years. When he looked back, it seemed that one day everything was fine. Then the next day, he'd woken up and discovered that every bitch and her sister wanted to wear pants and drive a forklift. Joe couldn't understand the attraction of hard manual labor, or even office work, for that matter. Men did it because they had to, to feed their families. Women did it because they wanted to fuck things up for the men in their lives.

One thing he knew for sure. The country was going to hell in a handcart ever since women stopped staying home and taking care of their families. Phillip wouldn't have had half as much trouble with Caroline if he'd kept her at home where she belonged instead of allowing her to parade down to Wall Street every day, hanging around men who should have known better than to do business with a woman. As far as Joe was concerned, a good-looking woman like Caroline who worked in finance was a freak of nature, as unnatural as a woman with a beard and just as undesirable.

Felicity Ames didn't have a job, of course—at least not one that paid money. She worked full-time organizing charity balls and getting her name in the society pages of the glossy magazines. She was still a ball breaker, Joe thought resentfully, just like Caroline. They were sisters under the skin, even if they happened to be on opposite sides of the Dayton Ames situation.

Felicity didn't offer him a drink. Didn't even ask him to sit down. He sat anyway, feeling better for the minor defiance. God knew, Felicity had plenty of reasons to fear him. Trouble was, with these high-class bitches, nine times outta ten they never recognized when they needed to be frightened.

He decided he'd keep everything friendly if he could. Then he'd come down on her real hot and heavy if he needed to. ''Nice place you got here, Mrs. Ames.''

Her light hazel eyes rested on him as if he was a piece of dog dirt that she didn't want to step in. "I'm glad it meets with your approval, Mr. Rossi. Dayton told me that you have some interesting decorative pieces yourself."

Joe wasn't stupid, and he heard the mockery in her voice. To hell with trying to be tactful with this uppity bitch. She certainly had nothing to be so proud about, as he knew damn well. "I didn't know you and Dayton still talked to each other, Mrs. Ames. From what my boys told me, he never spent much time here with you in Winnetka. Seems like he preferred watchin' Caroline Hogarth in those ceiling mirrors he got fixed up in his other place."

"There's no accounting for taste, is there?" Felicity took a cigarette from an ebony box and tapped it on the coffee table. "I assume you came here for some more urgent reason than to discuss my late husband's execrable taste in furniture and women?"

Joe had no idea what execrable meant, but Felicity Ames sure managed to sound snooty when she said it. "I decided it was time for us to have another talk about your husband's murder," he said. "The police are gonna ask a lot of awkward questions once they get that autopsy report, you know. Are you ready to give them the right answers?"

"We've discussed this before, Mr. Rossi. I shall, of course, do my best to assist the police in their inquiries."

"Assist all you want. Just make sure you don't mention Caroline's name until I tell you. We got different interests in this case. You want to make sure Caroline fries for your husband's murder. I'll see that you get her in the end, but we got some problems to solve first. Thanks to your failure to deliver the bank access codes as promised, I got to talk to Caroline before the police do."

Felicity lit a cigarette using the heavy silver lighter that stood on the coffee table. It was the only sign of nervousness she revealed. "I have already apologized for the fact that the security codes I delivered to you were incorrect. Obviously, Dayton chose to keep false records at home, to deceive my father, as well as at the office, to deceive the authorities. However, as I told you when we spoke on the phone, all Dayton's files and papers are now in my possession, and it should be only a matter of days, perhaps hours, until I'm able to tell you precisely where Dayton has been hiding his illegal profits."

"I hope so, Mrs. Ames, I really hope so. Because those safety deposit boxes you sent me to in downtown Chicago, they didn't have shit in 'em, if you'll pardon my French. And now it turns out that the person who knows where Dayton was stuffing his money is Caroline Hogarth. Not you, Mrs. Ames. His mistress."

Felicity took a quick drag of smoke. "I am well aware of the unexpected problems we've encountered, Mr. Rossi, and I understand the need to keep Caroline's name out of police files, at least for the time being. However hard the police press me, I shall stick to my story that I never saw Caroline Hogarth in my husband's company. If she was in the apartment at the same time as me the morning after Dayton died, then she must have kept herself hidden. I realized my husband had spent the night with a woman, of course, but I had no way of knowing with whom."

With whom. Jesus H. Christ! She talked like she had a dictionary stuffed up her ass. He looked at her closely. "You saw the police bulletin about that tall blond woman they wanted to talk to?"

"Yes—"

"Did the police tell you they picked up the woman they was looking for? Michelle Roche, they said her name was. Seems she's an old friend of Dayton's."

Felicity blew out a slow curl of smoke. "Yes, Mr. Rossi. The sergeant in charge of the investigation was kind enough to tell me that Michelle Roche had turned herself in. They asked me if I had been aware of the fact that Michelle was Dayton's mistress. I told them, with complete truth, that I had absolutely no idea she'd even spoken to my husband, much less slept with him." She stubbed out her half-smoked cigarette with careful deliberation. "Naturally, they didn't believe me."

Joe should have been reassured. He wasn't. Timing in this case was everything, and he didn't trust Felicity Ames to follow the agreed timetable. 'Course, if Steve and Gerry hadn't lost track of Caroline, Joe wouldn't be running around like a headless chicken, trying to clean up their mess. He leaned forward in his chair, taking out his irritation on Ames's widow.

"Just remember, Felicity honey, that your husband stole five million dollars from my organization, and I view theft as a real serious crime. Unless you want that pretty little daughter of yours to see certain pictures of her mommy in bed with another lady, you better make sure you do *exactly* what you've been told."

"Please don't bring Lucy into this, Mr. Rossi. I admitted several weeks ago that I don't want my daughter to see those photos. That's why I agreed to help you. Your blackmail worked." Felicity reached for another cigarette, but didn't light it. Joe noted with satisfaction that her hand was trembling.

"Blackmail's a real nasty word, honey. I just offered you a business proposition and you agreed to work with me. That's all."

She tapped her unlit cigarette against the edge of the table. "This conversation is superfluous, Mr. Rossi. We've already agreed that where my husband's death is concerned, your interests and mine coincide, at least in their ultimate goal. Further threats are unnecessary."

"I wasn't threatening, sugar. Just telling it like it is."

Felicity rose to her feet. "Is there anything else you want to discuss with me, Mr. Rossi? I have a dinner engagement, and I would prefer not to be late."

"You keep your dinner engagement, honey. I hope your date's a real cutie. She treating you nice, is she?" Joe stood up, finally feeling a little better. Other people's fear and failures always calmed him. "By the way, I'm gonna have the pharmacist call the police right around the time the autopsy report comes in. Just so's you know."

"The pharmacist?" Felicity looked momentarily puzzled.

"Yeah, the pharmacist who sold Caroline Hogarth the digoxin she needed to kill your husband. He's a nice guy, with his own neighborhood pharmacy up in Evanston. Got a dreadful coke habit, but nobody knows that yet. Except my people who supply him, of course. Soon as I give him a call, he's ready to swear that he filled a prescription for fifty milligrams of digoxin and sold it to a tall, attractive blond woman using a phony name. He was real devastated when he found out the prescription was a phony. Terrible to think Caroline must have been planning to kill your husband for weeks, isn't it? Premeditated murder sure is a horrible crime. They do still have the death penalty here in Illinois, don't they?"

"In theory, I believe, although rarely in practice."

"Yeah, well, I guess that means you won't have her death on your conscience. Juries don't often convict young and pretty women. Snooty, middle-aged wives having affairs with other women, now that's a different situation altogether."

Felicity drew in a deep, trembling breath. She walked across to the door of her den and held it open. "Goodbye, Mr. Rossi. I'll see you out."

Joe left the Ames house feeling almost cheerful. One of his bodyguards fell in behind him, the other rushed to open the door of his waiting limo. Felicity Ames hadn't been hard to handle, after all. Women

like her led such cushy lives they couldn't stand it when
you turned up the heat. The next time they met, she
would know she needed to show him proper respect.

He climbed into his limo and called Gerry on his
new car phone, the one that had an automatic built-in
scrambling device. Joe liked new technology, although he knew better than to trust it. "You found her
yet?" he asked without preamble.

"No, boss, but we got a dozen men out at the airport. If she takes a flight to anyplace, we'll know it."

"Twelve men? There's got to be three hundred gates
at O'Hare airport! How you gonna cover three hundred gates with twelve men?"

"I know there's a lot of gates, Joe, but she can't get
to the gates without going through security first. No
way she can bypass the security screen, and we got a
man stationed at each checkpoint."

Joe grunted, not really appeased. He'd seen O'Hare
airport, seen the thousands of passengers thronging
the concourses. It would only take one of the men to
screw up, and Caroline would be on her way to the islands, with Joe none the wiser.

"What about Michelle?" he snapped. "She and
that high-priced lawyer of mine still doin' what they
were told? She isn't screwing things up?"

"They're doin' their best," Gerry said, and from the
tone of his voice Joe knew they had more trouble.

"What's the problem?" he demanded. "How did
she screw up?"

"She didn't screw up, Joe, but the police are out
lookin' for Caroline Hogarth again, and this time they

got her name. They're not just lookin' for a blonde, they're lookin' for Caroline."

"How the hell did they get her name, for Christ's sake?"

"Real easy, Joe. She's been foolin' with Dayton Ames for six months, and she's been seen all over town with him. She's a good-lookin' woman, and seems like there's a dozen different people in the city who've already told the police she was his mistress."

Joe swore long and viciously. How come the police only took their fingers out of their ears and moved fast when you didn't want them to? He wanted the police to bring Caroline in eventually, but not yet. Now all his plans were messed up.

He'd had the whole thing worked out in his mind, like one of those mystery movies on TV, only better. He'd planned the murder of Dayton Ames, knowing suspicion would fall on Caroline. He'd planned to let her squirm in jail without bond for a few weeks, maybe as long as a couple of months, while he took care of getting back the money Dayton Ames had stolen from him.

Then he'd intended to send in one of his fancy lawyers and get Caroline out, and arrange for the lawyer to throw Felicity Ames to the wolves. He sure as hell never planned for that bitch to get away with offing her husband. Joe didn't approve of wives who made trouble for their husbands.

And the best twist of all was that when Caroline walked out of the courthouse a free woman, she would realize she'd gotten off from a murder rap because of him, Joe Rossi. Even now, when his plans were knee-deep in trouble, he could smile at the thought of her rage, at how she would hate the knowledge that she owed her freedom—even her life—to him.

But his plans had all come to nothing because that bitch Felicity Ames failed to keep her side of the bargain. The safety deposit boxes she'd gotten him access to were full of financial documents, all right, but nothing he could convert to his use. Everything they found needed the witnessed, notarized signature of Dayton Ames or his legal executor. The bearer bonds with Joe's stolen money were all hidden somewhere else.

Joe believed Felicity when she swore up and down that Ames had told her these were the boxes where he kept his bearer bonds. Obviously, Ames had been screwing his wife over in more ways than one. But the fact that Felicity hadn't been able to deliver the codes meant that Joe hadn't been able to reclaim his missing money, and so his lovely, clever plans for Caroline's arrest were in a state of turmoil. Now, horror of horrors, he needed *her* instead of the other way around. Joe Rossi needed his stupid bitch of a daughter-in-law to lead him to the missing five million dollars. Add to all this the fact that the idiots who worked for him had lost her—so she could be anywhere this side of the moon for all they knew—and it was no wonder he was feeling like hell. Jesus, what was he gonna do if she got locked up before he could find out where Ames stashed his liquid assets? Joe had payments due in the next couple of weeks, and in his line of work, they didn't take credit cards. Dayton Ames had screwed him over but good.

"So what are they doing about finding her?" he asked, keeping his voice real nice and low so Gerry wouldn't realize Joe was damn near messing his pants, he was so wild with anger. "Are the police gonna issue another bulletin?"

"Far as I can tell, they've quit with the public announcements. Now that they got her name, they're sending one of their detectives over to her apartment some time this evening. He wants to have a personal chat." Gerry tried to sound encouraging. "'Course, they won't find her there, we know that."

Joe finally lost his temper. "Yeah, but we have no more idea where she is than the police do, you stupid asshole!" He threw the phone at the bullet-proof window separating him from his driver. His bodyguard caught it and sat nursing it in his great paw of a hand.

Joe scowled. He had really wanted the satisfaction of smashing something. Some days, he thought morosely, it seemed like nothing went right.

The line of people waiting to buy tickets was short; there were only three people ahead of her. Caroline tried to appear as bored and impatient as everyone else. She pushed Kathleen's suitcase along with her foot and cast another surreptitious glance around, trying for the hundredth time to see if she could identify anyone from Joe's organization among the bystanders. Logically, she knew his men would most likely be posted at the security checkpoints, not wandering aimlessly around the concourses. However, in her current state of jitters, everyone looked suspicious—from the seven-foot, well-toned man surrounded by a cluster of excited children to the wide-eyed preschooler trying to wriggle away from the middle-aged woman holding her. Grandparent and grandchild? Or someone working for Joe who'd been smart enough to use a child as a disguise?

Something that sophisticated would be too expensive for Joe to set up a thousand miles from his New Jersey turf, Caroline decided. Here in Chicago, her father-in-law probably didn't have the resources to command more than a basic deployment of out-of-work petty criminals. She wondered if she should feel better knowing she was most likely being pursued by unintelligent armed thugs rather than higher-paid, smarter criminals.

"Next," one of the two counter clerks called.

"I'd like your cheapest round-trip ticket to Grand Cayman," Caroline said after casting a final nervous glance behind her. The preschooler had stopped wriggling and was clinging to the woman who held her, and the amazingly tall guy was autographing a basketball. She decided that only somebody in an advanced state of paranoia could consider them suspicious characters.

"When would you like to leave?" the clerk asked.

"As soon as possible. I think you have a six-thirty flight, don't you?" Caroline gave a nervous smile. "I've got some unexpected vacation time and my cousin lives on Grand Cayman." Careful, she warned herself. Don't elaborate too much. You don't want him to remember you.

"Lucky you." The clerk tapped swiftly at his computer keys. "Yes, we have space on our flight leaving at six thirty-five, connecting via Miami. How long can you stay? The seven-day return is the cheapest fare we have at the moment. Three forty-seven fifty including tax."

"Fine, I'll take that." Caroline opened her purse and started to pull out dollar bills.

"A credit card would be easier, if you don't mind. I don't have any change in my drawer."

Caroline handed across the cash. "Sorry, but I got overextended last year and nowadays I like to pay cash whenever I can."

The clerk gave her a sympathetic look. "You're smart. Wish I could train myself to stop using so much plastic. My monthly bills look like the national debt. I'll get some change in a minute. Right now, I need your name and address."

"Kathleen Williams, forty-five Spring Street."

The clerk keyed in the name and waited for the computer to print out a ticket. "I can check you in right here, if you like, Ms. Williams. How many bags are you taking today?"

"Just one." This was too easy, Caroline thought, glancing over her shoulder. When would something go wrong? Something was bound to go wrong. Surely she wasn't going to escape from Joe and the Chicago police with no more hassle than this? And as for escaping from Jack, never seeing him again . . . well, it was better not to think about Jack.

He and the boys would have returned to the apartment half an hour ago. Jack would have looked for a note, a message, some clue as to why she'd left and where she'd gone. He wouldn't find one unless he checked the trash. Is that why she hadn't shredded her pathetic attempts to write him a farewell explanation? Because she wanted him to know that she'd at least tried to apologize—

"You change planes in Miami," the clerk said, putting Kathleen's suitcase onto the conveyor belt. "There's a forty-five minute connection time, so you and your luggage should both make that, no problems. Do you have your passport? You'll need that for the next flight."

Now, Caroline thought, beginning to sweat despite the icy air-conditioning. This is when it's going to go wrong. She pushed Kathleen's passport across the counter, heart jumping into her throat.

The clerk barely made a token gesture of flipping through the pages and looking at the picture. "Great. Here you are," he said, stapling a baggage claim check to the ticket, tucking it inside the passport and handing them both back. "Enjoy your flights, Ms. Williams. Thank you for choosing to travel with us. Oh, wait a minute, I forgot. I have to get your change; you need two dollars fifty." He locked his computer and disappeared through the door behind his work station.

Caroline returned her documents to Kathleen's purse and sneaked yet another look around. The crowd still seemed the usual mixture of vacationers and businesspeople, all of whom appeared frazzled, hot and intent on their own business. She had to get rid of the paranoid sensation of being under constant scrutiny. She was sure it caused her to give off nervous vibrations that made her conspicuous.

She realized she was drumming her fingers on the counter and stopped at once. She checked her watch. The clerk had been gone for almost five minutes, which seemed a heck of a long time to find two dollars and fifty cents. Unless he'd used the excuse of needing to find change in order to call the police. The line of passengers waiting to buy tickets was growing. The clerk must know what would be happening to the length of the line. Why would he risk annoying his customers just to make such a tiny amount of change? Wouldn't he at least have come out to explain that he was having difficulty?

Maybe the clerk was so experienced at checking travel documents he'd needed only a brief glimpse of Kathleen's photo to know Caroline was an impostor and the passport was stolen. Her stomach lurched in terror. Through sheer willpower, she managed not to turn tail and flee for the nearest exit. But she didn't need to hang around and risk capture for the sake of two measly bucks. Better to head for one of the security checkpoints, overcome that minor hurdle, then hide herself in one of the boarding areas. She wouldn't approach the Miami departure gate until the very last boarding call.

Body stiff, her face muscles locked into a smile, she walked away from the counter, trying to keep her stride casual until she passed out of sight of the customers still waiting to buy tickets. Once she'd safely filtered into the crowd heading toward the security gates, she began to move faster.

Adrenaline pumped hard and fast through her system. The people moving through the terminal faded into a single faceless blur while at the same time her vision seemed to become oddly sharpened, honing in automatically on potential dangers. Every deviation from the expected leapt out at her: the woman who kept pace with her however fast she walked; the two men wearing heavy leather jackets despite the high summer heat; the man draped with gold chains, lounging against the wall, apparently in no hurry to get anywhere; the short, dark-haired man with skinny hips and extra-broad shoulders just like Steve's standing by the security checkpoint with his back to her.

Caroline froze. The man didn't have muscled shoulders just *like* Steve's. The man ten yards ahead of her *was* Steve. She'd spent two unpleasant car journeys staring at the back of his neck, and she didn't need to see his face to recognize him. The tilt of his head, the breadth of his shoulders and the curl of his hair over his collar were all too sickeningly familiar.

Caroline scanned left and right, searching for an inconspicuous escape route. She saw the sign indicating rest rooms and immediately cut across the flow of passengers. At least there she'd be hidden from Steve and able to take five minutes to recover her cool and organize her thoughts.

God alone knew what caused Steve to turn around at the crucial moment when she stepped free of the river of people and stood isolated from the protective cover they provided. She couldn't have been visible in the brightly lit entrance of the rest rooms for more than three or four seconds. And yet something intangible caused him to turn and survey the crowd behind him at precisely the moment she was most exposed.

Their eyes met and his face broke into a delighted grin. Panicked, she couldn't think of anything better to do than dodge into the ladies' room, even though she realized she would have to come out eventually— and Steve would be waiting for her when she did.

She should have known better than to think Steve would risk losing track of her just because the rules said men weren't allowed to enter the women's rest room. He dashed across the concourse and followed her in, ignoring the frowns, gasps and shocked complaints of the women who were waiting to use the facilities.

Dodging toddlers and senior citizens, Caroline zigzagged through the rest room, not thinking or planning, simply running. Away. Anywhere Steve wasn't.

She realized as she pushed past a gaggle of teenagers and emerged onto the main concourse that she'd been lucky: the rest room had two exits, each one facing a different side of the concourse. Steve had followed her into the rest room through one door and she'd just come out the other. She'd also gained a few yards on him, mostly because women had stepped aside for her, but nobody had stepped aside for Steve.

Caroline took off at a dead run, noticing that people were beginning to turn and stare but afraid to stop and ask for help. How could she ask for protection from Steve and Joe unless she was willing to talk to the police? And there were a thousand reasons *that* was impossible.

"Ms. Williams! Ms. Williams, what's the problem?"

She recognized the voice of the counter clerk who'd issued her ticket to Grand Cayman. She swerved to avoid him and continued to run as fast as her legs would move and as long as her heaving lungs would provide oxygen.

At some deep, subliminal level, she knew that this frantic run through the airport had effectively destroyed all hope of getting to the Cayman Islands using Kathleen Williams's documents. But the overwhelming fear that gripped her blocked out thought, leaving her free to concentrate on the need for immediate escape. If Steve captured her now, Joe would probably kill her. At the very least, he'd torture her until she revealed the access codes to Dayton's safety deposit boxes, then he'd turn her over to the police. In either event, Andrew would grow up never knowing any parents but Joe and Angela. He would become a replica of Phillip, and she couldn't allow that to happen. Not while there was still life in her body.

Dread gave power to her lungs and wings to her feet. She bolted down the moving stairs, then came up the other side, dashing toward the giant doors of the exit. She thought she could hear the thud of Steve's footsteps no more than a few steps behind, but she couldn't be sure with the roar of blood pumping in her ears. She didn't waste precious seconds turning to check.

She ran out of the airport into the hot, exhaust-scented humidity of the summer night. The pounding in her ears was getting louder, and now she *was* sure it was Steve she heard. She stepped into the road, dodging the traffic that approached the curb, her pace scarcely slackening.

She ran around a limo unloading a trio of businessmen. Out of the corner of her eye, she saw the trunk of a cab pop open a few yards ahead. The driver and his passenger got out. Simultaneously, she saw a cop and registered the way his head jerked up at the sight of her. He must have noticed she was being chased. For a split second, she almost appealed to him for help. Then sanity returned. She was on her own, just as she had been for the past year. Just as she would always be.

She couldn't keep running forever. Sweat was dripping into her eyes, and her throat was sore from sucking in gasps of air. Born of desperation, the realization came that there was only one way she was going to escape both Steve and the cop.

The cabby slammed the lid of the trunk. The passenger paid him and walked toward the airport entrance, and the cabby pulled out his wallet to tuck the bills inside.

Caroline's body had turned into a machine with no purpose other than to save herself so she could rescue her son. The cabby started to walk toward the driver's seat of his car, but she reached the door moments before he did. She flung herself behind the wheel and slammed the door, leaving the man to pound on the window and howl his rage and disbelief.

Steve ran up and pushed the cabby aside, hanging onto the handle and clawing at the partially open window. The cop was already running up on her right.

Caroline didn't wait any longer. The engine was on and she accelerated away from the curb, not allowing herself to slow down when she saw Steve lose his grip and fall onto the road. She swerved to avoid his body and cut across three lanes of traffic, ignoring the sounds of skidding vehicles and honking horns exploding behind her.

The cab, thank God, was relatively new, and responded with a welcome surge of speed when she stepped on the gas. She drove at reckless speed, concentrating fiercely. She had just enough conscience left to recognize that she had no right to cause any accidents, not even to save Andrew, and she slowed down marginally. She guessed she might have two or three minutes at most before the airport police would have every highway entrance from the airport cordoned off. Cabs couldn't be stolen with impunity, and if Steve was conscious, which seemed likely, heaven knew what story he might have spun to incriminate her.

She sped past Mannheim Road and made a spur-of-the-moment decision not to take the Tri-State Tollway. The toll booth, she remembered, was only about a mile down the road, which was much too close for comfort. A quick phone call from the airport police, and she'd be stopped as she tried to get onto the highway.

That left her with the obvious choice of taking the Kennedy Expressway toward downtown Chicago. The police might be out in force looking for her, but the expressway had no tolls and plenty of other cabs to provide protective confusion while she lost herself in the flow of traffic.

Five miles sped by, five miles of consuming fear, climaxed by a moment of almost perfect terror when she heard the wail of a police siren, distant but closing fast.

She didn't wait to find out if the cop was chasing her or somebody else. She took the first exit she came to, swung south on Cumberland, then doubled back and drove north until she got to Niles, a crowded suburb she recognized only by name. If the cop had been tailing her and not some other luckless speeder, it seemed she'd successfully shaken him from her tail. Two cars followed her off the Cumberland exit ramp. Neither of them pursued her to Niles.

She toured the side streets until she found a crowded supermarket and abandoned the cab in the middle of the lot, hiding the keys under the seat and locking the doors from the inside. The cab was conspicuous in this suburban setting, and the police would soon be notified of its whereabouts. She hoped that by tomorrow morning, the cabby she'd robbed would have his car back.

Shaking, her muscles limp with the aftermath of stress, Caroline stumbled toward the supermarket, seeking cover with the instinct of a wounded animal going to ground. She supposed that she had some cause for self-congratulation: she'd avoided arrest, escaped from Steve, thwarted Joe—and she hadn't even scraped the paint on the stolen taxi. Which was all terrific, of course, except that she hadn't the faintest idea what to do with her hard-won freedom. She was right back to square one, lacking the money and the documentation to get her to the Cayman Islands.

Her eyes were burning with a dryness that was beyond tears; her brain felt totally devoid of anything that might pass for intelligent thought. She slunk into the supermarket, automatically grabbing hold a trolley and pushing it ahead of her. She kept bumping into people and muttering apologies. Finally she realized that she needed to sit down before she fell down.

She pushed the trolley toward the pharmacy section, located in the back corner of the supermarket. She could see a couple of chairs by the dispensing window, presumably for customers waiting to pick up prescriptions. Maybe she could sit there for a few minutes and get a grip on herself.

There was a public phone hanging on the wall next to the take-your-own-blood-pressure machine. After two or three minutes of sitting and staring blankly ahead of her, Caroline acknowledged that her gaze was focused with hypnotic intensity on the phone. Suddenly she knew what she was going to do.

She bought a bottle of aspirin and asked for change to make a phone call. Then she looked up the phone number she needed and dialed before she could change her mind.

The phone rang five times before it was answered. She was about to hang up when she heard the familiar voice. "This is Jack Fletcher."

She drew in a deep breath and wondered if she was making one of the biggest mistakes of her life.

"Jack, this is Caroline. I'm in big trouble and I need your help."

Eleven

"**I** found this under the sink," Marcus said, handing Jack a crumpled and somewhat soggy piece of notepaper. "I guess it fell out of the trash. Maybe you want to take a look at it. I read it already." He went into the kitchen, where he and Antoine had just started to clear the dinner plates and stack them in the dishwasher.

Jack smoothed out the paper, experiencing a jolt when he realized it was a letter written by Caroline.

Dear Jack,

I want you to know how much I appreciate all you've done for me these past few days. I hope Marcus won't be very disappointed that I can't be there to serve him and his friend the special dinner I promised. He's a kid whose life has been too full of broken promises, and I'm really sorry to add my name to the list of adults who've failed him. A missed dinner may not seem much, but I know that little failures add up so in the end they hurt almost as much as the big ones.

I guess I'm taking so long to apologize about Marcus and dinner because that's easier than telling you how sorry I am that I have to leave. I truly wish I could tell you where I'm going, although I don't understand why I have this crazy urge to confide in you. Ignore that last sentence, I shouldn't have written it.

You've probably already noticed that I've stolen Kathleen's suitcase, and her purse, too. All I can say—again—is that I'm sorry. If her parents had asked you to send home her things, I swear I wouldn't have taken them. But they asked you to donate her clothes to a good cause, and I decided nobody could need them more than I do.

The next paragraph was scratched out, but Jack finally managed to read it.

I guess I have to be honest—I would have taken her wallet no matter what, even if her parents had asked for it to be returned. But I promise to make a cash donation to Goodwill when I get back from

The letter broke off and started again with another paragraph she hadn't scratched out.

I keep trying to convince myself that if Kathleen knew the truth—if you knew the truth—you would both understand why I have to

The letter ended in midsentence, and this time it didn't start again. Jack stared at the sheet of notepaper for several seconds before he crumpled it into a tight wad and threw it at the wall, a childish gesture that did absolutely nothing to improve his mood. He was concentrating on his clenched stomach and the tight feeling in his throat when the buzzer to the outside door of the apartment building sounded.

He picked up the phone and flipped the intercom switch, glad of a diversion. He was mad as hell and hated that he was. "Yes, who is it?"

"It's Frank Donohoe. I need to speak with you, Father."

The formality of his tone was unusual. Jack frowned. "Sure, Frank, I'll buzz you in."

He opened the apartment door and waved the detective sergeant inside. "You look like you've had a rough few hours since we last met," he said. "Take a seat, Frank. I have a beer in the fridge, or I could rustle up a cup of my famous instant coffee."

"I won't take anything right now, thank you, Father. Fact is, I'm here on official business."

"I see," Jack said, and he did see, all too well. One look at Frank's tight, tense expression told him that he was the bearer of bad news. "Something more to do with Kathleen Williams?" Jack asked.

Caroline, he thought, cold with fear. Caroline's in trouble.

"No, I'm not here about Kathleen," Frank said heavily. "This is about Caroline Hogarth. Are you expecting her back any time soon, Father?"

How did he know she was gone? What had she done to bring herself to the attention of the police in the three hours since he'd last seen her? "I'm afraid I can't help you, Frank." There was no reason for him to conceal the truth, no reason at all to shield Caroline if she was in trouble with the law. "She ducked out on me earlier this afternoon," he said. "I've no idea where she's gone or what she's up to."

"Damn and blast!" Frank muttered a few ripe curses under his breath, then shook his head. "Sorry, Jack. I don't mean to offend."

"It's okay. I've heard the words before, and a great many that are a lot worse." Jack gave a wry grin. "I've even been known to use a few of them on occasion." He gestured to the recliner. "Come on, Frank, you know you love that chair. Sit down for a minute, wipe that official look from your face and tell me what this is all about. Is Caroline Hogarth okay? What's she been up to? Since you're out looking for her, I gather she's not... You haven't come to tell me she's dead, have you?"

"She isn't dead, but I wouldn't say she's okay. Far from it. Basically, I'd say your lady friend is in deep, uh, trouble."

Jack started to protest that Caroline wasn't his lady friend. At the last minute he got smart and shut up. "What sort of trouble?" he asked.

"There's a warrant out for her arrest," Frank said, running his hands through his thinning hair. "Multiple charges, including murder."

Jack's head jerked up and his heart thudded faster. "Murder? Good grief! Who is she accused of killing?"

"Dayton Ames," Frank said.

For a split second, the world stopped in its tracks. When everything started moving again, Jack wondered why he felt no more than a quiver of surprise. He went into the kitchen, murmured a few encouraging words to the boys who were elbow-deep in soapsuds and came back out carrying two beers.

He popped open one of the cans and handed it to Frank. "I need this even if you don't," he said. "Last time I checked in with the TV news, the police weren't calling Dayton Ames's death a murder."

"We are now. The autopsy results came back. According to the coroner, Dayton Ames died of cardiac arrest following the ingestion of five milligrams of digoxin. Apparently he suffered from congestive heart failure, complicated by recurrent atrial fibrillation, so he was very vulnerable to any drug that affects the heart rhythm."

Jack had enough medical knowledge to make a translation. He frowned. "Presumably, with the sort of condition you've described, Dayton Ames was taking medication on a regular basis. What makes you so sure it was murder, not an accident? Or even suicide, for that matter? Digoxin is one of those drugs where there isn't much of a window between a beneficial dose and a lethal one."

"The drug had been injected through the cork into the bottle of red wine Ames drank that night at dinner. Unless Dayton Ames chose a real elaborate method of committing suicide, he was murdered. The digoxin couldn't possibly have gotten into that wine bottle by accident."

"Even if Caroline wanted to kill him, what makes you think she has the medical know-how to plot that sort of a death? It requires quite a bit of pharmaceutical knowledge."

Frank shook his head in disagreement. "Nothing all that special. Ames was under a doctor's care for his heart condition. Anybody with a few brains and a bit of determination could have found out that digoxin isn't a medication to be messed with."

"Provided they knew about his medical condition. A healthy person probably isn't going to be killed by digoxin, not unless it's administered in a larger dose than five milligrams."

"Caroline was Ames's mistress for six months. She would have known about his condition. He didn't broadcast his heart problems to the world, I guess. On the other hand, I doubt if it was a state secret."

Caroline had been Dayton's mistress for six months? Jack took a long gulp of beer. "Nothing you've said explains why Caroline would have wanted to inject poison into his wine. What motive could she have for doing something so terrible to the man who was presumably paying her bills?"

"I can't tell you what her motive was. But I can tell you she sure had the means and the opportunity to kill him."

"How did she get the digoxin? It's a prescription drug."

"Dayton Ames had a plentiful supply lying around, and Caroline had the run of his penthouse, remember. But we're checking with pharmacists to see if any of them recall filling a prescription for a woman answering to her description."

"If there was digoxin in the apartment, dozens of people probably had access to it, not just Caroline."

"Yes, but Caroline Hogarth's the only one who also had dinner with Dayton Ames the night he died. She met him in his penthouse every Friday night without fail for the past several months, and they always had a meal delivered by the Grand Gourmet catering service. Apparently their Friday night dates were an open secret around town with the folks who move in those sort of rarefied social circles. Gossip has it Dayton Ames was crazy in love with her. Would have married her in a heartbeat if she'd been willing to say yes."

"That doesn't explain why she would want to kill him. The opposite, in fact."

Frank took a final swallow of beer. "It might not provide motive, Jack, but it sure shows that she had plenty of opportunity. The woman who delivered their dinner saw Caroline. Seems Caroline helped her set the table, and this woman watched her personally select a bottle of wine from Dayton's private stock."

"You're not convincing me, Frank. Caroline is a smart woman. If she'd planned to kill Ames, do you really think she'd be dumb enough to make sure a witness saw her handling the murder weapon?"

Frank gave him a quizzical look. "The DA's office doesn't go for fancy double bluffs, Jack. We have a witness who puts Caroline Hogarth at the scene of the crime, with access to the bottle of wine that was later found to be poisoned—with a substance Caroline had easy access to. What's more, she's the only person who was there in the penthouse with Ames for the rest of the night. Put all that together, and it's more than enough to satisfy the DA.''

"You've stacked a lot of circumstantial evidence together. You haven't begun to suggest a motive."

Frank shrugged. "You're letting your heart get in the way of your head, Jack. Who can tell what makes somebody decide to commit murder? We're talking about a woman who was following the world's oldest profession. Maybe she wanted to move on to someone who paid better before Ames's heart condition did him in. Maybe she decided he was getting annoying with his offers of marriage. The guys downtown are handling this case, so they must have come up with some sort of a motive that satisfies the DA. As for me, I don't have to make the case against her." His mouth twisted wryly. "I just wanted to buy myself some cheap glory by being the working stiff who brought her in when none of the hotshots could find her."

There was absolutely no reason on God's green earth for Jack to feel any sense of personal involvement in what Frank Donohoe was saying. He *certainly* had no reason to feel protective toward Caroline Hogarth, or to leap to the conclusion that she was being wrongly accused. In fact, he had a bunch of good reasons for accepting that she was guilty as hell. She'd lied to him from first to last.

He had a vivid mental picture of her looking at him, her gorgeous, long-lashed eyes swimming with unshed tears as she whispered a husky, heartbreaking denial of ever having been involved with Dayton Ames. Yeah, right, Jack thought in disgust. She'd only been warming the guy's bed for the past six months. From Caroline's point of view, maybe that meant their acquaintance was too slight to be worth mentioning. So why did he keep hoping to hear something that would convince him of Caroline's innocence?

"I thought you already found the woman who was Ames's mistress," he said to Frank. "Danny—the cop we met down at the station this afternoon—he told us the woman you were looking for in connection with Dayton Ames's death had turned herself in. Michelle Something."

"Roche," Frank said absently. "Yeah, she turned herself in, all right. Volunteered the information that she'd gone to Mr. Ames's apartment to have breakfast with him. Claims to have left again lickety-split when she realized his wife was in the apartment. But our witness insists she isn't the woman he saw. They did a lineup just to be sure."

"Why in the world would Michelle Roche say she'd visited a murdered man unless she's telling the truth? What's in it for her? It's not like she's going to walk off with a prize if you accept her story."

"I can't answer that, but I'm twenty years on the force, and I've learned to spot the phonies and the crazies. I can tell you this for sure—Michelle Roche didn't come forward because she's a public-spirited citizen who wants to help the police in their inquiries. Michelle is what you might call connected. She turned herself in downtown with Mr. Clive Reese Burroughs, Esquire, right at her side.''

"Who's he?" Jack asked. "Am I supposed to be impressed or disgusted?''

"Who's Mr. Burroughs?" Frank said. "Ha, if you were in my line of work, you'd know the answer to that one. Mr. Burroughs is the mob's favorite lawyer in Cook County, that's who he is. Take my word for it, Clive Burroughs, Esquire, doesn't take on any client who hasn't been approved by the folks who pay for his thousand-dollar silk suits and his annual new Mercedes. Which means that Michelle Roche is about as civic-minded as your average sewer rat—and slightly less pure.''

"If Michelle has mob connections, why in the world do you suspect Caroline of being the woman who poisoned Ames? Good grief, if Dayton Ames had links to the mob, surely the odds are that they're the ones who'd have wanted him dead?''

Frank seemed to hesitate for a moment. "What makes you so sure Caroline doesn't have ties to the mob?" he asked. "For all you know, she may have been their hit man for the job.''

"*What?*" Jack would have laughed if Frank hadn't looked so serious, almost as if he knew something he wasn't telling. "That's crazy," he said with more conviction than he really felt. "Caroline Hogarth couldn't possibly have connections to the mob.''

"Why not?" Frank asked softly. "Because she's pretty and says please and thank-you like a real lady? Everybody who works with the mob doesn't wear oversize pinkie rings and talk like they just stepped out of the pages of *Goodfellas,* you know."

The case against Caroline sounded more compelling by the minute. Jack wondered why he still didn't believe a word of it. Intuition? More likely a rush of testosterone to the brain, he thought ruefully. In fact, for a thirty-eight-year-old man, he was doing a great job of impersonating a teenager in an advanced state of hormonal idiocy.

"I'm sorry I can't help you," he said, crumpling his empty beer can in his fist. "But I have no more idea where Caroline Hogarth is than you do."

Frank's gaze shifted uncomfortably. "Are you sure, Jack? Not that I want to accuse you of aiding and abetting a criminal, but why didn't you report that Caroline had stolen Kathleen Williams's suitcase and travel documents?"

"Not because I was in a conspiracy with Caroline," Jack said, wondering how the police already knew that Caroline had made off with Kathleen's belongings. "I figured you and your colleagues had better things to do than chase after a suitcase of clothes that were destined for Goodwill."

"But Kathleen's passport *wasn't* destined for Goodwill," Frank said sharply. "If we'd known Caroline had stolen all Kathleen's travel papers, we might have put out the word, so when Caroline turned up at O'Hare airport this afternoon, using Kathleen's name and Kathleen's documents, airport personnel would have been on the lookout for her."

Kathleen's documents. So that's what Caroline had been trying to weasel out from him, Jack thought numbly. She'd been planning all along to flee the country. While he'd been baring his soul about Beth and his months in prison, deluding himself that Caroline was getting ready to exchange confidences, she'd been stringing him along while she planned to escape a murder rap using Kathleen's passport and stolen identification.

"Caroline..." He cleared his throat. "Did she get away?" he asked.

Frank shook his head. "She booked a flight to the Cayman Islands, but she never made it on board. She's most likely still somewhere in the Chicago area, unless she's managed to hitch a ride out of the city." He gave Jack a pointed look. "Or she gets help from someone who's willing to smuggle her out."

"I plead not guilty," Jack said tiredly. "I haven't helped Caroline and I have no plans to help her. What happened at the airport?" he asked. "How come you know she was out there but you didn't arrest her?"

"Seems it's quite a story," Frank said, some of his normal friendliness returning. "Right out of the Keystone Cops, as far as I can tell. We reckon Caroline must've arrived at the airport around five o'clock. She pays cash to buy a ticket to Grand Cayman, checks in Kathleen's luggage and hands Kathleen's passport over for inspection. From her point of view, everything is going great. Nobody suspects the documents are stolen. Nobody suspects anything, in fact. The clerk doesn't have change, so he goes into the office to try to find some. He comes out and she's gone.

"God knows what spooked her. But next thing you know, the whole concourse is in an uproar. Some guy chases Caroline into the ladies' room. Goes right in and knocks a little old lady flat on the floor in his effort to catch up with Caroline. He doesn't get her, though. She dodges him, and eventually fetches up outside the terminal. A traffic cop sees her running, sees that there's somebody chasing her. He's just about to step forward and ask what's wrong. Next thing you know—and this part you aren't gonna believe—Caroline jumps into a waiting taxicab and drives off, right under the noses of the cab driver, the cop and the guy who was chasing her! Half the airport was on her tail, and she still got away!"

"She did?" Jack exclaimed, wondering what was wrong with his moral sense that he felt a crazy urge to cheer Caroline's success.

"Clean away," Frank agreed gloomily.

Jack tried to think like a sober, responsible citizen instead of a man drowning in hormones. "What about the guy who was chasing her? Isn't he willing to talk? Did you find out why he was so anxious to catch her?"

"The answer to all of the above is no, no and no." Frank's voice revealed his disgust. "The traffic cop was just a rookie. He ran after the cab Caroline had stolen, trying to catch up with it, and by the time he realized that was a fool's game, the guy who'd been chasing Caroline had disappeared. When the cop tried to describe him to put out an APB, all he could come up with was·slender, brown-haired and middle-aged. The woman he knocked over in the rest room says he was a boy—which she defines as less than thirty—tall, with huge shoulders and hair as dark as pitch. Which means that we have no effective description and no idea why Caroline Hogarth was being chased. And in the meantime, she's vanished.''

"She can't hide from you for long."

"Not without help, but she's probably getting help." A note of weariness entered Frank's voice. "There's something big going on here, Jack, and it pisses me off when I think that Mr. Clive Burroughs, Esquire, and his employers are sitting in their penthouses, raking in their illegal millions and laughing their heads off while we screw around trying to catch them out in some misdemeanor so's we can haul 'em inside for a few months.''

Was Caroline working with Mr. Burroughs and his mob friends? Or was she being set up as their victim? Jack prided himself on being an insightful judge of character, and he couldn't believe Caroline had the sort of corrupt, hardened core that would enable her to function as a willing servant of organized criminals. On the other hand, he'd realized in prison that the most successful criminals got away with their crimes because they believed in their own righteousness and therefore projected a convincing aura of innocence. Caroline's letter had made it clear that she considered herself a woman with a mission. It was amazing—frightening—what crimes ordinary people could be persuaded to commit if they thought right was on their side. She might be an example of the most dangerous and convincing type of criminal, using her stunning good looks to play the role of victim.

Jack reminded himself that however much he might be convinced of Caroline's innocence, society would never survive if all people took the law into their own hands and tried to dispense their own particular versions of justice.

"If Caroline comes back here, I'll let you know," he promised Frank with complete sincerity. "But I doubt she will. She knows I'm a friend of yours. She realizes I'd turn her in."

"Would you?" Frank said. "Are you sure you would, Jack?"

"Of course I would. I run a youth program at the church where I spend most of my time trying to convince the kids that civil society can't survive unless citizens cooperate with the law. If they think a law is unjust or a particular situation is unfair, they have to work to change the law or the situation, not disregard it."

"Sounds great, and I'm sure you're a swell teacher. But the trouble with you, Jack, is you're a regular bleeding heart, the ultimate sucker for everyone's sob story. Anybody down on their luck only has to squeeze out a few tears and you're convinced God loves 'em and wants you to take them under your wing."

"God does love them," Jack said quietly. "He does want me to care for them. That doesn't mean it's my job to conspire with them to break the law."

Frank sighed. "I suppose it's no use asking you if Caroline Hogarth told you anything that might help us with our inquiries?" he said. "I'm sure you're going to plead professional privilege, seal of the confessional and all that other annoying crap."

Jack smiled. "This time you're in luck, Frank. Caroline Hogarth never had any conversation with me that could be considered even remotely privileged. She never approached me as a priest, never told me anything she asked me to keep confidential. On the contrary, far from confiding in me, she swore to me that she'd never met Dayton Ames. The fact is, I know absolutely nothing that would help you find her. I don't know anything at all about the real Caroline Hogarth, except that she has the world's greatest legs."

Frank looked briefly disapproving. Good Catholic that he was, he could never quite accept that Jack wasn't bound by the same vows of celibacy as a real priest. He'd often said that only the English could have come up with a church that looked and sounded like the real thing but had gutted most of the worthwhile rules and regulations.

With another heavy sigh, Frank lumbered to his feet. "Well, it was too much to hope that I'd be the guy to find her, I guess. I'd better get home and stop dreaming about gold stars on my report card. It's been a long day, Jack, but thanks for the beer and the loan of your recliner—"

The phone rang and Frank gave a mock salute. "You get that, Jack. I'll let myself out. If you remember anything at all that might help us find Caroline, give me a call.''

''Sure will.'' Jack grabbed the phone just before the answering machine picked up. He nodded to the sergeant, simultaneously speaking into the phone. ''This is Jack Fletcher.''

The voice that answered him was breathless and thin with fright. ''Jack, this is Caroline. I'm in big trouble and I need your help.''

Twelve

Jack heard the car door open before he saw Caroline. She slipped into the passenger seat, and he immediately felt chilled by the sense of fear that surrounded her.

"Thanks for coming, Jack." Her face was paper white, her eyes feverish and circled by huge purple shadows. "You didn't tell anyone where you were going, did you?"

"No. I can't believe it, but I let Frank Donohoe walk out of my apartment without saying a word."

"Donohoe? Why was he with—" Her question cut off in a strangled gasp. She squirmed down in her seat, tucking her head beneath the dashboard, cowering out of sight for no reason that Jack could fathom. A split second later, he heard the wail of a police siren and realized what had terrified her. Her nerves must be stretched to their limits, he thought, if she'd registered such a distant threat.

"It's okay," he said, reaching down to grasp her hand and pull her up. "The cops aren't coming in this direction. Listen, the siren's getting fainter."

She waited until the siren had faded completely before she sat upright in her seat. "We have to get out of here,'' she said tautly. ''They'll find me. They'll see the cab and they'll know I'm somewhere in the neighborhood. Jack, go, drive! Get us out of here.''

He reversed out of his parking place, infected with her panic. Ironically, the weight of her fear seemed all the more oppressive because she was trying to hold it under such rigid control. ''Where are you taking me?'' she asked.

''I have a place in mind.'' He spoke absently, concentrating on avoiding the police squad car as he eased into traffic, but she flinched away from him, her eyes darkening with a despair so profound that Jack recoiled from the impact.

''What does that mean?'' she asked. ''Are you taking me to Joe's? Do you work for him? Is that what this is all about?'' She made a strangled sound, somewhere between a laugh and a sob. ''Oh, God, have I been so stupid that I actually started to trust one of Joe Rossi's hired hands?''

''I doubt it,'' he said. ''Seeing as I don't have the faintest idea who Joe Rossi is.''

''He's my father-in-law,'' she said.

Her father-in-law? ''So you're married after all,'' Jack said flatly. ''Where's your husband? How does he fit into all this? Is your father-in-law trying to bring the two of you back together?''

More to the point, perhaps, *who* was her husband? The mysterious Andrew she'd mentioned once, then immediately clammed up about? Jack didn't need to waste any time wondering why the news of Caroline's marriage disturbed him. He'd realized when he came home this afternoon and found his apartment empty—hollow with the echoes of her absence—that his feelings for Caroline went way beyond those of a minister trying to help a troubled soul, or even of a man experiencing a major case of lust after too many years of self-imposed celibacy.

I'm not appreciating your sense of humor, Lord. Ten years for You to send me a woman who pushes every single one of my buttons, and she's married?

"I should have said my ex-father-in-law," Caroline corrected herself. "I was divorced two years ago."

"I'm sorry," he said. And he was, both for Caroline's failed relationship and for himself. Despite vigorous debate in the House of Bishops, the Episcopal Church remained uncompromising in its belief that marriage lasted until death. In the eyes of his church, Caroline was still married, whatever the state might declare.

"My husband died last year," she said. "He was murdered."

Thank you, Lord, thank you. A touch belatedly, Jack realized how inappropriate that sentiment was. But the truth was, he was falling in love with Caroline, a state that tended to produce mental confusion.

Caroline drummed her fingers on her knees as he slowed for a traffic light. She noticed what she was doing and put one hand over the other, stilling the nervous tattoo. "Oh, God, Jack, I'm so scared," she whispered.

He wanted to pull the car over to the side of the road, take her into his arms and comfort her with murmured promises that he would protect her forever. Most of all, he wanted to hold her. Even in her present distraught state, he found Caroline almost unbearably attractive.

He contented himself with mumbling a platitude about everything turning out all right in the end. Reluctantly calling to mind Frank Donohoe's accusation that he was far too susceptible to sob stories, particularly sob stories from Caroline, he forced some steel into his flabby backbone. It was okay for him to be falling in love with her, despite all the questions about what she might have done and the mystery about her background. It *wasn't* okay for him to shove moral and ethical issues to one side because his emotions were in turmoil.

"I need to know just what we're dealing with here, Caroline," he said. "Am I helping you conceal a crime? Did you kill Dayton Ames?"

She hesitated for a crucial second. "No, I didn't kill him."

"Not even by accident, or in a good cause, or because he was threatening you, and you acted in self-defense?"

"I didn't kill Dayton Ames," she said through clenched teeth, this time without any hesitation. "He would never have threatened me with physical violence. He wasn't that sort of man."

"What sort of man was he?"

"Charming, sophisticated, with a conveniently flexible moral code. Probably as honest as Henry Ford or John D. Rockefeller or a bunch of the other millionaires we've chosen to admire. At least until he made the terrible mistake of going into partnership with Joe."

"So why was he murdered? Any ideas?"

"Just one," she said. "But it's the right one. He annoyed Joe Rossi." She shook her head angrily. "If you want to know something really pathetic, it never once occurred to me that Dayton had been murdered until I was watching television at your place and saw the news report about the police waiting for autopsy results." One of her hands tightened into a fist and pounded the palm of her other hand. "God, I've been so blind! For six months, I deluded myself into believing I was stringing Joe along, and all the time he was stringing me."

Jack swung the car onto the interstate and headed north. "Who exactly is Joe Rossi?" he asked. "Other than your former father-in-law?"

She smiled bitterly. "Allow me to introduce you to Joe Rossi, *consigliere* of the Family in New Jersey. Regional chief mobster, in other words. Super pimp. Drug czar supreme. Gambling king. Owner of ten percent of the state's politicians, twenty percent of the union bosses and God knows what percentage of the corporate executives. You name the crime, Joe has his feet sunk in the muck and his bloody fingers stuck deep into the money pile."

"Sounds like a really charming fellow."

"If you have an affection for cockroaches and disease-bearing rodents."

"How fortunate that he's now an *ex*-father-in-law, rather than the current model."

Caroline closed her eyes. "I don't think I'll ever in my whole life be rid of Joe Rossi."

If her revulsion was an act, it was one of the most convincing Jack had ever seen. Still, the fact that Caroline had ties—close family ties—to organized crime explained why the DA's office was so ready to believe her capable of murder.

He waited to speak until they'd been safely overtaken by a convertible and a sports car, whose drivers seemed intent on using the highway as a private race track. "There's a warrant out for your arrest on the charge of murdering Dayton Ames," Jack said. "Did you know that? Is that why you ran away this afternoon?"

He'd thought her face was white when she got into the car, but he'd been wrong, he realized. She'd merely been pale before. Now she turned white, the blood visibly draining from her face.

"Oh, my God!" she whispered. "Then there's no doubt any more that Dayton was murdered? And the police think I did it?"

"He was really murdered," Jack said. "And, yes, the police are convinced you did it. Fact is, Caroline, they seem to have a pretty strong case against you."

She shook her head, as if struggling to break free from shock. "How can they have a strong case against me? It's ridiculous. I mean, he had a heart condition and he died in bed, in his sleep. How am I supposed to have killed him? Enticing him into overenthusiastic sex?''

''He was poisoned.''

She absorbed that news in silence. ''Well, even so, I didn't kill him.'' She turned and stared out the window.

''Since you didn't kill him, that leaves us with two interesting questions. Who did? And are they deliberately trying to implicate you?''

''Those aren't interesting questions,'' she said bitterly. ''They're both no-brainers. Joe did it, and of course he's trying to implicate me.''

Jack saw a police car in his rearview mirror, and slowed to two miles less than the speed limit. The cruiser filtered into the right lane, then turned off at the exit ramp. Jack realized he was sweating. Guilt and fear were not comfortable traveling companions.

He spoke with an edge of sharpness. ''Accusing Joe may make you feel better, Caroline, but even if you're right and he's the guy behind Dayton's murder, that sure doesn't address the question of how he managed to pull it off.''

She shifted tiredly in her seat. ''If you'd met Joe, you'd know the answer to that. It's simple, Jack. He sent for one of his hit men and said, 'Dayton Ames is a problem. Take care of him.' Then Joe went right back to whatever he was doing before, planning a campaign to sell more crack to grade-school kids or making a donation to the church fund for widows and orphans. Either activity would be likely. Joe isn't big on seeing irony in life's little details.''

Her bitterness when she talked about Joe was corrosive, distorting her ability to see facts. "You're not thinking straight, Caroline. Dayton wasn't gunned down on a street corner, he was poisoned in his own home—hardly the mob's favorite method of eliminating problems. What's more, you were with him when he died. If Joe sent in his hit men to kill Dayton Ames, how did they do it? How did they kill Dayton without you seeing or hearing a thing?"

"I . . . don't know," she admitted. "That's why it never occurred to me he'd been murdered, because we were together, just the two of us, for hours before he died." She rubbed her forehead and blinked fiercely. "All right, I get your point. If I'm going to accuse Joe of murdering Dayton Ames, I have to explain how his hit man administered the poison when I was there all night, eating more or less the same food as Dayton, breathing the same air, drinking the same wine and coffee—"

"Actually, we don't have to speculate. We know precisely how the poison was administered."

Her eyes widened in surprise. "We do?"

She really had the most spectacularly beautiful eyes, a rain-washed shade somewhere between blue and gray, but Jack refused to succumb to their lure. He fortified himself against the urge to tell her that of course she was innocent, and he'd fight the world on her behalf until everyone believed her. "The forensic evidence apparently leaves no doubt about how the poison was administered. Dayton Ames suffered from recurrent atrial fibrillation, complicated by mild congestive heart failure. He had a weak heart, in other words, and he died because he drank at least three glasses of wine that had been laced with digoxin. About five milligrams, the pathologist said. That proved fatal because he'd already taken a prescribed dose of the same drug. The overdose in the wine did him in."

Face blank, Caroline stared at him in stupefaction. "No, Jack, that can't be right," she said finally. "The lab... the pathologist... has made a mistake."

"The autopsy report was unequivocal, Caroline. Dayton Ames had ingested an excessive quantity of digoxin, which is a cardiac glycoside with a very narrow window between lifesaving benefits and deadly dosage. Because of his heart condition, he didn't stand a chance once he drank his second glass of wine."

"He may very well have been poisoned with di-whatsit," Caroline said. "But it can't have been put into the wine." Her brow wrinkled in thought. "The food, maybe. Yes, that's much more likely. Our dinner was sent in from outside, by a catering firm, and Joe could easily have gotten to that. Or relatively easily, anyway. But he couldn't have doctored the wine."

"Why not?"

"Because *I* chose it. I opened the bottle and I poured it out, so I know it can't have been poisoned. I even drank a glass of it myself, and I'm not dead."

"You don't have congestive heart failure. A single glass would have made you feel unwell. It would be unlikely to kill you."

"Okay, but you're not listening to me, Jack. I chose the wine. Nobody could have known in advance which one I would select. Dayton kept half a dozen bottles of white wine in a small fridge by the bar, and half a dozen red in a special wine rack nearby. I always tried to choose whatever seemed best suited to our meal. Dayton was a wine connoisseur and he was trying to improve my hopelessly inadequate palate. Trust me, Jack, the wine couldn't have been the problem. Nobody could have tampered with the wine that night except me. And I didn't, so that means the di-whatsit wasn't in the wine."

"Unfortunately, that's exactly where it was." He smiled at her without a trace of mirth. "You know what you've just done, Caroline? You've done a really great job of making the DA's case for him. The wine was indisputably poisoned, and according to you, you are the only person in the world who could have poisoned it. You just spent several minutes convincing me of that."

For a moment there was total silence. Then, to his astonishment, she started to laugh. "Good old Joe," she gasped. "He's so much smarter than anybody ever remembers. How the hell did he do it, I wonder?" Her laughter stopped as abruptly as it had begun. Jack could see that she was teetering on the edge of hysterics.

She pressed her hand against her mouth, fighting for control. "Well, that's that, then, I guess." She squared her shoulders. "Where are you taking me? To the police station, to tell them I've just incriminated myself in the murder of Dayton Ames?''

"Not yet." He spoke curtly. He hadn't quite come to terms with the conflict between his emotional conviction that he was helping a woman who'd been brilliantly set up and his intellectual conviction that he ought to drive her straight to the city and hand her over to Frank Donohoe. He was a priest, not a cop or a lawyer, and she needed a good lawyer to straighten out this mess, not a well-meaning do-gooder whose experience of the law came mostly from the wrong side.

To hell with rationality! He didn't doubt for an instant that she was telling him the truth, so if Joe Rossi was the murderer, how had he insured that Caroline would select the bottle of poisoned wine? Not by putting it at the front of the fridge or by bribing the caterers to prepare food that demanded a certain wine choice. There was simply no way to guarantee that Caroline would pick the correct wine.

"From what you've told me," Jack said, "there's only one way Joe could have poisoned the wine."

She looked up, curious. "What's that?"

"He had digoxin injected into all the dozen or so bottles you had to choose from. Bingo! Whichever wine you select will kill Dayton."

"Of course!" Caroline shot bolt upright behind her seat belt. Then she slumped down and shook her head. "That wouldn't work either, Jack. What about the bottles I didn't open? They'd still be poisoned, sitting there in the fridge. Surely there's a good chance the police have already checked those bottles to see if they've been tampered with? Or supposing Felicity opened one of the poisoned bottles at a dinner party and served it to her guests. Or gave it away to the cleaning crew or whatever. One of them could easily have heart problems, and then he or she would die, just like Dayton. Joe couldn't risk killing off anyone else."

"Why? Would he care if a stranger died?"

"No, but he'd care about the police investigation that would inevitably follow. Presumably, if another person died in just the same way as Dayton Ames, it would cause people to question my guilt in relation to Dayton's murder."

"All right," Jack agreed. "Then we have to conclude that Joe made arrangements to get rid of the extra bottles before they could be used by Felicity or spotted by the police or drunken by a cleaning woman."

"How could he? Felicity Ames was in the apartment almost before I was awake on Saturday morning. Felicity wouldn't have allowed anyone to go to the kitchen and start emptying wine bottles while she was mourning her husband's unexpected—"

"What is it?" Jack demanded. "What have you just remembered?"

"Nothing. It's crazy." Caroline brushed her hand across her eyes.

"It's not crazy. You've remembered something about Saturday morning. About Dayton."

"Not about Dayton. About Felicity."

"Tell me."

"It's not what I've remembered, it's what I never thought about before." Caroline drew in a deep breath. "It was an open secret that Dayton and I spent Friday nights together. In the six months Dayton and I were involved, Felicity Ames and I had managed to never once cross paths. She and Dayton led completely separate lives, you see. Felicity lived in their house in Winnetka, and Dayton stayed in his penthouse in the city. The only time they got together was for a charity function or for outings with their daughter."

"So you're wondering why Felicity suddenly turned up at Dayton's penthouse on the very morning he'd died?" Jack suggested. "It sure is an amazing coincidence."

Caroline nodded. "Felicity practically threw me out of the apartment," she said. "She couldn't wait to get rid of me. At the time, I wasn't surprised. Under the circumstances, I didn't question her behavior, not even when she informed me that she wouldn't tell the police I'd been with Dayton the night before—"

"That didn't strike you as odd? It didn't set off loud warning bells that this woman was behaving strangely?"

"None at all," Caroline admitted. "Not even very small and quiet warning bells. I wasn't thinking straight that morning. I was upset about Dayton, and my head felt as if it was only loosely attached to my shoulders. I couldn't focus sufficiently to think coherently. In fact, I wasn't feeling well at all..."

"Which isn't surprising," Jack said grimly. "Remembering back to my medical school days, you could have given yourself a lifelong heart problem if you'd had more than a single glass of that wine. Digoxin is a powerful drug. Did you feel sick, do you remember?"

"Horribly sick," she said, realizing for the first time just how profoundly ill she'd felt the morning of Dayton's death. "I'd slept heavily, completely unaware of Dayton's problems, and yet I vaguely remember having nightmares that I was suffocating. I woke up feeling disoriented and giddy. My heart was racing, my eyes weren't focusing too well, and I kept being swept by these ghastly waves of nausea."

"And it never occurred to you that you might have been poisoned?"

"No, never." She gave a small, wry smile. "Dumb, huh? But at the time, I assumed that waking up next to a dead man and having his wife turn up before I was out of the guy's bed were more than sufficient reasons for why I felt sick to my stomach."

"Well, putting two and two together and coming up with a neat, round four, it sounds to me as if we've just solved the mystery of who killed Dayton Ames," Jack said crisply. "It wasn't your father-in-law, Caroline. It was Felicity Ames. Presumably, for whatever bizarre reason, she decided that this was a more efficient way to end her marriage than filing for divorce."

Caroline's cheeks suffused with a heated, guilty flush. Stricken, she turned to Jack. "I didn't mean to hurt her so badly, Jack. My God, I never realized how much she cared about Dayton. He swore their marriage was over, that she wouldn't care if he took a dozen mistresses." She closed her eyes. "I guess I wanted to believe him, so I didn't let myself think about Felicity and what she might be feeling. I can't bear to think that I may have driven her to murder."

"Stop wallowing in misplaced guilt," Jack said. "The fact that Dayton claimed his marriage was over doesn't excuse the fact that you chose to commit adultery. And the fact that you and Dayton committed adultery doesn't explain or excuse the fact that Felicity Ames committed murder. You're responsible for your own sins, and she's entirely responsible for hers."

"It must be nice to be so damn morally perfect," Caroline snapped. "But we lesser mortals have this tiresome tendency to get tangled up in our own emotions. Excuse me for a minute while I straighten out my various guilt complexes."

"Okay, I'm sorry. I'm behaving with all the tact and subtlety of a herd of elephants." Jack ran his hand through his hair. "Let's start this part of the conversation over," he said. "Don't let yourself be so overwhelmed by misplaced feelings of guilt that you stop seeing straight. Your father-in-law sounds like he's a really bad guy, Caroline, but that doesn't mean he's the cause of everything that goes wrong in your life. Logically, given the evidence, it seems to me we have to assume Dayton Ames was killed by his wife, not by Joe Rossi."

Caroline was silent for a while. When she spoke

again, her voice was flat, as if she expected to be disbelieved. "Maybe you're right, Jack, and maybe I'm crazy. But despite the fact that I can see exactly how Felicity could have murdered her husband, and I've no idea how Joe could have done it, I still think Joe Rossi was behind Dayton's death. I can just smell Joe's involvement in all of this."

"Can you? Two days ago—two hours ago—you weren't entirely convinced that Dayton Ames *had* been murdered. Now you're sure Joe's the murderer, and to hell with the facts."

"That's not fair. I know Joe of old—"

"Maybe that's the problem. You know him of old. If we're going to beat this murder rap, Caroline, we not only have to come out fighting, we also have to come out with our big guns all pointing in the right direction."

She turned her head away so all he could see was the heavy thickness of her blond hair. He felt no anger from her, just dull resignation. He had the uncomfortable feeling that she'd set him a test, and he'd failed. Miserably.

"We're almost to the Wisconsin state line," she said, glancing at a roadside sign. "Where are we going, Jack?"

"The Warzaks, Beth's parents, have a small cottage up near the lake, about five miles off the main road just this side of the state line. They're spending the summer touring Yellowstone in their Winnebago, and I have the key to their cottage. That's where I'm taking you. It's a nice place, very peaceful, lots of trees and birds around and not too many people."

She closed her eyes. "The not many people sounds especially terrific. I'll take the greatest care of everything, Jack, and I won't stay more than a few hours, just time enough to rest up a little and make up my mind where to go next."

"I plan to stay right there with you," he said.

She opened her eyes, pulling herself up in her seat. Far from looking dismayed, which he'd almost expected, she looked oddly hopeful, as if she wanted him around, despite his failure to accept the guilt of Joe Rossi. Then her expression darkened.

"You've done enough," she said. "I can't ask you to help me any more, Jack. Except to maybe not report to the police that you've seen me. You can always say I stole the key to your in-laws' cottage. That way, you don't have to implicate yourself in my escape."

"But that wouldn't be true, since you didn't steal the key. I'm giving you the key, so I am implicated."

"Honest Jack, who never tells a lie?" she queried, her voice laced with familiar sarcasm.

He smiled. "Semihonest Jack, who tries never to lie unless it's really necessary."

She made an attempt to smile. "Define really necessary."

"Do you have a couple of days to devote to the discussion?"

"I wish I did. It might be fun." She touched him very briefly on the cheek. "You know, you look like a real tough guy, Jack, especially when your stubble starts to grow, but you're a marshmallow at heart.

Even if I didn't mind putting you in the position of breaking the law, I couldn't let you help me. Joe Rossi eats marshmallow men for breakfast. He'd chew you up and spit you out in a hundred pieces.''

"Frank Donohoe claims I'm a bleeding heart, and you're accusing me of being a marshmallow. For a guy who spent two years in jail proving how tough he was, I obviously need to do some work on my macho image. I could develop a complex real fast around you two."

Her smile this time was a bit less forced. "You're a million times better than macho, Jack. You've been a real friend, and I thank you from the bottom of my heart. You took me in at a moment in my life... Well, anyway, if this turns out all right..."

She breathed deeply and corrected herself, her mouth tightening into a grim line of determination. "When this is over, and we're safe, I'm going to write and let you know what this was all about."

"No, you're not," he said mildly. "I'm not letting you walk out of my life with nothing more than the promise of a thank-you card. I'm taking you to the cottage and staying with you until you tell me why you're so convinced Joe Rossi is out to get you, and why you still think he murdered Dayton Ames. Now. Tonight. No arguments accepted."

She stared at the pleats she'd just folded into her skirt. "Don't offer again, Jack. Right now, I'm weak enough to accept. Trust me on this one—you don't need my problems tossed into your lap."

"I'd say they're already there." He turned off the highway and headed north. "It's settled, Caroline, so save your energy for something more important. Before I left to come and meet you, I made arrangements for Marcus to spend the next couple of days at a friend's house. Does that convince you I never intended to let you handle this situation by yourself?"

She closed her eyes, fighting a silent battle. When she turned to him, he knew he'd won. Her face seemed softer and younger, showing all the vulnerability she'd struggled so hard to conceal. "Jack, I don't know how to thank you. Not just for offering to help, but for believing the best about me when it would have been so much easier for you to believe the worst. I know I haven't always sounded completely rational these past couple of days, much less honorable."

"Fortunately, in my job you don't have to weigh evidence by the same strict standards the DA uses. Sometimes I get to take a chance and follow my instincts."

"What happens when your instincts are wrong?"

"Human beings are wrong all the time," Jack said. "Sometimes I think being wrong is what we do best. I guess I've reached the conclusion that you don't achieve much that's worthwhile in life if you allow yourself to be paralyzed by the memory of all the mistakes you've already made. Not to mention fear of all the mistakes you're certain to make in the future. If you're human, Caroline, you'll make mistakes. Lousy mistakes. Big ones. Giant-size whoppers. That's guaranteed. So learn to pick up the pieces and move on.''

"But what happens if you make a mistake that's so terrible it not only destroys your life, it destroys the lives of other, innocent people?"

"I've been there," Jack said. "I found out the hard way that you still have to pay your debts and move on."

"I wasn't talking about you."

"Are we talking in generalities, then? If we are, I have several great philosophers and theologians I can quote for you."

Her voice was low. "No, we're not talking in generalities. We're talking about me. About how I wouldn't listen to anyone's advice, and so I ended up destroying the life of the one person in the world I most wanted to protect."

"Who was that?" he asked.

"Andrew," she said, hugging her arms around her waist.

He could feel the air between them filling with the ache of her regret. "Your husband?" he asked.

"No," she said. "My son."

Thirteen

The cottage, surrounded by a wide deck and fringed by evergreens, stood in rough grass about a quarter of a mile from the shore of Lake Michigan. The setting sun turned the sky into a symphony of deep pinks and purples and burnished the wooden shingles on the cottage roof with a fiery glow. Jack drove over the bumpy graveled driveway and parked the car in back, where it wouldn't be easy to spot from the road.

The cottage wasn't air-conditioned, so as soon as they were inside, he flipped the breakers on the electrical panel and walked around opening the windows and started the ceiling fan in the living room. "It'll take a few minutes for the place to cool off," he said.

Caroline scarcely noticed either the heat or the faint musty odor. The cottage was a fantasy taken right out of her childhood dreams of how a home was supposed to look.

The decor would have horrified Caroline's adoptive mother, Mrs. George V. Hogarth IV, longtime doyenne of Chicago society, who had never come to terms with the concept that furniture was supposed to be comfortable. Mrs. Hogarth favored priceless antiques from the late eighteenth century, preferably inherited from the original owners. Caroline's nursery and childhood furnishings had all been exquisite museum-quality imports. She'd been seven years old before she realized most kids were allowed to play with their toys.

In contrast to the home where she'd grown up, the decor of the cottage made no pretension to any style of any epoch, not even Sears Modern. The furniture was early seventies shabby, with lots of brown and gold tweed and giant daisies and sunflowers blooming on the curtains and crewel-embroidered cushions. Crocheted doilies covered the arms of the sofa and the two rockers, and a long lace scarf trailed over the top of the sideboard, which was jammed with photos of brides, graduations and people holding up fish and babies.

Other than the screened porch, which had been recently painted and outfitted with new white wicker loungers, the major items of furniture all looked as if they'd been brought here when they got too bedraggled to keep anywhere else. Despite this, the overall effect was of coziness and intimacy, as if the cottage had been the scene of innumerable happy, easygoing family vacations. Caroline wished she could have shared in the warmth of those imagined family gatherings with an intensity that left her stomach aching.

Once he was sure that water was pumping from the well, Jack took her into one of the two small bedrooms. It had an old-fashioned armoire stuffed with a random collection of male and female clothing and a chest of drawers filled with misshapen T-shirts, mismatched white socks and assorted shorts in every size.

"Take a shower and find yourself something to wear while I mix up some lemonade," Jack suggested. "It's been so hot for the past week that the water should be at least tepid even before I switch on the heater."

By the time Caroline had showered, shampooed the snarls out of her hair and found something to wear, the living room had cooled down, and the mustiness had been swept away by a night breeze blowing off the lake. Jack whistled in appreciation as she came out of the bedroom.

"Wow! Cinderella is transformed into a princess."

His compliments were always offered with a casual smile, and they always made her stupid, gullible heart sing. Just being with him made her remember the time, a million years ago, when she had thought the world was a place full of possibilities, with love waiting to be taken and given easily in return. It was difficult to imagine that she'd ever been so hopeful. And so naive.

He held up a coffeepot in one hand and a pitcher of lemonade in the other. "Which one?"

"Lemonade, please. I'm still dehydrated from running so hard this afternoon."

He poured a glass and handed it to her. "Yellow suits you," he said. "I'm glad you could find something to fit. Something so pretty."

She sat on the sofa in a billow of yellow cotton. "Does your mother-in-law sew? This dress looks as if it's homemade." The dress had a full flared skirt, cinched waist and the sort of perky white collar and cuffs that had been the height of fashion in the late fifties. Caroline, whose taste normally ran to tailored slacks and unstructured linen jackets, found the outdated style feminine and oddly appealing.

Jack chuckled. "My mother-in-law believes in sticking to what suits her, and to heck with the dictates of fashion, so she sews most of what she wears. Beth and I once bought her this fancy designer outfit for her birthday. She wore it to church all winter, just to please us, but she hated it, really. She thinks human beings reached the summit of civilization when we invented polyester. She always said that when Beth and I had children, we'd finally understand the appeal of clothes that even a seven-year-old boy couldn't destroy."

He stopped abruptly, turning away to look into the darkness beyond the porch windows. Caroline hesitated for a moment. "You're thinking about Beth," she said at last.

"Yes." Jack cleared his throat. "She was five months pregnant when she died. The baby was a boy. It's crazy, but sometimes I miss the son we never got to see almost as much as I miss Beth. I wonder what sort of a child the two of us might have created together. It hurts like hell that I'll never know. That Beth never had the joy of holding her baby in her arms, where she could see him. Feel him."

Caroline wished desperately that she could comfort him, but she'd lost the knack of consoling other people. "Did Beth's parents know about the baby?" she asked. That was the best she could do—just prompt him with questions, then listen while he kept talking.

"It must have made their grief even worse, knowing they'd lost a grandchild as well as their daughter."

"Maybe, at first," Jack said. "But not in the long run. The fact that they have half a dozen other grandkids helps some. But they're much more accepting than I am, anyway. They always say how grateful they are that their final memory of Beth is such a wonderful one. We'd invited them to our place for a special dinner and shown them the ultrasound the obstetrician had just taken of the baby. That was the week before Beth was murdered, and it turned out to be the last time they saw her alive."

Caroline could visualize that special get-together all too vividly. She realized there were tears in her eyes, and she blinked them away, frightened because all her defense mechanisms seemed to be on the verge of collapse.

"I can't understand how they coped with losing a child," she said hoarsely, her grief threatening to break the dam where she'd kept it bottled up for almost a year. "How could they bear to carry on with the routine of daily living when they'd lost their daughter and a potential grandchild in one fell swoop?"

"They were devastated for a long time, but they have a truly remarkable faith, and they were able to say that God has a reason for everything, and eventually we would understand what that reason is."

"Is that what you believe, Jack? That God has a reason for everything that happens?"

He grimaced. "I'm a priest, so I should be able to say yes, right? Unfortunately, I don't have an easygoing temperament like my in-laws, and I'm not at all good at pious resignation. I get mad at God all the time. Fortunately, He seems to refrain from getting mad back. I struggle a lot with questions like why some children have to suffer so much from the second they're born and why evil so often seems to be rewarded. Saying that it all comes right when we're in heaven doesn't work for me. We've got eighty or so years of living in this life to get through first, and I'd like the good guys to win a bit more often than they do. So I guess the only answer that works for me is to try my damnedest to put in my two cents worth on the side of the angels. I can't end hunger and negotiate world peace, I know that. I can't even stop gang warfare in the inner cities. But maybe I can help make the streets of my city a little safer to walk at night. If we all took care of our own family, our own street, our own neighborhood, then maybe we wouldn't need to keep looking for a savior to float down on a white cloud and rescue the world."

He picked up his mug of coffee and took a sip. "Sorry. End of sermon. Not one that would go down well with the bishop, by the way. He sometimes has serious doubts about the orthodoxy of my theology."

"Theology be damned." Caroline blinked. The tears were gathering again, any minute now they'd start to fall. "You're a good man, Jack Fletcher, do you know that?"

"I have a lot of past mistakes to make payment on." Before she could move, he cupped her face in his hands and gently brushed the tears away. "Now it's your turn to share something with me, Caroline. Tell me about Andrew.''

Andrew. The name exploded inside her with a mixture of pain and pleasure. How could she begin to explain to anyone, even Jack, how the mere fact of Andrew's existence had filled all the empty places in her heart and wrapped her life in a haze of happiness? Not because he was cute, or bright, or sunnynatured, which he was, but because he loved her unconditionally and trusted her completely, the way she had always longed to be loved. Just for herself.

Outside, the last mauve moments of dusk were fading into the indigo darkness of night. The cicadas' song rose and fell in soothing, irregular rhythm. One day soon, when she and Andrew were reunited, she'd be able to find enjoyment again in such simple, everyday pleasures as sitting on the porch and listening to the cicadas.

If they had cicadas in New Zealand. One of the penalties she would pay for stealing Andrew out from under Joe's nose was that she would never again be able to live in the United States. Sometimes she wondered if she and her son would be able to find safety anywhere. Even New Zealand, eleven thousand miles away, sounded too close to Atlantic City to provide adequate protection against the long reach of Joe's arm.

She remembered the day when Andrew was born with brilliant, sharp-edged clarity. She'd woken at dawn with a dull ache in her back that quickly escalated into the regular contractions of true labor. She checked into the New York Hospital at seven in the morning, scared stiff but full of excitement that the long-awaited birth was about to happen.

Her labor lasted nine grueling hours. She thought it was the worst, most painful labor in the history of the universe. Her obstetrician, a monster in green scrubs who had previously managed to disguise himself as a friendly, decent man, laughed frequently and told her that for a first-time mother, she was having a pretty easy time of it. If she'd been able to spare even a smidgen of energy, she'd have given him the sock in the jaw he so richly deserved.

At three-twenty in the afternoon, Andrew was born. The doctor announced that her son was not only healthy but also cute and a hefty eight pounds. "You did a great job, Caroline," he said, thus instantly transforming himself back from monster to decent guy. He put her baby into her arms. "Unwrap him if you want. Take a good look."

During her pregnancy, Caroline had read what seemed like every book ever published on the subject of labor and delivery. All the authors had described the euphoria a mother feels when she holds her newborn infant for the first time. Until the doctor placed Andrew's squirming and bloody body into the sheltering cradle of her arms, she thought she understood what the books were talking about. As soon as she held Andrew, she realized that nothing she'd read even came close to describing the wonder and the joy of that incredible moment.

Phillip had been with her throughout her labor. He'd refused to attend any classes to prepare himself for the experience, but he'd summoned the courage to defy his father's proclamation that giving birth was women's work and had joined Caroline in the delivery room.

Looking at his newborn son, Phillip fell instantly in love. Handsome features working, his perfectly shaped lips quivering, he stared in wonder at the pink, squalling infant who was his own flesh and blood.

With infinite gentleness, he touched the translucent skin of Andrew's cheek. With his other hand, he stroked Caroline's tangled hair. "He's beautiful. He's so perfect. Look at his fingernails." Phillip's voice cracked. "I do love you, Caro, you know that, don't you?"

Her heart contracted with pity—for her husband and herself—at that tiny glimpse of the man he might have been rather than the man he'd actually become. "Yes," she said, allowing herself to hope one more time. "I know you love me, Phillip."

Of course, the tenderness of that hospital scene had lasted for all of three weeks, at which point Phillip felt in the mood for sex and demanded that Caroline accommodate him. She complained that she was still too sore for intercourse, and he beat her up for being so stubborn and frigid, a typical WASP bitch. In one night, all the old destructive patterns of their marriage were restored. And yet she knew the real tragedy was that Phillip had told her nothing but the truth the day of Andrew's birth. To the extent that he could love another adult human being, he loved her. The problem was, his father had taught him that marriage meant using fear and abuse to dominate your partner.

Loving baby Andrew was a lot easier for Phillip than loving his wife—Andrew posed none of the threats to his fragile self-esteem that Caroline presented. Phillip showered his son not just with material gifts, but also with personal attention. It was Phillip who read Andrew bedtime nursery rhymes, Phillip who built turrets of blocks so that Andrew could have the supreme pleasure of knocking them down, and Phillip who plunked his son on his lap and instructed him in the finer art of watching "Sesame Street."

Andrew accepted his father's attention in the spirit in which it was offered. He loved the turrets, loved the nursery rhymes, and despite the fact that he could barely talk, much less count and sing songs, he would gurgle happily for the first four or five minutes of "Sesame Street" before drifting peacefully to sleep in Phillip's arms.

One of Phillip's other favorite activities was to walk in Central Park with Caroline and Andrew. He enjoyed showing off his wife in one of her new designer outfits, chosen by him, just as he enjoyed showing off his son in his fancy imported Italian stroller, with the hand-embroidered blankets and pillows tucked around Andrew's plump and contented body.

Sometimes, during those long walks in the park, Caroline managed to join in her husband's game of Let's Pretend and could almost forget the pathological jealousy and ugly brutality that formed the flip side of their marriage. Unfortunately, reality was often too fresh and vivid in her mind for the pretense to work.

Their marriage lurched from crisis to crisis for the first eighteen months of Andrew's life—until she'd walked out of the house the day Phillip lost his temper with Andrew and threatened to hit him. She'd never gone back, despite Joe's vicious threats, and Phillip hadn't contested the divorce or her petition for sole custody of Andrew. She'd always wondered if that might not have been the noblest act of her husband's tragic life. When Phillip died, gunned down in a back alley in Atlantic City, she'd mourned more than she would have believed possible. She even found herself hoping that Andrew retained deep in his subconscious the memory of a father who had truly loved him.

Jack ran his hand lightly down the side of her cheek. "Bad memories?" he asked. "You look so sad. Is Andrew dead?"

"No, he's not dead," she replied. It was a moment before she could say anything more. The bitterness of her loss still had the power to leave her almost paralyzed with rage. "He's living in the sole custody of his grandfather, Joe Rossi."

"With Joe!" Jack exclaimed. "How the blazes did that come about?"

"We had a custody battle after Phillip died," Caroline said. "I lost."

Jack looked startled. "Joe must have had a hell of a lawyer," he said. "A paternal grandparent winning out over a child's mother is almost unheard of. What about your visitation rights? How often do you get to spend time with Andrew?"

"I don't," she said flatly. "Never. Not once since early last summer."

He shook his head. "I don't understand."

"The court has declared me an unfit and abusive mother."

Whenever she thought about the court proceedings that had taken Andrew from her, Caroline became sick to her stomach. Her anger and grief were all the more powerful because she was so completely impotent to change the verdict. "I'm enjoined from trying to see Andrew again until Joe and his wife, Angela, decide that I've reformed my wicked and abusive ways."

"You need a new lawyer," Jack said at once and with absolute certainty. "You can get the visitation clauses in the custody judgment changed. Good grief, even mothers in jail for child abuse can petition to see their kids from time to time."

"But they don't have Joe Rossi fighting against them," she said. "My attorney told me I was lucky to avoid a jail sentence with the evidence that was presented during the court hearings."

Caroline was positive another trip to family court would be useless. When Joe had threatened to gain custody of Andrew, she'd been scared but not terrified. After all, Phillip hadn't protested her claim for custody at the time of their divorce, so the previous judgment was in her favor. When her adoptive parents volunteered to pay the bill for a high-powered attorney, Caroline had allowed her confidence to blossom.

Her parents' offer of support had been important not only for practical reasons, but for emotional ones, too. It had always been a source of joy to Caroline that her son had captured the aristocratic hearts of Mr. and Mrs. George V. Hogarth IV as effortlessly and completely as he'd captured everyone else's. When she left Phillip and came home to Chicago, it had seemed as if her rocky relationship with her parents had finally reached some sort of equilibrium. She forgave them for not being Mr. and Mrs. Cleaver. They forgave her for being the daughter of an irresponsible cousin of George's and a dirt-poor girl from the Kentucky backwoods who had planned to be a famous model and had ended up a drunken whore.

With her superefficient lawyer working hard, Caroline had gone through the pretrial process nervous and on edge, but nowhere near frantic. In her screwed-up life, the one thing she'd really managed to get right was raising Andrew. He was bright, precocious, healthy and above all, happy. His day-care teachers were willing to testify she was a concerned and caring mother. Her parents were willing to testify that she earned a sufficient income to support him and that they would always help out in a crisis. Her employer and her landlord were on her side.

Despite all she'd learned about Joe's methods during the years of her marriage, Caroline had retained much of her naive faith in the American justice system. The battle over Andrew had taught her the harsh truth: justice and the courts had little to do with each other.

Joe had manipulated the legal system without breaking even a mild sweat. He'd let the custody case wind its way through the long, tortuous passages of the pretrial hearings, not attempting to pervert its progress. The case had ended up in Judge Long's courtroom, a great advantage to their side, Caroline's attorney assured her. Judge Long was deeply sympathetic to the rights of women and mothers, unimpressed by which side in a custody dispute had more money.

Even in those relatively innocent days, Caroline had been smart enough to wonder why Joe was allowing the case to be heard in such an unfavorable venue, why his team of attorneys had made no attempt to get the hearing moved. She questioned her lawyer, trying to find out if Judge Long could be bribed. Her attorney was horrified. Judge Long was a model judge. Caroline should get over her paranoid belief in the omnipotence of her father-in-law and the corruptibility of American justice.

The case had barely begun when Caroline realized why Joe hadn't needed to do anything as risky as bribing a judge of impeccable reputation. He'd simply fabricated the evidence. The legal juggernaut thundered ahead, all the way to rendering a verdict that was not only a massive and damaging injustice to Caroline, but clearly put Andrew's well-being—and even his life—at risk.

She noticed that she was shaking, trembling from head to foot. Jack put his arm around her, drawing her close, offering silent sympathy. Caroline knew she should resist such dangerous intimacy. What would happen when she grew to depend on it? But instead of pulling away, she let her head come to rest against his shoulder, and her hands splayed over his chest, drawing comfort from the steady thud of his heartbeat beneath the tips of her fingers. Until this moment, she hadn't acknowledged how incredibly, terrifyingly lonely she'd felt for the past year.

"Why did the court declare you an unfit mother?" Jack asked quietly.

"Unfit *and* abusive," she corrected him, rubbing salt in the wound of Joe's victory.

"Okay, why did they make such a decision? Courts are normally prejudiced in favor of the mother, particularly one who's well educated and able to support her child. They must have heard some pretty strong evidence of abuse."

"They did," she admitted. "They heard from a bunch of very talented and convincing liars."

"Who? How? Where from?"

"Well, let's see. There was Joe's housekeeper, who testified that she'd seen me beating my son in a drunken rage on more than one occasion. Then there was the psychiatrist who claimed that I'd consulted him because I was suffering from postpartum depression, experiencing feelings of murderous rage toward my baby because I'd gained ten pounds that I couldn't lose. He described this session in which I'd supposedly become hysterical because I could no longer fit into a size-eight pair of jeans."

"Had you consulted the psychiatrist for depression?" Jack asked. "I'm not suggesting that you beat and neglected Andrew, but were you depressed or fed up at not losing weight? I remember from med school days that a mild attack of postpartum blues is much more common than most people realize. Giving birth really messes with the hormones.''

She shook her head. "Jack, until the man walked into that courtroom, I swear to you I'd never seen him! I didn't suffer from even a mild case of the baby blues, and the few months I was nursing Andrew must be the only time in my entire life I've lost weight without consciously dieting. My size-eight jeans have never looked that great before or since! As for Joe's housekeeper, I don't believe she ever saw me with Andrew when there weren't at least half a dozen other people in the room. Everything those witnesses said was sheer, unadulterated fabrication.''

Jack frowned. "What was going on with your lawyer while all this false testimony was being given? Quite apart from the question of whether it was perjured, I don't understand why the psychiatrist was allowed to testify in the first place. How did Joe's legal team get around the laws governing professional confidentiality? How could the psychiatrist get away with betraying his doctor-patient relationship?''

Caroline derived a perverse sort of comfort from the knowledge that even somebody as street smart as Jack couldn't begin to fathom the extent of Joe's power to corrupt and distort. "Jack, you have to stop thinking within normal legal and moral limits. The psychiatrist simply produced release forms, signed by me, giving him permission to discuss my problems. Of course I never signed those papers, but it would have taken a crew of experts to get them declared forgeries.

And if I'd found ten experts to say they were forgeries, Joe would have paid off eleven experts to declare that they weren't."

"So what about the witnesses your side produced? You must have had some friends and colleagues willing to testify that you were neither depressed nor cruel to Andrew."

She shrugged. "They tried, I guess." She preferred not to think of the halfhearted support of her adoptive parents, who had turned increasingly hostile during the course of the trial. No doubt because they began to believe the stream of testimony produced by Joe. "Any points my team managed to make were overwhelmed by Joe's parade of witnesses. There were nine men willing to claim I'd slept with them—although *slept* doesn't seem to be the correct euphemism for what I'm supposed to have done with them. By the time my fourth 'lover' had finished testifying, you could tell my attorney was hoping he'd lose the case because I didn't deserve custody of Andrew. By the time the fifth lover had finished, the judge decided she didn't need to hear any more testimony. God knows, I can understand why. All the men swore under oath that I was a whips-and-chains freak, and that I had an insatiable appetite for oral sex."

"I won't bother to ask if you'd had an affair with any of the men, but had you at least met some of them?"

"No, not a single one, but who cares about a trivial detail like that? Everyone, including my parents, was too busy listening to how I found it especially diverting to play my morbid sexual games while Andrew was watching. That, my lovers testified, was why they'd all chosen to end their sordid affairs with me. It bothered their tender consciences to indulge in sadomasochistic intercourse with a two-year-old baby watching."

Caroline felt the nausea swell up from her stomach and into her throat. The memory of the courtroom was unbearable, which was part of the reason she'd spent the past year trying not to remember it. She pushed away from Jack and ran to the bathroom where she was helplessly and horribly sick.

When she came out, Jack was waiting with a glass of club soda and a graham cracker. "We don't have to talk about this if you aren't ready," he said. "We can take things more slowly."

"No," she said, teeth chattering on the rim of the glass. "It's never going to get any better, and I need to tell you everything so you'll understand why I have to go through with my plan, why I'm so sure it's the only way to get Andrew back."

"Okay. I'm ready to listen. I just don't want you to feel coerced or pressured. It sounds as if you've had enough of that to last a lifetime." He put his arm around her shoulders and guided her to the couch in the living room. "Start where you want and go from there, Caroline. Remember, you can stop whenever you want, and I'm on your side."

She managed a smile. A shaky one, but at least it was a smile. "I guess it all starts with Phillip Rossi," she said. "The handsomest man you'd ever want to meet, recent graduate of Harvard law school, with sexy brown eyes and the world's cutest dimple. My roommate, Anna Marie, was a distant cousin on his mother's side. Phillip stopped by our apartment for dinner one night, and I fell instantly in love. He asked me to marry him six weeks after our first date, and I couldn't wait to say yes. Anna Marie knew enough about the Rossi family to be worried, but Melissa, my other roommate, warned me I'd better marry him fast or she'd steal him from me. I suppose it's some consolation to know that I wasn't the only idiotic female around."

"And did you marry him quickly?" Jack asked.

"A couple of months later, with Anna Marie and Melissa as bridesmaids, in front of three hundred guests, in a dress with a ten-foot train, all arranged courtesy of Phillip's family. My parents attended, under protest, and walked around looking as if they had a very bad smell under their noses."

"But Joe obviously approved of you as a bride if he paid for the wedding."

She nodded. "Joe was temporarily thrilled by the idea that his son, the Harvard lawyer, was marrying a woman whose family helped found the college. And for my part, I thought Joe and Angela were just the neatest folks around. As soon as we were officially engaged, Phillip took me home to meet his family. He has three sisters, all married, and a bunch of little nieces and nephews. I shared Sunday dinner with them and saw exactly what I wanted to see, a big, noisy, blue-collar Italian family, living in Atlantic City, who worked hard and made good. The American dream personified."

Looking back, Caroline still found it hard to credit her own willful blindness. "I came away from that Sunday gathering convinced I was about to marry into the family I'd always dreamed of having. After that, whatever objections my parents made, I just ignored them."

"Parents don't stand much of a chance against true love," Jack said wryly. "They keep talking about boring things like compatibility and shared interests and lifetime goals. Those aren't subjects that resonate real loud over the drumming heartbeats of two kids who've just discovered the greatest sex in the universe."

Caroline smiled. "I wish you could have seen my mother after I introduced Phillip to them." She looked down her nose and lowered her voice. "'My dear, we had no idea he would be so... Italian. And Catholic, of course, which means endless babies and absolutely no discipline in the home.'"

Jack chuckled. "So their objections weren't based on insight into Phillip's character, just prejudice?"

Caroline's eyes opened in mock horror. "Just prejudice?" Her voice assumed a clipped British accent. "'My dear, you can always tell what sort of character a man has by the clothes he wears, and you must have noticed, my dear, that the suit Phillip wore to dinner actually shone. What's more, his cuff links had *diamonds* in them.'" She said *diamonds* as if it was some form of socially unmentionable disease.

Jack grinned. "I'm getting the picture. Your parents not only came over on the *Mayflower,* they believe that Puritan plain living is the highest form of earthly virtue."

"I doubt if Mr. and Mrs. George V. Hogarth IV had anything as modest as mere Pilgrims for ancestors," Caroline said. "Their folks probably owned the damn *Mayflower* and had one branch of the family providing provisions in England while the rest sailed on ahead in a private yacht. They were probably waiting on shore in Massachusetts to make a profit when the Pilgrim Fathers climbed down the landing ladders."

A laugh rumbled in Jack's chest. Caroline found the sound oddly comforting. "So you married Phillip despite the fact that your parents disapproved," he said.

"I married him in the teeth of my parents' undying opposition," Caroline said. "They had his background investigated, and my father called me into his study to present me with the report. Phillip Rossi, he informed me, had just been hired by a law firm with known links to organized crime. What's more, he was the only son of Joseph Rossi, *capo* of the Mafia in New Jersey, subordinate only to the *consigliere* who controlled all of organized crime in New Jersey."

"I thought you told me Joe was the *consigliere.*"

"He is now. He fought his way to a promotion."

Jack gave her hand a comforting squeeze. "Let me guess what happened. You weren't impressed by your father's 'evidence.'"

"Impressed? I was furious. I yelled and stamped my feet and told my father to put his damned report away before Phillip and I sued him for slander and libel."

"Then you stomped off and married your true beloved?"

Caroline winced. "Something like that. Nowadays, I look back and marvel at the fact that I was foolhardy enough to run headlong into a marriage totally ignoring such a crucial piece of information about the man I planned to marry."

"I can understand why you wouldn't back down in front of your parents, but didn't you have a few secret worries? A suspicion that maybe you ought to check out this information for yourself?"

She shook her head. "I was twenty-three years old, and I still knew everything. Whereas my parents were in their sixties, which meant that the few useful things they'd known in the past had long since slipped away into the mists of senility. Besides, I was fathoms deep in love, and what could my parents possibly know about love? They'd married because they wanted to merge their respective family fortunes, so how could they understand the passion blazing between Phillip and me?"

She pulled a face. "In other words, I had the emotional maturity of a ripe tomato and no qualms whatsoever about marrying Phillip. Jeez, how could a cute guy with a law degree, not to mention twinkling eyes and a dimple, be a bad husband? What did his parents matter, even if Joe Rossi *was* connected to organized crime, which I didn't believe for a minute. My parents were WASP snobs, with etiquette books where they should have had hearts. But I wasn't a snob, no sirree, and their outdated standards had nothing to do with the way I behaved." Her voice took on a note of sarcasm sharp enough to cut. "Phillip and I would set up our own rules and blaze our own little path through the world, just the two of us, hand in hand, into the sunset."

"So how long did it take you to discover that you'd made a mistake?"

"About a month." Caroline's voice went flat. "We'd been to a Christmas party at Phillip's law firm, and one of his colleagues mentioned how much he liked my dress. When we came home, Phillip went berserk. He was incoherent with rage."

"He beat you?" Jack asked quietly.

"Yes." Caroline hurried on. "There's nothing to say about that part of my life, Jack. If you've done any counseling in the area of spousal abuse, you know the sort of thing Phillip and I put each other through. The recriminations, the broken promises, the reconciliations, the threats." She drew in a quick, shallow breath. "I guess I was a lot luckier than most battered wives. I had a great job and I knew I could support myself financially. I made plans to leave him."

"What stopped you?"

Caroline stared into the darkness, remembering. "I discovered I was pregnant. I'd had the flu, I hadn't taken my pills for a few days, and I paid the price. Maybe I even used the flu as an excuse to forget the pills. Phillip was thrilled—he'd been begging me for months to start a family. He swore everything would be different from now on, that he'd get a legitimate job and learn to control his temper. I was eager to be persuaded that things would change once we had a family. I agreed to stay."

She looked at her hands and saw that her fingers were threaded through Jack's. Strange, that his touch felt so natural she hadn't even noticed the contact. She forced herself to meet his gaze and saw no condemnation, only understanding and silent sympathy. "At every crucial stage in my relationship with Phillip, I knew deep down what I should do, and every time, I made the wrong choice."

He drew her closer, hugging her gently. "Caroline, if we all lived our lives through the perspective of a rearview mirror, the world would be a vastly different place. When you get too upset about your past mistakes, you need to remind yourself that if you hadn't married Phillip, Andrew wouldn't exist."

"If Andrew has to grow up in Joe Rossi's household, maybe it would be better if he hadn't been born." Her throat hurt from the pain of admitting something so devastating.

"You're exhausted and you're scared or you wouldn't have said that." Jack framed her face in his hands. "Look at me, Caroline, so you can see for yourself that I'm telling you the truth. We're going to get Andrew back. And we're going to get him soon. That's a promise."

She had no idea why she believed him, but his words unraveled the knot that had kept her emotions tied in a stranglehold of silent grief and rage. It was so long since anyone had offered to help her, so long since anyone had believed she was fit to take care of her son, that she had forgotten what it felt like to receive support. She stared at Jack, unable to speak, her voice muted by the force of her emotions.

Sensing that she was overwhelmed, he squished her nose with his finger, deliberately lightening the mood. "Your expression of stunned gratitude is great for my ego," he said. "But honesty compels me to point out that I only leap tall buildings in a single bound on alternate Tuesdays. We'll have to do some in-depth planning if we're going to pull off this rescue successfully. I won't pretend it's gonna be easy."

We have to plan. We're going to rescue. Caroline couldn't answer, couldn't even smile, because if she moved the muscles in her face, she would start crying and not be able to stop.

Jack brushed his thumbs along her cheekbones. "I've always found that talking is a real helpful way to communicate," he said. "But we can just hold each other if that's easier right now."

She tried to make the paralyzed muscles of her mouth shape a few coherent words. Instead, she leaned forward, gasping for air as her lips parted and a giant wave of...something...rushed over her.

"Caroline." Jack's eyes darkened and his voice was suddenly hoarse. He shifted away from her, his movements jerky. His hands, which were usually so gentle, gripped her arms with unexpected force, holding her away from his body. "Caroline, honey, I don't think we want to start this right now."

Start what? Caroline wondered dazedly, her gaze fixing hypnotically on Jack's mouth. He stood up, and she reached out to him, pulling herself into his arms.

"Don't go," she said, recovering her voice. "Jack, I need you to hold me." When she realized what she'd said, her stomach started to churn, and her mouth went dry, just like it did when she thought about Joe and her defeat in the custody case. Oddly, though, this time the sensation didn't seem entirely unpleasant.

Jack didn't walk away, but he looked nothing like his normal, good-humored self. He stared at her, his mouth drawn into a grim, tight line. "This has been a rough few days for you, Caroline. Neither of us is in the best state to be making important decisions. I want you too damn much to be thinking straight...."

He wanted her.

Desire, Caroline thought with an inward gasp of astonishment. That was what Jack was feeling. What she was feeling, too. It had been so many years since she'd experienced anything that came close to sexual desire that she hadn't recognized it when it touched her. She blinked and looked straight into Jack's eyes, startled out of all her normal protective stratagems.

Her new awareness of what they were both feeling must have shown in her face. Jack held himself very still, as if any movement on his part might precipitate a disaster of unknown dimensions. Caroline didn't move, either. Instead, she dropped her gaze to his mouth, consumed with memories of how she had felt the night he kissed her. She hadn't realized the memory of that kiss had been stored in such complete and erotic detail. She certainly hadn't realized how badly she wanted to repeat the experience.

She ran the tip of her tongue over her lips, feeling hot, flustered and absurdly shy. She'd seduced Dayton Ames using every trick that life with Phillip had taught her. But with Jack, she couldn't even summon up the bravado to lean across a few inches of space and kiss him. How could she presume to make a pass at a man who'd been married to a wife as perfect as Beth? Caroline wasn't even sure she remembered how to kiss with feeling, as opposed to calculated expertise. If she made love to Jack, would he be disgusted by the evidence of her past activities? How could he forget that she'd slept with Dayton Ames? She needed something from him, a sign, some clue that he harbored more for her than lust spiced with a little pity.

Jack broke the brittle silence, his voice low and tightly controlled. "Caroline, I want to make love to you, but I can't. This isn't the right moment for us. You're vulnerable, and I'm not sure either of us is capable of sorting out how much of what you feel is gratitude and how much is something else. I may not be your priest, but in many ways, I'm acting as your mentor."

With her brain dissolving into pea soup and her emotions tumbling in freefall, she was in no condition to produce a logical response to one of Jack's sermons. Could she believe him? Was it possible that he was hesitating solely out of consideration for her and not because he found her sexually damaged goods? She grabbed the remnants of her courage and ended the discussion in the only way that made sense. She kissed him.

She'd anticipated feeling excitement; she was prepared for passion. She hadn't even contemplated feeling a hunger so deep and immediate it totally engulfed her, consuming her senses and sapping her reason. She was the one who initiated the kiss, but Jack claimed her mouth with an urgent, forceful thrust of his tongue. She tipped her head back and arched against him, quivering with pleasure when she realized that he was already significantly aroused. His hands ran up and down her back, urging her closer, making her skin prickle with a yearning fierce enough to be uncomfortable—and yet infinitely pleasurable.

She ground against him, hips swaying from side to side, not in an act of conscious seduction, but in mindless response to the desire building explosively inside her. For three years, she'd lived in a marriage made hollow by the absence of love. For six months, she'd been faking intimacy with Dayton Ames. Only now did she realize how much of herself she'd been forced to sacrifice in order to make two such deep-seated violations possible.

Jack kissed her until she trembled in his arms, until she forgot the past. He kissed her as if she was the only woman in the world he would ever want to kiss in the future. He kissed her . . . as if he loved her.

Caroline knew she had no right to take what Jack was offering. Her life was too dangerous to be shared, too tainted to contemplate new beginnings. But her defenses had been shattered, and Jack was giving her no time to mount them again. She returned his kisses with all the longing and the hunger that had built up during the past year of bitter exile.

"This isn't enough," he said huskily. "I want to take you to bed and make love to you properly. All night, with nothing to interrupt us."

She might not be thinking very clearly, but she knew there were a dozen reasons—a hundred reasons—she ought to refuse him. In a minute she would say no. As soon as she caught her breath. And her willpower.

He looked at her, his gaze tender. Willpower slipped far away, replaced by a rush of longing. "Yes," she said softly. "Take me to bed, Jack. Make love to me."

He didn't reply with words, just picked her up and carried her into the bedroom. He pulled the patch-work quilt off the bed and laid her down among the pillows, reaching for the buttons on her old-fashioned dress with hands that shook slightly. When he kicked off his shoes and lay beside her, there was no awkwardness, no hesitation. Her body fitted against his as if they had been designed to come together, two imperfect halves that miraculously made one perfect whole.

Caroline was naked under her borrowed dress. Jack kissed her and stroked her breasts, then bent his head and licked slowly around her nipples. She was so instantly aroused that her back arched off the bed and her arms tightened convulsively around his neck.

She felt her cheeks flame with heat, and she burrowed her head into the pillow, her hands curling into fists so she wouldn't reach up and clutch him again or hold his head to her aching breasts. She couldn't let him see how intensely she was responding to him, or he would conclude she was an easy lay, someone who got turned on at the first touch. She desperately didn't want him to think she was an easy lay.

The absurdity of her situation made her want to laugh, or perhaps cry. Dammit, it was ridiculous that she, the woman who had driven her husband nearly crazy by her inability to respond, was now writhing on the bed in an agonized attempt to conceal her state of arousal.

Jack leaned across her, the hard muscles of his chest assuaging the throbbing in her nipples. Her flesh jumped at his touch. "Sweetheart, don't hide from me," he said. "You're so beautiful, I want to see your face when you come."

He turned her head so she was facing him again. Heat burned in her cheeks—some of it embarrassment, but most of it sheer, unadulterated desire. Her breath panted in and out of her lungs, and her eyes misted over. Her skin prickled and burned as his fingers traced a swift, sure path across her breasts, over her stomach, and sought the opening between her thighs.

Instinctively, she clenched her legs together, but he kissed her hard, his tongue thrusting deep into her mouth, and she forgot why she had been resisting. When he finally stopped kissing her for a moment, she remembered that she was trying to prove she wasn't an easy lay, but by then it was too late. He already knew she was hot and slick with need. She moaned and moved restlessly against his hand, silently pleading for release.

"Yes," Jack muttered. "Yes, sweetheart, yes."

Abandoning her attempts at modesty, Caroline let her hands clutch his shoulders, returning his kisses with aching, passionate abandon. Her body arched against his. "Jack, please, I want you inside me."

Panting, his skin sheened with sweat, he pressed his forehead against hers. "Wait, Caroline, honey. We need some protection."

She was wild, trembling, mindless, waiting for the touch of his hands to make her complete again. She could scarcely breathe, and she certainly couldn't think. She linked her arms around his neck, waiting impatiently while he tore open a foil packet and put on the condom. His fingers sought her again, then delved deep inside. She shook in bewildered pleasure. Oh, God, this was heaven! No, it was scary. What was happening to her? Joy and longing were cresting together inside her—

"Not yet," Jack said hoarsely. "Wait for me, sweetheart. You're not quite there yet."

He slid into her. She wrapped her legs around him. He pushed deeper and her entire body shuddered in response. His eyes, bright with desire, locked with hers. "You look beautiful, Caroline," he said. "Even more beautiful than I imagined."

"Jack."

"Mmm."

"I...you..." The enormity of what she was thinking terrified her into silence. "I never felt this way before," she muttered.

"Neither have I." His voice was so low, she wasn't sure she'd heard him.

He thrust deeper inside her. She closed tighter and tighter around him.

When he climaxed, Jack gave a long, low cry of pleasure.

When she climaxed, Caroline made no sound at all. Shock at reaching the first orgasm of her life had paralyzed her throat muscles.

Fourteen

Caroline floated slowly and blissfully back to earth. At twenty-nine years of age, it was a minor miracle to discover she wasn't sexually frigid. At long last she understood why the rest of the world made such a fuss about sex. It was certainly worth fussing about, she thought with an attack of smugness. She could really get into this lovemaking stuff.

For a few euphoric seconds, she let herself lie in the shelter of Jack's arms, her head resting on his shoulder and their legs still intertwined. This, she thought, is what it means to feel cherished. This is what it feels like to come home.

Jack shifted on the bed, tucking her into a more comfortable position against his chest and lifting a strand of hair out of her eyes. She snuggled against him, and her eye caught the gleam of a discarded foil packet crumpled on top of the sheets.

Instantly, the warm fuzzy glow of their lovemaking congealed into something harder, smoother and much more familiar. It was the ache of betrayal that returned to its accustomed niche somewhere in the region of her stupid heart. Good grief, how could she have ignored the obvious? Who had she been fooling, kidding herself that Jack really cared about her as a person? He'd evidently brought her here with the express intention of getting her into bed. She couldn't think of any other reason a priest would have a condom stuffed in his jeans pocket.

Her stomach roiled sickly, although she had no reason to be surprised. She'd spent the past six months playing the whore, and Jack had believed her act. He'd assumed she'd be his for the taking—that she'd be more than happy to pay for his help with her body. He was just a typical man, after all, with the usual male blindness. Why had she been dumb enough to hope he would see the real woman behind the stereotype?

She moved out of his arms and sat up, hugging her knees to her chest. "That was great," she said, flicking her hair away from her face. "Thanks for a terrific performance, Jack. You're a talented lover. How many more condoms do you have?"

His expression was blank for a moment. "Four," he said, his voice clipped. He sat up, reaching for her, but she jerked away, unable to bear the thought that her body might betray her if she allowed him to touch her.

"Caroline, let me explain—"

She cut in ruthlessly, afraid to let herself listen to his rationalizations. "Four more packets, huh? Gee whiz, since you took such care to come equipped with all that protection, I hate to disappoint you, Jack. We'd better get busy. You must be feeling like a superstud. Or did you just hope that with an old pro like me, I'd really be able to show you some exciting tricks of the trade? Get the old ticker really ticking, so to speak."

He captured her face between his hands and forced her to look at him. "Stop it, Caroline, sweetheart. I understand why you're feeling hurt. It's my fault, I know, but I'm not going to let you turn what we just shared into something tawdry—"

"We had sex," she said tautly. "That's what we shared. And it was real smart of you to remember the condoms. With a woman like me, you sure need them. God knows what you might catch."

"We didn't have sex," Jack said. "We made love. Both of us, I'm damn sure of it. Your feelings were as involved as mine. And I didn't plan to bring condoms, I just happened to have them with me."

She laughed in mocking disbelief. "The tools of your trade, Father? Condoms for a guy who took a vow of chastity? I'm sure the bishop would be amused by that one. And what about the good old chastity vows, by the way? Our little tumble into the sack should make for an interesting session when you next go to confession."

"Chastity isn't the same thing as celibacy," Jack said. "But you're absolutely right, my bishop wouldn't approve of what happened. I can only hope that God is more generous. As for the condoms, I got them from Marcus."

She stared at him, revolted. "*That's* an explanation? You asked the fifteen-year-old kid you're supposed to be caring for if he'd share his stash of condoms with you?"

"No, of course not." Frustrated, Jack ran his hand through his hair. "I just hope Marcus will understand why I'm betraying his confidence in telling you this.

The fact is, he and I had a heart-to-heart chat this afternoon when we got home from the pool. Antoine was watching TV and we were setting the table. It turns out Antoine has been teasing him because he's still a virgin. So Marcus decided it was time to get prepared for any hot opportunity that might come up. I told him it was great to know he was planning ahead for safe sex, but there was only one good reason to start a sexual relationship, however hot the opportunity, and that was because you cared deeply about your partner. Marcus eventually agreed he wasn't ready to take on the responsibility of a committed relationship, so he surrendered his supply of condoms. I shoved them into the pocket of my jeans, and then Frank Donohoe came around—and you know the rest of the story. That's why I had the condoms, Caroline, not because I was crass enough to plan a sexual encounter with you, but by sheer coincidence.''

Jack had no way to prove his explanation was true—any more than she could prove she hadn't killed Dayton Ames, or that she hadn't slept with a bunch of men while Andrew watched. Sometimes, Caroline realized, you just had to take people on trust because there was no other way to keep hope and friendship alive.

She hadn't offered anyone her complete trust since Phillip performed his hatchet job on their marriage vows. During the past year, whatever tiny seeds of faith in human goodness she still possessed had been starved into dormancy. But somehow, in the end, trusting Jack came surprisingly easy.

"Four more condoms, huh?" She was smiling.

He eyed her warily. "Yes."

"I'm sorry for yelling," she said huskily, reaching out to take his hand. "I was scared by how you made me feel, so I lashed out at you." She was amazed that she could confess her uncertainty without feeling unbearably exposed and vulnerable.

"I was scared, too," he admitted. "Sharing that much passion with you, so quickly, seemed like a betrayal of Beth's memory."

"I know how much you loved her," Caroline said, swallowing the lump in her throat. "It's okay, Jack. I know the two of us could never come close to duplicating what you had with Beth."

"That's true," he said quietly. "But that's because our relationship is unique, not because it's a second-class rerun of something that's already gone before. You're not Beth Warzak, and I'm sure as hell not the same man who married her. I'll always cherish the memory of what Beth and I shared, but my marriage to her has got nothing to do with the way you and I feel about each other right now. We're different people, in a world that's ten years older."

Caroline became preoccupied with pleating the starched white sheet that lay across her lap. She cleared her throat. "How— Um, how do we feel about each other?" she asked.

"Good question." Jack gave one of his quick grins. "Speaking for my part of the we, I'd say we're falling in love." He crooked his finger beneath her chin and tilted her head upward, gazing at her with very blue eyes. "What does your part of the we say?"

Caroline tried to ignore the dazed feeling of happiness shimmering around her. "My part of the we says, get real, we only just met, and everything you know about me is bad. We can't be falling in love, Jack. H-how did you reach such a crazy conclusion?"

"I'm not sure." His mouth quirked into another grin. "I guess the fact that I'm struggling with an almost irresistible urge to murder Joe Rossi might be a clue. Or the fact that I can't wait to meet Andrew and get to know him, simply because he's your son. Or there's always this." He took her hand and carried it to his mouth, kissing the tip of each finger. "Yeah," he said, his voice not quite steady. "I guess the fact that I can't touch you without wanting to make love might be a sign that I'm falling hopelessly in love."

She tried to ignore the line of fire that streaked from his mouth, across her stomach, and deep inside her. "I hate to break this to you, Reverend, but despite your lectures to Marcus and the other kids, sexual desire and love don't always go together."

"I know. But this time, for us, I think they do."

She was scared that he was wrong, even more scared that he might be right. "Jack, how can we...you're a priest. My life is such a mess."

"Not any more. We're straightening everything out. We'll fix Joe Rossi, you'll see. As for the murder rap—hey, what's an arrest warrant for murder between lovers? I already have a plan worked out to get you off."

The pathetic part was that she believed him. What's more, Jack knew she was weakening, willing to accept the nonsensical premise that together they could make everything in her screwed-up life turn out okay.

He took her hand and cradled it against his face, pressing a tender kiss to her palm. "We can do it, Caroline."

She closed her eyes as she felt desire pulse through her veins. "It's crazy to believe we can defeat Joe Rossi."

Jack leaned forward, brushing his mouth against hers and threading his hands through her tangled hair. "First things first," he said. "We need to get our priorities straight. What do you think? If we make love now, could we manage a repeat performance that was as spectacular as before?"

She shook her head, knowing it was impossible ever to feel sensations that amazing again.

"Let's try anyway," he said softly. "I bet we could have a lot of fun trying."

She was still clutching the sheet as if it was a security blanket that could protect her against heaven knew what. The intensity of her foolish desires, most likely Jack stripped the sheet away. She shivered at the chill of the night air, and he gathered her into his arms, kissing her with a passion that warmed her soul at the same time it heated her body. She kissed him back, her mouth open and full beneath his as they collapsed together against the pillows. She wondered why, with Jack, everything that in the past had seemed so complex and difficult suddenly seemed so easy and natural.

He pulled her on top of him and told her how beautiful she was and how much he wanted her. He touched her everywhere, and she touched him in return, exploring his body, inviting him to discover hers, her need for him expanding so far and so fast that it swallowed up every last remnant of her inhibitions.

This time, when he thrust into her, she cried out. When she climaxed, he held her head between his hands, kissing her with a passionate urgency that matched the shuddering force of her orgasm. And then, when she thought there was no way in the world to make the sensations she was experiencing more intense or more powerful, Jack came.

Caroline realized there was only one explanation for Jack's ability to make her feel this way.

She'd fallen hopelessly, irredeemably in love.

They woke with the dawn, both of them recognizing that the euphoria of the previous night needed to give way to hard, practical planning. Caroline raided the pantry and made coffee and instant oatmeal for breakfast, using bowls decorated with big yellow sunflowers. They carried their meal out to the porch, which was refreshingly cool at this hour of the morning.

A cardinal swooped past them in a flash of scarlet and black, heading for the trees. Caroline sipped her coffee, wondering if there were windows in the women's state penitentiary. She wondered when the last woman in Illinois had been given the death penalty. Her hands started to shake, and she set her mug down, afraid of spilling her coffee.

Jack laid his hand over hers in a brief, almost impersonal gesture of reassurance. "Okay," he said. "I guess our party's over for a couple of days. Time to get down to business. What's your plan for rescuing

Andrew from Joe Rossi and how did Dayton Ames fit into it?''

A couple of days? Caroline almost smiled at Jack's sunny optimism, except that even he must realize Joe Rossi wasn't going to be defeated that easily or quickly. "I'm planning to bribe one of Andrew's bodyguards," she said. "Joe tends to rely on money to buy loyalty from the people who work for him. That means more money can sometimes buy their loyalty away."

"Seems reasonable. How much do you figure you'll need?"

"A million bucks seemed like a nice round number. Then I'll need at least another half million to buy forged papers to get myself and Andrew out of the country and established somewhere else."

"I see." He made no comment on the fact that her plans provided no role for him in her future. She'd been all lined up and ready to point out how impossible it would be for him to abandon his parish and come to New Zealand to live under an assumed name. She was perversely irritated when he didn't even suggest he might go with her. In fact, all he said was, "Do you have a specific bodyguard in mind?"

Caroline stared into the trees. The cardinal was nowhere in sight and the sun had disappeared behind a cloud. "I did have someone," she said. "Joe must have found out. His name was Lionel. Joe had him murdered."

"At least he killed him before you paid out your million dollars," Jack pointed out.

Caroline was oddly relieved by Jack's brisk approach. When talking about her father-in-law, she couldn't handle sympathy on top of everything else. "That's where Dayton Ames fits in," she said, trying to imitate Jack's crispness. "He was my money source."

There was an infinitesimal pause before Jack spoke again. "Dayton Ames paid you a million and a half dollars to become his mistress?" he asked.

"He didn't pay me anything," Caroline said. "He bought me a lot of expensive gifts, but I never let him pay me actual money." She shrugged, trying very hard to appear indifferent. "I liked to pretend that as long as he wasn't actually handing over fistfuls of cash, then I wasn't exactly prostituting myself." Jack started to speak and she held up her hand. "No, don't say it. You don't have to point out that I wasn't fooling anyone, not even myself."

"You do a lousy job of guessing what I'm going to say, sweetheart. I think you need to stop punishing yourself for what happened between you and Dayton Ames."

"Do I? Maybe. When I'm safely in my new home with Andrew, I'll be sure to bring it up with my shrink."

"Great. Or you could save yourself a few thousand bucks and have a private word with God. But, in the meantime, I hope like hell you're not gonna tell me the money to bribe the bodyguard is coming from Dayton's will. Because if you're about to inherit a million dollars from Mr. Ames, that would be the icing on the

DA's cake as far as his case against you is concerned."

"I'm pretty sure Dayton hasn't even left me the time of day in his will. My method is much more direct and simple. I'm planning to steal the money I need from one of Dayton's secret accounts in the Cayman Islands."

Jack choked on his coffee. "Excuse me? Would you like to run that by me one more time?"

She stood and walked to the screened windows. "Dayton has in excess of five million dollars' worth of bearer bonds hidden in safety deposit boxes in a bank on Grand Cayman Island. I plan to steal them. When I have false papers ready for me and my son, I'll bribe the bodyguard and we'll all three leave the country. Any money left over once Andrew is safely hidden I plan to donate to various charities that benefit children."

"This is your—quote—direct and simple method of rescuing Andrew?"

"Yes."

He came and stood behind her, wrapping his arms around her waist. "Honey, it's an interesting plan, and I sure hate to sound like a moral stick-in-the-mud, but I guess I have a few reservations about robbing Dayton Ames now that the poor guy is dead. Or even when he was alive, for that matter."

"We'd just be taking back stolen money," Caroline explained. "Dayton Ames was not only being paid to launder money for Joe Rossi, he was stealing from Joe and socking the proceeds away in his accounts in the Cayman Islands. Personally, I rather like the thought of rescuing Andrew by using money stolen from Joe."

"There's a certain appealing symmetry," Jack agreed. "I didn't realize Ames's nest egg was stolen." He turned her within the circle of his arms so they were face-to-face. "Is that why you became Ames's mistress?" he asked. "Because you knew of his connection to Joe and figured there would be some way to get the money you needed out of him?"

"Sort of," she agreed. "After the custody hearing, the only thing that kept me sane was my determination to find out how Joe had managed to produce so much perjured testimony against me. I had this crazy hope that, if I could discover how he'd bought off the witnesses, somehow I'd be able to use the information to appeal for a new hearing. I was trained as a financial analyst, and I have a lot of experience in uncovering facts people would rather keep hidden. I started burrowing into the backgrounds of the men who'd claimed to be my lovers. The only link I could discover was that they all had a connection to Dayton Ames. That seemed very surprising because Dayton Ames was considered a pillar of establishment respectability."

"He still *is* considered a leading and respected Chicago businessman," Jack pointed out. "A dead one, of course, but still respected."

"Yes, but that's just because he was very clever at maintaining his facade. The more I investigated, the more convinced I became that Dayton Ames was the person who'd helped Joe set me up, which meant he couldn't be the squeaky-clean person everyone assumed. Once I suspected a link, I burrowed deeper and started to uncover irregularities in the record keeping of Dayton's supposedly respectable investment fund.''

"If you could do that in a matter of weeks, working on your own with no official resources, how come the FBI or securities and exchange people were never suspicious?"

She shrugged. "I had nothing else to do, so I spent eighteen hours a day investigating him and watching the fund transactions. Besides, I'd been married to Phillip and had spent years watching Joe Rossi, which taught me more than I care to know about how to hide dirty money and where to look for links to organized crime. Plus, Dayton Ames's biggest asset was that nobody suspected him. I did, and that made all the difference.''

"Then why didn't you turn your information over to the DA's office?" Jack asked. "Suborning witnesses is a major crime.''

She shook her head wearily. "After years of living with Phillip, I seem to have developed this sixth sense for spotting people who are involved with organized crime. Dayton Ames stuck out like a cockroach on a white hospital bed, but none of the evidence I had against him would have caused the DA to blink an eye, much less launch an investigation. I decided to arrange a meeting with Dayton. That was easy enough—I knew his schedule by then, and it wasn't difficult to breeze into one of the charity functions he attended and look as if I belonged there. As soon as we were alone, Dayton made a pass at me.''

"It never occurred to him that you might have an ulterior motive? That was careless of him, since he'd been involved in major perjury against you."

"Arrogant, not careless," she said. "Dayton probably derived a piquant satisfaction from knowing I was the woman he'd helped set up. For him, the knowledge that he wasn't the man everyone assumed him to be was like a secret power source, something that added spice to his life."

"So having decided that Dayton Ames was a marginal psychotic with definite criminal tendencies and a murky financial history, you naturally decided to move right in and become his mistress."

"I figured I didn't have much to lose," she said quietly. "I'd already abandoned any hope of getting Andrew back through the courts, and I decided blackmail was probably the best way to go. At that point, I'd developed a new plan. I hoped to persuade Dayton to help me by threatening to reveal that his fund was drawing half its investment capital from organized crime."

Jack kissed her softly. "You do know you're crazy, don't you? You, of all people, ought to know what happens to the guy in the middle when fights break out between various branches of a criminal organization."

"Yes, I know very well," she said flatly. "That's how my husband got killed."

"I'm sorry, sweetheart, I'm so sorry." He wrapped his arms around her waist and held her close for a moment.

She was beginning to like the feeling of being held and cosseted and offered sympathy. Too much, Caroline decided, hardening her heart. It wasn't as if this relationship with Jack had anywhere to go. She moved out of his arms, hoping physical space would help remind her of the emotional barriers she needed to start creating. Loving Jack was one thing. Acting on her feelings was something else again.

"I have a degree in finance," she said, trying to sound brisk. "I've worked as an analyst with investment bankers in New York and Chicago, so I have a lot of firsthand experience in analyzing financial data. Dayton's heart condition tended to make him sleepy, and every time we were together, as soon as he was asleep, I started to make a systematic search of his private files. It didn't take me long to realize he was skimming twenty percent off the top of all the money he was taking in from Joe. It took me a bit longer to discover he was hiding that skimmed money in the Cayman Islands, and I only discovered the access codes to those accounts the week before Dayton died."

"Wait a minute." Jack swung around, eyes hard. "Who else knows the access numbers to those accounts? Ames's wife? His legitimate partners?"

She shook her head. "I doubt it. I'm pretty sure I'm the only person in the world who knows the numbers now Dayton's dead."

"And what about Joe?" Jack asked softly. "Do you think he knows Dayton Ames opened those accounts on the Cayman Islands? Does he know Ames was ripping him off?"

She understood exactly where this conversation was heading. She shifted uncomfortably on the wicker sofa. "I always assumed he didn't. Now I'm not so sure." She cleared her throat. "Dayton was murdered, after all, which is the way Joe invariably takes care of his problems. I suspect that Joe discovered Dayton was ripping him off."

"So, to sum the situation up in a nice small nutshell, Dayton Ames stole several million dollars from Joe Rossi. He squirreled that money away in secret accounts in the Cayman Islands. Joe knows the accounts exist. Dayton Ames is dead, probably murdered by Joe. And you're the only person in the world who knows the numbers that will give Joe access to his money."

Caroline stared at her bare toes. "Er, yes," she said. "I'd say that about sums up the situation."

"Well, that takes care of the first thing we need to do this morning," Jack said briskly. "We'd better get you arrested as soon as we can. A nice, maximum-security jail cell is the safest place for you right now."

"What!" She jumped to her feet. "Jack, for heaven's sake, I can't go to jail! What are you talking about? You promised to help me get to the Cayman Islands! I need that money if I'm going to bribe Andrew's bodyguard—"

"Caroline, get real. How the hell do you plan to evade Joe, the police, the immigration people, customs in the Cayman Islands, bank security wherever Ames has his accounts, and then all the same people in reverse order when you try to get back into the country?"

She couldn't allow herself to feel despair, so she let her temper erupt instead. She spun around, eyes flashing. "I'll make it work," she said. "I didn't ask you for advice, Jack. I just need you to get me on a plane to the Cayman Islands, that's all."

"All right," he said. "And suppose by some amazing piece of good luck your scheme works and you get your money, and the bodyguard doesn't run off with it to Hawaii, and you and Andrew actually escape into the sunset—what do you think Joe's going to do? Cut his losses and move on? I don't think so, and neither do you. We both know Joe will pursue you and his grandson with every resource he can command. He'd even have the law on his side, because you have a murder warrant outstanding against you. Not to mention the minor detail that Joe was legally awarded custody of Andrew."

"So what do you want me to do?" she demanded through clenched teeth, hating him because he was right, hating herself because she was crying and helpless and all the things she'd sworn she wouldn't be. "Do you expect me to sit back and resign myself to having Andrew raised by a monster?"

"No," he said quietly. "I want you to sit back and listen to the plan I have in mind."

Fifteen

It was almost four o'clock when Jack returned to the cottage. "It's done," he said, looking tired but triumphant. "Donohoe took my information straight to his captain, and the captain took it to the commissioner. They know what I'm trying to do and they've agreed to help."

"I guess that's good." Caroline paced nervously. "Is Donohoe absolutely sure he can trust his captain?"

"He's positive. He's known the captain and the commissioner for years, and he insists that whoever else in the department may be on the take, they're not."

"I can't believe the police commissioner agreed to help—"

"They're willing to adopt a wait-and-see attitude about our accusations. Why not? From their point of view, what I suggested is pretty low risk. You're their chief suspect in the Dayton Ames murder case, and I've told them where they can pick you up. Once you're safely in jail, they have no objections whatsoever if I try to bring down a major organized crime figure at the same time they pursue their case against you."

Caroline's mouth twisted wryly. "Do any of them really believe I might be innocent of Dayton's murder?"

"I doubt it," Jack said calmly. "But that doesn't matter at the moment. They're willing to ask Felicity a few tough questions, and they're going to see if they can turn up any evidence that the other bottles of wine were poisoned. That's enough to start with. We already knew we couldn't count on the police to make the case against Felicity Ames."

"How about them making a case against Joe Rossi?"

"All we need is cooperation from the commissioner, and they've promised me that. With any luck, Joe will incriminate himself. Frank Donohoe's already laid the groundwork for the first leak. Most of the cops have been told nothing except that a hot tip was called in revealing your location. A couple of privileged insiders—cops they suspect of having links to organized crime—have been told I'm the tipster."

Caroline paced, too full of nervous tension to stay still. "If Joe's contacts in the Chicago police department are even half as good as they are in Atlantic City, he'll know before morning that the Reverend Jack Fletcher turned me in."

"Let's hope so," Jack said, his voice grim.

She glanced toward him. "What aren't you telling me? You're on edge."

Jack took her hands and held them tightly. "We don't have long to wait before they'll be here, Caroline. When I left the commissioner's office, Donohoe was already coordinating with the detectives downtown who are in charge of the case. They'll be coming before five to arrest you.''

She swallowed hard. "So soon?"

"They want to make their move in broad daylight, and I didn't try to discourage them. That way, there's less chance of some rookie getting jumpy and putting a bullet through us. Or through one of his fellow cops.''

"There's that," she said. "On the other hand, I'll probably be the lead story on the local evening news."

The look Jack gave her was cool and steady. "Yes, I'm hoping you will be."

Caroline tried to sound brave and confident, but her voice came out small, shaky and timid. "Jack, do you think there's any chance in the world that this plan of ours is going to work?"

"We'll make it work," he said. "Remember, in this game, we're the ones who have most of the cards hidden up our sleeves."

"But Joe never plays by the rules, so he doesn't care who has the best cards. And if he thinks he's losing, he'll chop off your arms. It may not be subtle, but it's a surefire method of finding hidden aces."

"Sweetheart, we came up with the best plan we could. Now we have to stop second-guessing ourselves." He took her into his arms and kissed her long and hard. "Joe Rossi is a greedy man. We're going to make him an offer he won't be able to refuse. He'll walk into our net, and then he'll be caught. Scams always work best if they take advantage of a person's weakness. We're doing that."

With Jack right by her side, with his arms around her and his kiss still warm on her lips, she could almost believe they would be able to slay the dragon. She knew she wouldn't feel quite so confident this time tomorrow, when she'd been locked up in jail for twenty-four hours and the full weight of the law was arrayed against her.

"Don't worry, sweetheart." Jack stroked her hair. "I promise, this time we're going to win one for the good guys."

In the distance, she heard the faint drone of an engine. She looked at him questioningly. He crossed to the window, raised a corner of the flowered curtain, then nodded once.

She wrapped her arms around her waist. "This is it then."

"The beginning of the end," Jack said. "Hang on for a couple more days, sweetheart. That's all it's going to take."

He kissed her again, not hard this time, but with a slow and tender passion that made her throat ache. When she opened her eyes, the distant drone of the engine had faded into an ominous silence, but some of her paralyzing fear had gone.

"I love you, Jack." She'd had no idea she was going to say the words until they were spoken.

Jack smiled, his startlingly handsome face suffused with warmth, his sexy green eyes shadowed with tenderness. She wondered how she could ever have thought, even for a moment, that he looked like Phillip. "I love you, too," he said. He grinned. "I like saying that. It feels good. I love you, sweetheart."

Leaves rustled. A twig snapped, followed by an abrupt silence. Jack sneaked another quick glance from behind the curtains. "I can't see the police," he said, keeping his voice low. "But there's a TV roving minicam parked a hundred yards down the road. I guess Frank decided to give the local news people a ringside view of your arrest."

Caroline rubbed her hands up and down her arms, still finding it difficult to make the mental switch from hiding to actively seeking the glare of publicity. "I guess we should pretend we didn't hear anything."

"Yes. Why don't you start packing? Make it look as if we're getting ready to run."

Right at this moment, Caroline thought, running sounds like a really desirable option. She resisted the temptation to suggest that maybe they should just make a dash for the airport, after all. Numbly, she walked into the bedroom and began to stuff underwear and T-shirts into a backpack they'd found in the mudroom. Jack brought her purse and cosmetic pouch from the bathroom.

"You have the key to the safety deposit box, right?" she asked.

He fished in the back pocket of his jeans, then held up the key she'd given him.

She gave up the pretense of packing. "They're moving into position," she whispered. "They're surrounding the cottage. Can you hear them?"

"Yes." He put his arm around her. "Think about Andrew," he said. "Think about having him home in just a few days."

Heavy fists pounded on the front door. "This is the police, open up! We have a search warrant."

The police allowed her no chance to comply with their demand. She and Jack had barely made it halfway to the door when she heard the crash of an ax, splintering the panels and sending wood chips flying.

"Hey!" Jack gave a convincing roar of outrage. "What the blazes is going on? What are you doing?"

Three armed policemen burst through the door. One of them made a dive for Jack, the other two ran straight for Caroline.

"Don't shoot!" she yelled, holding her hands high and wide, scared damn near witless.

"What's going on?" Jack demanded, panting. "This is private property. What right do you have to break into a home—"

"Stow it, Reverend Fletcher. You know you're harboring a wanted fugitive. Keep your mouth shut, or I'll have you arrested for aiding and abetting." Frank Donohoe strode into the cottage, waving a sheaf of papers, looking nothing at all like the friendly Irishman Caroline had met the day before.

"Caroline Hogarth, we have a warrant for your arrest for the first-degree murder of Dayton Ames."

"I didn't do it," she said, instinctively turning to flee. "You're making a terrible mistake," she protested, struggling as a police officer grabbed her arms and slipped on a pair of handcuffs. "Jack, don't let them do this to me! Tell them I'm innocent. Oh, my God, I didn't do it!''

Jack tugged against the restraining arms of the cop holding him. "This is outrageous—"

"I've warned you, Reverend Fletcher, keep your mouth shut tight." Frank Donohoe glared at Jack, then spun around and gave Caroline a look she imagined he reserved for the scum bags of the world. Was he acting? Or did he still believe she'd murdered Dayton Ames, despite what Jack had told him about Felicity and the wine?

"I'm making you aware of your rights, Ms. Hogarth. You have a right to remain silent, but any statement you make can be used in evidence against you. You have the right to an attorney, and if you can't afford to pay for one, the State of Illinois will appoint one on your behalf—"

"I know my rights," she said, her voice shaking. From the corner of her eyes she saw that police officers were swarming through the house, searching for heaven knows what evidence of her criminal activities. Her stomach knotted into a tight ball of fear, and she had no doubt her face was white as a sheet. *Please God, let this plan work!* If she and Jack couldn't manage to incriminate Joe Rossi, how in the world was she going to beat the rap for Dayton's murder? It was unbearable to think Joe might win the final victory and incriminate her for the murder of his own partner. What in God's name would happen to Andrew if she was convicted of murder?

Her throat was already so dry she had to swallow twice before she could speak. "Who told you I was here? How did you find me?"

"We had a tip from a public-spirited citizen," Frank said, taking her arm and propelling her toward the ruined front door. He didn't even glance toward Jack when he spoke.

Through the haze of her fear, Caroline saw that four TV journalists were lined up outside, microphones at the ready, cameras waiting to whir.

Caroline looked into the cottage. "Jack!" she called out, her voice trembling. "Jack, help me! Please tell them I didn't kill Dayton Ames! Oh, my God, tell them I'm innocent!"

The reporters pressed forward, delighted that for once they'd captured an arrest on tape in which the suspect was providing a welcome touch of melodrama. Caroline, unlike most suspects, hadn't even had the smarts to cover her head with a jacket, which meant this would make for a really terrific piece of film.

Frank Donohoe waved the reporters aside. "No comment," he said in answer to their barrage of questions. "The department will be issuing a statement later this evening."

Just in time for the late-night news, Caroline thought, seized by a gasp of wild laughter. She sure was making it big tonight. Pictures at six and again at ten.

She was bundled into a waiting squad car, with police officers wedged on either side. Her last view of the Warzak cottage was of Jack, surrounded by policemen, declaiming into the TV cameras that Caroline Hogarth was a wonderful woman, terribly misunderstood, and that he was utterly and completely convinced of her innocence. If that naive speech didn't convict her in the minds of the general public, Caroline thought wryly, she couldn't imagine what would.

Jack placed his phone call to Mr. Clive Reese Burroughs at nine o'clock sharp the following morning. A snooty female voice responded. "Burroughs, Greenaway and Henderson, good morning."

"Hello, sweetie. Good morning to you, too. I'd like to speak to Mr. Burroughs."

"Mr. Burroughs is not available to take calls this morning." The snooty voice was cold enough to flash-freeze any turkey who addressed her as sweetie.

"Sure he is, sweetie. You can tell him I'm a real impatient guy. In fact, why don't you tell him that in two minutes, I'm gonna hang up and call the police instead."

The threat caught her attention immediately, which suggested Ms. Snooty was well aware that her employers didn't pay her wages with money earned representing the innocent and the oppressed. "Mr. Burroughs is in conference. He's left strict orders that he isn't to be interrupted."

"Then you're gonna have to disobey orders, sweetie, or Mr. Burroughs will be real mad at you. Tell him I need to talk about his client, Mr. Joseph Rossi."

"Who is this calling—"

"You have one minute and ten seconds to get him to the phone. And counting."

The line went dead for a full minute. Jack started to sweat. Finally an irate, cultured male voice spoke. "Who are you? I trust you have something very important you wish to discuss with me."

"Sure do, Mr. Burroughs. My name's Jack Fletcher. The Reverend Jack Fletcher of St. Luke's Episcopal Church. I want to meet with Joe Rossi. This afternoon at three-thirty would fit in well with my schedule. It's after my vestry meeting and before Evensong."

There was a moment of astonished silence, followed by a quick bark of laughter. "You have balls, Reverend Fletcher, I'll grant you that. However, you've approached entirely the wrong man. I have no idea who Joe Rossi might be, much less how to arrange a mee—"

"Tell Mr. Rossi that I'm a friend of Caroline Hogarth's," Jack said. "Tell him I might be interested in setting up a joint venture with him in the Cayman Islands."

"Reverend Fletcher, I am a busy man. No doubt this Mr. Rossi you speak of is also a busy man—"

"Yeah, I guess he is, Mr. Burroughs. That's why I want you to make sure he's expecting me. Tell him to arrange for his bodyguards to let me in without any hassle. Three-thirty this afternoon at his apartment."

Jack hung up the phone without giving Burroughs a chance to respond. He leaned against the wall of his living room, shaking as memories of bad times in jail crowded in. There was nothing like dealing with a sleazy lawyer to remind you of how it felt to be part of the slime such people fed on. He'd better get his emotions under control before his meeting or Joe would make chopped liver out of him.

Jack stuck his head under the bathroom tap, sluicing himself with cold water. He decided that when he went visiting this afternoon, he'd wear his full dress uniform. Dog collar, cassock, fringed sash, silver crucifix, the works. He suspected that there were few things Joe Rossi would enjoy more than planning the corruption of a minister of religion. And if Joe was having fun, he might become careless. Jack sure as heck hoped so.

The news of Caroline Hogarth's arrest sent Joe into such a predictable paroxysm of rage that the *consigliere* for Chicago called and apologized for Steve and Gerry's incompetence. Not that Joe believed the apology was sincere, not for a minute, but the politics of working on somebody else's turf forced him to keep his anger under tight control and pretend that it was no big deal. It would be no advantage to him if word got out that he was losing his grip, that a woman—a girl, a member of his own family—was causing him so much trouble that he couldn't keep a civil tongue in his head.

He was sick and tired of Illinois, sick and tired of incompetent fools like Steve and Gerry. He longed to get back to his home in Atlantic City, to be among familiar people, in familiar places. There'd been two major state highway contracts awarded in New Jersey during the past month, and not one of his construction companies had been given a piece of the action. Jesus, he needed to go home and bust some ass.

Between Dayton Ames and that bitch who'd married his boy, he'd been screwed, but good. God! His stomach was eaten away with acid just thinking of how Caroline was the only living person who knew the codes that would enable him to get back the money Dayton Ames had stolen. And she was in jail, for Christ's sake! How the hell was he gonna get those damn bank codes from her? The problem gnawed away at him, day and night, destroying his peace of mind.

Joe pulled back his starched cuff and glanced at his Rolex. "Three-thirty. That asshole priest of yours should be here by now."

Clive Burroughs coughed. "He's not my priest, Joe. I just reported to you what he said when he telephoned. That he was a friend of Caroline Hogarth's and that he was interested in considering a joint venture with you in the Cayman Islands."

"You checked him out? He's really a priest?" Joe had already heard from his sources inside the police department that the Reverend Jack Fletcher was the guy who'd tipped off the cops as to where Caroline Hogarth could be found. Still, he always liked to double-check his facts. Information, knowledge. That was what made for power these days, not muscle. Joe was proud of the fact that he'd been the first *consigliere* in the country to run a fully computerized operation. Now every branch of his organization was stacked out with corporate suits, playing with spread sheets and establishing cost control systems. That had been the trouble with Phillip, Joe reflected sadly. He'd been so hung up on what had happened in the past that he couldn't see the possibilities for the organization in the future. With Andrew, though, it would all be different. For Andrew's third birthday, Joe had bought the kid his own computer. Andrew was not only smart—Joe would see to it that he was prepared to lead the organization into the twenty-first century.

"Yes, Fletcher's a priest," Burroughs said. "Not Catholic, you understand, but he's an ordained minister. Graduated from theological seminary eight years ago, after he got out of the state pen."

"He's been in jail? What for?"

"Manslaughter. He beat a vagrant to death with his bare hands."

Joe grunted. "So now he's got religion, is that what you're telling me?"

"I have no idea, Joe. I've only had time to run a quick background check. He's been working at St. Luke's Episcopal Church for the last six years. He's established a slew of neighborhood youth programs, and he's active in the city's AIDS awareness campaigns."

"Then he's probably a faggot," Joe said sourly. "A priest should be telling people that if they're living right, they won't catch AIDS. Instead, they put condoms in high schools, tell the girls they don't need to be virgins when they get married, and then they wonder why the country's going to hell."

The intercom on his phone buzzed and he depressed the speaker button. "Yes?"

"I got a Reverend Fletcher waitin' with me, Mr. Rossi. He passed inspection with the boys downstairs and I frisked him good. He's clean. No wires, no weapons, no nothin'."

"Send him in."

When the priest walked into the room, for a split second, Joe's stomach cramped with pain. He was so damned clean-cut and handsome that it was like looking at a taller, less swarthy version of Phillip. While Joe was still staring, Clive Burroughs stepped forward.

"You're five minutes late, Reverend Fletcher."

The priest's gaze flicked briefly, almost dismissively, over the lawyer. "There was a lot of traffic."

Burroughs cleared his throat. "Mr. Rossi has agreed to meet with you, despite the fact that he has no idea why you would expect him to be interested in a joint venture in the Cayman Islands."

"Is that so?" The priest nodded toward Joe, and the illusion of likeness to Phillip vanished. Unlike Phillip, Joe realized at once, this guy was smart and tough and knew exactly what he wanted.

"I'm glad you could free up some of your valuable time to meet with me, Mr. Rossi."

"Yeah, well, not very much time." Joe decided that with a cocky bastard like this there was no point in beating around the bush. "Mr. Burroughs tells me you're a friend of Caroline Hogarth's."

Fletcher smiled. "I'm happy to say that Caroline considers me a very good friend, Mr. Rossi."

There was a definite undercurrent to the simple statement. Joe's gaze locked with the priest's, and a flash of understanding passed between them. The Reverend Jack Fletcher had turned Caroline in to the police. Joe knew that. And Fletcher knew that Joe knew. But Caroline still believed Fletcher was her friend. Oh, yes, Joe thought, clamping down on a twist of excitement. This guy's smart, all right.

Clive Burroughs steepled his fingers and peered over his reading glasses at the priest. "Caroline Hogarth may be your friend, Reverend Fletcher, but it pains me to state that she is also a whore and an accused murderer. Hardly a suitable companion for a minister of religion."

Fletcher smiled with so much cynicism that Joe couldn't help but like him. "As a minister of religion, Mr. Burroughs, it's my duty to consort with the whores and murderers of the world. We can always pray that I may be able to guide them toward repentance."

"Er, yes, I suppose you can." Clive Burroughs recovered and tried to look like the sort of attorney respectable people invited to dinner. "Reverend Fletcher, I'm not at all sure why you phoned me this morning. Why do you need to speak with Mr. Rossi?"

"Because I have a proposition to make to him, what else?"

"Then make it," Burroughs said.

Fletcher's gaze switched to Joe. "Mr. Rossi, I believe this interview would be more productive for both of us if you sent your attorney to check on your corporate tax return, or whatever it is he does to earn his retainer."

Joe glanced toward Burroughs. "Mr. Burroughs gets real nervous when I listen to business proposals and he's not around."

"Five million dollars," Jack said. "From the Dayton Investment Fund. Currently stored in a numbered account in the Cayman Islands. Don't you think it would be better if we talked about this alone, just the two of us?"

This time Joe didn't even bother to look around. "Go push some papers, Clive. I'll call you if I need you."

"Joe, I think I should warn you that in my considered opinion the Reverend Fletcher is not a man to be trusted—"

Joe wondered why it was his destiny to be surrounded by assholes. Stupid assholes. "Get out," he said to Burroughs.

Fletcher spoke politely. "Goodbye, Mr. Burroughs. Thanks for arranging this meeting."

Burroughs left the room without answering, his heavy brows drawn together in a furious scowl. Joe beckoned Fletcher over to the window and gestured toward the lake. "Admire the view, why don't you, Reverend. I reckon it must have cost me about a million bucks, because it sure ain't the facilities of the apartment that I'm paying for."

Fletcher walked over to the window, deliberately positioning himself with his back to the view. Joe liked that. Fletcher leaned forward. "This meeting's taking too long, Mr. Rossi. I'd like to talk to you about reclaiming five million dollars' worth of bearer bonds sitting in a bank on Grand Cayman Island. Are you interested, or should I take my information elsewhere?"

"Don't try to get smart, Father. You burned your boats when you arranged this meeting. You aren't taking your information any place. If you need to sneeze from now on, you better ask me first."

"Seems to me, Mr. Rossi, that you're confused about the situation we have here. I happen to know you want to get your hands on that five million dollars even more than I do. And there are only two people alive today who know where the money's hidden. One of them is Caroline Hogarth, and we both know you could kill her before she'd talk. And the other person is me. So you'd better hope nothing happens to my health over the next few days, Mr. Rossi, or you're gonna be out of luck."

Joe gave him a sharp look. "Are you willing to be more talkative than Caroline, Reverend Fletcher?"

"I might be, Mr. Rossi, under the right circumstances. And for the right price."

Joe was too old and too wise to jump right in just because somebody suggested the water was refreshing. "Let's make sure we both understand what we're talking about, Reverend. Seems like we both know Dayton Ames stashed five million dollars that he stole from me in a bank in the Cayman Islands. Caroline Hogarth knows how to access the accounts. So far, so good. But don't expect me to believe you know the name of the bank, much less how to get at the money. These past couple of years, Caroline hasn't trusted anyone with the name of her hairdresser, much less with the secret of where she's hidden five million bucks."

"Vincent's on State Street," Jack said.

"What?"

Jack gave a long, slow smile. "Caroline's hairdresser, Mr. Rossi."

Joe gave a crack of laughter. "Okay, but that doesn't prove anything about the bank."

"I think it does," Jack said. "It's a touching story, Mr. Rossi, and I'll spare you the details, but it seems Caroline has fallen in love. With me. And as a result, she trusts me. Completely."

"I know my ex-daughter-in-law, Reverend. Somehow, I find it real hard to picture her head over heels in love with anyone, even a handsome son of a bitch like you."

The priest shrugged. "She's a woman, right? Press the right buttons, and you can have any one you want."

He sounded bored, almost indifferent. Joe was impressed. "If Caroline trusted you with the access numbers to five million bucks, looks to me like that was her first big mistake."

"No, Mr. Rossi. I'd say it was her last."

Jesus, but this guy was sending chills down his spine. "If you know where she's hidden the money, why don't you go get it? What you comin' to me for?"

Fletcher sighed. "I'm a realist, Joe— You don't mind if I call you that, do you? And of course, you must call me Jack. I have no experience in smuggling bearer bonds into the good old U.S. of A. I have even less idea how to cash 'em without bringing the police and the IRS crashing down on my neck."

"Most people would be prepared to take the risk, if they really knew where the money was hidden."

"Well, Joe, I know where the money's hidden, all right, but I sure don't like the thought of spending the next twenty years in jail if I'm caught smuggling those suckers into the country. It's a funny old justice system, you know. Kill a guy and they give you four or five years with time off for good behavior. But do something that upsets the fat cats, like messing with their money, and they send you away for so many years you go senile waiting for the parole board to give you a hearing. I had a real unpleasant stay the last time I was a guest of the State of Illinois, so I figured this time I'd let somebody else do the dirty work, and I'd sit back and take a percentage of the profits."

"What makes you think I'm willing to do your dirty work for you?" Joe asked.

Fletcher gave Joe's arm a friendly punch. "Like I said, Joe, I have a hunch that you want this particular five million dollars real bad."

Joe didn't bother with any more denials. If Jack Fletcher knew where to find the money, then Joe would go get it. If he was lying—hell, he might stay alive just long enough to realize that he shouldn't have messed with Joe Rossi. "What do you expect your cut to be?" he asked, shaking off Jack's hold on his arm.

Fletcher smiled. "A lot of folks might think that I deserve half. But I'm a reasonable man, Joe, and you're going to have a lot of expenses bringing the money out. I figure a straight million bucks would be fair payment."

Joe laughed, pretending to be shocked. He was already figuring out various ways to screw Fletcher over and pay him nothing at all. "A million bucks! What you been smokin', Reverend? If I paid you a hundred thousand bucks, cash, my associates would tell me I'm crazy. And you're askin' for a million!''

The priest stood up very straight, making Joe aware of just how tall he actually was. "All right, Joe. I'll make this easy on both of us. No wasting our valuable time haggling. I'll tell you my bottom line. I want two hundred and fifty thousand dollars, paid into my personal account in Zurich, Switzerland, and I'll take the other two hundred and fifty, same place of payment, when you've cashed the bonds and cleared your money. That's my bottom line. No negotiations.''

"You gotta be kidding!" Joe protested, outraged. "A half a million bucks, and fifty percent of it up front! You're outta your mind! By the time I pay the courier and meet the other expenses, I'll be lucky to clear three million. And it was *my* friggin' money in the first place!" He thumped his fist on the desk, genuinely aggrieved despite having no intention of honoring any deal they might negotiate.

Fletcher shook his head, feigning sympathy. "Some investments just don't work out like they should, do they? Mr. Dayton Ames looked like he had such a reliable investment fund, too.''

Joe's temper snapped. He shook his fist in Jack's face. "Listen, you little prick, you get two hundred thousand when the deal pans out. And you better come across with those friggin' account numbers right this minute, or I'm gonna turn you over to my boys and have them work some sense—" He broke off in astonishment. "Where the hell do you think you're going?''

"I have another meeting," Fletcher said. "Sorry, Joe, but you have to realize that there's more than one party interested in making five million real easy dollars."

"Not so fast, smart ass. You don't think I'm just gonna let you walk out of here, do you?"

Fletcher leaned against the door, folding his arms across his chest, real casual. "Your boys can beat the shit out of me, Joe, and I'm not going to tell them those account numbers, for one very good reason. I don't know them. Not yet. You didn't let me finish explaining the deal."

Joe felt a little ball of pain explode behind his left eyeball. He breathed deeply. "Then what the hell are you wasting my time for—"

"I said I could get those numbers for you, Joe. And I can. But I don't have them right now. I know which bank the funds are hidden in, but I don't have the codes I need to access the safety deposit boxes where the bonds are hidden."

"And just how the hell do you think you're gonna get the access codes?"

Fletcher smiled. "Caroline is going to give them to me. Naturally."

Joe felt bitterly disappointed. This guy was as dumb as all the other people he had to work with. "Caroline isn't going to give you the access numbers," he said. "Why would she? Just because you ask her real nice? Trust me, pretty as you are, you ain't pretty enough to persuade her to talk."

"Caroline's going to give me those account numbers for one simple reason, Joe, and it's got nothing to do with how I ask her or whether she thinks I'm pretty."

"What, then?"

"I'm going to visit her in jail first thing tomorrow morning, and I plan to tell her you've agreed to return Andrew to her in exchange for the account numbers."

"Give her my grandson?" Joe realized suddenly that he felt old and tired and discouraged. "That's no plan at all," he said wearily. "Caroline knows I wouldn't give up Andrew for five million dollars. Hell, you couldn't pay me enough to give him up. You can't swing the deal, Jack, because Caroline won't believe you can deliver."

He reached for the intercom buzzer, but Jack crossed the room and grabbed his hand, stopping him. "Caroline knows she won't get Andrew back for five million dollars, Joe, she's not a fool. But when I went to hear her confession last night, she told me she has something else you want even more than you want the five million bucks Dayton Ames stole from you."

"More money? Even if she has it, I told you, my grandson's not for sale."

"Not money, Joe, information. Caroline's willing to give you the name of the man who murdered Phillip. Your son."

Joe was silent for a moment, absorbing the enormity of what Fletcher was suggesting. He wondered if there was a chance in hell that Caroline actually knew the truth. Joe had offered rewards, promises, bribes and threats. He'd gotten nothing in return, not even the name of the trigger man, much less the name of the man who'd ordered the hit. There'd been a hundred rumors on the street about who killed Phillip. And no facts, not a one.

He'd be damned if he was gonna let this guy see the tears in his eyes. Jesus, he still missed Phillip like it was yesterday the boy had died. He stared out the window, his back toward the priest. "How will I know she's giving me the true name?" he asked finally. "Has Caroline got some proof that she's telling the truth? Otherwise, how will I know she isn't just messin' with me to get Andrew back?"

"She has proof," Fletcher said. "She's willing to surrender that proof to you at the same time you give her back her son."

Joe had years of experience in assessing deals. Something told him this one was for real. Jack Fletcher could deliver on his promises. Which meant that Joe needed to work out an effective double cross to ensure he got five million bucks *and* the name of the man who'd murdered Phillip—without surrendering Andrew. First step was to accept the deal without looking too eager.

"You talk good," he said. "So far, I've seen no evidence you can deliver."

Fletcher cupped his hands around his crucifix. For a horrible moment, Joe thought he was going to start praying. Instead, Fletcher must have pressed a concealed spring in the side of the crucifix. It sprang open, revealing that it was hollow inside.

A small brass key tumbled out of the crucifix into Jack Fletcher's waiting hand. He held it up, letting it catch the light from the giant picture window, then he tossed it to Joe.

Joe caught the key, turning it over in his hand. "What's this?" he asked.

"A gesture of good faith, Joe." Fletcher gave another of his chilling smiles. "It's the key to the safety deposit box where Caroline has stored the documents concerning the murder of her husband. Your son."

"Caroline gave it to you?"

Fletcher nodded.

Joe fingered the key. "It's no good to me if I don't know which bank the box is at."

"It's no good to you even if you know the bank, Joe. Caroline's the only person in the world the bank will allow to open that box. If you want that information, Caroline will have to go to the bank with you."

"But she's in jail!" Joe exclaimed. To his annoyance, he realized he'd once again lost control of the conversation.

Fletcher grinned. "Right, Joe. And that's why you're going to send your Mr. Burroughs to get her released. But not until we're ready for her, of course."

Burroughs would have no difficulty getting Caroline released. Hell, the guy could probably spring a parakeet from the jaws of a hungry tiger. Why hadn't it occurred to him to use Burroughs to get Caroline out of jail? Joe wondered. These days, he just didn't seem to be thinking as quick and as smart as he had in the old days. Truth be told, it scared him a little that Fletcher seemed to be always one step ahead in their conversation. Still, there was no harm in listening to what the guy had on his mind, was there? Once he knew what Fletcher was proposing, Joe would come up with some neat, efficient way to screw him over. If all else failed, he could always arrange to have him eliminated. Lure him down to the Chicago projects, and he could be knocked off for the price of a month's supply of crack.

Joe put the key in the center of his desk and gave Fletcher a brief, friendly smile. "All right, Reverend, you got my attention. What's your plan? I'd like to hear it."

Sixteen

Four reporters had waited outside the cottage to see her arrested. It seemed to Caroline there were at least a hundred and four waiting to see her emerge from the courthouse when she was released on bail. Clive Burroughs, looking like the star of a TV miniseries in his thousand-dollar suit and two-hundred-dollar haircut, didn't attempt to hustle her into his waiting BMW. Instead, he stood on the courthouse steps, his arm clamped around her shoulders, and stared solemnly into the ranks of cameras. She suspected he'd learned long ago that viewers were suspicious of lawyers who looked too cheerful.

"Ms. Hogarth thanks you all for your interest and concern on her behalf," he said, blandly ignoring the fact that ninety percent of the American public considered her a coldhearted killer. "She has naturally found the past forty-eight hours very trying, and she is anxious to go home and rest."

One reporter's question rose over all the others. Caroline recognized Ms. Perky from Chicago's superstation. "The prosecution didn't oppose your request for bail, Counselor. Given that your client refused to surrender voluntarily two days ago, have you any idea why the prosecution no longer considers her a flight risk?''

Burroughs didn't even blink. "It's not for me to second-guess the DA's office," he said, his voice smooth as heavy cream. "However, we did suggest a couple of new lines of inquiry that the DA's investigators might want to pursue in relation to the murder of Mr. Ames." His bland, all-purpose smile shaded into malice. "You might care to address your future questions to Mrs. Felicity Ames. I believe the police are expecting her to shed some very interesting light on their inquiries. Thank you, ladies and gentlemen, that's all we have to say."

The reporters were stunned into silence. While they were still trying to calculate whether they'd get more mileage from pursuing Dayton Ames's mistress or setting tracks to harass his wife, Clive Burroughs hustled Caroline into his car. The chauffeur, well versed in the art of courthouse getaways, drove off without waiting for instructions.

Caroline leaned back in the far corner of the gray leather seat. She should have been grateful to Burroughs for the masterful way he'd liberated her and set the authorities and the public sniffing on Felicity's trail, but she found it hard to be indebted to a man with all the moral integrity of a sea slug.

"Where are you taking me?" she asked, knowing that Burroughs would have had his orders from Joe and that she didn't have a hope of countermanding them.

"My offices downtown," he said.

"I see." She glanced toward the driver, then decided she could safely ignore him. Nothing she planned to say could be used against her, and she wanted to find out how much Joe had told his lawyer. "Why did Joe decide to have you spring me?" she asked. "He went to such trouble to set me up, I can't understand why he's letting me go."

"You have your tame priest to thank." Burroughs didn't sound as if he liked Jack very much, but she couldn't tell how much he knew about the deal between Jack and Joe Rossi. "Your priest has persuaded Joe you're more valuable out of jail than in. So Felicity's been fed to the wolves to distract them from you."

"What does that mean?" Caroline asked. "Why are the police going to believe Felicity had anything to do with Dayton's murder?"

Clive Burroughs gave a thin smile. "Mrs. Ames has a taste for tall, muscular blondes. Female blondes. Which Dayton Ames discovered last month and wasn't at all happy about."

Caroline's eyes opened wide. "Felicity was having an affair? With a woman? I didn't know . . ."

"Multiple affairs, multiple women. Joe's been keeping an eye on her ever since he and Ames became partners, and he's collected a package of real interesting photos. He sent the photos to the police, along with the information that Ames was planning to file for divorce and claim custody of their daughter. He's also alerted the police to the fact that the pharmacist who claimed to have sold you that digoxin has a severe cocaine habit, and that his word isn't to be trusted." Burroughs smirked. "I think you could safely say Joe has cooked Felicity's goose."

Caroline felt a moment of sympathy for the hapless Felicity Ames. "I guess she's learning her lessons the hard way," she said. "If you decide to murder your husband, don't hire a criminal as your partner."

"Or take more efficient steps to cover your ass," Burroughs said dryly. "But let us move on to another subject, leaving the police to discover for themselves that Felicity Ames is not quite the devoted and grieving wife they believed her to be. Mr. Rossi has asked me to inform you that arrangements have been made to bring his grandson from the family home in Atlantic City to Chicago. Andrew will be arriving late this evening. I believe discussions are currently under way between the Reverend Fletcher and Mr. Rossi as to the precise terms and conditions under which Andrew will be delivered into your custody."

Caroline closed her eyes, emotions rioting inside her so violently that she didn't dare speak or even look in Burroughs's direction. Andrew! Dear God, she could barely allow herself to hope she would see him tomorrow for fear she would go insane with longing. She gulped in a couple of lungfuls of air, trying to recover her voice before her silence became too revealing.

"I hope Joe remembers I'm not a fool," she said finally. "Just because he's dangling Andrew as a reward in front of me, he needs to realize I'm not going to agree to any arrangement that gives him the money he wants before I have physical custody of my son."

"Joe hasn't seen fit to include me in the negotiations he's conducted with Jack Fletcher," Burroughs said, his voice tinged with genuine resentment. "However, from what I've seen of the results, I'd say your priest is doing an excellent job negotiating on your behalf."

"That's because he loves me and wants what's best for me," Caroline said, aware that the lawyer would report their conversation to Joe and that it could only be advantageous to appear besotted. The more she appeared to trust Jack, the more Joe would delight in counting on him to betray her.

She faked a wistful sigh. "After all those terrible years of being married to Phillip, it took me a while to understand what it means to be loved and valued for the person I am. Jack's shown me the meaning of true love."

"Very touching," Burroughs said. "Makes me want to run right out and get in touch with my inner child. But we've just arrived at my offices, so I guess I'll have to concentrate on more practical matters for a while."

They drove into an underground parking garage and took the high-speed elevator to the thirtieth floor. Burroughs hustled her through the reception area and straight into a private suite of rooms, where Jack was waiting for her. She flew into his arms, not entirely pretending when she clung to him, her eyes filling with unexpected tears.

Jack's arms tightened around her. "Hi, sweetheart, it's wonderful to see you again. I've missed you so much. I guess you had a rough couple of days."

She stepped back, wiping her eyes with the heel of her hand. "Not too good." She grimaced. "What I want to do most of all is take a shower. I smell of disinfectant.''

"You shall have a shower, sweetheart, in just a minute. But first things first. We need to talk. Mr. Burroughs, would you mind giving us a few minutes of privacy?''

"Not at all." The lawyer managed to sound like a kindhearted old gentleman whose sole purpose in life was to make Caroline and Jack happy. "I'll arrange for some refreshments to be sent in. Shall we say in twenty minutes?''

"Great." Jack closed the door, then took Caroline into his arms again, this time kissing her without any pretense. When they finally broke apart, he continued to hold her in his arms. "Sweetheart, we need to talk.''

"Jack, we can't speak here. The place is sure to be bugged, otherwise Burroughs wouldn't have been so agreeable. Joe's probably sitting in an office down the hallway, waiting for us to say something interesting.''

"No, dearest." Jack patted her on the back. "This office isn't bugged, I promise you. I checked it out myself.''

From the way his eyes gleamed, she knew he was warning her he was lying. She debated for a split second and decided she'd better not appear naive enough to accept his word.

"Jack, you still don't understand what sort of a man Joe is and what sort of people agree to work for him. Burroughs would never have left us alone unless he could hear what we're saying. Trust me, anything we say in this room is going to be recorded. Accept the fact that Joe and his snake-oil lawyer are listening to us right now.''

''As a gesture of good faith, I persuaded them to turn off all the recording devices,'' Jack said, taking her hand and leading her to the desk. He picked up a paperweight and showed her the electronic mike stuck into the base. ''See, honey? It's turned off. The red light isn't glowing. There's another one over the picture up there. It's turned off, too.''

She pretended to be persuaded. ''Well, if you're sure...''

''I'm sure. Caroline, honey, let's not waste time discussing this any more, okay? You have to take my word for it. The room's clean and we've got better things to do than worry about hidden mikes. Lots of better things.'' He reached out and pulled her into his arms with unexpected force, pressing his mouth against hers and grabbing her hips as he trailed hot, openmouthed kisses along her jaw line.

''Cameras,'' he murmured into her ear. ''Kitty-corner from the door and the desk.'' He groaned, reaching for the buttons on her dress, making sure her back was to both cameras. His hand inched up her thigh, then slipped between their bodies and slid up the front of her dress. Something cold and hard pushed against her breasts. She realized he'd stuffed a tiny tape recorder into her bra.

''Tomorrow,'' he breathed, lips not moving, his fingers busy tucking the end of a cord into her bra. ''Wire yourself up.''

''Mmm... Oh, God, yes, Jack. Do that some more.''

"Voice activated," he murmured into her ear.

"Recording time?"

"Lasts two hours." His kisses trailed toward her breasts. "Caroline, you drive me crazy. I want to make love to you right now."

She dragged his head up and bit his ear. "FBI?" she whispered. She clutched his hair, tossing her head back and moaning as he slathered kisses on her neck. "Oh, Jack, you make me feel like a new woman. I'm on fire with wanting you."

He jerked her head up, his eyes rolling in disbelief as she gave an especially throaty moan. "Er, me, too, baby. I'm burning up." He trailed his kisses to her other ear. "FBI agents will be at the bank." He gave a hoarse cry and buried his face in her neck, writhing against her suggestively. "Take me to the sofa and say no," he muttered.

She obediently kicked off her shoes and moved toward the sofa, which she guessed was right at the edge of camera range. Jack immediately propelled her against the leather cushions and she succumbed for twenty seconds or so before pushing him away. "Jack, no! I want you, but we can't do this, not here! Burroughs will be coming back any minute. He'll see us. Besides, we have to talk. This may be the only chance we get to be alone."

"Afterward," Jack said passionately. "We could talk afterward."

"No, Jack. You have to stop." She squirmed determinedly away and after a few more minutes of wrestling and arguing, Jack sighed and allowed her to win.

"I'm sorry, sweetheart," he said. "I didn't mean to be such an aggressive brute, but when I'm with you, I just forget everything except how much I love you."

"Oh, Jack, you're such a wonderful, caring man. So sweet and gentle." She intended to reach up and stroke his cheek, but his exaggerated expression of soulful nobility was too much for her and she was overcome with a fit of the giggles. Burying her face in his shoulders, she tried to get control of herself while Jack stroked her back and murmured sweet nothings.

"You were right about Joe Rossi," he said solemnly when it was safe to let Caroline sit up. "He's truly an evil man, and we'll have to be very careful how we set up our deal, otherwise I'm afraid Joe is going to end up walking off with the money and with your little boy."

"I won't let him have Andrew," Caroline said, and the hard note of determination in her voice was entirely unfeigned. "Did you follow my instructions? Have you explained to Joe how the deal has to be set up?"

"Yes, and Joe has agreed to almost everything."

"*Almost* everything?" Caroline asked sharply. "What does he want to change?"

"He insists on bringing his bodyguards with him when we make the exchange."

"Jack, we can't agree to that!" Caroline's panic was sincere. "Don't you see? He's planning to double-cross us. His men will kidnap Andrew at the first opportunity."

"No, sweetheart, they won't be able to." Jack squeezed her hand hard. "The bodyguards will all stay outside the church. I explained to your father-in-law that I'm a man of God. I couldn't possibly allow thugs carrying guns inside my church.''

"But how do you know the gunmen will stay outside?" Caroline demanded.

"Look, honey, I'm sure Joe would like to double-cross us, but he can't," Jack said. "The way we're setting things up is foolproof. Angela, Joe's wife, will bring Andrew to the church tomorrow morning, and I'll be there waiting for them. Clive Burroughs will bring you to the church at eight-thirty, and you'll be able to spend five minutes or so with Andrew. Then Angela and I will remain inside the church to take care of Andrew while you and Joe go downtown to the bank where you've stored the keys to the safety deposit boxes on Grand Cayman and the information on who murdered your husband—''

"No," Caroline protested. "I don't want to leave Andrew behind with Joe's bodyguards posted all around the church. Jack, they'll simply come in as soon as I've left with Joe and take him away. You'll be powerless to stop them.''

"Naturally, I've taken care of all that," Jack said smoothly. "Caroline, honey, when you reach the bank, you must call me on Joe's car phone. Unless Andrew is still safely with me, you won't open the safety deposit box. Joe can't pull anything underhanded. And once Joe has the information about his son's murderer and the keys to Ames's safety deposit boxes on Grand Cayman, he'll call his bodyguards and tell them it's all right for me to leave the church with Andrew. So I'll have your son, and Joe will have the keys and account numbers he needs to access Dayton Ames's money."

She knew the elaborate plan was meaningless, because neither she nor Joe intended to honor it. Even so, panic blossomed inside her at the myriad possibilities for failure. If she saw Andrew again and then lost him a second time, she wasn't sure she would be able to survive.

"I don't know, Jack," she said. "It all sounds okay, but—"

Jack put his fingers against her lips. "Hush, sweetheart. It has to be this way, don't you see? Joe leaves his wife and his bodyguards behind to make sure I don't run off with Andrew. You leave me behind to make sure Angela and the bodyguards don't take him back. Joe trusts Angela and you trust me. That way, you and Joe both have insurance while you complete your business downtown."

"Joe's so slippery, that's the problem." She leaned back against the cold leather, suddenly exhausted. "I hope to God this is going to work, Jack."

He pulled her to her feet, put his arm around her shoulders and walked her across the room until they were within optimum camera range. "Trust me," he said with a smile that set his dimple flashing and caused Caroline's hackles to rise in sheer reflexive terror. Sometimes he acted his role of traitor so well it was scary. He kissed her lightly on the end of her nose. "All you have to do is trust me, sweetheart, and everything will work out just fine."

* * *

Joe was still laughing when Jack walked into the room where he'd been watching the screen with Clive Burroughs. "Trust me, sweetheart, and everything will work out just fine. Jack, I think I gotta hire you on a permanent basis. I could turn you loose to practice your charm on a few lady judges and politicians I'd like to get rid of back in New Jersey. What do you say, Reverend? You want to apply for a transfer to a parish in my part of the country when this is over?"

"I was thinking of retiring," Jack said. "I hear half a million dollars buys a real comfortable life in Mexico these days."

"We'll talk about it later," Joe said. "Hell, Jack, you're too young to retire. Besides, I can always spot a man with talent, and you got it, Jack. You got it in spades."

"I'll think about your offer," Jack said. "I'll give it real favorable consideration when I've got my half million bucks in a nice, safe account in Switzerland."

"My boys are working on that now," Joe said smoothly. "You'll be able to call and check on it in another couple of hours."

"Okay." Jack paced the office, waving away the offer of a drink. "What's happening with Caroline? Where's she going to spend the night?"

"You wanna take her home?" Joe asked, grinning. "Hoping for a few hours of off-camera sex?"

"Hey, on camera or off, makes no difference to me. I'd just like a few hours alone with her, that's all."

Clive Burroughs intervened. "She's taking a shower and changing into the new clothes I had my secretary buy for her. Joe, I think it would be best if we took charge of Caroline for the rest of the day. We don't want any nasty surprises now that we've sprung her from jail."

Joe rubbed the back of his neck. "Yeah, you're probably right. Caroline's a smart little cookie—we don't want her to start worrying about whether Jack here is as loyal and loving as he seems. Can't have her throwing too many questions at him. She'd soon realize that the only security in the plan for her is that Jack is a hundred percent reliable."

"I think I could keep up the pretense for a few hours," Jack said. "But no big deal. One woman is pretty much like any other once you've had them a couple of times."

Joe chortled. "I'm surprised Caroline didn't freeze your pecker off. That little girl is one icy piece of tail."

Jack walked to the window, pretending to admire the view. When he had his voice under control again, he turned around. "Did Andrew arrive yet?" he asked. "Whatever else I can scam Caroline about, she isn't going to move from that church tomorrow until she's seen her son."

"He's arriving with my wife about an hour from now," Joe said. "In fact, I'll go to the airport myself to meet him. He's a great kid. About the only thing that stuck-up bitch did right—she sure popped out a great kid. You wanna come to the airport, Jack?"

Jack was aware that Clive Burroughs's gaze was still fixed on him with disconcerting intensity. He had a disquieting suspicion that the lawyer was a much more perceptive judge of character than Joe.

"No, thanks," he said, wondering if he was smart to trade off the chance to meet Andrew against the chance of Burroughs suspecting him of planning a double-cross. On the whole, it seemed wiser to show minimal interest in Andrew, despite the fact that tomorrow it would be vitally important for the child to accept him.

He fixed his mouth into a cynical smile. "I think I'd better get back to my priestly duties. I have all the old folks coming to the parish hall for a beetle drive tonight, and they prefer me to show up in person."

"What the hell's a beetle drive?" Joe asked.

Jack got to his feet. "If you don't know, Joe, don't ask. Just drive out to the airport, pick up your grandson and count your blessings. You've never done hard time and you don't know what a beetle drive is." He rested his hand on Joe's shoulder. "God loves you, my son."

Joe laughed. "This time tomorrow, you're gonna be a quarter of a million dollars richer. Sounds to me as if God loves you, too, Reverend."

"I sure hope so, Joe. Just make sure you don't try to screw me over."

Clive Burroughs pushed back his starched, monogrammed shirt cuff and stared at his Mondavi watch. "Take your own advice, Jack. People who try to mess with Mr. Rossi have a tendency to end up dead. Get smart and play this deal straight."

"I'm a priest," Jack said. "How else could I play it?"

* * *

Caroline had barely slept all night, and she got the shakes whenever she thought about seeing Andrew, but nobody had searched her and she'd managed to get herself wired up while she was in the shower. She'd even found some Band-Aids under the sink in the bathroom and taped the wires to follow the line of her bra. So far, so good. Fortunately, Joe Rossi and Clive Burroughs seemed to believe any treachery this morning would come exclusively from their side, and they'd been almost casual in their supervision of her. Still, they weren't fools and they always traveled with enough firepower to make any encounter lethal.

The prospect of seeing Andrew kept her on the edge of her seat. By the time Burroughs's driver turned the BMW into the asphalt parking lot next to St. Luke's, Caroline was bathed in cold sweat—and very close to losing it. If Joe had tricked her and Jack and Andrew wasn't at the church, she really thought she might die of a broken heart.

She followed Burroughs out of the car, willing herself to stay calm. Joe's bodyguards were already stationed outside the imposing fake-Gothic entrance to St. Luke's. There were three guards, she noted as she climbed the flight of shallow stone steps, and another person who was probably a guard lurking at the side entrance. Four guards plus Burroughs's driver, and all of them undoubtedly armed. The odds of Jack escaping with Andrew did not, on the surface, seem very good. On the other hand, Joe's people didn't know about the basement corridor leading from the church to the parish house.

Joe's black Lincoln town car, parked at the curb, engine running, was attracting surprisingly little attention. Maybe it was too early for the neighborhood kids to turn out in force, or maybe they assumed it was there for a funeral.

Burroughs was waved through the screen of bodyguards, Caroline at his side. He pushed open the heavy oak door that led into the vestibule of the church. The iron hinges creaked, then creaked again as the door closed, shutting out street noises and sunshine. Caroline walked past the baptismal font and into the nave of the church, the lawyer at her heels. The lights illuminating the altar had been switched on, but the body of the church was lit only by the early morning sun, which shone through the stained-glass windows and cast patterns of bright emerald green and sapphire blue on the little group of people clustered in the front pew.

Joe, his wife, Angela, Jack. And a little boy with brown curly hair, burnished with a red halo of filtered sunlight.

Oh, my God! Caroline thought. Joe's really brought Andrew to Chicago. He's really and truly here.

Her heart stopped beating. Silence buffeted her ears. Her vision contracted until she could see nothing except Andrew. Her son. Her baby, who wasn't a baby any more.

Jack stepped into the aisle, holding Andrew's hand. Jack was wearing his cassock, and Andrew was dressed in blue shorts, new socks and sneakers and a white sport shirt. They waited for her, backs to the altar, not speaking.

Caroline's heart resumed beating, thumping so hard and so fast she was propelled forward by the force of it. She ran down the aisle, falling to her knees and folding Andrew in her arms, tears pouring down her cheeks and trickling into his soft curls. She was happier, more full of joy, than she'd ever been in her entire life. And she was so full of sorrow for their lost time together that she thought she might die of the pain.

"Andrew," she whispered, rocking back and forth. "Andrew, I've missed you so much. Oh, my God, I've missed you."

He didn't say anything. She hugged him some more, whispering how much she loved him and how she'd longed to have him home again. Jack touched her lightly on the shoulder. "You might want to let him breathe for a few seconds, Caroline, honey. His face is turning purple."

"What?" Caroline relaxed her grip on Andrew, and registered that her son was standing stiff and unresponsive in her arms. His hands were clapped flat against his sides, and his huge brown eyes were staring at her with a mixture of curiosity and anxiety.

He didn't recognize her.

The realization that her son didn't know who she was nearly snapped the frail threads of her self-control. Somehow, though, she managed not to start ranting and raving at Joe for the wickedness of what he'd done. She reminded herself that Andrew was the only truly innocent person in all of this, the one whose feelings had to take precedence over her terrible sense of loss. She couldn't lose her temper because that would only make Andrew more wary of her than he was already.

Fighting for control, she rocked on her heels, holding Andrew's hands but allowing him to put a little distance between the two of them. "Munchkin, I'm sorry if I scared you. I was so excited to see you again, I forgot everything else." Her hand shaking, she touched the top of his head. "Wow, you've grown to be so big. You were still just a little kid the last time I saw you."

He looked at her speculatively. "I'm not...what you said."

"Not big? Not a little kid?"

"No, not that. I'm not Munchkin. My name's Andrew Phillip Rossi. Soon, I'll be four." He held out four stubby fingers in proof of his claim.

Caroline stared at her son's chubby hand and wondered how she had endured three hundred and seventy two days away from him. She squeezed his hand, struggling against the urge to smother him in more hugs. "I'm sorry, of course I know you're Andrew Phillip Rossi and I like your name a lot. I used to call you Munchkin a long time ago, when you were just a baby."

He viewed her silently for a moment, then held out one of his feet. "These are my new sneakers. They glow in the dark. Are you my mommy?"

There were some questions that should never have to be asked, Caroline thought. She swallowed the hurt. "Yes, Andrew, I'm your mommy, and I love you very much."

"What about my sneakers?" He jiggled his foot.

She held onto her smile, but her voice broke. "They're nice, too."

He considered her answer. "You went away," he said finally.

She didn't correct him. Instead, she reached out and stroked his face. His cheeks were thinner and more defined than when she'd last seen him, but still baby soft. "I couldn't help it, Andrew. Truly, you're the most important person in the whole world to me, and I didn't want to...go away."

"Nanna and Poppa take care of me now." He glanced worriedly toward Angela and Joe, as if not sure he should be talking to this unfamiliar woman without their permission. Caroline tried to draw some comfort from the fact that he had made no attempt to remove his hands from her clasp or to distance himself from her.

She drew in a shaky breath. "Nanna and Poppa looked after you for a little while, Andrew. Now you're going to come home and live with me. Little boys usually live with their mommies."

"With you?" Andrew asked, mulling over the idea. "You're my mommy, right?" He obviously felt a need to get the important points clarified beyond any possibility of doubt.

He wasn't quite four years old, Caroline told herself. He didn't know he was slashing her heart to pieces with a sharp serrated knife. "Yes," she said, giving him another hug. "I'm your mommy, Andrew, and I'm going to look after you for always."

"Are Nanna and Poppa coming to live in your house, too?"

Fortunately for Caroline, Joe had obviously endured all he could of this discussion, which, from his point of view, was entirely pointless, since he had no intention of honoring his side of the bargain. "All right, Andy, it's time for your mother—" He almost choked on the word. He began again. "Caroline and I have to take a trip downtown. Nanna will take care of you, Andy, just like she always does. Caroline, let's move it." His gaze flashed from his wife to Clive Burroughs. "You two know what you have to do, right?"

Caroline couldn't let that remark pass. "What does that mean, Joe? I hope you're not planning anything I wouldn't like."

"Of course not," he said impatiently. "I'm just warning Angela and Clive to keep an eye on my grandson. Jack, be ready to take a call from Caroline in about fifteen minutes."

Jack reached into the pocket of his cassock and drew out a small cellular phone. "I'm ready," he said.

Caroline gave her son a kiss and a quick hug. "Father Jack will look after you, Andrew, and Mommy will be back very soon." She prayed she was telling the truth. She spared a pitying glance for Angela, Joe's wife, who was sitting in her accustomed meek silence, huddled into as inconspicuous a position on the pew as she could manage. "Goodbye, Angela. I don't suppose we'll see each other again."

"Goodbye, Caroline." Angela's gaze slid away. Then, with a surge of amazing bravery, she looked up and met Caroline's eyes. "Andrew's a lovely child," she said. "I've tried . . ." She saw Joe looking at her and quickly bent her head. "I've done my best to raise him right," she whispered.

Joe marched out of the church, Caroline keeping pace beside him. He paused on the steps and addressed his bodyguards. "You boys make sure nobody goes in and that the Reverend Fletcher doesn't try to bring my grandson out, okay? You got that?"

"Yes, boss. We got it. Nobody goes in and the priest isn't allowed out."

"What about the side entrance to the church?" Joe asked.

"We got it covered, boss. Vic's taking care of it."

"There's just two entrances, right?"

"Just two, boss. It's a real old building. They didn't worry about fire exits or nothin' in the old days."

Joe's eyes narrowed suspiciously. Then he grunted and Caroline released the terrified breath she was holding. Jack planned to wait no more than two or three minutes before making some excuse to take Andrew into the vestry, which backed onto the old-fashioned furnace room. From the furnace room, a basement passage connected to the parish house, where police would be waiting. Andrew's arrival would be the signal for police to move in and arrest the bodyguards on charges of carrying concealed weapons. The basement link between the church and the next-door building was crucial to the success of their plans, and a thorough search might have revealed it. Thank God Joe's bodyguards hadn't exerted themselves to find other entrances to the church, Caroline thought.

Joe pushed her toward the waiting limo. "Get in," he said. As she bent forward to slide across the backseat, she slipped her hand inside the buttons of her blouse and activated the tape recorder. From now on, voices would automatically set the tape rolling.

Joe fumbled in his inside breast pocket and took out the key Jack had given him the day before. "Okay, Caroline, here's the key to your safety deposit box. Now it's payoff time. Tell my driver where we're going."

Caroline spoke to the chauffeur through the glass partition. "Take us to the Fourth Federated Bank of Chicago, please. Michigan Avenue and Pearson, near Loyola University."

"Don't take all morning gettin' us there!" Joe ordered. He pressed a button on his armrest and the partition glided closed. He leaned back, trying to appear relaxed, but his eyes glittered and his body was tense with anticipation.

"You seem to want this money very badly," Caroline said. "Do you have some hot creditors breathing down your neck, Joe?"

He scowled. "Dayton Ames stole this money from me. Five million stinkin' dollars. Of course I want them back."

"Not stinking dollars, Joe. Nice clean perfumed ones. Dayton Ames washed each and every one of them for you, remember?"

"Yeah, right. He laundered the money through his investment fund and then hung me out to dry. I didn't send him my hard-earned money just so's he could skim twenty percent straight off the top."

"It's touching to see you still have so much faith in your fellow criminals, Joe. Once a thief, always a thief. You knew Dayton Ames was a thief, otherwise he wouldn't have agreed to work with you. You were crazy to trust him."

"I don't need moral lectures from a whore," Joe said. He thumped on the window separating them from the driver. "What the hell you takin' so long for? Get us out of this traffic."

The driver wove his way across two lanes of slow-moving traffic, dodged around a truck, and ended up a hundred yards ahead of where he'd started. "Angela doesn't look well, Joe." Caroline spoke abruptly, the topic unplanned, surprising her.

"She's all right most of the time." Joe's fingers drummed impatiently on his knees. "She took Phillip's death real hard. We all did, in the family."

Caroline looked out the car window, not sure what to say. Absurd for her to feel sorry for Angela—even more absurd than the pity she felt for Felicity Ames. She was relieved when the traffic started flowing more freely. They were almost at the bank. "What are you going to do, Joe, when I give you the name of the man who ordered the hit on your son?"

Joe's voice was cold. "I don't believe you have the name, Caroline. The day after Phillip died, I put word out all over New Jersey that there was a million dollars in cash, no questions asked, for anyone who could tell me who ordered the hit and who pulled the trigger. I never heard nothing. Not a name, not a word, not a hint. How the hell could you have information nobody else could bring me, not even for a million bucks? I think you're blowin' smoke.''

"No smoke," she said quietly. "Phillip told me."

"That's crazy talk," Joe said. "How could Phillip tell you who killed him? You been tapping out messages on the Ouija board or something?"

"Nothing that fancy," she said. "He sent me a letter."

Joe grunted, clearly unimpressed. "Yeah, well, you can show me the letter, but I'm not holding my breath. If Phillip had known there was a contract out on him, he'd have told me." He peered out the window. "This it?" he demanded. "It's taken long enough to get here."

"Yes, this is the bank," Caroline said. "Give me your phone, Joe. I'm not moving a single step closer to that safety deposit box until I've heard from Jack that my son is still safe."

"Be my guest." Joe handed her the phone, not quite able to conceal his smirk. It was giving him real pleasure, Caroline knew, to think that Jack was about to trick her. "Here's the number to call," he said.

Jack answered on the second ring. "Hello."

"Jack, it's me, Caroline. We're at the bank. Do you have Andrew safe?"

"Very safe," he said. "No worries, Caroline. None at all. Everything's gone just as we planned."

Joe could hear every word. He looked amused. Caroline shifted slightly so she wouldn't have to look at him. "No problems with the bodyguards?" she asked Jack.

"None at all. They've stayed outside the church, just like Joe promised they would. Andrew and I have been having a good time exploring the church. It's an interesting old building."

That was as close as he could come to saying that he and Andrew had made it through the basement passage. Caroline repressed a sigh of relief. "Then I'm going to take Joe upstairs and open my safety deposit box. Okay?"

"Perfect," he said. "Go right ahead. Take care, Caroline."

"Just watch out for Andrew."

Joe snatched the phone out of her hand and hung up. "Enough already, this was supposed to be a business call, not an episode in a soap opera. Let's get moving, Caroline. I've got boys standin' by, waiting to fly down to the Cayman Islands. That money's singin' out to me to come and get it."

They walked into the bank, heading straight for the section in the far corner that housed the safety deposit boxes. The slender, middle-aged woman behind the counter greeted her with a bored smile. "Good morning, how may I help you?"

"I need to access my safety deposit box," Caroline said. Joe handed her the key and she slid it across the counter to the clerk.

"Sign here, please, and give your social security number." The clerk barely looked at Caroline, much less at Joe. She took the signed form, compared it cursorily with a signature card from the file index at her desk, then buzzed to release the electronic lock on the door that gave customers entrance to the room-size safe.

Joe started to walk through. "Sir, excuse me, you can't go in there! Box holders only."

Joe glared at the clerk and started to swear. Caroline put her hand on his arm, hastily calming him. "Wait, Joe, you can't expect her to break the rules for us." With a strained attempt at a smile, she turned to the clerk. "I expect you have a room where we can take the boxes to examine documents at our leisure? This is my father-in-law and I have some papers I need him to see."

"Oh, yes, we can arrange that. You can take out whatever documents you require and carry them through into the room just to the right of us here. You come through here with me, miss—er, ma'am, and if you'll walk around to your right, sir, I'll be able to let you both into the same room without violating bank policy and procedures."

"She can bring the actual deposit box into the room where I'm at?" Joe demanded.

"Yes, sir. First, though, I have to go into the secured area with your daughter-in-law. We need both her key and mine to open any of the boxes. We won't be more than a couple of minutes. If you could just be a little patient, sir, I'm sure this will all work out."

Joe scowled and muttered, but eventually complied. Caroline walked into the claustrophobic, windowless, steel-lined room that housed the safety deposit boxes. She was no sooner inside than the bank clerk flashed an embossed badge at Caroline.

"FBI," she said very quietly. "Federal Agent Kirsch. Do you still want to go ahead and open the safety deposit box?"

"I sure do," Caroline said, her knees a little shaky with the relief of knowing law enforcement officials had arrived as promised. "Are there more agents close at hand? When Joe Rossi sees what's in the box, he's going to be mad enough to kill me. When he realizes what isn't in the box, he'll dismember what's left of my dead body."

"My partner's not more than thirty feet from the room where I've sent Mr. Rossi. You're wired, right?"

Caroline nodded. "Yes, I hope everything's working. I've never wired myself up before."

"May I?" Agent Kirsch took a quick glance at the tape recorder. "It's working just fine. My partner will be able to hear everything you and Mr. Rossi say. Any trouble, and he'll come in. Let's get the box. We're taking too long."

Agent Kirsch put her key into one of the locks guarding the slot that held Caroline's box. Caroline used her key to open the other lock. The door sprang open, and Caroline tugged the long, narrow box out of its rack.

"Check the contents," Agent Kirsch said. "Show me what's there, so I can testify if needed."

Caroline lifted the steel lid. Inside the box were two letters, one scrawled on a sheet of ruled note paper, the other written on several thick, expensive sheets of monogrammed personal stationery. PJR, the monogram said. Caroline ran her fingertips over the engraving, caught off guard by the intensity of her regret.

"No time to read them," the agent said. "Seven pages, right?"

Caroline smiled tightly. "That's it," she said. "Seven pages of dynamite. Let me into the room where Joe's waiting, please. I don't want him to get suspicious."

Joe stood up as Caroline walked into the frosted glass cubicle next to the safe. "You got it!" he said, flush with satisfaction. "Where's the clerk?"

"Back at her station. She can't hear us from where she's sitting."

"Are the keys for Dayton's safety deposit boxes still in there?"

She was scared, even though she knew there were two FBI agents within fifty feet of her. Bullets traveled a heck of a lot faster than people, and Joe might soon be angry enough to shoot first and worry about the consequences afterward.

She drew in a deep breath. "There aren't any keys," she said.

For once in his life, Joe didn't shout or bluster. He turned to stare at her. "What do you mean, there aren't any keys?"

"Dayton's money isn't in a safety deposit box," she said. "It's in an account. A numbered account. You should have realized I didn't need any keys to get his money, Joe. Why do you think I was going to O'Hare and trying to fly to the Cayman Islands if I needed to get to this bank and pick up keys first? I always planned to make an electronic transfer of the funds."

"Then give me the account number," he said.

"The identifying number of the account is 19-384-227. Dayton used his birthday as his access number, although the bank told him not to—11-17-48."

"How do I know you're telling me the truth?" Joe demanded.

"You don't. If I'd given you a set of keys, how would you have known they were the ones you wanted? You're no worse off than you were before, Joe."

"Why did you lie?"

"Would you have brought Andrew to Chicago if I'd told you the account numbers you needed were in my head?" He didn't answer and she smiled grimly. "Just what I thought, Joe. You'd have tortured me to death if you thought I had everything you needed inside my head."

"Why are you giving me the numbers now?"

"Because I have Andrew," she said. "That was all I ever wanted from you, Joe. Nothing else. No revenge. No payoff. Just my son."

He brushed her remarks aside. Caroline assumed he was drawing some consolation from the belief that, for all her plotting, she didn't have Andrew, that Jack had been bought off, and her son was already being sped back to the airport and New Jersey.

Joe gestured to the safety deposit box. "If you didn't have keys to Dayton's money in that box, what *do* you have in there? Nothing? Garbage?"

"I have important papers, Joe." She picked up the sheet of ruled notepaper and held it out to him. "This is a signed confession from the gunman who shot Phillip."

"I don't believe you." Joe's face turned white, then purple with the force of his rage. He snatched the paper from her and read the scrawled words.

"Lionel Silva!" He spat out the name, ripping the page into shreds. "So much for his confession. The guy was crazy. Even you can't be stupid enough to believe this pile of garbage."

"But I do believe it," Caroline said softly. "And I don't think I'm in the least stupid." She finally spoke the words she'd kept bottled up inside her for more than a year. "It's too late for bluffing, Joe. The man who shot my husband was Lionel Silva, but the man who ordered him to pull the trigger was you. You ordered Lionel to kill your own son, and we both know it."

Joe stood stock-still in the center of the little cubicle. The only sign of emotion was the vein throbbing at the side of his head. "You really have gone crazy," he said at last. "Why would I kill Phillip? He was my only son. I loved him more than anybody else in the world."

"The tragedy is, I think you did love him in your own twisted way." Caroline held out the six-page letter from her ex-husband. "Phillip wrote this to me the week before he died. He said he'd been doing a lot of hard thinking since our divorce and he told me about his plans for the future. He was planning to make a fresh start somewhere out west where the tentacles of your organization couldn't reach him. He promised us a new beginning if I'd agree to join him. My biggest regret is that I never answered his letter. He died before I could make up my mind what to say."

Joe took the letter, but he read no more than the first page before he threw it down on the table, crashing his fist into his palm. "It was *your* fault," he said, his voice trembling with rage. "You destroyed my boy. He was a good son, respecting his father, until he met you. After you divorced him, he was never the same. In the end, you had him so mixed up, he actually threatened me, his own father. Said that unless I retired, he was going to turn me in to the Feds, give them the information they'd need to bring me up on charges of racketeering."

Joe's shoulders slumped and he rested his weight on the edge of the table, his face twisted with pain and hatred. "*You* made me do it, Caroline. *You're* the one who's responsible for Phillip's death, not me. You! You stuffed him so goddamned full of your own dumb-assed ideas about life that he didn't know which way was up no more. He told me he was going to get a no-account job in a regular firm so you'd think he was good enough to come back and live with you and Andrew. *Good enough.*" Joe spat at her in his rage. "You're scum, Caroline, that's what you are. Scum that broke up my family and killed my boy."

She took a tissue and wiped the spittle off her cheek. "No, I'm not scum, Joe. I'm just a wife who saw her husband ruined by his father's corruption. I'm also a mother who's determined not to let her son grow up under your influence."

"You haven't got a chance in hell of getting Andrew back," Joe said. "And if you're counting on that priest of yours to help you out, forget it. I didn't even have to buy him. He sold himself at the first opportunity."

"You're wrong, Joe, but that doesn't matter. You're going to federal prison, and I'm going to get an official reversal of the custody order. Andrew will be living with me from now on."

"Me? In prison?" Joe laughed. "That'll be a cold day in hell, babe."

"Then I guess it must be close to freezing down there right now," Caroline said, backing toward the door of the cubicle. "I'm wired, Joe, and you just confessed to ordering the murder of your own son."

He gave a howl of rage, cursing and swearing as he lunged for her, clawing for her neck or the wires of the tape recorder—Caroline wasn't sure which. His hands fastened around her neck, pressing against her windpipe with his thumbs.

"This is how I killed my first man," he panted. "And it's how I'm gonna kill my first woman, too. You'll be dead before the Feds can get to me, Caroline. Thirty seconds, that's all it takes."

Scarlet stars danced before her eyes, and her tongue suddenly felt too big for her throat. She heard noises. Voices. Running feet. God, she needed air. Joe's hands were clamped around her throat, tightening like a metal vice. He gave another vicious squeeze to her windpipe.

Andrew. Jack. She saw their faces and knew she wasn't going to let Joe kill her. Not now. Not when she was finally so close to happiness.

Her left hand was free. She smashed it upward, in a hard blow to the underside of Joe's jaw. His hold on her throat loosened enough for her to draw in a single shallow breath.

And then she was free. Agent Kirsch caught her just in time to prevent her falling. "Don't faint," Kirsch said. "Have the pleasure of watching while they put the cuffs on him and read him his rights."

Caroline watched.

Joe turned to her as he was being led away. "You won't get Andrew," he said, his eyes wild with hatred. "You'll never even find him. Jack's already handed him over to my bodyguards."

Caroline smiled. "You always were a lousy judge of character, Joe." She walked past him to a waiting squad car. "St. Luke's Episcopal Church," she said to the driver. "And please hurry. My son is waiting to see me."

Epilogue

Andrew climbed onto the bed and insinuated himself between his parents. Neither of them moved. He bounced several times on his mother's stomach, in case she hadn't realized he was there. She opened her eyes and smiled at him sleepily. She smiled a lot, and Andrew liked that.

"Hi, Andy. What time is it?"

"Late. Breakfast time." It wasn't dark any more, so that meant it must be time to get up. He held out his drawing. "This is a dinosaur. His name is Max and he wants pancakes for breakfast."

His new daddy pushed himself up on one elbow and stared at the drawing. "Great picture, Andrew." He squinted at the clock and groaned, flopping back against the pillows. "Six o'clock. I can't stand it." He tousled Andrew's hair. "Hey, kid, I'm a night person. That means I growl and turn into a bear if you wake me before eight o'clock on my days off."

"I like bears," Andrew said. In fact, Andrew liked almost everything about living with his mommy and his new daddy. He especially liked that they didn't shout at each other, like Poppa had always shouted at Nonna, and sometimes even hit her. At Nonna's house, he'd had his own bathroom and two rooms of his own, one to sleep in and one just for toys. He liked it better in this apartment, which only had a few rooms, but he felt safe and warm. He didn't mind sharing a bathroom with Marcus, and he didn't need two rooms any more because he didn't have many toys.

He didn't mind not having many toys. Marcus played with him instead, and he went to preschool, where there were lots of kids to play games with and he was never bored. Marcus was teaching him to be a cool dude. Andrew didn't know what a cool dude was, but he wanted to grow up just like Marcus. And his new daddy.

His mom was showing alarming signs of falling asleep again, so Andrew clambered off the bed and retrieved his other offering. He rummaged around on the floor and handed his mom and dad the sections of the newspaper that had survived the journey from the front door to the bedroom. The pictures in the newspaper were all boring, but his parents liked to read it. "Here," he said. "For you."

Caroline hugged her son, aware as always of a tiny burst of happiness that he was with her, not doing anything special except being there. Her eye was caught by the newspaper headline. *Joe Rossi Guilty.* She'd already heard the verdict on the late news, but she read on anyway, Andrew snuggled comfortably at her side, his toes wriggling against her.

The front-page lead article reported that Joe Rossi, head of one of New Jersey's major organized crime syndicates, had been found guilty on charges of conspiracy to commit murder in the death of Dayton Ames. The judge had congratulated the jury on returning their verdict in the face of threats and intimidation from various associates of the accused. Joe Rossi had been sent to state prison to wait for his trial on racketeering and tax evasion charges, which was pending in Federal court.

Silently, Caroline handed the paper to Jack. "Felicity's already in jail, Joe's on his way. Seems you were right. Sometimes the good guys win one, after all. Thank God it looks as if that part of our lives is finally over."

Jack read the article, then put the newspaper to one side and took her into his arms, with Andrew squished between them. "It's not quite over," he said. "There's still one loose end. You're not going to like what I'm about to suggest, Caroline, but I want you to think about it, okay?"

She looked at him warily. "I hate it when you get that look on your face. It means you're going to expect me to do something noble and uplifting."

He smiled. "Not too noble," he said. "Just generous."

"You're making me more nervous by the second. What?"

"I want you to let Andrew call his grandmother."

She stared at him, appalled. "No! You can't ask me to do that—"

He pressed his finger against her mouth. "Caroline, she's a tired old woman with chronic asthma and nothing much to look forward to except failing health and loneliness. For the rest of her life, she'll have to live with the knowledge that her husband murdered their child. You can imagine better than most people what a terrible burden that must be. She loves Andrew and she did her best to care for him after Phillip died. Be generous, Caroline."

Caroline stared stubbornly at Andrew's soft brown curls, refusing to let herself feel pity. "She should have left Joe years ago. Angela made her own bed, however lonely and uncomfortable it's turning out to be."

"Maybe, but that's not what we're discussing. Andrew misses her, you know he does. Are you sure you couldn't manage to handle the occasional phone call to Angela? Once a month, maybe, just so she could hear his voice?"

Caroline sat up in bed, sighing. "Damn it, Jack, don't do this to me. I don't want to sympathize with Angela—"

He grinned. "You already do." He kissed her lightly on the tip of her nose. "Think about it, okay?"

She grunted. "I'm not promising anything."

She knew Jack was too smart to press the victory he sensed right around the corner. He jounced Andrew on his knee, to their mutual noisy satisfaction, and they ended up rolling on the floor in a raucous pillow fight.

"You guys want me to kill the little kid?" Marcus arrived bleary-eyed in the doorway of their bedroom.

"It's a tempting thought," Caroline said, sliding down in the bed and pulling the covers up to her chin.

"Maybe you could help him get dressed?" Jack suggested.

"Okay." Marcus jerked his thumb at Andrew. "Move it, kid. Your Mom and Dad want to go back to sleep."

As always, at a word from his idol, Andrew scrambled obediently toward the door. Marcus held out his hand, and Andrew took it trustingly.

"Oh, by the way, my gran called last night while you guys were out," Marcus said. "Evonne's had her baby. It's a girl."

Caroline smiled. "Oh, wonderful! Right on time, too. How much did the baby weigh? Did Evonne decide whether to call her Tonya or Marie in the end?"

Marcus looked utterly blank. "I don't know," he said. "Jamal's bringing Evonne and the baby home from the hospital this afternoon, and taking her to his sister's place," he added, obviously trying to make up for his previous lack of information. "You can call them for all that baby stuff, I guess."

"We'll do that," Caroline said, waving as Marcus and Andrew left the room. She propped herself on one elbow, looking worriedly at Jack. "Is it going to work out, do you think?" she asked. "Jamal's sister and her husband already have two kids of their own, and Evonne's baby is going to be a huge drain on their time and their finances."

"Jamal's sister wasn't nagged into taking the baby, she volunteered, so that's a promising sign, and her husband's supportive of the idea, which is even more promising. Giving them temporary custody of the baby was a better solution than anything else we could come up with." Jack picked the pillows off the floor and sat on the edge of the bed. "At least Jamal finished school and Evonne's hanging in there, despite everything. I'd say her odds of graduating and getting that scholarship look better with every day that passes. It's less than nine weeks to the end of the school year."

Squeals from the bathroom suggested that Andrew was having much too much fun with the toothpaste. "I'd better get up," Caroline said. She scowled at the clock. "I'll never get used to being bright and cheerful at six-thirty in the morning."

Jack grinned. "Sweetheart, trust me, nobody would ever accuse you of being bright and cheerful in the morning." He leaned across the bed and kissed her before she could protest. "We both have the day off work, and it's raining. How about you cook our son the pancakes he seems so set on, then Marcus can drop him off at preschool. That way, you and I can come back to bed and take a morning nap."

"By the time I've cooked breakfast and helped Andrew to get dressed, I won't be sleepy any more."

"Great," Jack said. "Neither will I. Maybe, if we think about it, we'll be able to come up with a way to fill the time."

She faked another yawn. "I doubt it. What do people do in bed when they've already been married for nearly six months?"

Jack's eyes gleamed. "Stick around, sweetheart. I can't wait to show you."

Bestselling Author

JASMINE CRESSWELL

Invites you to play a deadly game of

CHARADES

The killer has struck twice already. Abigail Dean is to be his final victim, taking to her grave a secret she doesn't even know she possesses. Realizing that her life's in danger, Abigail turns to Steve Kramer, a man she believes she can trust. Now the killer must silence two instead of one. And by working so closely together, Abigail and Steve have become an easy target.

Find out how it all ends, this June at your favorite retail outlet.

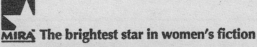

Take 3 of "The Best of the Best™" Novels FREE
Plus get a FREE surprise gift!

Special Limited-time Offer

Mail to The Best of the Best™

3010 Walden Avenue
P.O. Box 1867
Buffalo, N.Y. 14269-1867

YES! Please send me 3 free novels and my free surprise gift. Then send me 3 of "The Best of the Best™" novels each month. I'll receive the best books by the world's hottest romance authors. Bill me at the low price of $3.99 each plus 25¢ delivery and applicable sales tax, if any.* That's the complete price and a savings of over 20% off the cover prices—quite a bargain! I understand that accepting the books and gift places me under no obligation ever to buy any books. I can always return a shipment and cancel at any time. Even if I never buy another book from Harlequin, the 3 free books and the surprise gift are mine to keep forever.

163 BPA A2P5

Name	(PLEASE PRINT)	
Address		Apt. No.
City	State	Zip

This offer is limited to one order per household and not valid to current subscribers. Terms and prices are subject to change without notice. Sales tax applicable in N.Y. All orders subject to approval.

BOB-288

©1990 Harlequin Enterprises Limited

MIRA Books presents the newest
hardcover novel from

New York Times bestselling author

CHARLOTTE
VALE
ALLEN

Experience the compelling story of

CLAUDIA'S
SHADOW

When her sister, Claudia, dies mysteriously,
Rowena Graham cannot accept the verdict of
suicide. Desperate to find out the truth, and to
discover why Claudia had been so difficult and
cruel, Rowena moves into Claudia's house—their
old family home. As she sorts out Claudia's affairs
Rowena discovers a trove of dark family secrets. And
finally sets herself free from the shadows of the past.

Look for *Claudia's Shadow* this May, wherever
hardcover books are sold.

Readers just can't seem to get enough of
New York Times bestselling author

Sandra Brown

This May, a mother searches for

A Secret Splendor

(previously published under the pseudonym Erin St. Claire)

Arden Gentry is searching for the son she was forced to give
up. But finding him could resurrect all the half-truths, secrets
and unspeakable lies that surrounded his birth. Because it
means finding the man who fathered her baby....

Find out how it all turns out, this May at your favorite
retail outlet.

MIRA **The brightest star in women's fiction**

MSBASS